MIRACLES
OF THE
HEART

Blessings,
Monica Coglas

Monica Coglas

WINEPRESS WP PUBLISHING

This is a fictional work. The names and situations of characters in the story are solely a product of the writer's imagination. Any corresponding identity to a living person is purely coincidental.

Some actual locations and facts about Seattle, WA are referenced, only with the intent to preserve the authentic ambiance of the city.

ISBN 1-57921-264-6
Library of Congress Catalog Card Number: 99-68311

I humbly dedicate this book to the Greatest Storyteller of all time: Jesus Christ. Thank You, Lord, for revealing to me Your precious truth and life, and thanks for giving me a gift of writing. May You find pleasure in this work.

I also dedicate this to Debby McNeill, my partner in prayer. You and I have encountered many mountaintops and dark valleys. Thanks for walking alongside of me. You have a heart of gold. Your encouragement and friendship are precious treasures to me!

Acknowledgments

Len—Thank you for loving me. Words can't express how much I appreciate your support of me and my dreams! I love you, honey.

Kaitlyn—You are the sweetest daughter! Thanks for praying for Mommy's book. Love you always!

Mom & Dad—Thanks for providing the wind in my sails. Your confidence in me is priceless! I cherish you both.

To Robin Kelly—Your belief in my writing has been invaluable! Without your inspiration, I would not have achieved as much, I am sure. Thank you for almost 12 years of friendship.

Thanks to my draft proofreaders: Loraine Rieken, Michelle Southern, Tina Carter, Debby McNeill, Dorothy Lawter, Sheila Lampe, Beverly Young, and Korri Ostheller-Munyan. I appreciate all your time and comments. Thanks for noticing the diamond in the rough!

To Rita Bennett and Shirley Wilson—Thanks for your dedication in teaching others about Inner Healing Prayer. It is a much needed ministry.

To Susan Young—Thanks for the tour of the hospital. It was perfect!

To Duane and Carol Perron—Thank you for carrying on a worthy endeavor. The carousels you restore are a joy and a wonder to all who ride them! I hope you (and everyone who is engrossed in this restoration) will never give it up.

To American Carousel Society, and National Carousel Association—I applaud your admirable commitment to keep these wonders alive for all.

To Dr. Richard Ellenbogen—Thank you for granting me some of your valuable time to answer my questions on neurosurgery.

To pediatric hospitals and neurosurgeons everywhere—God bless you for using your skill and talents to help the suffering little ones. You are truly fulfilling a mission of mercy!

Preface

While some liberty was taken in describing a few medical procedures identified in this book (to support the storyline), on the whole I strove to investigate and accurately describe these amazing techniques, and the difficult and demanding roles of both a neurosurgeon and hospital administrator. Equally, I attempted to reveal much of the complex and fascinating history behind the treasured carousel, and portray the exemplary efforts of those who restore the magnificent designs.

My hope is that you will find this story complimentary of these esteemed professions. The "healing" and "restoration" they endeavor to bring others is truly remarkable!

It is my deepest prayer, however, that through this written work you will also sense the restorative and healing love of God, Who is ever calling this wounded and broken world back into His embrace.

May you discover and accept His redemptive truth, for the Lord Jesus Christ is gracious and wonderful, and He desires to bring you the greatest of all miracles . . .

A miracle of the heart.

He heals the brokenhearted
and binds up their wounds.

Psalm 147:3

Chapter One

Early December, present day—Los Angeles, California.

"**A**re you in the perfect will of God?"

Daniel Brakken glowered in response to the TV evangelist. He hated pointed questions like that one. Besides, he thought, how can anyone know God's will for sure?

He blinked his tired, swollen eyes. Another sleepless night. It neared two-thirty in the morning. He was weary beyond measure, but hours of restlessness had forced him up and he'd flipped on the television, searching the channels for something to put his mind at ease. His button-pushing scan had finally landed on the only program that hooked him.

He watched the fired-up man. In ways, the preacher vexed him—he was too loud and paced habitually. Yet, in other ways he intrigued Daniel. This man had *something*. And it was no act. He held his Bible like it meant more to him than the air he breathed. He spoke with conviction, an assurance that was real—and missing in Daniel's life. The lack of it made his heart pound with want, and his mind swim with questions.

For Daniel Brakken, hearing this man out was no small feat. It had been over a year since he could actually sit and listen to a sermon. Since then, anguish clenched his insides. The words from the scriptures called him with an unmistakable plea . . . but blame flooded in, an overwhelming, nauseating sea of condemnation. Accusations stabbed mercilessly at his vanquished soul: *You messed up. It should've never happened. Now it's over. You can't go back. You failed. . . .*

He would always limp away. Wounded. Broken. Too much in despair to believe that hope—forgiveness—still existed for him. Facing his failure was too painful, and he'd learned to run.

Not tonight. He stayed put and really listened.

It wasn't so much that he wanted to. He felt compelled this time, *drawn* to hear what the preacher was saying. Riveted, Daniel watched on.

"You need to know," the evangelist droned, a desperate, urgent summons. "If you don't know, you need to ask God. . . . If you don't ask, . . . you'll never be sure of what God has intended for your life, *and life will lose its meaning*."

The closing words branded Daniel's heart. Life had lost meaning. That was sure. The question was how—rather—if he could get it back. He was continually tossed by doubts, and dangerously close to crashing on a reef of remorse.

He knew it. He just didn't know what to do about it.

He pressed the remote's off button. The TV screen *blipped*, leaving him to sit in blackness. After a long, quiet moment he rose from his leather easy chair, turned, and did something he hadn't done in years. He knelt to pray.

There in the dark he bared his soul. "Lord, . . . if You still want me, . . . show me Your will for my life."

Simple words. Brief. Desperate. He laid down a burden he no longer wanted to bear and waited for an answer. A sign. Anything to show him God had heard.

Silence.

Several minutes passed. Finally, Daniel hung his head and grimaced. He rose from his knees disappointed. Now his wounds were beyond exposed. They throbbed with rejection.

He trudged onto the back deck and watched the moonlit Pacific Ocean below. Waves rolled in and slapped the beach methodically. Strangely, with each crash on the sand they seemed to be waving goodbye.

It wasn't an illusion. Daniel sensed the need to go. There was nothing left for him here. No job. No future. And, with the absence of divine guidance, apparently God didn't want him anymore.

He had one alternative: take the job offer from Seattle and move to Washington State. The purposeful call last week from a retiring Executive Administrator in the Northwest had almost made Daniel laugh. Being asked to consider an administrative position over a private Christian hospital for mostly terminally ill children was more than a step down from practicing neurosurgery. But then—he *wasn't* practicing anymore.

So, he had listened to the offer.

Surprisingly, their salary proposal was high for a small organization, and the whole idea had caused Daniel to reevaluate his professional goals. After a complete briefing and a few interview steps by telephone and fax, they had offered him the position and were waiting to take him on—immediately. If he accepted, he would train under the current executive for a few weeks of transition, until Christmas. Then he'd be on his own.

Directing medical staff would be a challenge, but this opportunity meant more than a new career. It was quite possibly the change he needed: All business. No emergencies. No more jeopardizing others' lives.

A clean slate, the idea soothed his scarred soul.

Ocean waves crashed again, lifting him from his musings. A gale picked up and blew against his face. Its salty, seaweedy smells potent and familiar. Strange, he thought. Even the wind seemed to be urging him to move on.

Daniel closed his eyes and nodded. The tides of his life were changing. He had longed for a break like this, an opportune crack in the wall of despair he'd lived behind for too long. A chance to start his life over.

Bits of resolution settled, pieced together in his mind. He knew what he should do, and he missed the beach house already. He loved living here. But that was before the pain. Since then, the solitude had become an escape, a fortress where he could hide from defeat and lick his wounds. He'd spent the last twelve months running from his disgrace—and that had seemed an eternity.

It wasn't like Daniel Brakken to stay down, though. His present anguish had rocked him considerably more than any previous trial, yet something inside drove him to move on.

Massaging his bleary eyes he shuffled back inside and slumped onto the supple, leather couch. He stared into the blackness, void of hope. Needing a miracle, yet certain he was unworthy of one.

You're on your own, he thought, feeling his prayer had been a waste of time—something God had ignored with due justice. Daniel's throat tightened at even considering that, but he'd been the one to walk away first. He erected a wall against the building emotion. If God was still interested in him, God would have to track him down. He had humbly given the Almighty an honest chance to guide him—

Nothing.

That left one option.

"It's all you've got, *Doctor* Brakken," he mocked the former prestigious title and staked an end to indecision. Tender Loving Care Hospital in Seattle wasn't a chief pick—certainly not the high-caliber medical career he was accustomed to—but it was all he had. He would call Henry Freeman in the morning and fax his acceptance letter. Then he would carry out his hopes for a new life, the same way he'd learned to cope these long, twelve months. . . .

Alone.

Chapter Two

One week later—Seattle, Washington.

*K*ate Montgomery stood stiffly at the back of the meeting room. Her tailored, mauve suit bore a few wrinkles, but it was fine for the announcement. She crossed her arms over her waist, trying to keep her butterflies at bay. She couldn't bear to sit down. Her pulse raced and her ears buzzed from adrenaline. Why couldn't Henry have mentioned their decision before this? she wished. Regardless, if Henry didn't get on with things, she was certain she'd faint right on the floor.

Hospital personnel filed in eagerly. At 4:30 on Friday afternoon, the room was packed with nurses, doctors, personnel, and volunteers—both on and off duty. Only a skeleton crew watched TLC's three floors during the brief assembly.

Kate clenched her hands. She'd waited five years for this day—this meeting—the declaration of Henry's replacement as Executive Administrator. It just had to be her!

They'd interviewed for two months and several applicants had been turned away in the final consultations. She'd been told a week previously that only two were left, and she was one of them. The other candidate was a man from California, some stranger the rest of the staff knew nothing about.

Surely they wouldn't want an outsider, she reasoned. Kate felt confident. Besides, the Board always made their decisions based on Henry's recommendations, and she'd been groomed for this position under his tutelage. He'd always supported her desire to direct this hospital in his footsteps. She couldn't lose, as long as she had his vote.

Two charge nurses sat in the last row of available seats, right in front of where Kate stood. They turned, giving her smiles and thumbs-up signals. "We're pulling for you, Kate," Jocelyn Greenbeck whispered.

Kate smiled nervously and nodded. "Thanks."

The staff was being terrific. Most had already voiced their wishes for her to be chosen. It encouraged Kate to know they actually wanted her to be in charge.

She wanted it too. Overseeing the care of these children was more than a job to Kate. It fulfilled something in her, satisfied a calling in her life. She knew she would never rest content with anything else.

The jabbering crowd silenced when Henry Freeman finally strode through the door and stood before his audience. He smiled, briefly, but his face seemed unusually pale to Kate. Though in his mid-sixties, Henry's age was rarely noticeable to her. Now, at that moment, he looked weak. The loss of zeal made him appear frail. Old.

Troubled.

She tried discerning his mood, but he wouldn't make eye contact with her. No reassuring smile in her direction. No usual fatherly wink.

Something's wrong. Kate's heart rate doubled. For the first time all week she realized what made him look so downcast: He was being elusive. In retrospect, his behavior had been very unusual since Monday. He'd even cancelled his weekly status meeting with her without explaining why.

"As you all realize," Henry began, "we will have a new Executive Administrator at TLC beginning next week. First of all, I want everyone to know that the board gave tremendous consideration to the final nominees. Both of them are extremely qualified, and we are honored to have had two splendid candidates from which to choose."

Dr. Michael Reid, standing beside Kate, patted her shoulder. She blushed at his approval, and her breathing grew choppy.

Henry continued. "Although having wonderful applicants made our selection more difficult, we believe we've chosen judiciously for our exceptional hospital. I hope you will receive Daniel Brakken, and support him as faithfully as you have me. He'll arrive Monday from Los Angeles and . . ."

The remainder of Henry's speech faded from Kate's thoughts. Her heart slowed to a painful thudding. The surrounding room blurred over. Had she heard correctly?

". . . Thank you for coming." Henry ended his speech and finally glanced her way. He looked grieved. His bluish-gray eyes were somber, remorseful. Then he excused himself from the hubbub and left the meeting.

Kate's lungs craved oxygen, but she was practically in shock. She felt as though the wind was knocked from her.

A warm hand rested on her forearm. "Sorry, Miss Kate."

"Yeah, next time, Lady." Zinnia and Jocelyn, her closest co-workers, tried consoling her as they left the meeting.

"Thanks," she forced a strangled reply, trying to inhale normally and respond with good nature.

Others shuffled from the room, past her, their faces considerably more melancholy than when they'd arrived. Several extended their lamentations. She returned polite thank-yous but felt numb to it all. Her attention was arrested, imprisoned by the memory of Henry's solemn visage, and those three unbelievable words: *Mr. Daniel Brakken.*

She contended with the lump in her throat while questions deluged her mind and emotions gripped her insides. The impossible had happened. But how? How had the tables turned so quickly? She didn't understand.

After the attendees filed out of the room, she made her way back to Henry's office and stood in front of the closed door, hesitating. She drew in a bolstering breath and examined her motives. She wasn't jealous—just dumbfounded. And she had to know.

She knocked.

"Come in, Kate."

"You knew it was me?" she asked at hearing her name.

She stepped in and closed the door behind her. It latched with a soft snap. Henry sat in his brown leather chair, looking even more pale close up.

"I knew you'd come," he answered in a subdued manner.

Silence fell between them for a moment. His face reflected compassion, understanding, like a father who could easily discern his daughter's moods. Many times Kate had felt like he'd adopted her. When she had blundered nursing school by fainting over some bloody procedures, he'd taken her under his wing at TLC, encouraged her that there were other, equally blessed ways to minister to infirmed children. He'd helped her, trained her, watched her progress—and mostly—encouraged her to apply for his position once he retired. He'd praised her continuously for her ideas and zeal, claiming she had exemplary capacity to direct the hospital. How had all of that failed to make any difference in their selection?

She crossed her arms, attempting to hold in check the ricocheting emotions. "Then, you know what I'm about to ask."

Manifold wrinkles creased Henry's brow and around his eyes. Their rumples intensified his sorrowful expression. He laced his spotted, aged fingers together in a prayer-like fashion. "Yes." He paused, and waited.

"Why didn't you tell me, *before* the meeting?"

He looked her in the eye. "Because you wouldn't have come."

His answer caught her off guard; she acknowledged the truth in it. Ordinarily she admired his perceptivity; now it irritated her. "Even so, do you have any idea how embarrassed I was? You should have informed me first."

"I couldn't. Besides, you needed to be there to see how hard it was for me to announce."

"Hard for *you?*"

"I'm sorry, Kate. I know you're disappointed. It's warranted. But please, . . .
give this a little time."

His soft, blue-gray eyes held her attention. She blinked in dismay, wondering what the last half-decade of personal training was all about.

"This will work out. You'll understand. . . . later," he added.

"Later? I've walked in your footsteps for five years. How much more time
should I have on my résumé?" Bitterness pricked at her, and she tried to ward it
off.

Henry sighed. "You need to give him a chance. Things will look different in
a few months."

She neared losing control of her voice. "A small hospital like this can be
ruined by then. Come on, Henry. What do you know about this man, anyway?
What is his background?"

"Daniel Brakken is very . . . *accomplished.*"

"In what?" she pleaded, insisting on impressive credentials but also knowing they could put her own experience to shame.

Henry paused. She sensed he was withholding something—maybe a lot.

"In real-life trauma," he finally responded.

"What's that supposed to mean?" Her attitude grew sardonic. "Just tell me
the truth—is it because he's a man?"

"Heavens, no!" he said, shaking his head deliberately. "Look, I know you're
not happy with this decision, but the Board is confident. They believe Daniel
Brakken is the right person. For now, anyway."

His meaning was clear. His tone absolute. She saw there was no chance for a
reversal at this stage.

"Kate, I really hope you can accept this because Daniel is going to need
you to support him. . . . *you* need to support him."

She grimaced, unconvinced. "Why is that?"

Henry stared at his desk. "Because there is more at stake."

Needles of fear pierced her remaining hope. "What?"

"Well, . . . he's not in favor of your Wellness Program."

She blinked, then swallowed hard. "Why not? It's breaking medical records
in recovery stats. We're getting national media coverage."

"I know, I know. Unfortunately, I'm not the one you'll need to convince
anymore. Daniel is your new superior, and he wants to review your program reports first thing Monday morning. And Kate . . ." He glanced up meekly, pain
etched on his face. "He intends to auction the carousel."

Her indignation rose like boiling water. "He *what?*" She paced the office
floor, hands flailing. "He—he can't! Don't you realize—? No—the children!
They'll be absolutely crushed."

"I realize what it means. But he's got big ideas on expanding and upgrading
the ER, and he plans to use profits from selling the carousel. Those horses and
other figures are worth many thousands apiece, and he's definitely aware of it. I

know the ER needs improvement, but I'm with you on this. The carousel should stay." Henry sighed and hung his head. "I wish we'd known this before making him an offer, but we learned of it after his acceptance was voted on."

She ceased pacing. Her lungs felt taught with pressure.

Henry looked straight at her. "You have got to convince him not to do this. If anyone can persuade him, you can. *That's why* you need to stay on here." Henry looked desperate. "Don't give up on this program, Katie. I think he will turn around."

She knew when he called her Katie that he was sincere. She couldn't blame Henry for what was happening, and she finally gave him a nod. "OK," her lips answered, but her heart wasn't in support of it.

She turned to leave, then stopped and looked back. "Henry?"

"Yes, Katie?"

"Do . . . do you still believe in me? For this position?"

Henry looked choked, forlorn. He cleared his throat and smiled, his eyes moist with emotion. "You are clearly my best choice. You always have been. And when the time comes, you will be the Board's. I hope you'll be patient until that time."

She nodded again and left.

Heading back to her desk, she tried to accept his supportive words, to let them sink in. Still, it couldn't diffuse her ire over Mr. Brakken wanting to sell the carousel.

The "Miracle Machine," as the kids lovingly called it, was more than financial capital. It really belonged to TLC's children. Kate's grandfather had willed it to the hospital, but he had intended it for *their* benefit—not for administration to use as a business asset. Unfortunately, the will hadn't specifically stated just that.

Initially, Kate had begun helping Grandpa Joe restore it to help pass the hard time following her mother's death. When she started working at the hospital, the kids continually asked to see pictures of the carousel. That's when she proposed the idea to her grandfather to bring the carousel to them. They tried coming up with a plan, but two months later Grandpa Joe died, never realizing the medical "miracles" that would follow his generous gift of joy.

Now, repulsed by the new administrator's greedy desire for money, Kate collected her coat and purse to leave. She had one weekend to brainstorm, and the clock was ticking fast.

She strode out of the office wing and through the hospital's automatic doors. Frigid December winds buffeted her face. She pulled her coat tighter and glanced beyond the covered loading zone to see the night sky. No stars. Only thick, black clouds hovered ominously above, threatening snow.

She scorned the nimbus shroud. As if a private hospital for children fighting terminal illnesses didn't face enough trials. Snow especially complicated matters in the hilly terrain of Seattle.

The freezing wind and draping clouds symbolized more, however, than ill climate. They paralleled the dark adversity standing in her way. Mr. *Daniel Brakken*. She frowned and tried to picture the coldhearted man. "Accomplished," Henry had said. It was probably just a nice word for old codger, she mused as she continued around the annex and toward the hospital's unique, glass pavilion. Beneath the sidewalk lamppost, she stopped to gaze at the grand machine within the dome. Her throat tightened. Her fist clenched so hard around her car keys that they jabbed into her palm.

"I can't let him sell it." Her breath fogged the frosty pane in front of her. For seconds it clouded her view of the carousel inside, then dissipated quickly with the wind. Cast with shadows, the large contraption sat motionless, a lamentable, arrested display. Horses and animals hung frozen on their poles. She envisioned them as captive exhibits in some home or office. Collector's items. Forever void of animation, music, and—most of all—children's laughter.

The mournful idea made her nauseated.

Then it strengthened her fortitude.

Mr. Brakken would be here Monday morning. She had roughly sixty hours before then to come up with a strategy. He may have snatched away the promotion due her—there was nothing she could do to change that—but he wasn't waltzing up to Seattle and eliminating her nationally-acclaimed program. She would rival with all she had before letting anyone auction their Miracle Machine!

"Don't worry, kids. . . ." She squeezed her eyes shut and pledged in faith to the children within the medical center. They relished the therapy rides on the ornately carved wonder horses. Sadly—short of a miracle—they would soon learn of the program's jeopardy, and it would dash their spirits.

". . . Christmas is coming," her voice broke with emotion. "It's the time of miracles." Sending a prayer to heaven for help, she took a bolstering breath and finally released her vice grip on the keys. She believed in miracles. Nevertheless, she hoped, desperately, she could make good her promise.

She forged on toward the staff parking lot, desiring to get home before any snow arrived. With each careful step on the icy blacktop she rehearsed her objective for the next two days: *Find a plan. Find a plan.*

Before she faced Mr. Brakken.

Chapter Three

"Wow!" Andrew Tucker sat up in his bed.

A frequent resident on TLC's second floor west wing, he shuffled his flannel pajama-clad body over to the window and gaped—eyes wide, mouth open—through the double-pane glass. Thick flakes spiraled down in promenade, flurrying occasionally from a blustering gale.

"It's snowing!" he squawked in his tired, youthful voice.

The descending veil of dotted white gladdened his eight-year-old heart, and his glee hoisted a huge grin on his face.

"Allllright! Thanks, God!" he chirped.

"Hey, Champ? It's after midnight," a friendly female voice called. He turned to see Nurse Jocelyn, his favorite night charge, standing at his door. "What's got you up, kiddo?"

"Snow!" he piped again. "I asked God if He would make it snow, and He did!"

She came up beside him and placed her hand on his shoulder. They peered out the window together. "Did you doubt He would hear you?"

Andrew's joyous smile faded somewhat. "No, I think He listens. It's just . . ."

After a long moment, she asked, "Hmm?"

He faced her, a knot of frustration tying up his insides. "Well, I've prayed before and He didn't answer me."

Her dark eyebrows curved sympathetically. "I see." She tucked her hands into the pockets of her rainbow-striped jacket—the cheery, uniform piece that all the nurses and volunteers wore. "May I ask what you prayed for?"

Andrew admired the snow again, fighting inner pangs of sorrow. "To take away my tumor."

She didn't respond right away. He figured it had stumped her, too.

"You know, Andy," Jocelyn knelt beside him and placed her arm around his shoulders. He turned to look at her. Soft white glow from the window's string of Christmas lights graced her face. The tiny dots sparkled in her eyes. "I'd like very much for God to do that, too. But, sometimes He answers our prayers in a different way than we'd like. So, when you don't see the answer you wanted right away, it doesn't mean He has stopped caring about you."

Andrew watched her silently, searching for the truth behind her words. She seemed confident, certain of them.

"Why, I bet He's working on it right now," she added.

He wanted to believe her—really. But the brain tumor was growing. He knew they'd tried everything. No one could hide that after four years of testing and three surgeries. He knew the headaches would return. Eventually.

Unless God stepped in.

Andrew swallowed at the tightness in his throat. "You really think so?" he asked, daring to hope.

"Yes. I really do." She nodded.

She looked sincere to him, and he was heartened by her faith. He smiled. "OK. But I hope He answers by Christmas."

"Me too." She smiled back at him and ruffled his hair. "Now, time for bed, Champ. You still need your sleep."

Kate sanded the wooden horse leg until her lap was layered in fine dust. She blew. The scent of pine filled the room. Then she smoothed her hand down the length of the leg, checking for rough spots. *Like satin.* She beamed. "Ready for painting," she said, and brushed her palms together.

Then she wiped her brow with a forearm and slumped back in the chair. Her shoulders ached, her hands felt knotted. After spending most of Saturday in her usual manner—restoring another carousel animal—she recognized the warning signs to call it quits.

She stood up from her chair, brimming with satisfaction but stiff as a crowbar. Though comfortably dressed in gray stirrup pants and her favorite navy sweatshirt with embroidered roses, her leg muscles were beyond taut—they twinged. She endured a painful stretch until she gained some relief.

Kate patted the horse's wooden nose. "Enough for today, pal. Soon you'll get your first coat."

Her painstaking efforts were noble, but she wondered if they were now in vain, with Mr. Brakken coming to town. It incensed her to even think of him nonchalantly deciding to sell TLC's carousel without asking the children or the hospital staff what they wanted. Without even seeing it first. And all *before* he started the position!

She couldn't agree with his reasoning. He had to be blinded by something. Yes, TLC needed a sizable bundle of money to expand and update their ER. Kate admitted it seemed a respectable business decision to raise money as quickly as possible. But TLC wasn't a business. And a hospital needed to enact major changes with far more care than a company. Lives were at stake with every transition—especially big ones.

Besides, there were more features to the Wellness Program than the carousel. To withdraw the Program in the interest of the ER would be like cutting off their right leg to fix the left.

She let her recollection trail on. . . . Kate remembered how the Program had greatly benefited the small hospital. Being privately owned and operated, many of TLC's staff were strong Christians, especially Henry. As his Assistant Administrator, Kate suggested that the Board allow the children to receive prayer if they wanted it. Wisely, to quiet any opposition, she backed up her proposal—as she always did—with several medical journal studies and psychology reports concluding that prayer was a significant positive influence in recovery.

One recent California study showed that church attenders had lower death rates than nonattenders. Another study, for cancer patients, revealed seven out of eight people with a strong religious commitment had fewer symptoms and better outcomes.

By not using government funding, religion couldn't be restricted in their hospital. So, it wasn't long before the Board expanded their policies to offer prayer to the children as regularly as other caregiving. And the kids favored the change. They often said prayers for one another, more than for themselves.

How Henry had battled the press! She recalled their victory wasn't without resistance. Nevertheless, TLC's recovery rates soon ranged considerably higher than other conventional hospitals in the Northwest region. The impressive statistics began silencing their critics, and the media gave up the chase.

Beyond prayer, the Wellness Program also offered a few less controversial activities, like their in-house petting zoo. Provided the activity wouldn't exacerbate a child's condition, their physicians allowed them to play with a few domestic and exotic animals sequestered in one annex. The creatures were cared for by a staff zoologist and two volunteer veterinarians. Everything was kept very sanitary. Visitation was closely monitored, and restrained only if medically necessary. Children who were not permitted inside the isolated "zoo" could still enjoy watching the animals through a large glass wall. Over all, the bonding with animals greatly helped the children's morale and made their hospital stay more enjoyable.

But as far as the kids were concerned, the carousel was the grand highlight. And it had effected some truly miraculous transformations in them. Not merely emotional lift, but physical improvements were discovered to take place after routinely riding the carousel. For a few, the special daily rides had actually helped promote recovery. New life! Undeniably, Kate knew God always imparted the healing, but she kept thoroughly documented medical reports to substantiate the program's benefit to each child.

"*Reports!*" Rousing from her deep reflection, she smacked her palm against her forehead. "Oh, no!"

The thought of them reminded her of Mr. Brakken's first mandate: Having her Wellness Program journals and stats on his desk Monday morning. Fortunately, the records were complete—except for the first week of December, which she needed to organize. But she really wanted to review them—all five years—before handing them over for scrutiny. It went against her nature to submit any report without meticulously double-checking facts and organizing the documents.

Unfortunately, in her distress yesterday evening, Kate had left the hospital without them. Now she would have to go back. There wouldn't be time to review them Sunday, with church services and her usual visit with Grandmother Rose. She would need at least six hours. Her compilations were so inclusive—with preliminary discussions, permits, and structural plans. Then, there were case studies, findings, interviews with physicians and psychologists on local television stations and newspapers to support the "new" treatment at Tender Loving Care Hospital.

Certainly, that would be enough to sway Mr. Brakken.

And if not? Doubt and fear slithered into her thoughts like evil twins, securing their undermining tentacles around her faith. She tried to reassure herself things wouldn't turn out adversely.

But what if things did? Qualms squeezed their way in again.

In that case, she determined she'd just have to pray for a Plan B!

Chapter Four

*K*ate pulled into the staff parking lot just as another sprinkling of snow floated down. Thankfully, the roads had remained clear, but the temperature was dropping with the onset of Saturday's evening skies.

Begrudgingly, she hoped the cold weather would send Mr. Brakken running back to his former job—whatever it was—in sunny California!

A twinge of guilt nudged her, and tender words captured her mind: *Love your enemies, do good to those who persecute you.* She gave them heed. Though the new administrator's decision against her program could hardly be considered persecution, Kate felt obligated to pray for him. Especially since he was her new boss.

"I'm listening, Lord. Please bless Mr. Brakken with Your grace in his new position. Guide him by Your hand. Please cause him to become an asset to TLC, and help me to serve and support him, as I would You. Amen."

Feeling more serene from the prayer, she left her warmed car and walked briskly toward the entrance, having forgotten her coat at home, in haste.

She noticed that several of the children's windows were now decked with colorful light-strings. They shone and blinked in the faint light of dusk, a sort of Morse code of peace. Kate thought it was actually beginning to feel like Christmas.

Once inside the South wing, she unlocked the door to Administration and strode through to her office—if it could be called that—the largest of five cubicles sectioned off with medium-high partition walls. It held the basics: desk, telephone, computer, printer, and an in-box piled high with paperwork. Only Henry's office had real walls and a door. When he went on vacations and left her in charge she always worked in there, relishing the quiet atmosphere.

Kate walked to the file cabinets and, one at a time, pulled down eight large three-ring binders from above. She stacked them into a single tower on top of her desk, then walked over to the office's air-compression door. After propping the door open, she relocked it, then went back to carefully lift the tall armload of binders. She waddled to the doorway. At the entrance she paused and scanned the floor for the rubber doorstop. Spying it, she gave it a swift boot from its position, and strode through.

Whump!

"Oh!" The impact stunned her. She blinked, relieved the binders didn't fall.

"What on earth—?" The deep voice of her doorway contender was definitely masculine, though she couldn't see him because of the binders. Kate backed up a step to turn, but suddenly the door's compression pulled forward and it bumped her in the backside.

"Oof!" She lunged into the man again. This time, the binders tumbled all around them.

They both stood, baffled by the mishap. His dark gold eyes locked on her, revealing his displeasure, and demanding an explanation. *Lion's eyes*, she thought, unnerved by his gaze. Yet, their intensity held more than agitation. They revealed inner fortitude and something else. *Need.*

"I-I'm so sorry," she declared, embarrassed. "Are you hurt?" She gaped at her surprised casualty in his chestnut suede coat. He resembled a fatigued Harrison Ford, only his facial features were younger—harder. Thick, light-brown whiskers revealed several days without shaving. Rumpled hair and dark bags beneath his eyes evidenced too many nights without sleeping.

His stubbly jaw clenched. "No, fortunately, I'm not hurt," he answered bruskly.

The man's irritation was obvious, and semi-warranted. Kate wasn't able to meet his chastening stare any longer. She knelt to restack her binders. "Really, I am sorry," she added. "I should've made two trips, but I was in a hurry."

After a tense moment of silence, he knelt beside her and methodically added a binder to her stack. "You know," his tone was lower, more restrained, "Hospital staff is supposed to help heal people, not injure them."

His admonishment was clear, but it carried a hint of forgiveness in the way he'd said it. Kate faced him and determined to accept his correction responsibly. His glower had tempered to a *you-should-know-better* look, and he reached for another binder.

"True," she answered. She acknowledged his mercy—though sparse—and suddenly felt awkward with his aid. "Thanks for helping, but I can get this."

"Actually, I hope you can help me," he said bluntly.

He was still crouched beside her, arms resting on his blue-jean-clad thighs. She smelled the rich leather of his coat. Its smooth scent was far too soft to match his rough demeanor.

Maybe he's having a bad week, she thought, giving him a generous benefit of the doubt.

"Yes?" she asked, willing kindness and patience. She placed the last few binders onto two evenly divided stacks, then straightened herself.

"I know it's Saturday, and you're obviously busy," he grimaced at the towers of binders, "but I'm looking for Henry Freeman. Is he here, by chance?"

"You found his office, but you're right, he's not usually in on weekends. I'll be happy to leave him a message." She went to unlock the door again and retrieve the secretary's message log. "Your name?"

"Daniel Brakken."

Daniel Brakken! The words exploded in Kate's brain like dynamited Ping-Pong balls. Her whole body stiffened. She blinked and looked him over again. *No—! He's supposed to be older, codgerly, and . . . unattractive.* This man in front of her was nothing like her envisioned rival.

"I can spell it," he added, obviously growing impatient with her sustained pause.

"Ahhh, . . . Mr. Brakken. . . . You—you're TLC's new Executive Administrator."

"Yes." He nodded, looked unhappy about the declaration.

Kate pasted on a nervous smile as her cheeks grew fiery hot. She further regretted her carelessness with the reports.

"I'm Kate Montgomery, your Assistant. It's a . . ." She offered a tardy handshake, still reeling that he wasn't the older man she'd expected, ". . . pleasure to meet you," she finished.

He shook her hand and, for the first time, observed the rest of her, casually dressed and still powdered with sanding dust.

"You work in Administration?" he asked. A paltry grin curled up on his lips.

"Yes," she answered, retracting her hand. "Not dressed like this, of course."

He now seemed accepting of her. His attempt at smiling made him almost pleasant. Kate started to feel a pull, a magnetism, she hadn't before. When he wasn't glaring, Daniel Brakken was genuinely appealing—in a vanquished, calloused way. Not many men remained handsome with tired eyes, disheveled hair, and a porcupine beard.

She pushed her musings aside, intent on keeping things "business" between her and her new boss. She had a lot of tough territory ahead to cross with him. Right now, she needed to redeem her image from that of a senseless broad. "Mr. Brakken, I'm not typically careless," she added. "It's just that, rarely is anyone around this wing on a Saturday."

He didn't look persuaded, so she tried for a more professional topic. "Henry spoke favorably of you. He claims, with your experience, you'll be a tremendous asset to TLC. I'm hoping we can make a good team." *Praying* was more accurate, but Kate sensed this man didn't lean on anyone but himself.

"Great. I need a good secretary."

Kate gave a short, surprised laugh. She cleared her throat and shook her head. "No, you misunderstand. I meant *Assistant Administrator*, Mr. Brakken. I'm the supervising director below you. I handle the hospital's Wellness Program, staffing, patient programs, and numerous other things. Lisa is *our* secretary."

He paused at hearing the words. The revelation seemed to sap him of strength, like a punch in the stomach. Tiny wrinkles emerged around his eyes, along with a bewildered expression.

Kate's pulse accelerated. Misgiving swelled inside her. She wondered why mentioning her position brought such a reaction.

"Henry explained your support staff, didn't he?" she asked.

"Yes—well, he said I would have a very capable assistant, but I thought—" He frowned again. "You're not what I imagined."

She raised her eyebrows. At least she'd been courteously silent about her erroneous presumptions. He was not only outspoken but seemed disapproving, as well. Slivers of fear pierced Kate's surety. She waited for him to explain, but Daniel only kept his golden gaze on her. He seemed caught in a mental struggle. It disturbed her that he couldn't even appear eager to work with her, especially after she'd gained Henry's laud all these years.

"Mr. Brakken," she folded her hands together and faced him. "Clearly, my actual capacity here is a surprise to you, but I'm confident that you'll be pleased with my accomplishments, as well as the Wellness Program."

He shifted his stance. One eyebrow tilted and his mouth curved a disbelieving arch. "Uh-huh. That is an . . . *interesting* program. You were the one responsible?"

She nodded, feeling condemned by the way he said it. "Yes. I've also kept it going, despite all our outside opposition." She could feel the fires of testing heating up, but she was proud of her efforts, just the same.

"Hmm . . ." His expression grew stern. "Did Henry mention I wanted to review this program when I arrived?"

Kate blinked. Adrenaline shot through her. She heard an imaginary timebomb start ticking. "He did," the answer sort of slid from her lips. Her assurance was crumbling. Daniel's so-called "interest" really put her on edge.

"Good!" he countered bluntly.

Boy! Henry wasn't kidding! she thought, evaluating her competition more closely. Now she needed every moment to prepare her reports—and herself—to defend the Program.

Growing uncomfortable, Kate turned and hoisted one of the two small towers of binders. "Well, Mr. Brakken, if you'll excuse me, I've got to get going. We can talk more on Monday." She left the hospital and hustled to her car through the increasingly snowy sheets, suddenly realizing Daniel was close behind her with the other stack. Stopping beside her car, she peered at him, silently questioning his assistance.

"You didn't want to make two trips, remember?" he said.

"Thanks." She unloaded her stack into the back seat of her gold Ford Taurus, then turned to unburden him.

"What are these, anyway?" Daniel asked, half-glaring again.

Adrenaline rippled through her. She wasn't yet prepared for a verbal defense of the program. But she couldn't lie. "Reports . . . on TLC's Wellness Program. I've kept meticulous records of its operation from the start. *Successful* operation, I might add." She glanced at him candidly while packing the last volume. Then she swung the car door shut.

A scant smile graced his face. Her plug seemed to amuse him. He observed her, his tired eyes alert with visible dare. "Well, if it's so successful, why are you absconding with the evidence?" he calmly charged. "Planning to alter the documents?"

Kate's jaw dropped. His teasing accusation made her feel guilty, though the notion was entirely unfounded. *He's tougher than I thought!* Although she knew he was probably trying to get her goat, her assurance of winning him over to the program cracked—significantly. She shivered without her coat and propped her numbing hands upon her hips, giving him her most contesting smile.

"Mr. Brakken, you asked to see my reports on Monday. That's *five years* of extensive data and records. I'm making sure they're all organized—for your convenience."

Daniel stared firmly, unmoving. His eyes were colder than the weather. Then, for a fleeting instant, their dark honey-gold glinted. His lips turned slightly upward, revealing a diversion in his attention.

But it lasted only a moment.

He reached for and opened the driver's door for her, indifferent once again. "See you on Monday, Miss Montgomery."

She nodded, and slunk down into the driver's seat. He closed the door and walked away.

While driving home, Kate analyzed the rising opposition. It made her grip the steering wheel even tighter as she navigated carefully through the increasing snow.

Daniel Brakken was single-handedly the most intriguing man she'd ever met. And the most frustrating! The amalgamation of his "push-me-pull-you" character seemed impossible to understand—yet it stirred her soul. She'd never met a man like him, one who sparked her determination, but in the tick of a second made her feel vulnerable to his gaze.

She sensed he relished challenge—faced it brazenly. Yielded *rarely*.

Yet, something else in his eyes indicated defeat. Maybe recent. Maybe a bad one. He bore evidence of scars, but she sensed he was normally a man who'd quit at nothing. He'd keep matching his rival, *mano a mano*, until he conquered it— or it conquered him.

Now, he wanted her territory. He was taking over and eliminating her program—all without remorse!

"Oh, why this, Lord?" she pleaded for wisdom. "Why the carousel?"

Kate didn't mind a little tribulation in life—she'd faced lions before. But this special program was so far her biggest ambition in life. It was more than just the Miracle Machine, it was her ministry to the hurting, sick children. If Daniel Brakken succeeded in removing it . . . he'd be doing surgery on her heart.

You have got to convince him not to do this, Henry's appeal from yesterday flooded into her mind. Strangely, it paralleled the way her Grandpa Joe had always bolstered her courage.

Fond memories resurfaced of her maternal grandfather. He was the kindest man she'd ever known, the finest carousel restorer on the West Coast, the only real "Daddy" she'd ever had. She recalled cheerful times, of playing on the wooden horses he loved reconditioning. She test-rode each one as it was finished and erected onto the flooring. Her smile was always Grandpa's gauge for approval, and she had loved him so for the restoration he'd brought into her broken, young life through his tender care.

Kate missed Grandpa Joe these long four-and-a-half years. Sorely! But the inner strength he'd imparted to her came back when she needed it most. Strength from knowing God. From believing in Him. From trusting Him—leaning on Him in everyday situations. All of them: the happy, the mundane, the sorrowful.

She'd learned to trust her Heavenly Father at an early age. She'd had to. Her earthly father had failed her miserably. He had shattered her heart and left it in pieces.

Now Kate's life was in upheaval again. She needed the Lord's help. Her career and her dreams were on the chopping block. Prayer and perspective were vital, but she'd have to do her part, too. And, with a clearer idea of what— rather—who she was facing, she desperately needed a plan. *Anything* that would keep Daniel Brakken from tearing down everything she had contributed to the hospital and to the lives of the children.

And she needed it soon!

Chapter Five

*D*aniel groped for the icy house keys. They clanked as he retrieved them from the metal newspaper bin where his new landlady instructed him to check.

Driving on snowy roads to the woodsy area outside of Issaquah had taken him over an hour. But earlier in the week, when he'd called on ads for a furnished rental house, *peaceful* topped his list. If this enormous three-story cabin in a virtual forest was the nearest serenity available, he'd take the commute over noise any day.

Even with his car headlights on, he couldn't see much of the huge house from the front. It was too dark and thickly surrounded by trees. It didn't matter right now, anyway. He was here and it was the right place, evidenced by the keys with his name tagged on them. He unlocked the heavy door and pushed it slowly open.

Daniel stepped inside the shadowy entry. Wood flooring *tap-creaked* beneath his heavy steps. He stood, expended from two days of driving, and sighed. The warmth of his face melted the snowflakes on his nose and cheeks. Keen cedar and sweet spice surrounded him with their hearthy aroma. The cabin seemed to welcome him, make him feel . . . at home.

Home. The soothing thought comforted his aching, weary frame. It made him wish for someone to greet him after a long day. Someone like Kate. He recalled her lush auburn hair, sea-green eyes. She was different. Genuine. Beautiful—exceptionally so—but not in the same way as the other women he'd known. Her attractiveness went beyond the physical and radiated from beneath the skin. Inner beauty.

She'd hooked his interest. For sure! And like a fool teenager, he could barely speak when she'd said they'd be working together. Day after day.

Yeah, someone like Kate would be nice, he yearned. But realistically, she'd never have him. Not the *real* him, tormented as he was. He wasn't good enough for her. Never would be. He knew it. And if Kate Montgomery was one gorgeous hair as intelligent as he sensed, she knew it too.

Daniel fumbled for and found the covered porch's light switch. With a flip, golden glow illumined the snow drifting down around the large alcove. Big flakes came down now. He shivered and stared in amazement. *Man!* It'd been a long time since he'd actually seen snow. Over fifteen years—while attending Med School at the University of Washington.

Although the separation from cold weather hadn't made his heart grow fonder toward it, he felt a renewed appreciation for how pure and peaceful everything looked under a blanket of heavenly white.

Too bad the snow couldn't transform his muddled life the same way, Daniel wished, then ambled back to his car.

He unloaded only necessary bags for now, and plopped them onto the spacious, circular, tweed-twisted rug in the living room. He then went back and turned off the headlights. The rest would wait until morning. He was beat. Beyond beat—fatigued. The bone-deep exhaustion paralleled bygone days in surgery when—

No! He flinched. Lightning defenses rose against retention. He willed the memory down . . . away . . . gone.

"You can't go back!" Daniel reproved himself. He stormed back indoors and flung the heavy door shut against the cold. It hammered into the latch. He winced at the *bang* and squeezed his eyes shut. How he longed for the guilt to cease tormenting him. Just once!

Massaging his temple, he collected his emotions. "Not a chance, Brakken," he strove to deal with the condemnation that afflicted him daily, and would for life. He had no choice but to live with it.

It was the bitter consequence of his failure.

Daniel swung at the blinding, halogen surgery light. "Move that—I can't see!" He tried to focus on the bleeding incision, but the overhead beam reflected off his tool and made it impossible to see. "Sponges! Now! We can't lose him."

Sounds—too many—beeped and clanged in the tile-floored sterile room. He kicked the utensil tray aside from obstructing him, and the nurse's resulting shriek heightened the hysteria. Daniel watched the sudden pooling of life-giving blood. His concentration wavered, plummeted. Panic raced through him akin to ice water poured into his veins.

"Pack him! Hurry up! We're *losing* him!" he barked orders while quickly but carefully filling and sopping with the surgical cotton.

The room then filled with a dreadful droning, an unrelenting, solid tone that stifled all other sounds, and rended Daniel's very soul. He glared at the heartbeat monitor screen as if he could will it back into the steady life-monitoring bleeps.

"No! *No!* Sammy, come back—you hear? Come back to me! Don't quit on me!" For a few more seconds, they packed the issuing incision. Then they quickly turned him onto his back and tried using defibrillators to command a returned pulse.

"Do it again!" Daniel yelled. The technician sent another shock.

They continued the effort. Crucial minutes passed.

But it was futile.

Daniel still called to the lifeless boy. The attending physician rested a hand on Daniel's forearm. "Dr. Brakken, he's gone . . . there's nothing more we can do."

Panting from tension, Daniel pulled off his cap and yanked his shield down in defeat. "NO!" he yelled.

Daniel's own holler woke him. He sat up with a start. The harrowing dream vanished, replaced by sunshine. Its warmth and radiance poured through the East window onto his face, causing the dark, choking waves of panic to retreat from the calming light.

Morning. Thank God! He blew out a sigh, gratefully aware of the new day.

Daniel needed the sleep, though fitful. Yet, locked in slumber, the torturous dreams once again had their way with him. They had developed over the last month, become constant—worse. His brief reflection last night on former days in surgery no doubt had watered the seed of remorse that was well rooted inside him.

Still, they had never been *this* bad, he thought. If only he hadn't remembered the OR.

But he could never forget. Why did he try?

Daniel pitched off the dampened covers. In the cold room he tugged on sweats and two pairs of cotton socks. With daylight beaming through the windows he finally took notice of his temporary, furnished dwelling. It was warmly decorated, obviously a woman's touch—but cold as a refrigerator! He rubbed his hands together and wished he'd bothered to turn on the furnace before collapsing into bed.

Carefully shuffling down the glossy pine staircase in his stockinged feet, he recalled the landlady's recommendation to use the wood stove instead of the furnace. She'd warned him the heat bills could be outrageous in the large house, as she had yet to switch to natural gas. Her promise that the wood stove made the place "toasty" in less time was enough to convince him. He was eager for heat. The stove it was.

Crumpling newspaper and stacking kindling, he formed a small teepee of debris in the iron unit. "OK, 'toasty'—I'm ready."

He struck a match. It fizzed, flamed, and tempered to a small glow. Biting sulfur awakened his nostrils and he coughed, then lit the newspaper. It easily ignited into flames that curled around the cedar sticks. They took, and started popping and snapping. Daniel huddled closer. He relished the modest instant warmth it offered. His still sleepy gaze lingered on the growing fire, and his thoughts drifted. Somehow fires were always meant to be shared with someone. Someone *special*. Someone like Kate . . .

The telephone sounded, a strange bird-chirping, electronic tweeting that annoyed him. "That will be the first thing to go," he muttered as he searched for the device. As a busy physician, he had never allowed his residence phone to ring. That was what answering machines were for.

Figuring it must be the landlady checking on his arrival, he answered politely. "Hello?" He rubbed his eyes, trying to stave off a yawn.

"Daniel?" a man's voice came through the line.

So much for the landlady. He wondered how anyone else got his new number. "Who's calling?"

"Henry Freeman. From TLC Hospital. Did I wake you? You sound half asleep."

"Oh—Henry. No, I'm up." Alleviated by the caller's importance, Daniel gaped in awe at the giant tree-trunk-sectioned clock that spanned a large portion of the fireplace wall. *Everything about this cabin home is so big!* he reflected.

Then he realized the time—12:15—with astonishment.

"Good. I figured you would be in town," said Henry.

"Yeah, but how did you get this number? I just signed the lease by fax two days ago."

"You left a message at the hospital switchboard. They contacted me."

"Oh." Daniel nodded. He'd completely forgotten about leaving his new number. Kate obviously passed it to someone else.

"Bet you're not used to this snow, huh?" Henry rambled. "Well, thanks to the sunshine the roads are clear and dry. I wanted to invite you to lunch today, with one of the other directors you should meet. Kate Montgomery. She's your Assistant."

Daniel's eyebrows arched. His mind, though fatigued, pictured her with ease. "We've met."

"You have?"

"Briefly. We sort of . . . bumped into each other at the hospital. She's the one that took my message." He couldn't deny the luring feeling as he recalled her . . . startled and lovely, her soft, peach face framed by a few escaped bangs, and the fitted, gray stirrup pants that outlined her figure. It made his insides knot—then and now!

The peculiar white powder all over her revealed she'd been up to her nose, *literally*, in something time-consuming. Even the blush of her cheeks had a dusting that dulled their glow of accomplishment. He had noticed how satisfied she'd looked, and it made him long to have that kind of gratification again through work.

". . . before you get saddled with introductions," Henry's voice drifted back into Daniel's thoughts, and he wondered what he'd missed. "That is, . . . if you don't have other plans on a Sunday," Henry concluded.

Daniel recalled a time in his past when every Sunday had a plan: Honoring God. But the memory was wrenching. He buried it within the recesses of his forsaken dreams.

"Is that OK with you?" Henry asked again.

"Sorry, I'm recovering from a long drive. What was that?"

"Lunch today, with us? Is that all right?"

"Oh, fine. Where at? And directions."

"There's a nice seafood place called The Shell House on Western Avenue. It overlooks the waterfront. Why don't you park at TLC, since you've already been there. Meet me by the office entrance, say around 1:30? We can carpool down to the restaurant in about fifteen minutes," Henry said.

"Fine. I'll be there."

Daniel punched off the cordless phone and placed it on the countertop, tempted to turn off the ringer. But he resisted the urge. He sat in the glider rocking chair beside the now hot stove. Somehow, he felt a bit nervous over seeing Kate. Thinking about her was easier. Safer. Being around her was anything but! She'd awakened something in him, something he hadn't dealt with before— even sensed before: Longing. A need to be close to someone. Maybe, to her.

At thirty-nine Daniel had never married. Never wanted to. His profession had contented him, actually *consumed* him, until life had turned a cruel twist a year ago. Now, for the first time he felt vulnerable to a woman. This woman.

And, he felt . . . alone.

Daniel sighed and drummed his fingers on the rocker arms. If these weird feelings kept up, it would prove to be very challenging working at her side. Nevertheless, until one of them quit, they would be together a lot.

And Daniel never quit.

Guilt stabbed him again as a memory of defeat surfaced. *Almost never*, he amended his personal mandate. Only when he was conquered—and that had been the case *that* time.

He squared his shoulders and mustered resolve. He was going through with this change, no matter how difficult it became. He had no other choice, so he was determined to keep a level head around Kate Montgomery. His future, his career, and his sanity depended upon it.

Luckily, there was one topic that would keep his focus on work and hold them at odds: Kate's carousel Program. Who'd ever heard of such a ludicrous operation in a hospital? he questioned the plan. It was hardly appropriate to delude children—especially those who had limited hope of living normal, happy lives—into thinking life was better with a carnival ride.

And praying for them? "Yeah, right," he scorned the thought and stood to stoke the fire. He'd tried that personally, and it had failed.

In spite of his scorn, Daniel recalled the early days when TLC's Wellness Program hit the covers of several national medical journals. In the interview, TLC had argued how prayer, among the other Program features, helped significantly with each child's recovery—sometimes bringing about unexplainable healing. Yet, the articles were discreet enough to caution that there was "no proven link to show that TLC's recoveries were tied to such aids" and the Program was deemed "medically undependable" by most of the columnists.

Being a believer in innovation himself—back then—Daniel had first thought the Program ingenious. Until raw experience soon radically changed his opinion. Especially regarding prayer. Medicine was more reliable than divine intervention—the last twelve months of his own life had confirmed that.

He stocked more wood into the stove, enough to keep the house warm for hours. Then he reached to close the iron door. It squeaked and banged into place. Daniel latched the handle down and stood.

"No way. Not with me responsible," he spoke firmly against Kate's risky concepts. Now that he was going to be in charge, her "medically undependable" Program was seeing its last days.

With that, he headed for the shower.

Chapter Six

$\mathcal{K}$ ate drummed her fingernails on the white table linen. She finished her water, poured more, checked her watch, drummed again. It was already well after 2:00. Valuable time was marching on. She had four more binders of reports to review this afternoon.

Henry and Daniel were beyond late. *Probably touring Daniel's new office*, envy's repulsive voice slipped into her thoughts. Her lips pressed to a thin line. By all rights, it should have been her office.

Kate tried reminding herself of a Biblical promise that "All things work together for good, for those that love God," but her heart wasn't convinced Daniel was the best choice. Not yet.

She felt strangely stripped of the promotion—and not by the newcomer. When Henry had announced Daniel's name at the meeting and then finally looked straight at her, more than compunction was etched on his face: Remorse. It was Henry's grievous expression that made Kate's stomach drop to her knees.

She lost out. But more than that, she couldn't put away the odd feeling that Henry'd had something to do with the outcome—firsthand—in spite of his saying he'd supported her. Yet, it didn't make sense. All her years of training, taking night classes to get a second BA in Business Administration after her degree in Health Care, encouraging her to submit her application to the board. He had wanted her to have it as much as she desired it herself. He knew of her plans and proposals for making TLC a superior, alternative hospital. He applauded them all. So why the switch?

She didn't know. And doubts were making her more edgy.

She checked her watch again. Almost 2:30. *Where are they?*

After committing her morning to worship services, she called Grandma Rose and regretfully postponed her visit until later in the week. She needed the remaining weekend to finish reviewing those reports. But Henry had insisted she come to the lunch. She checked her notes again for the restaurant name and street address: The Shell House, on Western. This was it.

A few minutes later, she finally saw Daniel enter and approach the hostess. The woman checked her chart, nodded, and offered to take his coat. He removed the leather jacket, muffler, and gloves, rubbing his hands as he parted with the raiment.

Kate watched, intrigued by this California man who was not used to cold. Not that Seattle had much snow! She and her mother had moved here from Idaho when Kate was only five, just after her father had abandoned them both. In Kate's thirty years as a Washingtonian, she remembered only a handful of winters when the white stuff lasted more than a few days.

The hostess led Daniel to Kate's table and left menus.

He looked tense, regarded her briefly. "Hello," he grumbled, and thrust a hand through his hair before he sat across from her.

My! She took in his freshened-up appearance, and a shiver raced through her. His sun-lightened bangs feathered into the tawny waves. It gave his tanned, shaven face marked appeal! The large mahogany sweater hugged his chest a little, and the white-collared shirt beneath was unbuttoned at the neck. Even dressed casually, Daniel Brakken carried a very commanding air.

She'd remembered him as good-looking in an expended sort of way. Now it was like meeting a different person, except for the scowl. "Good afternoon, Mr. Brakken," she said.

"Please—just Daniel," he advised her tersely.

She swallowed and tried to start intelligent discourse. "Glad you made it," was all she managed with a modest smile.

"Barely," he retorted and stared past her, scanning the view instead of making eye contact with her.

Daniel's eyes gleamed in the sunlight. She admired their golden intensity, how they invoked her attention. Yet, on closer glance, she again noticed a shaded depth—an obscure dullness—that belied their boldness. Kate recognized that lackluster stare. She knew it well, had seen it in the mirror a long time ago. Only one thing stripped eyes of vitality like that.

Inner pain, she contemplated the answer.

"What happened to Henry?" Daniel asked, flustered.

"Hmm?" Kate ceased her introspection. It finally dawned on her that he wasn't intentionally alone. "I thought you were catching a ride with him?"

"He never showed." Daniel grimaced. "I hope the rest of your personnel is more reliable."

Kate sighed. She didn't want another strike against her or TLC's staff. "That's really not like Henry. I'm sure he'll call if something came up."

Daniel looked placated but not convinced.

Again, she recognized his inner turmoil. It clutched at her sentiment, evoked her empathy. She was too familiar with anguish and bitter sorrow—lived with them for a sizeable part of her life. She was aware of how unremitting they were, no matter one's innocence. She knew the scars they left upon the heart.

He's been scarred, all right. Her compassion for him grew. She wondered what caused his wounds, if they were as deep-seated and agonizing as her own once were. Though he was really a stranger to her, she felt a kindred sympathy toward him. She ached to help, to somehow lead him toward the path of healing.

"Do you mind if we order?" he asked finally. "I sort of slept through breakfast."

"That's fine," she said. They turned their attention to the menus. Kate scanned the entrées, but the black calligraphy writing faded into loopy lines. Her thoughts were captured by the smooth, woodland scent of his cologne. It suited the earthy way he was dressed, but certainly not his mood—vinegar would have been a closer match for that!

Kate pursed her lips. How would she be able to work under him? When he wasn't making her uneasy from his glowering, his amiable side wreaked havoc on her concentration. She fixed her attention as best as she could on the menu.

The waiter appeared. Kate selected the fresh salmon in lemon-herb sauce, with steamed rice and vegetables. Daniel ordered steak and a baked potato, with sourdough bread and extra butter on the side. After the waiter left, Daniel poured a sizable dollop of cream into his coffee and took a sip from the taupe liquid. She grimaced at his consumption of unnecessary fat—although he didn't appear laden with any.

"So, Kate, tell me. How did you come up with this, uh, 'merry-go-round program' of yours?"

She bristled at his discourteous term. His tone warned her she was at a hearing. She wasn't supposed to face him about this until Monday, but he obviously wasn't waiting.

"I'd like to take full credit, but I can't," she began. "The carousel belonged to my Grandpa Joe. He had volunteered at the hospital since it's inception twelve years ago—and was a very benevolent donor when he died. The kids loved hearing about his work, they constantly asked us to bring in Polaroid shots to see." She used what facts she could to make Daniel reconsider selling it. "He finished it shortly before he died. After the hospital heard the machine was willed to them, they didn't know what to do with it. Knowing Grandpa Joe, I explained to the Board that my grandfather wanted the kids to enjoy it. Then I suggested they somehow make on-site use of it. Ideas flourished from there."

Daniel looked unimpressed, his expression flat.

She drew a bolstering breath and continued, "At the time, I was the Admin. Receptionist/Secretary. When Grandpa died, I'd just received my BA in Health Care and wanted to move into the hospital's Activities & Programming department. So, Henry asked me to take on the carousel project, since it was mostly my idea. After that, working on it became a fixation." She smiled. "Guess I'm a lot like my grandfather."

She examined Daniel's face for interest, still seeing none, and forged on, "Anyway, the hospital had some extra space. We transferred the cafeteria to the second floor and started assembling the carousel in what was once the outside dining courtyard. Then TLC had the glass dome built around it with a modest portion of the money Grandpa had willed them. It fit *perfectly* in the courtyard," she said frankly, underscoring her belief in the carousel's destiny at the hospital.

Having finished explaining, she sipped her water. All that time she had seen Daniel only blink, twice. She wondered if he was really listening, or preparing his speech to tell her it was over. He turned his head and peered out the restaurant's window.

Waiting anxiously for him to break the silence, Kate also glanced outside and viewed the snowcapped Olympics magnificently spanning the Western horizon. The afternoon sun made Puget Sound glisten in sapphirine waves. It was a gorgeous day. She really didn't want him to ruin it!

Daniel cleared his throat. He frowned. "I talked to Henry about this Program after I accepted the position."

She nodded, waited. Her heart pounded painfully in her chest.

"I explained I wasn't in support of the idea. Too many risks involved."

Kate's mouth was going dry. She took a drink of her water. "He said you were skeptical," she stretched the truth, "that you wanted to see the reports and any proof of its benefit. We have plenty."

Daniel looked her straight in the eye. "I respect your vision, Kate. Your drive and accomplishment are admirable. I'm just . . . not persuaded. There's a danger here you obviously don't see."

Dread washed over her. Adrenaline flashed like lightening. Her foot began bouncing nervously. "We have plenty of endorsements from physicians, not to mention credible statistics of the children's improvement when they're in the program. At least give those a fair reading."

He looked pensive. "I've read the articles that reached L.A. You received considerable press."

She was surprised, and wondered what he had read about her. She'd kept copies of as many as she had heard about, but surely there were other newspapers and periodicals across the nation she had missed. She couldn't dwell on that now. "That's press—not case studies and data. Reporters always slant stories and omit crucial information."

"These were *medical* journals," he responded, "and not entirely favorable of the program." He paused, looking serious. "It's a solemn time for these kids. Most of them are fighting to live. Some know they are dying. They need something real, *meaningful*, during this difficult stage of their lives."

Her defenses rose. "Daniel, the kids love the carousel. It's very real to them! They long to ride it. Many family members and friends can't visit them until evening; the carousel is the most meaningful thing they have each day—it's what they look forward to waking up for, despite their illness."

"Their lives are in a critical stage. They need better emergency care, something more beneficial than a fanciful carnival ride. Their physical health must come first. TLC desperately needs an upgraded ER."

"And we'll get it. TLC has never had problems meeting its financial needs."

He shook his head. "I'm sure they enjoy it, Kate. That's basically my point." His voice was now strained. He breathed sharply. "Their feelings are delicate, they should not be toyed with."

"*Toyed with?*" Her voice rose, and he glared at her. But Kate couldn't believe what she was hearing. "Their lives are filled with heartache. A few moments of joy are what they wish for each day they have left." She paused, then added, "Don't you think they deserve it?"

He looked cornered, indignant. "Of course. I'm just trying to do what's best."

"Well, they have a superb means of finding joy—a way that sometimes results in *recovery*." She kept her voice from escalating again, but she couldn't stop the tremulous reaction in her abdomen. "This program *is* best for them. In fact, I can't believe you'd even consider taking it away!"

Daniel wouldn't answer her this time. His steely, lion eyes returned, and they lit with offense.

Her breathing halted. She discerned—too late—that she'd overstepped her bounds. Maybe she'd challenged his authority too strongly. Or, maybe she'd made him realize something he didn't want to. She didn't know. She could only watch, wait for him to respond.

He stood, keeping his intense gaze on her. In a reserved and displeased tone he declared, "We'll discuss this again, at a more appropriate place. Excuse me." Then he turned and left, without regard for his food, or his bill. Daniel quickly retrieved his things without the hostess' help, without even stopping to put them on before heading outside.

Kate watched him disappear through the etched-glass doors. She hung her head and dug her fingernails into her forearms. *Terrific!* She sighed, and reflected on the whole ten minutes of conversation. Now her chances of having a decent working relationship with Daniel were minuscule—at best. And it was obvious he wasn't changing his mind about the carousel.

The waiter appeared and set two steaming plates on the table, not realizing Kate's other party had just exited the restaurant. She briefly thanked him and stared blankly at her food, then she drank only water. Her appetite had vanished and her nerves were jangled. She'd ruined the first business meeting with her new boss.

Lord, what did I just do? She silently prayed for understanding.

Despite her blundered encounter, Kate felt peace expanding inside. Serenity covered her heart. It soothed away the frustration. She knew she'd done the right thing. She had stood up for what she believed in, for what was best for the children—though it may have risked her employment.

And if she had to, she would do it all over, again!

Back at the cabin, Daniel popped the migraine medicine tablets into his mouth. He winced at their bitterness and washed them down with the coldest well water he had ever drunk. He closed his eyes. Head pounding, vision blurry, the pain weakened him, but the meds would help. They always did. He inhaled a few steadying breaths.

The severe headaches were a common affliction—since the incident. Their excruciating pressure fell without warning. They also hit easily with stress, and right now Daniel felt a noose tighter than a surgical glove stretched around his neck.

He had moved to Seattle to make a clean break. And he'd struck out already—the first day! *Before* he even sat at his desk. Who was he trying to kid? He wasn't adept at this administration stuff. It wasn't his "calling."

But he'd failed that.

His insides felt squeezed from the grip of remorse. Frustrated, Daniel *whacked* the plastic cup on the bathroom counter, then winced from the gunshot reaction in his head. He pressed his hand against his right eye. Slowly, blindly, he shuffled over to the wood stove to add a few logs as carefully and quietly as possible. Then he dragged himself up to bed.

Lying down, he groaned until his head adjusted to the lateral position. He despised weakness, and the conquering reality of it hit with sledgehammer-like blows. He had done what he could to mend his life, yet he was still a broken man. Without remedy. A year ago, after his tragic failure, his sights should have been set again on victory. But here he was, still licking his wounds.

Kate had seen right through him, too. She had straightaway sensed his ineptness, practically declared him unworthy to make the right choice for the children.

But unworthiness wasn't new. Daniel had lived without honor since Sammy Paredes. That is why he was here. If he still had honor, he would have stayed in California making a half million a year as L.A.'s most respected neurosurgeon, *saving* the lives of children, instead of—

"Aaauug," Daniel moaned from the pain. He turned on his side and doubled up, then towed the pillow over his face to block out all light.

Those days are over! he thought. He had transgressed honor. And there was *no* getting it back.

On his bed, he waited for the fitful sleep to overtake him. He was so tired. Tired of living in remorse and despair. Tired of paying for his failure.

Chapter Seven

*H*enry Freeman sat in his office chair. Reflective. Alone. He'd come in very early Monday morning to pack his personal items before Daniel arrived. And to pray.

Boxes were sitting open-ended around him, baring lots of hospital knick-knacks, pictures, personal files, and mementos.

Henry was glad to be retiring—deserved it well. Straight out of college, forty-five years in hospital administration was a long stretch. But he'd loved every one of them. Especially the last twelve at TLC; he was so honored when they had selected him to be their first Executive Administrator.

Now, with age, it was time to step down. Time for him and Louise to spend quality days together before they got too old. Time for someone else to carry on the vision of this notable hospital.

He frowned and suffered a twinge of uncertainty. Too bad it was Daniel, Henry sighed. He would only be training Daniel for a couple weeks, helping him make the transition until Christmas. Then it was time to let go and trust God. He leaned on the desk, folded his wrinkled hands together, and prayed.

"Dear Lord, help Kate. She needs Your guidance. Keep her here. Help her stick this out until Your plan is done. Please, God—for the children's sake."

He reflected on her call from the previous night. She had been extremely upset. First she'd questioned him about not showing up at the restaurant, and then didn't sound convinced that his tire blew flat on the freeway—though it was true. After that, she had recounted a half-hour's worth of reasons why Daniel wasn't qualified for the position. Henry tried rationalizing with her, but she just wouldn't agree . . .

"I'm telling you, Henry, he doesn't really care about what's best for the chil-dren, and they will be the ones to suffer."

"Now, Kate, you haven't given him a chance."

"I can already see his true colors. You've got to speak to the Board. He thinks that we're somehow hurting the children, leading them on. He doesn't understand how medically advantageous this Program is. And even when it can't help all the children, they still need the joy and hope—sometimes more than medicine!"

"But he will settle in, Kate."

"When? In four, five years? What will happen to the hospital—to the kids—by then?"

"I understand your uneasiness, but the Board—"

"Please talk to them, Henry. Tell them you disagree with his idea, that you see potential harm in stopping the program. They'll listen to you, Henry. *Please?!*"

Silence lingered on the line while his heart thudded in steady, aching beats. Attempts at calming her hadn't worked. Reassurance didn't seem possible. Kate was not persuaded—not completely. That troubled Henry. She was an excellent judge of character; he'd always trusted that quality in her. And he had never been disappointed. This time he'd stepped out on a limb, and he knew it would be shaky at first, but he had felt certain he'd made the right decision.

"Kate, . . . I'm sorry. We'll just have to wait and pray for the best."

More silence. Finally, Kate muttered, "Goodnight, Henry. I'll see you tomor-row," and hung up.

Having recalled their conversation from the night before made a new wave of regret flood in. Henry had yet to confess to Kate that it was *his* involvement in recommending Daniel that had swung the Board's position in his favor. Kate's voice carried a trace of her suspicion on the phone. Perhaps with Henry's sup-port to keep Daniel, it had already occurred to her that he had been endorsing Daniel all along.

That was OK, he thought. She would learn the truth—in time. He wasn't keen on withholding the information from her, but it was best for now that she not know all the facts. If she did, she would resign. And TLC needed her to stay.

Henry settled back in his chair. Warding off doubt, he rehearsed again his motive for encouraging the Board to select Daniel over Kate. He'd known the Board would designate whomever he proposed. How he'd felt like a traitor in doing so! Her destiny was altered by her closest friend. After training her fully for the position, Henry was now to blame for extinguishing her chance, her dream.

And it had torn his heart in two.

Henry had prayed long and hard upon hearing through the grapevine that one of the elite neurosurgeons in the country had left his practice and might consider settling in administration. Henry had felt *compelled* to call Daniel and offer an interview.

It wasn't that Kate was inadequate. Conversely, she was superior at administrative things: organized, levelheaded, creative, and relished detail. She had proven herself savvy in all the hospital's business matters, and ran the department better than him when he was on vacation. Most importantly, she was compassionate, gifted with the children. It was what he admired most about her. It seemed her love for them always propelled her in the right direction.

No—far from being unsuitable—Kate was perfect for the job.

His reasoning had stemmed from something else, something *deeper*. He had sensed the Lord had wanted him to select Daniel. And, though he didn't understand why, he still felt that way.

Naturally, he had thought it cowardly not explaining things to Kate. But he couldn't. Not yet. He couldn't give her a reason to quit. If she learned he had advised the board to select Daniel, she might lose hope and leave.

He didn't want that, with good reason. Henry sensed Daniel's stay was temporary. His deep impression of that was beyond peculiar. It was not so much a notion, or even a feeling, it was more like†.†.†. divine information. He couldn't discern how he knew. He just knew!

Doubtless, God had His reasons for selecting Daniel. And that had been reason enough for Henry.

Until now. Until the doubts resurfaced. And *before* Kate's lengthy discourse last night on Daniel's incompatibility.

Henry rubbed his chin in quandary.

She had sensed something off-kilter. She was very keen, always had been. Henry wasn't surprised. He just didn't know how to respond to this dilemma, other than to pray and trust God.

Still, he wrestled with misgivings. Not over endorsing Daniel—he'd been positive Daniel was divinely appointed to come.

No, it was over how difficult things could get before the Lord worked everything out! In Henry's lifetime of experience, great travail *always* preceded miracles.

Chapter Eight

*K*ate turned on the key to the carousel. Its motor *brrrrred* into action, vibrating with a resonant hum. The sound excited the children, already lined up with nurses, aides, and volunteers, They were eager for their daily ride, and their youthful voices rose above the engine noise.

Kate flipped another switch. Hundreds of tiny, bulbous lights flashed sequentially along the scalloped roof, the mirrored core strips, the ribboned side poles, and the ornamental sculptured base.

She glanced at the Mickey Mouse wall clock. His hands forthwith pointed to 9:00, and his eyes popped open. He gave a cheerful, high-pitched greeting along with the time, then waved mechanically.

"OK, kids!" Kate announced to the crowd of over thirty waiting children. Her decree was echoed by the usual cheers. She turned one more knob that controlled the carousel's music, and merry, band organ toots sounded from the center core.

The kids paraded slowly through the small gate. They were lined beyond the dome's glass doorway and partway down the hall. They came in wheelchairs, on crutches, with bandages, braces—even mobile I.V. stands. No matter what the apparatus, if their doctor approved the ride, they were escorted on. Daily.

In single file they loaded with the nurses' care and precision. Smiles expanded as children mounted horses, exotic animals, or even just sat in colorful carriage-like chariots. Once the machine filled, the others didn't mind the wait. They knew their turn would come.

"Hi, Miss Montrum'ry!" four-year-old Marissa Jane squealed. Strawberry-blond spindle curls bounced along with her impatience as she was wheeled through the entrance gate by her aide. Kate smiled and waved at the cheery, dimple-faced girl.

An older Asian girl approached the gate with a bandage covering her neck. Yet, her nine-year-old face was bright. "Guess what, Miss Montgomery? I got my stitches out!"

"That's terrific, Mei-Ling," Kate answered, knowing how long the precious girl waited to try an animal instead of the safer carriages. "Did you see Dr. Ward already?"

"Yes! He said I could pick a horse today! I'm going to ride the black mare with the pink roses on its mane."

"Great! I love that one, too." Kate gently cupped Mei-Ling's chin. Her own spirit soared. She loved bringing this moment to the children. More than that, she needed to.

What if Daniel takes it away? Her breath caught and her heart wrenched. She didn't want to dwell on that now. She'd grappled with that possibility for the last sixteen hours, without much sleep—since the moment Daniel had walked out of the restaurant.

Distressed over their ruined meeting, she'd tried pouring her efforts into reviewing the rest of the reports and brainstorming for a plan. But her efforts proved fruitless. She constantly found herself sidetracked by the memory of Daniel's dark, golden eyes and the lifeless, hurting man behind them. Each time, she wondered what caused him so much heartache.

That aching look—rather, the *reason* for it—was the key to why he couldn't accept the carousel, she felt sure. If she could learn what wounded him, she was bound to grasp that key. Then, she believed she could win him over to her Program.

"Morning, Kate," a lanky, freckled, blond-haired teenage boy stood in front of her, on crutches, his olive green eyes hopeful.

She refocused on the young fellow, a bit embarrassed for practically staring right through him. "Oh—morning, Eddie." She smiled. "How's the leg?"

He shrugged. "OK. It's great to be here, though." He loped on in, and stretched out on one of the chariots, laying his crutches beside him.

Eighteen children of various ages continued filing through. The 2-row machine filled up, and seatbelts were checked by the nurse chaperons. It was time!

"Ready?" Kate called out.

"Ready!" their collective response roared back at her.

She reached for the shiny black knob on the long-stemmed lever and pulled back, gently. The wooden contraption creaked and moaned into slow motion, starting to spin. Then it picked up momentum. The inside row of smaller, less intricate jumper horses rose and fell in conjunction with the rotation. Beaming faces and eager waves passed her, going round and round.

Kate smiled too. Her eyes moistened with the miracle of the joyful moment. *Oh God, please don't let Daniel destroy this. Please!* She blinked back her tears, willing herself to hope.

After two short melodies, she slowed the spinning until it ceased. The children dutifully filed off in another direction while more reloaded via the front. She checked Mickey Mouse: 9:30. The usual amount of time for one round of kids. She always conducted the opening ride before Harriet Dunlop, the hospital's most experienced and cherished volunteer, regulated the rest.

But not today. Kate told Harriet she needed to do one more.

Again, the machine began filling with children while its lively music frolicked along. She felt transported in time to some dream world where sorrow and pain didn't exist. And she knew, for a few brief moments, the kids went there too.

"Good morning, Kate," Henry's familiar voice called from behind the stunted picket fence outlining the dome's chamber. Daniel stood beside him. Stiff. Stern. Charcoal suit, smokey-gray tie. No color. No smile. Drab and cold-hearted, he was out of place amongst the rest of the joviality. His features would have been handsome if they weren't so obscured by his "business" air.

Kate inwardly sighed. He looked so hard. No doubt, partly due to their brief encounter at the restaurant. But there was more. Once again she sensed the answer lay in that key, the one beyond the nebulous depths of pain in his eyes.

"Morning, Henry. Daniel." She gave him a polite nod. From the corner of her vision, she saw Henry check his watch and excuse himself to leave. Daniel stood behind the gate. She wondered if he'd linger and watch. Or take off— like yesterday.

She hoped he would stay. Seeing it for himself could be her best ammunition at this point. If he saw how much the kids needed it, maybe it would shoot holes in his theory of "toying with their feelings."

Daniel watched reservedly as the kids continued to load. Then—to Kate's surprise—he came inside the gate to stand beside her! She acknowledged him, and tried to perceive his reasoning. It wasn't visible. She had no clue why he did sense was his wonderful aftershave. Its luring aroma teased her nose. The scent wasn't strong, just notable—and appealing. She contemplated whether there was a side to his heart more like it, more soft, . . . romantic.

"So, this is it?" he said, looking a bit dubious. Even so, a slight curve turned his lips upward, and a tiny smile escaped.

Her stomach did a flip. His sparse interest gave her some relief. But it was the hint of a smile that actually sent her heart racing. *He's impressed.* She couldn't believe it! She'd wished for it, alright—desperately prayed that God would touch his insolent heart. Yet, she hadn't really expected to witness the change.

Faith welled in her. Maybe he wasn't beyond convincing.

More children passed through with salutations and health updates. All were excited. Kate introduced Daniel to each one. He switched into a greeting role easily, as if there were no internal conflict simmering below the surface.

Kate knew better. In fact, it bothered her how he could act a part he didn't seem cut out for. When things got really serious, how would he be able to make sound, tough decisions for the hospital if his own life was in turmoil?

"Hi, Miss Kate!" A lean, seven-year-old boy patiently approached, awaiting his turn. He had no wheelchair or crutches; no bandages or equipment was attached to him. From the exterior he looked like a normal, healthy boy. *If only it were true*, Kate thought. She knew the type of sickness you couldn't see was often the most critical.

"Hey, Champ! How are you today?" She was delighted to see Andrew Tucker. He'd been restricted from riding for at least two weeks. Finally, his doctor had reapproved them . . . for a while. "Feeling all right?"

"Yeah. Still no headaches, for now."

"That's terrific news!" She beamed at him, compassion wrenching her heart and stinging her eyes with unshed tears. Andrew's case was the kind that outraged her most: fine for a while, then sudden unforgiving pain announced a new life-threatening battle.

He nodded. "Gee, I hope I can ride the white stallion." He glanced at the few animals still waiting for jockeys on the stationary outside row.

Kate spotted the horse. "Look! He's still available." She patted his shoulder.

Andrew erupted with excitement and bounded off to claim his steed before Kate could introduce him to Daniel.

Kate studied Daniel's reaction to Andrew. He watched the boy climb aboard, but he then seemed suddenly withdrawn, imprisoned in contemplation. She didn't know what had captured him, but something had seized his openness. His wrought-iron defenses were clearly back up.

The kids finished loading and seat belts were inspected. Kate was about to pull back on the lever when she hesitated. An idea sprouted in her mind; it budded quickly and unfolded promise and hope. *Get him involved.*

She turned to Daniel. "You try it." She didn't wait for his response. She reached for his hand. He flinched, frowned at her in dubious surprise. She ignored his glare and placed his palm on the knob, with hers atop.

He tensed. Whether at her bold move or the physical contact, she wasn't sure. It didn't matter. His hand was on the stick—he was committed. She tried to veil her enthusiasm, lest he pull his arm back altogether. "Ready, kids?" she called to them.

"Ready!" they cheered in unison.

"Just start slowly," she instructed. Securing her grasp around Daniel's, she guided the maneuver, gradually, . . . then increasing, until the lever rested above med-high and the carousel was rotating at near maximum speed. The music rolled into a new carnival tune.

Their hands bonded, creating a warmth—one Kate didn't realize would affect her so much. The simple union made her heart rate sprint, and a tingle danced in her toes. Now conscious of her lingering grasp, she released his hand.

The absence of his warmth made her palm feel cool. A desire sparked inside her to have the union again.

She crossed her arms, mollifying the simple yearning. He looked at her oddly, with apparent need in his eyes. Their golden intensity seemed to reveal a like struggle, reluctance to let go. Kate swallowed. She reasoned that it was impossible to assume his feelings would match hers. Then she wondered when the last time was that Daniel had held a woman's hand. By the way he had tensed, she was certain it was a long time ago.

His "involvement" was a meager start, but it was a breakthrough. At least he hadn't yanked his hand away and stormed out on her. Maybe, just *maybe*, it did something positive within.

"They usually ride for seven minutes. Unless someone gets dizzy or sick." Her pulse tripped. She regretted the negative details within a millisecond of mentioning them.

"Sick?" His brows trenched and the tiny smile crashed.

Real smooth! Kate tapped her fingertips against her forehead and tried, this time, to pick her words wisely. "It's not a problem, really. On rare occasions, the spinning doesn't mix well with their medication. That's all. The dizziness is mild, and very temporary."

"How temporary?"

"Mmm, a half-hour, at the most." She attempted a blithe tone, but it sounded weak and pitiful to her ears.

Kate wanted to kick herself. Thanks to her careless tongue, Daniel had stumbled over a minor glitch, and he looked more skeptical now than when he'd arrived. She'd spoiled the moment! No telling if she'd get another chance to influence him this directly before he revoked the program.

Soon the ride ended and the children began another exit/enter promenade. Kate noticed Harriet waiting patiently outside the gate with her generous grin. She would now monitor a few more runs until the children had gone through twice, at most. Then the Miracle Machine would retire for the day, having worked its own shift, just like one of the hospital staff.

Kate introduced Daniel to Harriet, who extended her rounded, dark brown hand to shake his. "Good morning, Mr. Brakken!" Her beaming smile was a literal gold mine, bearing two upper-front caps in gleaming yellow. Not that her forty-something enthusiasm didn't sparkle without them. She was walking effervescence, and Kate knew well why the kids loved her so.

"Harriet is our *model* volunteer, Daniel," Kate knew the commendation would make the humble woman feel bashful.

"Oh, Kate—" Harriet looked surprised and laughed.

"It's true," Kate continued. "She teaches the weekly classes to our volunteer applicants. She's been here longer than most of us, and she knows how much the carousel means to the children." Kate needed the extra pitch after her blunder a minute ago.

"Nice to meet you," Daniel responded courteously, but without his earlier charisma with the children.

They parted company from Harriet. "Let me buy you a coffee in the cafeteria," Kate offered, wishing for a sedative instead to calm him.

"Sure."

He followed her lead as she walked him down the empty hall toward the elevators. They waited alone.

Daniel glanced occasionally at her. Notable lines of distress were chiseled on his sun-darkened face. His eyes mirrored the torrent of emotion. *Of all things*, Kate thought. Daniel was so strong, she had been prepared to see any emotion from him, besides anxiety.

"Kate, who's the skinny little guy? The one called Champ."

"That's Andrew Tucker. He's been through several rounds of surgery, so we thought he deserved a conquering title."

"And his condition?"

Her remaining smile tumbled off her lips. She glanced up at the floor numbers above them, then back at Daniel. "Brain stem tumor. It's inoperable beyond this point." The elevator *dinged* its arrival. They entered the caricature-painted contraption, and Kate selected the second floor. The doors closed and the rectangular box tugged into sluggish motion.

Daniel looked like he'd suddenly become ill. His face contorted, turned ashen. She wondered if he would pass out.

"Are you alright?"

"Yeah," he gave a feeble reply.

"Daniel, with all due respect, you'll need a tougher skin being here. We're not calloused in our hearts, it's just that the children can't see you shaken up." She didn't mean to sound condescending, but he had to buck up soon if he was going to oversee this hospital.

Color finally returned to his face. "Have they tried Laser Extraction Duo-Therapy? It's a newer microsurgery treatment on brain stem tumors, involving two types of laser equipment."

Kate was baffled by his outburst of medical terms. "No, I'm sure that's one he hasn't had. Way too risky. And it doesn't sound like a favorable option at this point."

"But it's not as high risk as conventional cutting. You just—" he halted midsentence, cleared his throat. "That is, the neurosurgeon uses a microsurgery instrument to guide him, and the whole procedure is conducted with less invasion to the surrounding healthy tissues."

Now she was really intrigued by his detailed knowledge. "You know a lot about neurosurgery. Ever thought of entering the practice?"

His face paled again. The elevator *dinged* again, and Daniel nearly bolted through the opening doors, not waiting for her.

Kate shook her head in dismay and followed before the doors closed. She simply didn't know how to figure this man out. One second he was masterful and unshakable. The next, vulnerable and . . . wounded.

It was crucial that she understand his thinking. They'd never make it as a team if she didn't. Right now, picturing herself yoked with him as co-administrators hardly portrayed an image of teamwork. And concentration would be difficult—his handsome features often took her breath away.

Still, she felt something toward him. Mercy? Sympathy? Whatever it was, she couldn't evade it. For now, she clamped a lid on her attraction and caught up to him. "Daniel?"

He turned the corner, then halted part way down the corridor leading to the cafeteria. A pair of nurses passed them in the hall, glancing at Daniel, curiously. Finally he faced her, cheeks splotchy and pale.

He's scared. She blinked in dismay at his weakened appearance. "Was it something I said?" She longed to know about the inner turmoil he faced. More than that, she wanted to comfort him. The yearning stirred her, made her nervous and tingly. She clenched her hands, resisting the desire to touch his shoulder . . . console him.

He shook his head. "Sorry, I—" his words were strained.

"No, I'm sorry, Daniel. I was too hard on you back there. This hospital affects everyone. It should. When it stops affecting you, then you should worry. We just have to be careful not to let it show around the children."

He stood rigidly, hands on hips, then raised one hand to his brow. "It's not that."

Kate sensed the tension enveloping him and wondered what caused it. Men usually handled these things better, she thought. "Then what?" she asked, tenderly, watching him. For the first time, she felt like a comrade, instead of his contender.

Daniel looked strangled, like he wanted to say something yet couldn't. His eyes held a faraway gaze, his mouth parted to speak. But nothing.

Kate was beyond baffled. Frustrated! She knew something was churning below the surface, something he wasn't ready to share—yet.

And it was tearing him to pieces.

Chapter Nine

*D*aniel gaped at his pallid image in the men's room mirror. He tried denying that things were getting through to him. That didn't work.

"Where's your head, Brakken?" he attempted a stern self-chastening, instead, in the vacant area. He cast his reflection a disapproving glare. "You may as well hang in the towel if you can't get your spine back." The solitary lecture did next to zero, he knew, but he was desperate.

He pushed his hand through his bangs, unnerved, trying to think. He had almost let the cat out of the bag and told Kate what was stonewalling him. But if he'd done that, he could just sign his resignation letter. No other hospital that he had contacted in the last year was willing to take him on once they learned of his controversial departure from his practice.

He still couldn't understand why Henry Freeman sanctioned him before TLC's board, after knowing full well Daniel's suspension and obligatory resignation from L.A. General. As if offering him a position at TLC wasn't merciful enough, Henry and the board insisted Daniel keep knowledge of his former career undisclosed to staff, to prevent the spread of disreputable talk. It was the closest thing to a miracle that Daniel had experienced!

Nonetheless, he detested playing games. He loathed feeling like he was concealing truth from people. Worse, he hated feeling like he was running—still! Regardless, he had no choice other than to keep quiet. He had desperately hoped this move would eradicate his forsaken past, yet he hadn't foreseen colliding with a challenge to return to neurosurgery.

When Kate had mentioned Andrew Tucker's headaches and the location of his tumor in the brain stem—Daniel's former specialty—it nearly sent him through the roof. But when she teased him in the elevator about practicing neurosurgery, the spinning pressure in his head accelerated so fast he thought he would faint.

She had no idea what nerve she had struck! Daniel had always been the medical "master," the proven hunter on those life-and-death expeditions. He was heralded as the best Pediatric Neurosurgeon on the West Coast, possibly in the country. Now he was hunted. Beaten. Mocked by the tumors he spent nearly two decades learning to defeat.

Failure—combined with his inability to help any longer, to heal, to fight this killer malady—struck him at his very core. It stripped him of sustaining force. He began crumbling again.

"Your fortitude is a joke!" He gave himself another chastening. He'd expected to show more composure while resuming contact with the medical world, especially after so much time had passed. But little incidents piled heavily, building a tower of condemnation and judgment . . . hearing the praise substantiating Kate's innovative program. . . . Daniel's painful recollection of surgery. . . . Kate's stern talk about knowing what the children needed . . . learning of Andrew's situation . . . realizing he *could* help the boy, if—

The combined chain of events was more of an onslaught to his emotions than he'd presumed possible. As a result, foreboding kicked in—big time.

"Time to stand," he declared, once more giving his duplicate image the toughest coaching he could muster. He had at least fifty introductions to make today. He needed to shake this apprehension and get on with things.

Just then, a man strode into the rest room. Daniel's concentration broke. He briefly acknowledged the stranger and walked out. Fortunately, the man disrupted Daniel's private lecture, otherwise he might have stayed in there all morning, trying to will the strength to leave. He had become too used to being isolated.

And that was no longer an option.

Kate placed the telephone back on the cradle and took another message over to drop in Daniel's message slot. They were piling up fast. Two from local medical journals that learned of Henry's retirement; another from the Executive Administrator of West Point General, who wanted to have lunch with Daniel; and half a dozen others from various medical professions. He'd certainly become the object of attention.

She hadn't seen a hair of him since their impasse following the elevator ride, when he'd abruptly cancelled her offer for coffee. A short while later, Daniel and Henry had left to make more introductory rounds before she returned from her weekly meeting with the Wellness Program volunteer staff.

It was now well after noon, and Lisa, the Admin. Secretary, along with the rest of the office, had taken off to meet Henry and Daniel for lunch. Kate stayed behind, having brought her meal—leftovers from the restaurant meeting yesterday.

The lunchroom microwave *beeped*, and she retrieved her salmon with rice. While waiting for the steamy fare to cool, she picked up the newest Hospital Weekly circulation from the magazine rack and began perusing the list of articles.

Kate was a voracious reader. Always had been. Reading was initially an escape for her as a youth, transporting her somewhere else, somewhere outside her world filled with pain. But the influence it had on her was far more positive than her motivation for reading. She pulled straight A's all through school, and made the Dean's list every year in college, graduating with honors.

She loved stories on overcoming adversity, whether an autobiography or a novel. She also read a lot of nonfiction. Though medical periodicals at the hospital were ultrascientific, they were still fascinating and offered fresh hope.

She paused at one article on innovative surgical techniques. The bold title, "Hot Spot Surgery," and its leading paragraph caught her eye after a comment Daniel had made in the elevator about laser treatments. She read on:

> Lasers breaking unprecedented ground in successful tumor removal. New
> hot surgery is today's medical miracle. . . .

She read about the percentage of successful removals of malignant tumors now steadily increasing in the United States. Kate finished her lunch and retreated to the office to keep reading. The information on laser surgery was fascinating to her. She wondered if there was a small chance of it ever helping Andrew. But Andrew had been through so much. A new technique probably wouldn't gain approval from his parents.

She soon finished the article and wanted to share it with Henry, as she often did when something seized her interest with regard to the hospital. Then she reached for the December binder, now organized along with the others, and started charting the morning's carousel rides as recorded on a list by Harriet.

A while later, laughter grew louder outside the office door. It opened and Henry, Daniel, Lisa, Stephen, Nicole, Chang, and Mary strode through, all engaged by something entertaining.

"That's too funny, Mr. Brakken," Lisa commented.

Kate was stunned. Evidently, they'd witnessed a side of Daniel that she had yet to see. The group divided, still chuckling, and went to their separate workstations.

Henry walked up to Kate's desk and poked his head over the partition, with Daniel close behind. "Kate?" Henry asked, concerned. "Where were you?"

"I had plenty of leftovers I didn't want to waste." She couldn't help glancing at Daniel, hoping he'd remember that he'd left her with his food, *and* the bill, at the restaurant. "Did you enjoy your lunch?"

"Very nice." Henry smiled. "Daniel pulled a fast one with the waiter and paid for all of us. Now we still need to take you out for a welcoming." Henry gave Daniel a pat on the shoulder.

"It was my pleasure. Sorry we missed you, Kate," Daniel said. "Maybe I can treat you tomorrow."

She regarded him politely. His eyes showed a definite wariness. Perhaps he was attempting to bribe her to not spill the beans about how incompetently he'd behaved this morning. But his vulnerable moment was safe with her. Whatever misgivings she had about Daniel, Kate knew it wouldn't be right to use public embarrassment to make her point.

"Thanks, but I really need to catch up on several tasks. All these extra meetings lately have put me behind."

"I hear that," Henry quipped, and excused himself to start returning several calls.

"Well, I do want to make it up to you," Daniel added.

Kate looked to see if anyone was within earshot. "You're sure you want to keep track? That will make two lunches you owe me," she whispered.

He looked puzzled, then obviously recalled what she was hinting at. "You're absolutely right. I hope you'll allow me a chance to pay off my mounting debt." His deep, golden eyes yielded a spark, and her light sarcasm didn't seem to disturb him. She glimpsed again that side of him that welcomed playful challenge, the one she'd seen a glimmer of in the parking lot when he'd teased her about altering the reports.

"I'll think of something to make things even," she added.

"Good." He grew serious again and turned to join Henry in their temporarily shared office.

She wasn't sure if he appreciated her spirited comeback, but if he couldn't take a little teasing, he was wound up too tight to be acquiring this stressful position.

An hour later, Henry's office door reopened and they both emerged. Henry mumbled something to Lisa about needing to meet his wife, Louise, out front in a few minutes.

Daniel approached Kate's desk. "You ready to meet with me?"

"Sure." She grabbed a few accordion files, various folders and the December Wellness Program binder, and then followed him back into his office. He shut the door. "We have a lot of ground to cover," she began while sitting down, then opened her notebook. "Here's a list copy of items for this week. First, we have a new parent program date set for the Depression During Illness seminar. The flyers are going to be reproduced and distributed in the next general mailing. Also, here are the staff performance evaluations for December." She handed him a thick file. "They need to be reviewed and signed. And these are budget reports for all departments for next year." She placed another inch-thick stack of printouts on his desk. "The Accounting Department supervisor has already approved them, but they still need to be reviewed and approved by you, or adjusted if necessary. Then we have a membership meeting with the National Association of Hospital Development on next Wednesday—"

"Whoa—hold on!" Daniel looked distressed. "We aren't going to be able to cover all this today. I've got a 3:30 appointment with another hospital director in Bellevue. And at 4:30 I need to meet with one of the local papers for a publicity photo and interview."

Kate glanced at her watch and smirked. It was after 2:30 now! Boy—are his priorities out of balance, she mused but kept her opinions safely tucked away this time. "Daniel, that only gives us twenty-five minutes to cover several days worth of critical material, which doesn't even include the Wellness Program reports. At the very least, we need to discuss staffing issues, annual updates on state and federal regulations, new personnel policies, auxiliary information, and Friday's semimonthly Roundtable meeting with the physicians on how to combat the latest E. coli outbreak."

He looked a little shocked, then the color returned to his face. "Look, Kate, I see there's plenty to cover, but we'll need to be brief this afternoon. Maybe we could schedule a dinner meeting tonight . . . then I can start reducing my meal indebtedness." He eyed her earnestly, but his reference to owing her meals proved he hadn't taken offense to her earlier quip about lunch.

His offer sounding tempting, but Kate doubted much would get accomplished, after witnessing firsthand the last restaurant meeting.

"Thanks, but I have a date with a horse."

Chapter Ten

Daniel couldn't believe what he'd heard. "Pardon?"

She smiled at him with jest, and the pure beauty of it almost knocked the wind from him.

"I use a lot of my spare time restoring carousel figures at home. I just finished sanding a horse, and it's ready for the primer coat." She paused a moment. "You could, however, pay off *both* your meals by helping me. I have several others that need sanding."

"Really?" He didn't doubt the truth of her statement. He was merely stunned that she'd asked such a request.

"Yeah. You can bring some takeout. I love veggie pizza with mozzarella. After you finish sanding an animal, we can discuss business over some of my freshly baked banana bread."

Daniel was flabbergasted. He certainly had never before encountered that proposal from a woman! Although common sense told him sanding horses would be harder work than buying her dinner, his challenge was sparked.

He couldn't resist. "What time?"

Daniel found Kate's house just after 6:30, in an area West of Bothell. He parked his car at the end of the gravel drive and reached to unload his goods.

He tucked her directions into his wallet, then made his way to the door of the ranch house, with a large pizza box in one hand, bouquet of assorted roses in the other. He flipped the flowers behind his back and then tap-knocked on the door, using the toe of his shoe.

Footsteps sounded. Then Kate opened the door, smiling, her face softly aglow from the porch lighting. "Hi. Come in. You found it OK?"

He followed her inside. "Yeah, but I think my indicator blew a fuse from all the turns."

She grimaced at his wisecrack. "It's not that bad. Here, I'll take that." She reached out for the pizza, but he swung the flowers around in front of her to see.

"These are for you." Surprise lit up her face along with appreciation. It was the receptive response he'd hoped for. "They're sort of a peace offering for storming out on you yesterday at the restaurant. It wasn't professional." He swallowed the thick lump in his throat. "Or . . . kind."

She looked up at him, pleased, and Daniel sensed he was forgiven. *Good*, he thought. He needed Kate's support if this transition was going to work.

"Thank you. That was nice." Then she laughed. "For a second, I thought you wanted to make this a date."

Daniel felt like an idiot. Romantic notions hadn't occurred to him when he'd purchased the conciliatory flowers. How could he not realize she would see them as such a gesture? *You've sure been out of the loop with women!* he silently lectured himself.

"Well," Daniel broke his awkward pause, "that wouldn't be fair to the horse. Maybe another time."

She gave him another accepting smile, which melted him down to his toes.

"I'll put these in some water," she said and took the arrangement into the kitchen to retrieve a vase.

He placed the pizza box on the dining table, then glanced around her home. It was pretty—inviting. A far cry from the sometimes bizarre, Californian deco styles he'd grown accustomed to seeing. Kate's house bore evidence of special touches, personal decorating, and lots of country charm.

He removed his coat and stood by the fire to warm himself. The snow had all melted, but clear skies sent the temperatures back down to the high twenties. "Thanks for the fire," he called to her. "I'm not used to this below-freezing climate."

"Well, it doesn't snow much in this part of the Northwest," she answered from the kitchen, "but we do have occasional periods of wintry weather. Hang around, it will break in a few days. The rain always comes back."

She walked from the kitchen into the dining room and leaned across the table to place the flowers, now artistically arranged, at the center of the lace doily. Her angled posture in the soft, shimmery pantsuit caught Daniel's awareness of her pleasant figure. His pulse doubled in rhythm. Her deep auburn hair shone with tiny red highlights beneath the five-lamp chandelier. She turned to smile at him. "Ready?"

"Famished." He nodded, dimly aware that he was agreeing more to his captive state over her than to the meal. He approached to sit down and noticed her outfit looked like pink silk. "I thought this was a work party. Where are your overalls?"

She gave a soft laugh. "I don't host in my work clothes. I'll change after dinner."

Much to Daniel's surprise, Kate bowed her head and said a brief but reverential blessing for their food. He'd given up on prayer, but he politely listened, not wanting to offend her. Yet something about her simple act pricked his heart. It made him wonder. When had he last given heartfelt thanks for his food? Or for anything? With his affluence as a prestigious doctor, simple daily gratitude had somehow slipped away, years ago.

She said "amen" and opened the lid to the pizza box. Her mouth turned into part smile, part frown. "I recognize half of it. What's the other side?"

"Salami and anchovies," he said.

Kate looked ill. "Oh," she gave a feeble reply.

"It's actually very tasty. A lot like hors d'oeuvres. I got hooked on it back in college." Then he looked at her apologetically. "I, uh, couldn't bear the thought of just veggies on my pizza. Hope you're not offended."

"No! No, it's your stomach." She gave a semi-sour face but then attempted a smile. "You can eat whatever you like. I do have some antacid tablets—a whole bottle—if you need them. Just let me know."

They ate for a few minutes, until Kate asked, "So where is this college where students thrive on anchovies?"

"University of Southern Cal. Then I went through med school up here at the UW." He bit into his pizza again.

"Really?" She gaped. "You studied to become a doctor?"

Ooops! Daniel gulped his bite of food down. He realized he was letting the cat out of the bag without paying attention. TLC's board and Henry Freeman insisted no one on staff know of his former surgical career. They didn't want the L.A. scandal affecting their little hospital. Now he had to cover his tracks, though he hated lying. He drank some milk and wiped his mouth.

"You might say, *failed* becoming a doctor." His face heated from the twisted truth, but the failure part was accurate enough. "So I decided to switch gears and use the knowledge I'd gained."

She gave him a sympathetic look. "I know how you feel. I blew my chance at nursing when I fainted during a blood draw—twice in one week! The moment I saw red, everything went black. After the second time, I was politely asked by the Nursing Department supervisor if I shouldn't drop the program. But they weren't really asking."

Daniel didn't respond audibly, but his heart felt a kinship toward her in their common experience. He, too, had been politely asked to resign from L.A. General, though he knew he would be discharged if he had refused.

Kate shrugged it off. "It was for the best, though. The Lord knew I was much better at administrative things. Now that I look back, I wouldn't trade what I've done at TLC for any nursing career. I still help sick children, just in a different way. All I needed was a nudge in the right direction."

He nodded, contemplating her story.

They finished eating, and after clearing the table, Kate retreated to wash and change. She soon reappeared in an oversize maroon sweatshirt, sleeves rolled to her elbows, and white stirrup pants, socks, and tennis shoes. "This way," she called for him to follow her past the dining room and into the garage through an inside doorway.

Daniel eagerly ensued, trying to keep his focus on the work ahead and his gaze off of her shapeliness. Kate stepped down into the darkness and pulled the chain to a tiny overhead bulb. Then she walked in a little and flipped on two other sets of light switches. The large, expanded garage lit up like a small factory. Horses, animals, benches, poles, and equipment were everywhere!

"Whoa!" Daniel uttered, not expecting to see so much. Although he hadn't really given thought to what he would encounter, it didn't compare to the mini-warehouse before him.

The garage was warm, like the house. Surprised, he had to ask. "Does your fireplace heat all of this, too?"

"Yep. The warm air is piped in from those air ducts up there. She pointed to an aluminum box that lined the ceiling and disappeared into the house wall. "My grandfather constructed it when he was alive. This was my grandparents' house. Grandma Rose has Parkinson's, and she now resides at Peaceful Meadows Home, up the road a few miles."

Kate walked him over to a section of at least twenty animals with obviously worn paint. Horses in various profiles and trappings stood on bases. Daniel also noticed a menagerie of other animals—an ostrich, bear, two zebras, an antelope, two tigers, a swan, and a goat. The other side of the room held a frog, a wolf, rabbits, giraffes, a peacock, and a Monarch lion bearing a crown. All were faded, peeling, and scratched.

"I agreed to only one, right?" he let a little irony flow, making sure she wasn't going to keep him slaving all night.

She laughed and nodded. "We still have a lot of hospital business to cover." Kate told him to take his pick of the lot, while she gathered a stool, sandpaper, a drop cloth, and various sanding tools.

"How about the lion over there? I've always admired lions."

She glanced at him oddly, like she was amazed by his choice. Maybe he just didn't know what he was getting himself into. "OK, but save the mane and crown for last, and I'll show you a few special techniques that will make the waves and intricate sculpting easier to do."

She quickly explained how to hold the sandpaper over a small block of wood for the flatter parts. After a few *scritch-scritch* practice maneuvers, he had it down.

Kate sauntered over to her own horse project and placed the painting cloth down below it. Then she opened a can of white primer, stirred it vigorously, and dipped in the brush to begin.

Together they worked, side by side. After she had finished the first coat, she stood and came over to see his progress. Daniel had started to work up a sweat by now, and wished he hadn't worn a heavy sweatshirt. He stopped sanding to wipe his brow.

"Hey—that's great," she complimented his work. "You're very adept with your hands. Too bad that med school didn't work out. With this precision, you'd have made a excellent surgeon." She trailed a hand over the faultless, sanded area.

If only you knew. He thought about disclosing to her that she was right, but quickly decided against it. Instead, he smiled, surprised and pleased by her recognition of his aptitude. It felt good, like refreshing water poured upon his soul after wandering in the desert sands of guilt and failure. Daniel had never considered himself artistic in a conventional sense, but the exacting procedures he had faced as a neurosurgeon trained him to muster extraordinary patience and deliver flawless medical skill.

He wiped his dampened neck. "Could I trouble you for a soda pop?"

"I don't buy pop, but I have juice or bottled water."

"Anything cold." He gave her a pleading smile.

"Coming right up. I'll turn off the vents. It should cool down pretty fast with the temp outside."

Daniel stood up to stretch and dust himself. As he did, he realized what Kate must have been doing the day he met her at TLC's office, covered in a layer of the fine particles. It made him grin, recalling the dust on her nose and cheeks.

She returned and set down a hardwood tray with two glasses of orange juice on ice, and a bottle of chilled water. She handed both the bottle and a glass to him. "Keep the water for later."

"Thanks." He placed it down and drank half the juice. "Mmm—wow! That's fresh."

"Like that? I make it fresh every morning with my own juicer. I can't bring myself to buy the store kind anymore, it's too watered down and has too many preservatives."

"You seem pretty health conscious, always watching what you eat. I mean that in a good way."

"Well, I'm not a fanatic, but I believe you reap what you sow. Bad food inside, bad body outside. I like being healthy."

He had to agree that her model form was certainly in the *good* category. No fat, clear complexion, shiny hair, bright eyes. She was the picture of health. "That's smart. These days, you can't pick up a magazine without learning that something you eat is going to harm you."

"It's mostly from all the man-made things. Processed food. My Grandma Rose used to call them 'garbage edibles.'"

"What else is there?" he joked.

"God-made. Natural. You know, fruits, vegetables, grains, herbs—the things that come from the earth instead of being processed in some lab. We would see a lot less cancer and heart disease if people would eat more of the *real* food their body was made to live on."

He couldn't dispute that. Studies had long shown notable health improvements based on diet changes alone. "So, what about cows and anchovies? They're natural." He knew there was no defense in her mind for his choice of pizza, but he couldn't resist asking just to see her reaction.

Kate looked nauseated at first. "Well, meat is a subject of *great* debate. Personally, I'm not a vegetarian, but I think it's better for our bodies to limit eating lean meats to twice or three times a week. I don't eat much beef or pork, but I haven't been able to give up a juicy steak, altogether." She smiled bashfully.

"Aha!" he piped up. "*Now* I know your weakness. Watch out, I can blackmail you one day."

She laughed freely and smiled at him. "Daniel, I have to be honest. After the first few meetings with you, I was pretty concerned that you didn't have a sense of humor. Now I see you were hiding it."

He almost blushed. Something about being in this woman's presence brought out traits in him he hadn't witnessed since college. "It's just because we're away from the hospital. In the medicine field, I'm kind of a different person."

"Yeah, sort of like Dr. Jekyll and Mr. Hyde?"

"That terrible, huh?" He glanced sheepishly at her.

"Well, . . . you've had your moments. It's true, though, there's something about being at the hospital that changes your mood. Any idea what it might be?"

He really wanted to open up to her. She had such a way of making him feel at ease. "Guess I am just driven. Maybe that's why I never married. Too wrapped up in my medical career—" Daniel choked on the words, remembering once again that his past was off limits to TLC's staff.

"Ahh—I don't know." He slapped his knees free of some dust and stood. "Now I see I should have gotten a carousel horse for company, instead," he jested, to lighten the mood. "Well, I better get back to my lion before I'm here all night." He returned to his sanding.

When Daniel was ready to start the mane and crown, Kate had finished up her second coat and came over to show him how to use a small utensil to sand the small grooves and crannies. She guided his hand with hers until he got the hang of it. He appreciated the personal instruction, but the contact wreaked havoc on his concentration. It took him a few minutes to get his precision back. Even then, his mind was still relishing the feel of her touch.

Another forty minutes or so later Daniel finished and blew away the dust. "There. I think that's all I'm good for. My shoulders are getting a little stiff."

She looked at him and suppressed a giggle, but then laughed.

"What?"

Kate handed him a towel. "Your face is covered in dust."

"Oh." He wiped it off completely then guzzled some of the cold water. "Mmm! That's good, but my well water's got yours beat by at least ten degrees. It's like drinking from a melting glacier."

"Yeah, well water can be close to freezing in winter, but it tastes wonderful. Plus it doesn't have the chemicals in it. By the way, how do you like your place? You said it's in Issaquah?"

"It's huge—three stories—and very spacious. I think it was built for Paul Bunyan! A loft ceiling goes all the way to the top on the front side. It sits on a couple acres, practically buried in a forest. Nice, but . . ." he was about to say the word *lonely* but stopped. "It's obviously a family-sized house. Too big for just one person."

She didn't respond.

Daniel surveyed the warehouse-sized garage again. "This is quite an operation. How do you keep going, horse after horse?"

She tilted her head while she began cleaning her painting supplies. "I just know that each one that I finish is going to bring happiness to many children, probably long after I'm gone."

As he regarded her, a dull ache began gnawing at Daniel's insides—for dual reasons. Foremost, he knew precisely what she meant. It was the same motivation that had held him captive in neurosurgery for more than a decade. Alternatively, she'd made a similar point about touching children's lives during their discussion at the restaurant, but he hadn't then caught the real impact of her work.

Until now.

Daniel felt calloused. Worse than the heel of an old boot.

"Kate, . . ." he paused as she regarded him, "no matter what happens at the hospital, please understand that I respect, and even admire, what you are doing with all this."

She seemed saddened by his confession. It made him feel even more brutish, considering his imminent plan for TLC's carousel. But he truly believed the ER upgrade was for the best. Still, he wanted to comfort her somehow.

"Your work—" he looked around, gesturing for emphasis, "rather, your *mission* here is more than a talent. It's a gift you are sharing with others." He hesitated again. "I'm sure your grandfather would be proud."

"I know," she answered, looking choked up by his compliment. "But I'm very glad you see it too, Daniel."

Kate brushed her hair out after her late shower. Daniel had left a little after 10:00 p.m., loaded with an extra loaf of banana bread wrapped in foil, and his boxed lunch from the restaurant. They'd covered the essentials for the next few days, and Kate felt more at ease over relating to her new boss.

Now sitting at the dining room table, she gazed at the flowers and reflected on the evening full of surprises. For one, she had never expected him to apologize. Further, she couldn't have guessed his choice in pizza if it had meant her life! Then, he did a superb detailed job sanding the lion—as skillful as a surgeon—far exceeding her expectations.

Even his compliment about her "gift" to others pleasantly caught her off guard and nearly brought tears to her eyes.

Mostly, it amazed her how relaxed Daniel was outside of TLC. How kind, humorous, and appealing he could be when he wasn't coiled like a spring. Evidently he hadn't been fully aware of his tense reactions by the way he humbly received her "Jekyll and Hyde" comment.

Now she was more than curious. What was it that caused him such anxiety when he was at the hospital? Compared to tonight's suave mannerism, Daniel's behavior at TLC was akin to a spooked bull in a china shop. What unnerved her most was, How long before something of value crashed? She didn't want to know.

Sadly, he'd made it clear he had not changed his mind about selling the carousel. Not even after reviewing some of her reports tonight. He'd merely said he wanted to study them further.

At that, her hopes for softening his heart started to fizzle. She was back to square one.

Kate retired for the evening and spent some time reading her Bible in bed before sleeping. As she offered her nightly prayers, she remembered to lift up Daniel.

"Lord, please guide Daniel. May he accomplish Your purposes at TLC. In the meantime, *please* guard the entire hospital with your angels. Protect us from disaster while he finds his way!"

Chapter Eleven

A ndrew Tucker knelt beside his bed. He folded his hands and closed his eyes—but not too tightly. His head had been hurting most of the day.

He wanted to ignore it, but it only got worse. Although he was tired and tried to sleep, the increasing pain made him restless. And scared.

He had gotten up to sit by the window a while. Anything was better than lying in bed. Sitting took some of the pressure off, though not much. But he had become dizzy looking outside and shuffled his way back toward the bed. He was losing the battle—he knew. The headaches were returning.

As he knelt, he summoned all the faith a little boy could. His parents couldn't do anything more. Medicine had failed. A miracle was all he had left, if one was available.

"Dear God, I don't know how to say this, but I really need Your help. Mom and Dad don't believe much in miracles, but I do. I know You are there. Nurse Jocelyn knows, too. She talks to Jesus all the time. We both wanted to ask You a favor. I know I already asked You once, but I thought maybe I'd just send You a little reminder."

Andrew grew quiet. He tried to find just the right words. Maybe he had been too selfish the first time, he thought.

"I suppose You are very busy up there with all the sick people. I just wondered if . . . if You would please take away my headaches. They came back. Actually, I really wanted to ask if You would take the tumor, too. But if You're too busy, could You just take away the headaches? They really hurt, and they kind of scare me. I want to be brave like Mom says I am, but I think I'm more afraid than brave." He paused.

"Nurse Jocelyn says sometimes You answer prayer in a different way than we want. I'm not sure why, but You are bigger and smarter than me, and I think You know what's best. I . . . I wanted to ask You for a miracle—for Christmas? I know You're not Santa Claus—he doesn't do miracles, anyway—so I knew I needed to come to You. I've never asked for one before. Actually, I don't think I've even seen one. My friend Jesse said a miracle happened when his brother, Jake, passed his math test. But I wasn't so sure that was a *real* miracle. I think he just tried harder." Andrew wondered what else to say.

"Well, I better let You go. You have a lot of prayers to listen to. Thanks for watching over me. And please bless Mom and Dad, and all the kids in the hospital, and their families. Amen."

He started to get off his knees but remembered something. He bowed and knelt again. "Sorry, I forgot—please bless my sister, Caroline, too. Amen."

Andrew crawled beneath the covers and tried once more to sleep. The aching didn't leave, but it seemed less painful. He sighed, remembering Nurse Jocelyn's hopeful words from last week: "I bet He's working on it right now."

With that to comfort him, he fell asleep.

Jocelyn gave a heavy sigh. During her midnight rounds, she had approached Andrew's door just as he was kneeling to pray. Her hesitation to interrupt his prayer was not out of eavesdropping, but respect. Now she was glad she had overheard it. Andrew was a real champ and rarely let on when he was hurting or even just down in the dumps. She didn't want him to further conceal the recurring headaches. That would only cause him unnecessary pain.

She decided to keep a watchful eye on him through the night, and talk to him in the morning about going back on some medicine.

Nonetheless, before leaving his doorway, she sent her own request to heaven, pleading for Andrew's miracle.

Kate finished giving the first carousel ride on Tuesday morning. She continued humming the cheerful, windpipe melody that stayed in her mind as she walked to the petting zoo wing. The happy children and bright songs helped lift her spirits considerably from the misgivings that had crept in last night.

Sleep was elusive after Daniel had all but declared TLC didn't have a chance to keep the carousel. His tone was firm, albeit apologetic, when he'd said "no matter what happens at the hospital." Adding to her melancholy was that she still had not come up with a plan—even after worrying about it half the night.

Somehow, though, the sunny morning brought new hope. And being around the children again doused her in a fresh wave of courage.

She came around the corner and pushed the button on the wall for the zoo wing's automatic doors to swing open. After striding through, they closed behind her. The hallway inside the zoo wing was lively decorated with jungle terrain and painted creatures of all sizes. The multicolored mural not only blanketed the side walls, but also covered the ceiling and floors. Birds and animals of various kinds hung in trees, peeked through tall grass, or sailed through the sky. In addition to the artwork, plastic hanging vines, big leafy plants, and stuffed exotic animals lined the corridor. To top that, four small speakers, hidden behind plants in each corner of the hall, played a wild jungle soundtrack.

Kate loved it! Not solely for its fantasy—the work behind the creation was more meaningful to her. It was a community effort orchestrated by over twenty volunteers, several staff members, a few doctors, and a handful of the more artistic children in the hospital.

The mural took six months to create, but their efforts made the evening news, the local papers, and drew a special award from the city council, which hung at the entrance to the wing next to a large, framed, color photo of all who participated.

TLC never seemed to have problems getting support or funding for projects. The two major zoos nearby collectively donated twelve of their smaller creatures to TLC for permanent housing, and another twenty were rotated in on a seasonal basis. Only the zoologist was paid staff. Other volunteers on the small team of caregivers included two local veterinarians. The construction of the wing, domiciles, and viewing cages was done free of charge by a small Christian business. Even the paint supplies were given to them by the nearby Kaleidoscope Paints store.

Many believed the donations were given because people wanted to do something for the children. And that was true. But Kate knew, ultimately, it was the Lord supplying their needs, even though He almost always accomplished it through people. The hospital prayed regularly to request God's help, guidance, protection, and provision. Kate had seen more than one divine intervention take place that nothing else could explain.

That was why she felt confident now. She knew the Lord was watching over them, still. The Miracle Machine would never be removed from TLC unless God ordained for it to go. Nevertheless, she kept praying earnestly for Daniel to change his mind!

Kate walked down to the internal set of safety glass doors. The zoo's hours for viewing were from 10:00 a.m. to 3:00 p.m. daily, so she had a little more than a half-hour to go over the weekly stats with Zinnia before the kids started lining up.

Advantageously, Daniel agreed to join them. Kate wanted to involve him as deeply as possible, so he could witness firsthand what he'd be throwing away if he cut the Wellness Program.

Zinnia Katarubba was crouched behind the viewing glass of the first animal cove, and she saw Kate approach. She waved one dark hand cheerfully while she wrestled the recently added lion cub with the other. The male cub, Sassafras, was on loan for a month. He was no longer a newborn, but there remained plenty of playfulness in his young lion heart, though he was still fairly small. His growing strength, sharp teeth, and impulsive nature, however—which would have been too much for some children—kept him off the petting list. Still, he provided hours of entertainment for the kids by chasing his tail and playing with big-cat toys.

Zinnia rubbed his chin and patted him good, then exited out the domicile's back door, closing it behind her. Kate punched a combination on the electric keypad controlling the locks to the secured staff entrance. The door to the back area buzzed, indicating it was passable. She strode through to greet the zoologist. "Good morning, Zinnia."

"Mornin', Meez Katie!" her strong Jamaican accent flowed.

"How's our new little rascal on his third day here?"

"Oh! Heez ready to take on the world, that one!" Zinnia threw her hands up and beamed a mouthful of glistening white teeth. Long, raven dreadlocks swayed from her dramatic gesture.

"*Great.*" Kate teasingly wondered if they could use the young cub as a secret weapon to take on Daniel.

"Come, Meez Katie. I've another new resident to show you." She gave a broad, inviting smile and led Kate back into the open grooming room, where a tall cage in the corner held a brilliantly colored Macaw. The flamboyant bird clung sideways to the rails with its gray feet, while taking bites of fruit and seeds.

As they approached, the Macaw took note of them, turning his blue head sideways and giving a compulsory "'Ello." Kate smiled and admired his composition of blue, red, and green feathers. "He is beautiful! Or is it she?"

"'Tiz he." She opened the latch and, with a little coaching, the bird hopped to her forearm. "And handsome, true?"

"Dazzling! If I had feathers, I'd fall off my branch," Kate joked, and Zinnia laughed heartily. "Where'd you get him?"

"A good friend of mine eez leaving on a missionary trip to Zimbabwe for a year. He wanted to loan Tepo to our zoo. Tepo eez fully trained and very good with cheeldran. I assured my friend we would treat Tepo like royalty." She passed Tepo to Kate's hand.

Kate held and petted the docile bird, who then rubbed against her hand, begging for more strokes. "Zinnia, you treat all the animals here like royalty."

"So, he'ez in good co'pany!" She beamed.

"Well, I'm impressed," Kate said. "Two new residents in one week. We might have to expand. What do you think?"

"As the Lord wills," Zinnia answered, nodding.

The security locks on the door buzzed and the door opened. Henry and Daniel stepped through, both wearing suits and ties. "Good morning, Kate, Zinnia," Henry said.

"Mornin', Sir Henry!" Zinnia greeted him in her usual, charismatic way.

"Hi, Henry. Hello, Daniel." Kate smiled. "I'd like to introduce Zinnia Katarubba. Her homeland was Jamaica until she turned fourteen. Her parents then moved to the USA. Following graduation, Zinnia studied zoology at the UW. She came to us after working with Woodland Park Zoo for five years. She's our Zoologist on staff. The vets and caregivers are all volunteers."

"Meester Brakken," she took his hand and shook it firmly. "Such a pleasure to welcome you!"

"Thank you. Pleased to meet you."

The Macaw piped up in a song voice, "Pleased to meet you." He dipped his head forward several times, like he was bowing.

Everyone laughed.

Daniel eyed the bird curiously. "Well—thank you, too!"

"And this is Tepo," Kate said. Tepo raised up to flap his wings, then whistled.

Kate returned him to Zinnia. "We'd better let Tepo get back to his breakfast."

"Well, ladies," Henry remarked, "I'll leave Daniel in your capable hands. I just thought I'd better guide him down here, until he can find his way in the jungle." Henry winked, then chuckled at his own joke.

Daniel raised his eyebrows. "He's not kidding. That's the closest I've come to knowing how Tarzan must have lived."

Though Daniel seemed a little tense, Kate was pleased to hear a hint of last night's humor. She'd expected him to be on pins and needles again at the hospital. It was so much easier to relate to him in this temperament.

While Zinnia put Tepo back in his cage, Kate began telling Daniel the history of the petting zoo's inception and the community involvement in putting it all together. Then, they gave Daniel the grand tour, showing him the veterinary room, the glass wall coves, inner cages, the outside play arena, and the indoor "tropical pond," where some exotic fish swam lazily around.

Zinnia insisted Daniel bond with each creature to see how gentle they were for the kids. He was resistant at first, but she just starting draping them on his arm or shoulders, ignoring his verbal objection. Kate thought the personal touch was a great idea for other reasons: The more bonding, the harder it would be for him to send them away. By the time Daniel had been introduced to each animal, he actually looked like he was enjoying himself.

Ten minutes before 10:00 a.m., they met together in Zinnia's office—comparably decorated with the zoo's hallway—to review the weekly stats. Zinnia handed Kate a paperclipped stack of yellow slips with doctor approvals for the various kids admitted inside the zoo. Another collection of pink papers permitted "view only" candidates. Kate read each one carefully. Like the carousel arrangement, each child was allowed to be involved, even if it was merely watching. Only those in Recovery and ICU never made it down for a visit.

"What are the blue ones for?" Daniel asked.

Kate had forgotten about those. Her stomach knotted. She glanced to Zinnia, trying to send her a silent warning through desperate eyes.

"Eenjury reports," Zinnia said. "Sometimes there eez a bite or scratch. Nothing major. Yet, we record."

Kate tapped the pads of her fingertips together waiting for Daniel's reaction, and praying it wasn't volcanic.

"How *unmajor* are they?" he persisted, his face showing concern.

Zinnia looked matter-of-factly at him. "Usually we only need to saneetize the area. Occasionally, bandage the wound eef there eez a tear een the skin."

"*Bandage?* What about casting? Surgery? Any of those?" Daniel's tone had turned cynical.

Zinnia took a slight offense to his overreaction. Her mouth and eyes opened wide with surprise. "Of course not. We—"

Kate interrupted, "What Zinnia means by "bandage," Daniel, is a small *adhesive strip*." She didn't want the woman's imperfect English to magnify the matter beyond actuality.

Zinnia nodded her agreement with Kate's clarification. "My zoo eez very safe, Meester Brakken. We only have leetle problems." She held up her thumb and forefinger to show a quarter-inch space between them.

Daniel kept quiet, but Kate could tell his pot of worries had started to boil again. "There's no cause for alarm, Daniel. We've never had a major incident. The animals are monitored daily for aggressive behavior. If they show any, they are switched to isolated stations with no petting allowed."

"What about infections? Allergies? Diseases? You realize it only takes one thing these days for malpractice suits to fly."

Kate closed her eyes briefly. He was obviously headed for the deep end. "We've never had any infections, all wounds are cleaned immediately, and the animals have all been vaccinated thoroughly. The kids are charted for allergic probabilities and admitted appropriately. And as for diseases," she was beginning to lose her calm, "*unfortunately . . .*" she paused for added emphasis, "it is the children who are sick—*not* the animals."

"No zuits, either," Zinnia added firmly.

The jungle clock on the wall beside them blared an imitation elephant's trump, and two monkeys—one per side—swung back and forth on plastic vines, giving ten shrieks for the hour. Zinnia stood with a less exuberant smile than before. "Too bad we do not have more time. I must let een the cheeldran. Good day to you, sir." She reached out a hand, which he briefly shook.

As she passed by, Zinnia squeezed Kate reassuringly on the shoulder. Kate accepted it for what it was, a silent *don't worry* from her hospital comrade. She wanted to believe that, but Zinnia had not yet heard Daniel's plans for the entire Wellness Program—including the zoo. And Kate didn't want to be the one to inform her!

Kate collected the daily authorization slips, stood, and walked Daniel back through the jungle hall. They strode against the incoming flow of ecstatic kids—apparatuses and all. The noise of the happy children made Daniel's silence all the more evident. He was simmering, Kate knew, and she deemed it best to let him cool. She had set him off once before, at the restaurant, and knew what kind of reaction that brought.

When they reached the Admin. wing he headed straight into his office and closed the heavy door with a thud.

Kate sat at her desk in the nearby cubicle and tossed the clipped stacks of slips onto the mountain of things piling in her in-basket. With her morning ambition now dampened, she fell back into the chair, crossed her legs, and started rubbing her forehead with her fingertips.

The cloud of discouragement from last night returned.

Chapter Twelve

K ate saw Jocelyn walk into Administration, right at 1:00. She was dropping off the nurses' time sheets in Chang's office for payroll. They exchanged a swift greeting glance. From the corner of Kate's vision, she noticed
Jocelyn halt in her tracks, then approach. Kate peered sideways. Jocelyn stood by
Kate's desk with her hands buried deep in the jacket pockets, lightly tapping her
thighs. Kate waited for her to comment.

"You know," Jocelyn spoke cautiously, "I think we can get that troubled expression into the Guinness Book of World Records."

Kate offered a meager grin to her co-worker and friend. "Hi, Joce. I know—
it's not pretty, but I have my reasons."

Jocelyn glanced around at the empty cubicles. "I think everyone's still at
lunch. Want to talk about it?"

"Wish I could." Kate sighed and gave her an apologetic look. "But keep me
in your prayers, will you?"

Jocelyn nodded. "Always. Especially for the right man."

Kate looked at her incredulously. Jocelyn winked. "Gee, thanks," Kate said,
and laughed with disbelief.

"What? I prayed my husband here. I'll do the same for you."

"Thanks," Kate lowered her voice to a forced whisper, "but I'd rather you
prayed a man *away*, right now."

"Hmm . . ." Jocelyn also whispered. "That wouldn't happen to be . . ." She
mouthed the name *Mr. Brakken*.

Kate mouthed *Bingo!* back to her. "Careful," she added, whispering, "he's in
Henry's office."

"You mean *his* office."

Kate rolled her eyes. "Whichever."

Jocelyn looked suspicious. "Kate, tell me—this problem is not about professional jealousy, is it?" she asked softly.

"No! In fact, it is far more serious. If I could explain, I would, but I can't say anything, not yet." She didn't want to say anything *ever*. Kate didn't know when Daniel was going to bring the axe down, but she wasn't going to leak any bad news until he insisted on announcing his plans for the big change.

After a brief hesitation, Jocelyn nodded. "OK, I trust you."

"Thanks. Hey—I just realized you're supposed to be sleeping now. Are you working a double shift today?"

"Yeah, Diane and Char both have that nasty flu going around. I'm tired, but I can make it two more hours."

Lisa and Chang walked in, returning from lunch. Jocelyn glanced at her watch. "Will you make it to staff prayer today?" she asked Kate.

"I would never miss it," she replied and gave a firm smile of support.

"Good. We need everybody today. Round up any stragglers."

Kate felt troubled by her plea. "What's up?"

Jocelyn's expression turned to one of compassion. "It's Andrew. He's back upstairs, in ICU."

Two-thirds of the staff on duty filed into the meeting room, joined by two available doctors and a handful of volunteers. Henry addressed the gathering with a quick list of announcements.

"We need to keep the regulars in mind, plus our ER needs and our new Administrator. As you already know, our Oncologist, Colleen Huntsman, is moving to Colorado to get married in January. We still need a replacement for her position. Next, we had a successful bone-marrow transplant with Tad McKinney—" Henry paused as the room erupted in applause and cheers. "He's doing well in Recovery. Lastly, a few residents are coming out of remission: Anne Zowalski, Peter Niles, and . . . Andrew Tucker."

Sighs of disappointment and concern laced through the room at the mention of Andrew. Kate knew it wasn't that the other children weren't cared about, just that Andrew had suffered so much and fought for so many years. And, for a while, things looked as is they were improving.

"What is his status, Henry?" Kate asked from the front row.

Henry frowned. "His headaches have returned, he's heavily sedated, and that is helping with the pain. His parents don't want any more surgery. The remaining portion of tumor is too imbedded in the brain stem, where there is considerable risk. I'm afraid we've done all we can for Andrew." Henry wiped his eyes. All in the room held hands, by rows, while Henry and a few others prayed for each concern with fervor and sympathy.

After the prayer, Kate remained seated while everyone returned to their post. She was always touched by the brief yet powerful meetings. They lasted only about ten minutes, but they rejuvenated her faith and sparked fresh hope.

She had really needed the boost today. More than that, Andrew Tucker needed a miracle. If any boy deserved one, he did.

With Andrew's condition weighing heavily on her already burdened heart, she stayed a while longer to pray.

Undetected, Daniel had slipped out the back door of the meeting room at the onset of the prayer. He headed back to his office. He wasn't interested in praying, just the information.

What he wasn't prepared to hear, though, hit him like a brick squarely between the eyes: Andrew was much worse, . . . and they were giving up on him.

He paced the office like a caged animal, running his hand through his hair. He felt caught between two walls that were closing in—Pain and Need.

It wasn't the fault of the hospital, he knew that. He was certain they attempted everything they could, as Henry had said. But there was more available: Newer procedures and hi-tech options that reduced a great portion of the risk. Most he had used successfully. Others . . .

The guilt swirled around him again like a haunting demon that awoke whenever the memory surfaced. Daniel knew firsthand *other* procedures held a larger degree of risk and could claim the final days of the child. He'd learned his lesson: Some risks you don't take, even if you have a good chance at beating the odds. If you lose . . .

He sighed remorsefully.

Daniel's instincts wrestled with his judgment, and they started to get the better of it—as they invariably did. He had always followed his inner leadings in his practice; they were what made him rise so quickly to the top. The strong, intuitive guidance defined the gift in him.

Combined with the medical knowledge he had acquired, Daniel had always hit his mark. That is . . . all but once.

His confidence faltered beneath the resurfacing doubt and shame. He shook off the rising aspirations to save Andrew's life. Daniel refused—this time—to let pride and ego cost him another fatal mistake.

Besides, it was unthinkable! He wasn't even allowed to let TLC staff know that he was a surgeon. A *failed* surgeon. How was he supposed to waltz into this boy's life and work a miracle? And what if the local press learned of his past publicity? They would hang him before he could perform the operation. Then what? If his previous ordeal was exposed in this community, the boy's parents would probably not consent. His hands would be tied, even if he could help

Andrew. All would be for naught! That would surely end his new career here, which, he reminded himself, was his last and only option.

Daniel decided, no matter how sorely it disturbed him, no matter how his instincts berated him, there was *nothing* he could do for Andrew Tucker.

Chapter Thirteen

$\mathcal{F}$or the rest of Tuesday Kate saw virtually nothing of Daniel. Between his meetings with Henry and other medical professionals, he was swept away, hour by hour.

Fine, she thought. His touchy temper that morning at the zoo made her want to keep her distance. Too bad his mood from dinner didn't last, she reflected, longing for the congenial, easygoing Daniel that lay beneath the rough, lion surface. It was strange but true: Daniel Brakken was a drastically different person around the hospital, just as he'd claimed.

On the bright side of his mood swing, during Daniel's seclusion, Kate was able to do wonders with the backlog piled high in her in-basket, and she welcomed the lack of interruptions.

Besides, staying focused on her work kept her from thinking about him.

    🐦   🐦   🐦   🐦

For most of Wednesday, Daniel was equally engaged. Kate spent the majority of her time reviewing information about the new state and federal regulations, and checking their current policies against them—something Daniel should have been doing. She knew he would never get to them until next week or later. And that would be too late.

Now Thursday, she had just conquered a list of confirmation calls and preparations for Friday's semi-monthly Roundtable meeting with the physicians. This meeting's topic—recent E. coli eruptions—involved obtaining the most current data to be used for discussion purposes. She had spent the morning hours on it already.

Daniel was so busy getting familiarized, Kate was rightly concerned that he wouldn't get to the calls or the research. Now that she had tackled them both for him, all he would need to do was preview the materials and lead the discussion. She didn't mind doing the preparations for him—actually she'd always enjoyed helping Henry prepare for the Roundtables. But, it was also easier to take care of it than take a chance at it not getting done with Daniel's unavailability.

At the same time, though, she hoped it wouldn't be like this for the next month. These tasks were his territory. And if he was going to be the new Executive Administrator, he would need to buckle down and schedule less *engagements*. Based upon Henry's laud for Daniel's experience, he would hit the ground running by the end of next week. But, given what Kate had seen so far, it was going to be well into spring before she stopped covering for him by handling a large portion of his responsibilities.

Delving back into her own work, Kate still couldn't agree that Daniel was the best choice to direct the hospital!

Friday morning, promptly at 7:00, various physicians streamed into the assembly room for their meeting. After helping themselves to coffee, tea, juice, and muffins, they took random seats in the new circular arrangement of chairs, which Kate thought would be a good change to enable a "roundtable" discussion more easily. The meetings weren't mandatory, just a forum to discuss current topics and answer questions. Everyone's opinion was valued, and each doctor's specialty was respected.

The flow of attendees halted about five minutes later. Kate grew nervous; they were ready to start. Unfortunately, the only persons not present were those scheduled to lead the meeting—Daniel, and Henry to introduce him. Kate didn't want to make the physicians wait for nothing, so to pass time she handed out the compilations of E. coli data that she had photocopied for their information.

The doctors perused the handouts for another few minutes, then gradually they began making eye contact with her, showing inquisitive looks. Still no sign of Henry or Daniel. Kate's concern escalated. These meetings only lasted an hour. It would be embarrassing to cancel, making the doctors forfeit their valuable time.

She stood to begin the meeting herself.

"Well—" Kate broke the silence and all eyes turned to her, "I apologize for the delay. As you know, Henry is in a very busy transition right now with Mr. Brakken. So, may I propose a discussion on the E. coli material. Have any of you heard of these recent reports?"

Most of them shook their heads no. One man, Dr. Melton, TLC's longstanding Gastroenterologist volunteered, "Our office has recorded a mild increase in the number of cases we've seen this year, but it hasn't been pivotal," he mentioned. "However, this is something TLC should keep an eye on. It's my opinion that we have superior policies here at TLC, but I believe this data raises a few excellent new options for preventing liver damage and using new antibiotics."

"I agree," Dr. Winthrop concurred, an older balding man with half-lens spectacles. Heads around the room nodded in agreement.

"Kate, have there been many cases this year in the ER?" asked Dr. Harris, TLC's newest Pediatrician. Her light-blond hair was pulled back into a bun, professionally, outlining her comely facial features.

"Not as many as previous years," Kate responded. "But Dr. Winters is probably more prepared to give you an answer at this time. Dr. Winters?" She regarded the middle-aged Asian-American man.

Dr. Winters, head of the ER Department, set his paperwork down and folded his hands, "Kate is correct. We have not had a large-scale incident pattern. Only a handful of cases since last January. But I understand that larger local hospitals are still seeing about twice that, per year. Our lower numbers could definitely stem from being a smaller organization."

Several more questions arose, and various professionals responded. Kate was grateful they'd broken the ice and forged ahead without their intended leader. She glanced at her watch again and frowned. Henry and Daniel were over a half-hour late!

The discussion continued, crested, then quickly dwindled. Kate jotted down their suggestions for updated policies. And with that, she decided it was only fair to dismiss. At least she had taken advantage of fifty minutes. "Well, doctors, thank you for your time and expertise. Next meeting, we have planned for discussion on new technology breakthroughs and procedures using laser surgery. Have a pleasant day." She smiled at everyone.

Chairs scraped the linoleum flooring as they all stood to leave. Some shook hands and chatted with one another in the extra minutes. Most hurried off to resume their busy schedules. Eventually, all filed out.

Kate rearranged the chairs back to the standard meeting-row format while battling a mixture of emotions. She was aggravated with Henry and Daniel for their embarrassing absence. Even if one of them couldn't have made it, the other one should have been there.

Nonetheless, Kate wondered if the unexpected outcome wasn't for the best. If Henry had come by himself, it would have made Daniel look really bad. And if Daniel had shown up alone, he likely wouldn't have delivered anything close to Kate's cover job—she was certain. She had left one of her handouts of the E. coli data on his desk yesterday. However, she saw it this morning, pushed aside to a far corner and most likely unread.

To be honest with herself, Kate enjoyed undertaking the meeting preparations. Though the research had put her behind in her own work, collecting the data had been interesting, and fortunately, gave her a substantive jumpstart in igniting the discussion today. Had she known in advance that she would be managing the Roundtable, it would have run even smoother.

She beamed, and commended herself for handling it so well!

Nevertheless, Kate festered over Daniel's growing areas of incompetence.

Henry strode through the office just after 8:00 a.m., practically on the heels of Kate's arrival. He greeted her with his usual warmth and happiness. Then she asked about his absence. Henry looked dubious for a second, then abashed. He straightaway apologized. He'd forgotten completely about introducing Daniel, who was to conduct the meeting. And since Kate had given all her meeting information to Daniel directly, there was nothing to stir Henry's memory the previous day.

"I'm sorry, Kate. How did it go?" he questioned, curious.

Kate explained Daniel hadn't shown either.

"Oh . . ." he remarked, disclosing a trace of concern. "Well, aside from that?"

"Fine. The only glitch was keeping them waiting. If I'd only known in advance that I would be leading the discussion, everything would have run even more smoothly."

"That's my girl! Always hitting the mark." He patted her on the shoulder with a fair amount of pride.

"Thanks for the accolades, Henry, but this is Daniel's responsibility. And frankly, what concerns me more is I doubt he would have outdone me. Aren't you even remotely concerned about his performance—or, should I say, his *lack* of performance? Daniel was supposed to be the best choice for TLC, remember? He's been here a week, and all I've really seen him accomplish is attend receptions and publicity meetings."

"There's bound to be bumps during a transition."

"Easy for you to say, you're leaving." She looked matter-of-factly at him, then forlornly. "How long are these bumps going to keep appearing?"

Henry sighed. "Kate, I know you see things sharper than he does. Give him a little grace. You're used to how we operate; he's new in town. How would you have felt if I'd expected you to run your departments with a week's training?"

She felt ashamed at her intolerance. Still, something didn't settle in her stomach. Yes, Daniel had talents: Easy rapport with the kids, knowledge of high-tech procedures, concern for risks—but they weren't all that was necessary. Several more administrative basics were needed for this position.

Where was his motivation to hold a staff meeting? Why did his eyes gloss over when she tried to review policies with him? When would he show as much interest in the parenting issues and support programs as in his concerns for the ER upgrade?

Odd as it seemed, to Kate, Daniel functioned more like a physician than a hospital administrator.

And it greatly concerned her!

Chapter Fourteen

*D*aniel's heels echoed in the empty hall as he walked toward the Admin. offices late Friday morning. He was fully engrossed with a hospital equipment brochure for emergency room apparatus and supplies. The lengthy meeting he'd just had with the Chief of Emergency at St. Brendan's Hospital proved invaluable. They had upgraded their emergency wing six months ago with the latest options in high-tech equipment, and were swaggering at the change. Not only had their older instruments been replaced and sold for profit, but newer innovations were purchased, as well. The result was a big rise in patient treatment, with better technology at their fingertips than many of the hospitals in the surrounding region.

The only aspect the C.O.E. groaned over was their total bill: A stunning three-and-one-half million! With only one quarter of those changes being implemented at TLC, the small hospital would be looking at seven hundred thousand in necessary revenue. And that didn't include installation and training expenses.

But, Daniel knew there *was* a way to cover it all.

He had also conferred with another colleague recently, whom, he learned, was nearly as hooked on carousel things as Kate. The colleague informed Daniel that each piece—depending upon the maker, the age, wear, and quality of restoration—could carry an auction bid ranging from five hundred to forty thousand dollars. Daniel was betting that Kate and her grandfather would have wanted to preserve the better figures.

It didn't take him long to do the math. He found they could auction the entire carousel setup, piece by piece: base, music box, mirrors, side panels, top panels, and poles. Then, with each riding piece bringing an average of twenty thousand it would pull significant assets for the ER upgrade. Additional monies would come from eliminating the zoologist from the payroll.

Daniel rolled the glossy brochure into a tube. He felt satisfied with his findings. But there was something else brewing, an emotion he hated to concede to because it suggested a warning—compunction. He feared this auction was a bad idea and would cause Kate to write him off as soon as he unloaded his grand plans on her.

His face twitched. He wanted to believe that he was making a smart business investment, but the anxious feeling inside gave him the "willies." Probably because he had a bomb to drop, he reasoned. After all, no one likes to be a bearer of bad news.

He drew in a bolstering breath as he strode through the entrance to Administration. Surely, his apprehension would fade after talking with Kate. If he reasoned with her, explained the benefits clearly enough, she would come around he was sure. After fourteen years of practicing surgery, coaching people in what avenue they *needed* to take—though they were uneasy about doing so—was something Daniel executed well.

"Morning, Lisa." He approached his secretary's desk. She blinked and pushed her dark, long bangs behind her ears. She clearly looked unsettled by his late arrival.

Retrieving his telephone message slips, he viewed them briefly: Several inconsequentials, one important—Jerry Nabor. Just who Daniel wanted to hear from. Nabor, an Auction Master from the Pacific Northwest, was returning Daniel's call about setting a date to auction the carousel. *Perfect timing.*

"Is Henry in, Lisa?"

She nodded stiffly. "He's in the boardroom, Mr. Brakken. An interview with a new oncologist prospect. He'll be available in about another hour."

"Thanks."

As he passed Kate, who was on the telephone, he curled an index finger in her line of vision and moved on. She abruptly told the caller, "Excuse me—I'll call you back," then hung up the phone. She followed him into his office and closed the door behind her. Daniel had just picked up his phone to return Nabor's call, not expecting her to be done so soon. He replaced the receiver.

"We need to talk," she blurted.

He was surprised by her lack of usual charm. "Yes, we do. Please—have a seat." He gestured to the chair beside her.

"Before we begin, I want to make it clear that Henry knows nothing of me coming to you about this. So I would appreciate your keeping this confidential."

Daniel pursed his lips and then nodded.

She looked restless, strained. "I'll just be honest, Daniel. I've been having some real concerns . . . regarding your performance." Her green eyes sent a clear, bold message. She was obviously bothered, and her irritant had his name on the tag.

"Why don't you fill me in." He folded one arm over his chest and propped his chin up with his other hand, trying to stay open to her complaint.

"Well, frankly, since you've started this position, you seem very distracted."

"Really? How so?" he countered, wondering how long she was going to drag this out.

"Emotionally. And there is also some confusion about your priorities."

"Interesting." He narrowed his gaze on her. A sliver of offense started to fester, but he ignored it. She had her own surprises following this discussion. He needed to remain calm to deliver them successfully. "Why don't you explain a little. Give me some examples."

"Well, like neglecting to show up at the physician's Roundtable this morning. I gave you the handout for it yesterday with a note asking you to share the information with Henry. Henry never saw it. Did you even review it?"

Daniel looked unsure. He started to rummage through his in-box, which was now twice as high as when he'd left last night. It stunned him how rapidly the administrator's mail piled! "I'm not sure whether I recall that. . . ."

"I believe I see it laying over there." She pointed to the far corner of his desk.

"Oh." He plucked it up, scanned the note, and realized he hadn't read it thoroughly the day before. "Now I remember. I didn't notice that the Roundtable was so soon. I'll appreciate your pointing that out to me in the future."

She looked insulted. "It was posted on your calendar for today."

"Really? I checked it before I left last night." His eyebrows drew together. He was sure there were no meetings posted for this morning, having checked his daily electronic calendar after typing a note to himself in the to-do section. Daniel pulled up the system and clicked on the day. The meeting reference stood boldly in caps. His note was not there.

"Hmm. Strange." He clicked on the optional monthly view and saw the reference to his note, mistakenly written on Saturday, not Friday—he'd been working on the wrong day. He tried to hide his embarrassment, but was sure she'd see right through him. "It appears I got the days mixed up with tomorrow."

She nodded. "Daniel, I understand that everything is new here, but in case Henry hasn't mentioned it, you will normally be the one to furnish the data and direct these meetings. I took care of this month's research because I could see you were busy with transitioning. However, I reminded you of the meeting time when I gave you the handouts."

He remained calm. "My sincere apologies, Kate. It was a genuine oversight. And yes, I obviously have a lot on my mind." He tried to sound remorseful, but he didn't think one botched meeting was worth all her huff.

She grimaced; a scant acceptance of his confession. "The next Roundtable is December 31. They are held semi-monthly. Our topic is technology breakthroughs in laser surgery. I've placed a copy of an article in your box that is fairly substantial, and it should give you a headstart on the subject. You can search online for more."

He wanted to howl! If she only knew how many times he had already successfully performed such techniques, with acclaim. Suppressing a grin, he added, "I'm sure it will be fascinating. Is that everything?"

"Actually, no," she bounced back. "You are falling behind in interviews for the new oncologist. Henry met with Dr. Yulong Wang earlier, and he's meeting with Dr. Heidi Tams right now. Both interviews were scheduled with you—and were also on your calendar for today."

He was starting to get frustrated with her chastisement.

"You'll have two more tomorrow morning. One from 9:00 to 10:30. The next is from 11:00 to 12:30."

"Tomorrow is Saturday."

"I know. However, we are trying to make up for lost time. You haven't been available much this week."

"I don't plan to work Saturdays, unless it's critical. You'll need to reschedule."

"We can't. These two candidates are arriving from out of state just for the day. Dr. Scott Terrington is from Portland, Oregon, and Dr. Simi Arianke is visiting relatives in Tacoma. He has to fly back to New York on Sunday."

Daniel grew further annoyed. He did not want to forfeit the morning of his first day off. He'd been eager for a break.

"Next item?" he asked curtly.

Kate continued. "As soon as possible, you will need to review the new bulletins on state and federal changes. They have compliance dates posted—usually a few months after enactment. I've read through them and checked our policies against the updates. Fortunately, we still have time to comply with most, but there are two immediate issues that will cause a domino effect in our policies. Both have deadlines of January 2. You'll see the discrepancies when you review TLC's procedure manual." She spied and retrieved a very thick white binder from the shelf beside his desk. She placed it with the bulletins at the center of his desk, next to his growing stack of things to do.

Daniel shifted and dropped his hands to the arms of the leather chair. Then slowly he drummed his fingers, willing tolerance. Unbeknownst to him, this meeting had become a match that he was losing. If Kate wasn't near the end of her list of shortcomings, he was going to be at the office every weekend until April.

"Anything . . . else?" He felt more humbled this time.

"Yes."

He closed his eyes and sighed. Then tried afresh to hear her to the end.

"Well, this is actually more of a favor," her voice changed to a softer, friendly tone.

He cocked his head sideways, not sure whether it was safe to feel relieved yet. "Yeah?"

"Henry's retirement party is supposed to be held next Friday evening—on Christmas Eve. We'd like to keep it a surprise, and that means throwing it elsewhere. There isn't a place in this hospital that Henry doesn't roam—especially with it being his last few days, with goodbyes and all. We've had several offers for host homes, but none are big enough for sixty-five people. You mentioned that your cabin is very spacious. Would there be any trouble with our holding the party there? Don't worry—we would handle all the preparations and cleanup. Your place would be left spotless."

Daniel couldn't see it being a problem. It might be a bit tight for space, but they could manage it in the large cabin dwelling. "That's fine. You may arrange to hold it there."

"Great! Thanks." She looked relieved, then paused. Then looked slightly ill.

"That was all—right?" he ventured, unnerved by her change in countenance.

"Daniel, those are the scheduling items we needed to discuss, but there is something else . . . that I—personally—need to say," she answered more seriously, cautiously.

Now his stomach was hurting from tension. He gave her the most patient look he could muster, though he had mounting apprehension over what was to finally surface. "OK."

"You may as well know up front, I'm not the type of employee to play games. It's a quality Henry always appreciated. Regardless, I hope you won't be offended at my frankness. I've been at TLC awhile—almost eight years—and in the last eighteen months, I've practically run this hospital. Henry still does things, but for some time he's been delegating jobs to me left and right that were clearly outside of my job description—meaning, they are now *yours*. We operated like this with the assumption that I would be his replacement. Of course, now those tasks will need to be reverted to your charge."

Daniel nodded pensively.

"Since you haven't been around much this week, Henry has only one week left to train you from his perspective. Unfortunately, there exist about a hundred other duties, which he's bound not to recall, that I have been handling for a long time. To be candid, I don't see a smooth transition ahead. So, . . . I'm suggesting we work as a team for a period of time."

He blinked but didn't respond.

She took a deep breath, then proceeded with her concern, "*Unless*, that is, you would prefer to go for it yourself. If that's the case, I can understand your aspirations, but I believe the hospital will suffer. The facts are, at least four to five months of agenda remain regarding programs, policies, and legal procedures that you'll never cover with Henry by Christmas."

"Point made. What do you propose?" Daniel countered.

"Two items. First, that you let me advise you—not positionally, but in a pragmatic sense—until Memorial Day."

Without debate, he narrowed his gaze on her. "Second?"

"That you change no policies at the hospital until the advisory period is over—including the Wellness Program."

Checkmate! Daniel felt like he'd been shot. His strategy of dismantling that program had been completely stonewalled in less than fifteen minutes. Kate was handing him an ultimatum, and he was pinned beneath it.

Frankly, he didn't at all like the prospect of managing without her assistance. He needed Kate's expertise! Or, as she frankly pointed out, the hospital would begin to crumble. And his career would crumble with it.

He hadn't felt this trapped since he was forced to resign from L.A. General. But this time he wasn't backing down.

He tried steeling his gaze upon her to stay in control. "Just for the record, Kate, what should I expect if I can't agree to this proposal?"

The muscles in her face seemed suddenly tense. She looked away, bit her lip, tapped her knee with her fingers. "Then, I guess I'll have to do what I need to do."

She glanced back to him, and he could see the solemn look in her eyes. He tried to appear unmoved by her statement, but his adrenaline was already racing. "And what would that be?"

"Well, it would mean . . ." She faltered at the words and fought the tears rimming her eyes.

He felt he knew already from witnessing the pain on her face. Obviously, resigning from TLC meant more than a job change to Kate, just as his disengagement from practicing neurosurgery had been more devastating than anyone could have imagined. Daniel actually felt sorry for her, having called her ace. He empathized with the agony she was enduring. Such a withdrawal of personal vision and dream was akin to stripping someone from all life-support systems. He didn't want to press her into that. But he didn't have much in the way of alternatives.

"Yes?" he gently nudged her to answer.

"One month's notice of my resignation," she barely uttered the assertion through quivering lips.

Daniel dipped his head and swallowed hard. He had been hoping his assumption was wrong—that was why he insisted she spell it out for him. Not so. She was dead serious.

So much for your "talk" to her, he ruminated on the shriveled-up idea.

Plain and simple, if Kate quit, he was surely a dead man. Daniel couldn't see a way around that. On the other hand, if she stayed, he needed to keep the hand of power. Otherwise, the Wellness Program would never be withdrawn.

Candidly, he couldn't see her relinquishing that bargaining point now. Unless there was a reason for her to compromise.

He rubbed at his temple, strained by tension. He needed time to mentally work this out. A snap judgment would trip him up for sure. Daniel stood and opened the door for her.

"Give me the weekend to think about it."

Chapter Fifteen

*K*ate stared back at Daniel. She couldn't believe she'd said the words. It was tearing her to pieces. She wanted to retract them so badly, but they were on the table. And if she backed out now, he would surely never place the same amount of trust in her again. In his eyes, she'd merely be "crying wolf."

"Of course." She rose and headed out of his office. He quietly closed the door behind her.

Kate tried returning to her work, but it was practically a waste of time. Her mind was held prisoner by the preceding conversation. She rehashed it over and over, wondering what she could have said differently.

Nothing. She felt sure about following her convictions. Even though her stomach was doing flips!

She knew inside and out that Daniel didn't have the qualities or skills to replace Henry. Maybe the talk would motivate him to sprout some. If not, she was going to have to keep her word about resigning.

Besides, she didn't want to work for a man who was going to bring the whole hospital administration down around his shoulders. She wasn't so concerned over the children—the doctors and nurses would safeguard them with the care they needed. It was the hospital itself she worried about. Its remarkable legacy in the community, everything Henry had labored to build into it—all would surely collapse if Daniel wouldn't agree to train under her tutelage.

Kate thought of Henry and wondered if Daniel would keep her discourse under wraps. She didn't want to trouble Henry with a lot of worries now. He deserved to retire without fretting over whether the hospital, its prestige, and his hard work were being undone.

Furthermore, he'd be greatly disappointed in her. She hadn't waited two weeks before handing Daniel a time bomb.

But Kate felt strongly that she didn't have time to wait.

She wasn't sure what it was about this man that skyrocketed her determination, but something about Daniel's visible lack of expertise made her insides twist painfully. If he couldn't concede to the necessary training from her, she was certain he'd be a sailboat wafting dangerously toward the reef.

And if he was heading for a wreck, she was going to abandon ship!

It was after Noon on Saturday. Daniel finished making notes regarding the interviews with the oncologist prospects. At least those were something he felt competent doing! Physician talk he knew well.

Contemplative, he sat in his office. *My office? That's a joke!* he mused. It hadn't rightfully felt like his office since he'd arrived. He was doing his best to fit in here, but something unseen, something more powerful, kept usurping his efforts, making him a personified square peg in a round hole.

Again, Kate had him cornered, just like at the restaurant when she'd practically declared him unfit to make decisions for the children. Daniel wasn't truly sure that was her intention. It was believable enough that she was just being a "mother hen" over Henry's position, wanting to make sure Daniel performed well. He couldn't fault her for trying to protect her world from catastrophe.

In fact, he'd faced similar rivalries, year after year, training zealous new residents. Transforming the "greenhorns" from lofty *I-know-the-books* attitudes, to humble *you-show-me-the-best-way* perspectives, once their residencies were complete.

Daniel knew he was the short stick here in comparison to Kate. What bothered him most was sensing that she would be *far* better at running the hospital. And acknowledging that reality was no small feat! It chipped at his pride considerably.

It was obvious to him that Kate's ability stemmed not solely from having worked here. He recognized that she had those special traits of a gentle, but strong, leader—the Three C's in his book: Competent. Courteous. Cautious.

Now the pressure was on. He would need to relinquish his upper hand and forgo any changes to the Wellness Program. Or he had to forge ahead on his own, a path on which he could see only self-destruction. He didn't want that. He'd already messed up royally and nearly lost his ability to practice. He couldn't afford to fumble this pass. His future depended on it.

It wouldn't be easy, but he would have to keep Kate placated. At least for a time, until he had gained enough training to succeed on his own.

As for the ER and the carousel—he would have to find a way to turn the tables.

Kate prayed the entire weekend. No matter what she was doing on the outside, on the inside she was asking—pleading—for divine intervention. Not on behalf of the kids this time. This one was for her.

She arrived at the office early on Monday morning. It was better to be doing something than thinking about what Daniel was going to say to her. She came into the Admin. wing and unlocked the door, surprised to see the lights already on at 7:15. Since she usually opened up at 8:30, it could only mean someone else couldn't sleep.

Kate passed all the empty cubicles and placed her purse upon her desk. She glanced at the door to Daniel's office, which was closed all but an inch. The light was on inside, and she decided not to disturb him. After all, she didn't want to rush into the discussion she knew must take place.

Quietly, she sat at her desk and began going through the mail that had arrived in the drop slot on Saturday. She sliced envelopes with the razor-edged opener and unfolded the contents to view. Opening Saturday's mail wasn't a task she normally did for Lisa, but it helped to combat her nervousness over being alone in the office with Daniel.

She read each Christmas card and letter with the fondness and interest of a teacher reading her pupils' papers. Kate cared meticulously about everything the hospital encountered. Each note from a grateful parent, each medical periodical, each seminar opportunity—even the countless ads for ever-improving equipment and medicines—all links of communication were important to her. They received no junk mail in her eyes.

To Kate, staying informed was the healthy pulse of a good hospital. Countless advancements had been made at TLC over the years just by considering all that was available.

She perused a pamphlet on heartbeat monitors for intensive care. Medical service companies were always busy "repping" a new invention. Though TLC had made major upgrades to their Intensive Care Unit two years previously, a small portion of the equipment was already outdated. Regardless, that area would have to wait a while. The ER upgrade was next on the docket. And with Daniel leading the band, it would no doubt happen soon.

Kate opened the last envelope addressed to Daniel but not marked confidential. She unfolded the contents; its letterhead was boldly printed at top: Jerry Nabor—Auction Master. She read:

Dear Mr. Brakken,

Sorry I missed your visit to my office. Since I didn't hear back from you Friday, I wanted to drop you a note. I'd like to discuss the options with you, at your convenience, regarding placement of the carousel in one of our auctions. We have two available dates at this time. Saturday, January 8, is our first opening, due to a cancellation; the other is not until late February. My understanding was you requested to schedule as soon as possible, so I will pencil you in for January. Please confirm after receipt of this letter. I will hold the slot for 3 days. Given the short timeframe, I suggest you not wait too long, as we will need to have all advertising prepared by the end of this week. Otherwise, you will not get much publicity for your auction.

> Sincerely,
> Jerry Nabor

Kate sat motionless. She couldn't blink. Couldn't breath. She wanted desperately to crumple the letter and burn it in her garbage can, but she knew that wouldn't end her turmoil. Obviously, Daniel's array of meetings had included business other than local receptions. He'd searched out Jerry Nabor in less than a week. No doubt, her talk with him on Friday just bounced off his ears. He was probably only buying time over the weekend to keep from having to break bad news to her.

Daniel's door swung open and he strode through. Startled, Kate picked up the mail to bunch it together and straighten the edges. Nabor's letter lay on top, so she held the stack of mail against her, surface unseen.

Daniel noticed her. "Oh—good morning, Kate."

His lion eyes were tame, but they held their usual golden-brown intensity. Seeing him dressed in an attractive, blue pinstriped suit, she found it difficult to hold anything against him. But she wasn't about to let his suave appearance beguile her judgment. Now she knew he was "the enemy."

"Morning." She acknowledged him, then looked away. Although she often had opened letters not marked as private, Kate felt guilty—as though she'd snooped into personal affairs. Unfortunately, there wasn't a way to reseal the envelope.

"You're here early." He seemed concerned.

She nodded. "Mmm-hmm. Same as you."

He conceded by a roll of his eyes. "I had to do something about tackling my in-box. I can't believe all this mail!"

"Yes," she gave a grim look, "it's downright *shocking* sometimes." She was still reeling from Nabor's letter.

"Well, I just needed to run down the hall a second."

After Daniel left, Kate retrieved Nabor's envelope from her trash can and slipped the letter back inside. She wasn't going to keep it from him—that would be dishonest. But neither could she let Lisa discover it. Until Daniel made a formal withdrawal of the Wellness Program, she wasn't about to alert any staff members of his intentions. Kate's only option was to give the letter to Daniel, personally.

Then he would have to explain where he stood.

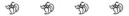

Later on Monday, after everyone in the office had left for the evening, Kate ventured over to Daniel's office and knocked. His door had been closed virtually all day. She'd rarely seen him slip out, except for occasional coffee and trips to the restroom. Once, after lunch, he'd stepped out to retrieve all of her Wellness Program data, then immediately returned to his isolation.

"Come in," he answered.

She turned the knob and opened the door. "Hi. Is this a good time to interrupt?" She could feel her nerves tightening. Approaching Daniel about Nabor's letter might not be an inoffensive approach, but it was best to do it in person.

"Sure." He placed his pencil down and leaned back in his chair, rubbing his eyes—obviously fatigued by the long day.

She sat in front of his in-box, immediately noticing how diminished it looked after his productive day. "Seems like you've made a lot of progress."

"I *can* be capable at handling matters. Although paperwork has never been one of my favorite tasks."

She nodded and bit on her lower lip. After a pause, she knew she had to take the step. "Daniel," she silently prayed for the right words, "I first want to mention that we received a letter today from Jerry Nabor." He steeled his dark-golden gaze on her, and Kate wondered where her courage had fled. "It wasn't marked 'confidential,' which is why it was opened along with our regular mail." She laid the envelope on his desk. He unfolded the letter and briefly reviewed the one paragraph message, then set it back down. He looked at Kate. No apology. No expression. No response.

"I don't think you realize how very difficult this is for me, Daniel." He remained unmoved; she forged ahead. "You know, it was hard enough losing out on a promotion I'd been trained for—and rightfully deserved—to a stranger whom no one in our hospital had even heard of. But, to watch you ransack an excellent program—one which our hospital has received tremendous acclaim and publicity over pioneering—I just don't think I can sit idly by."

"Kate," he responded, "my seeking out Jerry Nabor happened before our talk on Friday. And, as you no doubt recall, I said I would give it thought over the weekend."

She wasn't appeased. "Granted, but I had no idea how quickly you are bent on doing this. If I hadn't opened Saturday's mail this morning, I still wouldn't know your full intentions!" She gave him a frustrated look. "Why must this happen so fast? What is so unreasonable about waiting six or eight months? *Then* if you feel the need to auction the carousel, at least you would have a seasoned understanding of its benefit to the children. And—"

"I've reconsidered," he broke in.

She felt stunned. "You . . . what?"

"I said, I've reconsidered revoking the program—for now."

She tried to suddenly reel in her seismic wave of entreaties. "You *have?*"

"Yes. To put it bluntly, Kate, you have me on a hook. If I want to succeed here, I'll need your support. I know you realize that. So, if my success means postponing the ER upgrade, then that's what it means. We can't very well have a hospital without a functioning administration. So, let's face the facts: Without you here to back me up, I'm a weak link in the chain. I'm sure you agree to that."

She blinked, flabbergasted by his honesty. Her talk last Friday had become the lifeline she'd hoped for. "Yes," she tried to answer in a tone of voice that didn't sound condescending. But she was glad to see him come around to reasoning.

"Nevertheless," he continued, "we can't function without an ER either, so I'm constrained as the Executive Administrator to place a condition on my reconsideration. And that will also grant some balance to your proposal."

Her moment of peace started to fade. "And that is?"

"You can keep the program and the carousel, as long as the ER functions in a beneficial way. However, if that changes . . ."

"Then?"

"I will pull the plug on the program. Auctioning the carousel is the hospital's quickest way to finance an adequate restoration of the ER. I know this is not what you laid on the table last Friday. If you still choose to resign, that's the chance I'll have to take. At least I've tried to meet you half way." He looked soberly at her, "Hopefully, you'll consider staying on—for the benefit of the children, if not for me."

His last comment was indisputably meant to nail her to the wall. And it did! Kate knew it was a shaky conciliation, but it was all she had for the time being. She needed to stay as long as she could. As long as he made an effort to be reasonable.

"Alright. Agreed."

"Great." Daniel refolded Nabor's letter, stuffed it back into the envelope, and placed it within his top desk drawer—a warning to Kate that he wanted it close by, regardless. He looked at her amiably. "Now, I really have a lot more to finish before dinnertime. . . . that is, *if* I get dinner tonight."

His attempt at dry humor reminded her of their pleasant night together sanding the carousel animals. Kate stood to leave but turned toward him again. Her conscience wouldn't let something slide. "Daniel, I really appreciate what you're doing, meeting me half way."

His countenance softened at her show of gratitude. He smiled awkwardly. "It's only fair. Besides, I really don't want to lose you."

His eyes seemed to convey far more than regard for her work at the hospital. When he looked at her with that kind of favor, Kate's insides melted.

She smiled back. "Thanks."

"You're welcome," Daniel replied.

Chapter Sixteen

*D*aniel placed the telephone back into the cradle. He stretched and gave a low moan. Now 4:40 on Tuesday afternoon, he couldn't tackle another item. For two solid days he'd made himself bleary-eyed over reports, schedules, meeting agendas, and budgets—the list was endless. He listened to Henry's detailed explanation for each one. He'd eaten, driven, and literally slept with Admin. procedures flooding his mind, swallowing him in an ocean of bewilderment.

How did Henry do it? Daniel wondered often. He perceived that the nuts and bolts of his new career would always be something he'd merely execute—not seize passionately.

Like surgery.

Relentlessly, the inner voice reminded him of his failure. Only, it was more of a rebuke when it surfaced. Surrounded by the medical center atmosphere, his thoughts swerved often to his former career, carrying with them the howling winds of doubt and shame he'd grown used to contending. *If only . . . if only . . .*

Daniel strove to rise above the condemnation whirl-pooling in his mind. He got up and left his office to stretch his legs, telling Lisa he needed some air and would be back in a half-hour. Around the campus he took slow, deliberate steps, breathing in the fresh crisp air as a welcome replacement for the choking sensation he was experiencing inside.

After circling the hospital twice, he was chilled enough to brave returning, and decided to cut through the ER on the West entrance to the hospital. He entered the sliding doors, past an ambulance, immediately witnessing two nurses in an anxious exchange with the EMT. The unloaded patient lay motionless, strapped to the gurney with the other paramedic at his side.

"What do you mean you can't take him?" the older, dark-haired EMT implored the nurses. "You have to. He's got a head injury. We're another thirty minutes from Pediatric Northwest!"

"We would, but our CT machine is down. We can't do much without pictures. I'm sorry!"

The attendant seemed exasperated, but resigned at the nurse's final words. The two men briskly reloaded the patient into the aid unit, then soared back down the *Emergency Only* avenue, sirens wailing.

Daniel approached the nurses and glanced at nametags. "What's up, Lana? How long has our CT been down?"

"Since 4:15 this afternoon. It was giving us trouble yesterday, too. We called for urgent repairs, but the servicer doesn't usually show for a couple of hours."

"I won't be surprised if that old thing finally died," the shorter, plumper nurse, Jasmine, remarked. "We've been praying it through for three months! Now maybe we can get it replaced."

Nurse Lana added, "We didn't have room, anyway, Mr. Brakken. Our capacity is full. He's better off going to a larger ER."

Daniel was concerned, but at the same time he felt a wave of relief break over his dejected soul. It was the best "bad" news he'd heard all day. Kate had already left for the night, but he could wait until tomorrow morning to tell her.

"Well, ladies. Your wishes for new machinery are about to be granted," Daniel assured the nurses. They looked at him, then each other, curiously.

"Please excuse me," Daniel said and turned away. The two women hustled back toward the ER while he headed for the halls leading to Administration.

As he passed the wing to the petting zoo, he spotted Zinnia and two volunteers searching behind the tall, bushy plants throughout the corridor. Their odd exploration struck his curiosity.

He watched for a half-minute, then had to ask. "Zinnia?"

She gasped, bolted upright, and placed a hand over her heaving bosom, startled by his undetected presence. "Meester Brakken! You frighten' me."

"Sorry. Did you lose something?"

She looked distressed. "Uh . . . not exactly, sir."

"So what's the search party for?"

After a moment's hesitation she smiled admittedly and answered. "We looking for Sassafras. He took a leetle walk."

"Sass—you don't mean the *lion* cub?" Daniel stared in disbelief.

Zinnia's smile thinned to a tense band of shiny, plum lips. "Yes, sir. We were grooming heem on the observation platform. He managed to slip through zee door when Stacy brought the pellets for feeding."

"He managed?" Daniel took in the underlying meaning. "Terrific," he answered, both agitated and relieved. On the inside he was rooting, *Two for two!* On the outside, he wanted to maintain a professional air over the valid concerns. "Well, see that you catch him—soon."

"Yes, Meester Brakken. We catch heem. Don't worry."

"Right. Call me when you have him confined. OK?"

"Yes, Meester Brakken."

Daniel made it back to Administration feeling both like a victor and a villain. Within two days of his agreement with Kate, not only was the ER breaking down and turning away patients, but the zoo had a security problem! The tables had turned. He could engage his plan for the ER—and the carousel—all in fair play.

Still, his heart turned apprehensive. Daniel firmly believed the upgrade was best for the hospital. And yet, something didn't feel quite right about his strategy.

He tried to shake the quirky sensation. Right now, he needed to figure out how to break the news to Kate. It wouldn't be right to gloat.

Daniel walked into the office. When he saw that she had left for home already, he decided it was better that she find out in the morning, rather than make her upset all night.

He sat at his desk and retrieved the stowed letter from Jerry Nabor, then dialed the number at the top of the letterhead.

Kate's telephone rang during her overdue dinner, which was hours late from giving Daniel's lion piece a few primer coats. She turned down the classical CD that played from her stereo while she wondered who was calling at this time.

"Hello?" she asked.

"Meez Katie—eez Zinnia!" the zoologist sounded anxious.

"Zinnia? It's after 10:30. Is everything all right?"

"No—eez Sassafras—he escape. But we find heem."

Kate's mouth fell open, and she put a hand to her forehead. "Mercy! Is anyone hurt?"

"No. 'Tis late, and I don't like to trouble you, Meeze Katie. But Meester Brakken, he knows about Sassafras. That eez why I called. I tried you earlier, but no answer."

Kate closed her eyes. Her insides filled with dread. She could just imagine the look on Daniel's face at discovering a glitch with the Wellness Program. She'd have to do some fancy dancing tomorrow. At least the call wasn't about the ER.

"Thank you, Zinnia. I'm sure things will look better in the morning. Try not to worry. Good night."

Zinnia hung up. Kate went back to her dinner, but her appetite had vanished. *Try not to worry.* Right! It was all her heart had been doing since talking with Daniel two days ago. He'd given her a thin tightrope to walk. It wouldn't take much to make it snap.

Forcing herself to eat her salad greens, cottage cheese, and sliced melon, she tried to trust that her life was in the Master's hand—no matter what! God was in control.

At her next bite the telephone jangled again. Kate forced herself to swallow. She hoped this wasn't someone from the hospital.

"Hiya," Jocelyn's congenial voice came over the line.

Kate winced. No such luck. "Hi, Joce," she answered a bit anxiously, knowing Jocelyn was on shift now. "How're things?"

"Kate, I wish this were my usual friendly call, but I just came on here and found out we've got a real problem. I wanted to touch base with you."

Kate's heart was in her throat. She squeezed her eyes shut and prayed as she responded. "Not the ER, please."

"I'm afraid so. We've had a CT machine down since after 4:00 this afternoon, and the service man was finally here but says it can't be repaired yet. He claims we have two threadbare parts, both of which he called 'ancient.' And, it will take a minimum of two to three weeks to have them manufactured, the order filled, and then air-couriered to us for replacement."

"This can't be happening," Kate barely spoke with a vanquished whimper.

"Sorry, but it is. He actually mocked our keeping the thing so long. He said that design has been outmoded three times. I told him the hospital was being frugal."

Kate couldn't respond. The pain surrounding her chest was tighter than a steel band.

"Anyway, Lana said you've been asking about the equipment lately, so I wanted to give you a heads-up. Looks like we're going to be sending some kids to Pediatric Northwest for a while—for CAT scans, anyway."

"Thanks, Joce." Kate resisted the yearning to unload on her friend the full impact the two predicaments would have on TLC.

"Sure. See you." Jocelyn's line clicked.

Kate placed the phone down and pushed aside her dinner plate. She dropped her head into her arms. With a flood of tears, she poured out her heart to the Lord of the universe.

The following morning, Kate walked TLC's festive halls with purpose, but without her usual bounce and enthusiasm. The cheery Christmas decorations did nothing to perk her up as she made her way to give the kids their morning carousel ride. She dreaded seeing Daniel this morning and was thankful he had not yet made an appearance. After their little "agreement," there wasn't a chance in the world that he would overlook the prior evening's two misfortunes. Kate was now faced with a decision she had never before imagined making.

She unlocked the dome's gate and turned on the lights. The kids were already parading down the hall to line up. She knew she needed to keep up a smile—no matter the dread in her heart. The kids needed to see peace and joy on her face, even if none was springing up from inside of her.

She smiled as best she could while she watched them load, and she fought the stinging that rose behind her eyes. Here, in front of them, Kate *had* to hold the tears at bay. That was why she'd allowed herself to really cry it out last night. Even so, she was susceptible to the pain shredding her into confetti. After pulling the carousel's rotation lever, she waved while they passed, one merry face after another.

Then the dam broke. She tried to wipe away the cascading drops from her anguish, but she couldn't. Harriet, who could always read Kate's moods, stepped up behind her and handed her a large white handkerchief.

Kate turned her back to the kids. "Thank you, Harriet." She forced the strangled words and sopped at her flooding eyes.

Harriet pursed her lips and shook her head. "Now, I know better than to ask you if everythin's all right." Concern was etched on her round, dark face. "Why don't you let me take over, hon'. Mmm?"

"I'll be fine. I just need a minute."

Harriet looked disbelieving. "Girl—it's gonna take you a half-hour to stop that leak! Now go on, before the children get upset over seein' you upset. You know it ain't good for them."

Kate nodded with a tremulous, thankful smile and excused herself. Just as Harriet predicted, Kate spent a good while in the ladies' room trying to barricade the tides of emotion. Finally, she felt calm enough to return to the office.

She slipped in as quietly as she could, hoping to avoid looking at anyone. But from the discerning expression on Lisa's face, Kate's puffy eyes and nose were still a direct giveaway as to what she'd been doing.

"Miss Montgomery?" Lisa asked softly.

"Yes?"

"Mr. Brakken wants to see you ASAP, this morning."

Terrific! Just what she needed. A face-to-face meeting with him after bawling her eyes out in the bathroom.

"Lisa, would you do me a favor?" Lisa nodded. "I'm going up to the cafeteria for coffee. Would you ask him to join me there in fifteen minutes?"

Lisa looked puzzled. "Sure, I'll give him the message right away. but, Miss Montgomery, . . . you *never* drink coffee."

"True. But I've never had a meeting like this before."

Lisa gave a look of sympathy, and Kate left the Admin. wing.

In the cafeteria, she selected a table away from the windows and as much in the back corner of the room as possible. There were very few people in the cafeteria and none close to where she sat. She pulled her makeup mirror out of her purse and gasped at her reflection. Her nose was shiny red, and all her mascara had been cried off. Her eyes were glossy, swollen at the rims and pink-tinged.

Well, she thought, no sense in hiding her grief from Daniel—she didn't need to impress him with professional appearance at this point. Besides, she would be leaving soon.

A little while later, he approached her table and tugged out the chair across from her to sit down. Kate didn't look at him, but could tell from his prolonged silence that Lisa had wisely warned him of her delicate emotional state.

He finally spoke, gently. "You don't drink coffee, so I'm certain what you're about to say is critical."

She didn't respond verbally, just nodded while staring down at her steaming beverage. Daniel remained silent for a minute.

"I take it you heard about the ER," he mentioned.

She sipped her coffee, winced at the unfamiliar flavor, nodded again, and stared out the window. Her throat closed tightly, moisture swamped her eyes with pain. "And the zoo escapee. *You win*," she started to say, but it came out in a weak, bleating sound. More like a sick goat than a woman. She raised the tissue in her hand to wipe her eyes.

"Kate . . ." he talked softly, "this wasn't a game where we were contesting to see who won."

"Doesn't matter." She sniffled. "You got what you wanted fair and square. I agreed to meet you half way. My part just fell through the floor, that's all."

She hoped—desperately—he'd apologize for being a tyrant and then promise not to sell the carousel. But he didn't.

"I don't suppose you'll reconsider?" she asked in a low voice, but this time she braved making eye contact. Maybe if he saw how much anguish she was in he'd come around, she reasoned.

He frowned. "Would you have reconsidered if things were reversed?" he asked with seeming concern, as well as fortitude.

"I guess not."

"That's because you're supporting what you think is right for the kids. And I do admire that, regardless that you probably loathe me right now."

She looked away. "I don't loathe you."

He paused a moment. "Kate, I also strongly believe I'm doing what's best for them. Unfortunately . . . we disagree."

She looked at him again. "What if we're both right?"

He appeared uncomfortable with the mention of that as a possibility. She watched him toy with the sugar container, rotating it in short, ninety-degree turns.

"You know, . . . not long ago, I used to be a lot like you."

"How so?" She tried not to give a mocking laugh. So far, she'd noticed nothing the two of them had in common.

"Your drive for the finest plans, courage to battle the odds, brave new ventures—despite resistance. Yeah, I did it all." He rubbed at his forehead as though the memory caused a bitter headache. "Until one day, when I took a bold step over the edge and fell right off the top of my mountain."

"Sounds fatal," she murmured, and drank in some more coffee, curious what Daniel was referring to—specifically—and what it had to do with her Wellness Program.

"Nearly was. In fact, . . . it cost me everything. After that, my brilliant, fearless ideas didn't look so hot. I learned that sometimes it's better—safer—to stick the standard course and not always reach for the maximum."

"That may be true, but if every creative and gifted person took the safe route, we'd still be living in the dark ages—medically and otherwise."

He seemed frustrated by her sensibility. "My point is, the carousel can't save the lives of these children. Better, newer emergency equipment can. Look where we are, Kate: Right now, TLC can't even take CT scans. We're having to turn away ten to fifteen percent of injuries we would be able to treat. If another machine shuts down, our unit will be severely disabled. Those high-tech pieces cost multiple thousands apiece. Your grandfather's carousel can fund most of what we need done. The rest will be covered by not having a zookeeper on staff."

"Zoologist," she flatly corrected the title. Kate could see they were at a stalemate. His argument sounded sensible, but every cell in her body was set against it. She knew the Wellness Program aided the kids' recoveries. "Daniel, did you read through the documentation?"

"Every page."

"Then how can you deny the benefit of this program?"

"I don't deny its *secondary* benefit. I deny its primary importance at this facility. We are a hospital. Hospitals are supposed to focus on healing a patient."

"The carousel is helping to do just that. So is the zoo. And the prayer. Healing doesn't start or stop with medicine. There are many *other* ways to affect health, well-being, and recovery."

Now he appeared ignited by her daring defense. "Well—maybe we should just wheel them from the ambulance onto the merry-go-round."

She was shocked by his sarcastic reply but refused to let it stop her. Kate steeled her nerves and lowered her voice. "You know what I think, Daniel? I think you're scared. There's fear and pain in your eyes. You're running—hiding from whatever is in your past that you failed. You are letting it cloud your reason." She shook her head slightly. "You didn't give up the edge. You lost it with your backbone. And now, because of that, you question everything that doesn't promise a guarantee. Well, life has *no* guarantees."

Daniel's eyes appeared darker, as though suddenly blinded by the effects of trouble and pain. His lips—tightly closed—barricaded any response.

Agitated, Kate stood. "You are right about one thing. I *do* believe I'm doing what's best for these kids. In fact, I *know* it. I love these kids . . ." she started to choke up, "so much . . . that I can't stand by helplessly . . . and watch when things crash around your shoulders!"

She turned to leave him. Hands trembling, she clutched her fists to keep them from shaking. Her accelerated heartbeat pulsed noticeably in her chest, neck, and fingertips.

Kate was reeling from her bold move. She'd never taken such a daring step, especially in confronting authority. Yet, something compelled her to do it. She felt she had to take a stand, for the sake of the children.

Chapter Seventeen

*D*aniel sat pinned to the cafeteria chair. He wanted to leave, to walk out. To never return. But he knew he'd be throwing away his last chance at resuming a normal career.

He rubbed his forehead. The migraine was swiftly returning. He marveled at how Kate could be so alluring and so infuriating at the same time! She had him riled, almost to combustion point. Yet, he couldn't let this beat him. It would ruin him. He had to prove to Kate—to himself—that he could make this work. He believed he was acting in the best interest of the children.

But was he? Misgivings slithered in again. He despised the constant tossing they caused inside, a sickening sensation of confusion and uncertainty. Was he right? Daniel didn't know and love these kids as much as Kate. She had the winning hand on that point! But, with all the medical knowledge he had amassed over the years in surgery, couldn't he safely lead this staff into selecting what was foremost in their care?

He wondered now if it was even possible.

Languishing in reservations, he rose from where he sat just to conquer something—even if only from having been stuck in a chair. He had to move forward. If he didn't forge ahead, he was going to be annihilated by bombs of apprehension for sure!

He wandered back to the office, fighting the increasing pain in his head. His vision was clouded but not so much that he couldn't stay. Though he felt vanquished, Daniel had to show Kate that she hadn't defeated him.

He plodded into Admin., telling Lisa to hold all calls until further notice. Inside his office he begged Henry to excuse him for some badly needed privacy, then he reached to switch the telephone to "Do Not Disturb." Henry had, no doubt, noticed Daniel's troubled state, and he left compliantly. Daniel retrieved the medicine from his briefcase and downed two pills, hopeful the migraine would be gone after a while and he could resume normal functioning.

He turned out the lights and found his way back to his chair, then sank into the soft leather. He blew out a sigh, trying to relax in the dark, trying to arrest Kate's words that circled in his mind, vultures waiting out their victim: *When things crash around your shoulders . . . crash around your shoulders . . .*

A knock woke Daniel. He stirred in the darkness and saw the door open a ways. Henry stuck his head through the opening, "Feeling better?"

"Yeah. Come in, but don't hit the light yet. Let my eyes get used to the one out there first."

"Bad headache?"

"Migraine."

"Oh. Those can be terrible!"

"I can vouch for that, personally." Daniel's vision started to adjust, and he saw Henry sitting down into a chair across from his desk. "What time is it?"

"Noon. Everyone's gone to lunch."

"Good."

"You mind if we have a little chat, while we're alone?" Henry asked in a kind, fatherly tone.

"That's fine."

"Daniel, you'll have to excuse Kate. She's very passionate about this place. She can be . . . well, exceptionally *focused* sometimes."

"Wasn't the word that came to mind," Daniel responded.

Henry gave a soft laugh. "I guess what they say about redheads being stubborn may be true, huh?"

"We're all stubborn in some way. Did she talk to you?"

"She did. Kate and I go back several years. She needs someone to turn to. Not much of her family left anymore, just her grandma and some distant relatives in the Midwest. She would never expose personal conflicts to other co-workers, though."

"How'd it go?"

"I calmed her down a bit, but she's more upset than I've ever seen her. I think it might be a while before she comes around."

"Meaning?"

"That if you're doing what's right, she will realize it—down the road, yes— but she will. She is very intelligent. I trust her."

Daniel didn't explain that Kate was ready to walk out on him. "And what if I'm not right?" he dared to venture, just to pull Henry's thoughts on the concept.

Henry paused. "I'd hate to see the outcome of that, but only you can know for sure."

"How can anyone know for sure?"

"You have to look inside yourself. Listen to your heart, your *spirit*."

Disturbed, Daniel gave a snort. "What if it's not responding?"

"Then you need to ask the One who made it, for help and guidance."

"And I suppose that would be God?" Daniel asked, contempt flickering on the edge of his voice.

"I think you realize that, son."

He pondered Henry's sagacious words in the dim light of the office. They were pure wisdom, he knew. But how could he go back? God had turned down his last plea for direction. "I'm not sure that's possible."

"Daniel, I've known about you for several years. I heard about your discoveries in Pediatric Neurosurgery at least ten years ago. Since then, I've kept track. You pioneered some of the best breakthroughs in the nation, maybe even the world. I also read some of your distinguished articles in the med journals. For some reason God had me keep tabs on you a long time now." He paused. "I also know that you are a Christian."

Once was a Christian, would have been more accurate, Daniel silently countered.

"If that is true," Henry continued, "then you've tasted what's real. You have the Lord's light inside you. Might seem dim right now after what you endured in L.A., but it's there. You'll find God's answer—if you're agreeable to ask for His *will* along with His help."

"What if He's not interested anymore?"

Henry chuckled like Daniel should know better. "The Lord wouldn't have brought you here if that was the case."

Daniel had to agree. It was a wonder how this job opening worked out—another reason he didn't want to botch things.

"So, the reason I'm here is due to divine providence?"

"I believe there's a reason—yes."

"If it's so right, then why do I feel like I'm going to go crazy?" Daniel added, a little more vulnerably than he'd intended to be with Henry.

"Sifting," Henry answered. "Sometimes the only way for us to recognize truth is to see it sitting next to error. God has a way of crumbling us to remove the chaff, that way we can be left with wheat. It's not pleasant, but all the while it's happening, we are *still* in the palm of His hands."

Daniel fell quiet. Henry's sermonette was the closest thing he'd had to church in a long time. It almost inspired him. Something actually sparked inside that he'd thought was dead: his faith.

"Thanks, Henry," he eventually responded. "I'll think about what you said."

With only two days to Christmas Eve, and Henry's retirement, Daniel and Henry spent the remainder of the afternoon reviewing multiple procedures. They didn't talk personally again, but each time Daniel looked in Henry's eyes he felt the same beckoning sensation he'd had during their private conference. The luring rended his soul, but also offered him peace. He wanted to trust what Henry believed, but the part about still being in God's hand was too hard to accept.

Daniel had never felt more alone.

Maybe it was an indication that he was missing the right path. He presumed he had consulted God, but perhaps he'd only asked *conditionally*. Maybe, as Kate had charged, Daniel was making decisions based upon avoiding pain.

His insides wrenched. How he hated being wrong! A strong ego was always crucial to his being a successful neurosurgeon. If an aspiring surgeon didn't possess extraordinary self-confidence, he or she would never be able to pick up the knife.

Now, Daniel had to speculate whether this quality was hindering his judgment and his spirit. He reevaluated his motivation for selling the carousel. He wasn't being selfish. In fact, he was indeed trying to help the children in the best way possible. Hopefully, Kate would come around as Henry had indicated.

Nonetheless, he feared making a major error, *and* the cost it would bring. It had nearly destroyed him once before.

Kate walked into the impromptu staff meeting at 4:45 that afternoon. Lisa had sent an urgent e-mail from Daniel to all stations requesting as many as possible attend a brief meeting regarding the ER.

Kate took a deep breath, but it didn't loosen the knot in her stomach. The last time she'd been at an all-staff meeting the floor had bottomed out of her dreams. She now hung somewhere between paralyzed and petrified. She'd been hesitant about coming at all, and the only space now available was to stand at the front.

Daniel met her gaze. Apology seemed engraved across his face. She didn't have to read his mind to know what was about to take place.

He flipped on the microphone switch. "Thank you for coming. As I relayed in my message, I'll be brief. What I have to say will come as a shock to most of you, so I'm asking you to give it some time. And save your questions for an assembly planned after Christmas. I promise to address everyone's concerns at the assembly, after you've had some time to really evaluate this." Daniel paused and scanned faces across the room.

"Out of necessity, we are going to auction TLC's carousel," he brusquely stated.

Astonishment ricocheted through the room. Outcries erupted. One nurse stood to her feet and exclaimed, "You can't!" Another called out, "That's absurd!"

Daniel raised both hands up to hush them. "Everyone—please! If I could have your attention." The uproar quieted, but grumbling still filtered through the audience. "I warned this would be disturbing at first. Now, let me explain. TLC has a major crisis on its hands. The ER equipment, which is now nearly two decades old, is beginning to break down. With the temporary loss of our CT, we are not able to give care to a tenth of the children we are meant to benefit. Other machines badly need to be upgraded, as well. If we do not execute an immediate upgrade, we could be forced to decrease between twenty to thirty percent of our staff."

"*Thirty percent?*" a male technician hollered from the back row. "How're we supposed to operate at all with those cuts?"

Kate observed the troubled expressions around the room. Her own trepidation was rising.

"That's precisely the dilemma we are facing," Daniel continued, "If we don't have as many patients, we are not getting paid as much. Consequently, we cannot afford to pay all of you. That's why it's imperative that we overhaul the ER, immediately. At the present time, only the CT machine is down. It will take a minimum of two weeks to replace the worn parts, which may help it along for another year. On the other hand, we can purchase and install a brand new unit within a few days that will last ten to fifteen years. The unfortunate truth is, *all* of our ER equipment needs upgrading and will follow the same route unless we replace it." He took a deep breath.

"So, we need to look at financing options: Grants, loans, fundraisers, or income through assets. I am initiating the latter. Here's why: First, there are no grants available at this time, especially because TLC is a Christian organization. Second, a loan is a possibility, but we would be shooting ourselves in the foot to take this route and pay interest when we have expendable assets available to fund the upgrade. Third, fundraising will take too long to implement and may fall very short of what we need to bring in—plus, it will cost plenty to initiate the process. Our only reasonable option is the sale of *unnecessary* assets."

More outbursts resulted, but Daniel pressed on.

"The carousel, although not superfluous in the children's estimation, is a huge pocket of capital. As much as you all admire and enjoy the carousel, it does not contribute to the hospital in a monetary or medically proven way. Therefore, it *is* expendable."

Protests flourished. Still, Daniel forged ahead. "However," he nearly shouted over them, "it can contribute significantly by becoming the means with which we operate successfully once again."

The disturbed crowd finally quieted down again. He put his hands on his hips and took another steeling breath. "Look, I understand you may have objections to this strategy, and you will be able to voice them at the assembly. However, you are constrained from speaking of this to the children or their parents until after the next meeting. Following that, if the carousel is to be auctioned, a public announcement will be made in our community. That is all for now."

Daniel turned and headed out the door.

Kate wondered if a lynch mob would follow.

Chapter Eighteen

K ate sat at her desk. It was nearly 6:00 p.m. She'd put in an extra hour to make up for lost time this morning. Now, she had one thing left to accomplish before leaving. She resolutely typed an e-mail to Daniel:

I hereby give my 30-day notice of resignation.

She hadn't expected to stay so calm in doing so. Maybe it was because she had the foresight that it was inevitable.

Kate sent the message and signed off for the evening, feeling she'd made her only choice. She retrieved her coat and purse and walked out of the wing. As she passed the carousel dome on her way to her car, however, the restraining force inside of her broke and she was swept away with crying. She hastened to her car, wishing she could run from the pain.

A half-hour and many tears later, Kate drove into the nursing home parking lot to visit her Grandma Rose. Having driven the entire distance while weeping, she was amazed at arriving safely and whispered a quick thank-you to her unseen angels. Turning off the engine, she sat in the car a moment to pray.

"Lord, I can't do it anymore. I can't work with him. I hope you're not disappointed, but I tried, and I just can't stay. I'm sorry." She remained seated for a few moments of silence, to steady her breathing. Then she got out to go inside.

When Kate arrived, Grandma Rose sat in the room in her wheelchair, with her back to the door. The elderly woman was asleep in front of the television. Her roommate, Edna, was gone for the time being.

Kate gently touched her warm hand, "Hi, Grandma." She knelt beside Rose and kissed the aged woman's thin, soft cheek. Rose quivered awake, and a surprised smile spread over her face. Pale blue eyes lit with joy, sparked by the visit of a loved one. She sluggishly formed words that Kate knew came easily to her mind, "Ka-tie, my l-love!"

"How are you?"

The frail woman nodded slowly. "F-fine. How a-are y-you?"

Kate wanted to say everything was wonderful. But she couldn't. She told her grandmother the whole story, knowing Rose wouldn't have wanted it any other way. Her Parkinson's had disabled her muscles from working properly, but her mind was sharper than the average person her age. The doctors were very pleased with her mental capacities.

Rose absorbed the saga, and with tremendous effort, lifted a shaking hand to pat Kate's forearm. "I t-trust y-you. Y-you know b-est."

Kate's eyes clouded up and a couple tears seeped out. "I'm not so sure this time, Grandma."

Her grandmother looked saddened by the display of Kate's pain. "D-don't wor-ry, Ka-tie. Je-sus is w-with y-you."

Kate gave her a long hug. "I know, Grandma. Thanks." She sniffled, wiped her eyes, and stood. "It's time for you to head for the dining room. I can only visit through dinnertime, tonight, but on Saturday I'll be back to pick you up for Christmas."

Rose looked elated but didn't speak.

Feeling more at peace, Kate wheeled her grandmother down the carpeted hall to the facility's dining room. Her heart was encouraged by the simple truth spoken by an elderly, wise woman: Jesus was with her, and He was *all* she needed.

Daniel downed the last swallow of his second cup of coffee, trying to focus his thoughts. It was Christmas Eve morning. A day when most people were loving and happy, despite everything, just because of what the season presented: joy, hope, good news, peace.

For Daniel, this day meant utter failure.

He'd just finished reading his e-mail. Twenty-six messages—all rankled employees—all aggravated with him for "taking away" their carousel. He felt like the Grinch character from a Dr. Seuss book.

Topping those was Kate's resignation. It struck him worse than a knife wound to the heart. He'd assured himself that he could manage without her if she resigned, but now he didn't know if he could stand her leaving.

It wasn't so much losing her experience and competence that he feared—although that would cause him plenty of grief, he was sure! It was the absence of *her*: her graceful manner, her "Hello," her gorgeous auburn hair and sea-green eyes. The inevitable departure of her tenderness, intensity, and mission toward the children was what he lamented.

Daniel rubbed his tired eyes. He hadn't slept much lately. He'd suffered again through the recurring nightmare of his last operation—Sammy Paredes. How it ached to even think of the dying seven-year-old boy. So young, so trusting, so hopeful that Daniel would make him better and keep him alive.

It had always infuriated Daniel when desperate parents made him out to be like God. What were they thinking, anyway, pressuring him to save their child when all he could execute was a man-made procedure? But, when the kids placed their innocent and steadfast trust in Daniel—laying their life in his hands, pleading for success, healing—that's when he couldn't say no to their appeal. That's when he promised incredible things he wasn't sure he could deliver.

But he couldn't bear to tell them otherwise. As long as there existed a minuscule chance the procedure would work. He had to aim for the miracle, even if he didn't make it.

Just one year ago today, he'd made such a promise. He recalled the momentous conversation. . . .

"Hey, Sammy. Ready to do this?" Daniel asked the dark-haired, dark-eyed Spanish-American boy.

Heavily sedated with pain medication, he looked up and slowly responded, "I don't feel so good. But I know I'll feel all better after you fix me up."

Daniel only nodded. He wouldn't dare take away the little guy's hope. "That's my man. Your parents and I are proud of you being so brave."

"I guess. I'm kinda scared, though, . . . Dr. Brakken?"

"Yeah, pal?"

"Please—don't let me die? Promise?"

Sammy's slurred words were without intensity, but Daniel understood the panic behind them. He swallowed hard. This was the test he always dreaded, the crossroads that severed his heart in two. Yet he chose the same path every time. "I promise, Sammy. . . ."

Daniel's telephone buzzed, and he fell crashing back to present day. "Yes, Lisa?" he said, blowing out a sigh.

"It's Jerry Nabor, line two."

"Thanks."

Daniel confirmed the carousel auction date with Nabor and exchanged pertinent information. The call was quick, but not without impact. As soon as he hung up, he sensed a strange foreboding steal into the room. The thick, uneasy feeling of *finality* turned loose a discernible fear in Daniel—so real it made him shudder!

Suddenly uncomfortable, he stood and immediately left his office.

Chapter Nineteen

*K*ate arrived at Daniel's rented cabin a little past 3:00 p.m. The Admin. staff had been let off at 2:00 in honor of Christmas Eve. She had left a little later, telling Jocelyn and Lisa that she would meet them at Daniel's after picking up the party decorations, paper dishes, and supplies for punch and snacks. Fortunately, Jocelyn offered to pick up Henry's retirement cake at the bakery, freeing Kate from one more stop.

She approached the grand, wooden cabin door and found the key where Daniel had instructed her to look. Unlocking the door, she hauled her armload of provisions inside to place them on the kitchen counter. After emptying one sack the telephone rang.

She hadn't asked Daniel whether she could answer his phone, but with so many people driving to his isolated site she knew she'd better, in case someone was lost.

"Brakken residence. This is Kate."

After a small pause, Daniel's voice came over the line, "Sounds like you're moving in. Are you?"

"Cute," she answered dryly. His irony almost made her crack a smile. But she was still smarting over his continued plans for the auction—regardless how much he knew it tormented her and everyone else.

He cleared his throat. "Sorry. I, uh, thought I'd better make sure you found the place OK."

"Just fine. You were right about the size." She glanced around the spacious log dwelling. "This cabin home is practically a woodland mansion. I don't think we'll have any trouble fitting everyone."

"Good. I don't need any more strikes against me."

"No—you don't," she quickly added.

"I was hoping you wouldn't agree to that so eagerly," he remarked, a trace of sorrow evident in his voice.

She closed her eyes and sighed. When he did the sensitive thing with her, Kate's insides turned to jelly. But she wasn't swayed this time. "Daniel, you're not exactly on my "good-guys" list. To be honest, tolerance is about all I can offer you right now."

"That's fair. It's better than the list I'm on with everybody else. Think it's safe for me to show? I'd rather not deal with punctured tires or an egged car if I can avoid it."

"I think you'll be safe for tonight. The lynching isn't until after the holidays." She mused, imagining him running from a mob of irate nurses.

"Thanks for the advance notice." He paused. "Kate, I know you're upset with me, but I have been straight with you about this change from the start. I hope you'll at least give me credit for my candor."

She really wanted to give him a punch on the proboscis. Any administrator who mandated his own selfish ideas—despite a roomful of incensed vetoes from his staff—surely deserved one! But, she entreated the Lord instead. Kate knew His way was better. Besides, God had a powerful way of knocking the proud off their high horse. All she needed to do was pray and duck!

Kate sighed. "Daniel, you already know how I feel about this ordeal. It's not going to do much good for us to discuss it again—unless you're willing to reconsider."

"Right. Well, I expect to be done in a couple of hours. I'll see you after a while, around six o'clock."

"Please—don't be late. Louise is bringing Henry right at 6:30."

"Alright," he answered.

She pressed the off button on the cordless phone and placed it back upon the recharger.

That evening, Daniel turned onto the lengthy driveway leading to the cabin as "God Rest Ye Merry Gentlemen" coursed over the radio. He hit the brakes, then lowered the song's volume.

"Good night!" he said and stared in amazement. Cars were parked as far as he could see, bumper to bumper, down both sides of the lengthy passage. He decided to seize the remaining space available by the road and walk the distance, rather than take a chance and find no room in his carport. He'd envisioned a crowd in his house but hadn't expected to trek a quarter mile to his own place.

Served him right for being so late, he thought. He had told Kate he'd arrive by 6:00 p.m. But, anxious over the party, he stayed to work about an hour overtime, then shopped for a gift for Henry. When he finally made it to the freeway, he was caught behind an accident on the highway bridge over Lake Washington. Now—nearly 8:00—the party was likely winding down.

They're probably glad you haven't shown, he contemplated their displeasure, still a little tender from the chilly reception he'd encountered at the hospital all day. People said "Good morning" and "Hello," but their greetings were only obligatory, not cheerful. He knew he'd be on thin ice for a time, until he could convince the staff how essential it was to sacrifice the carousel for an improved ER.

At last, he made it to his front yard. Colored Christmas lights graced the windows in a scalloped pattern. Cheery holiday music and laughter could be heard through the glass panes. Daniel started up the cedar staircase to the large porch—but froze halfway, overcome by the immense respect and adoration they had for Henry Freeman. Daniel couldn't imagine making such a beneficial impact on TLC, as Henry had.

He stood riveted while fear pressed in, constricting his breathing. He wasn't wanted here. He wasn't one of them. They were without a black mark on their past. Daniel, on the other hand, was a refugee. Running from dishonor and grief.

After only two weeks, the pristine state of his new job had worn off. When he had arrived in Seattle he'd been offered a chance to make a good impact—the hope of a new beginning. Now in command, he was being ostracized, just like before.

His heart raced, thudding painfully. The revelation of his meager importance in their lives made him feel queasy and defeated. But he *had* to go through with things. If he let this crowd beat him, he was finished! No matter whether they loathed him, he needed to stake his claim.

They will have to get used to Daniel Brakken, he determined.

He managed the final two steps, still unnerved but without the panic of a moment ago. Turning the doorknob, he entered the room packed with festively dressed people, all conversing happily. "Chestnuts Roasting on an Open Fire" played through the house. As nearby heads turned and people recognized him, their smiles faded or looked compulsory, confirming his suspicion. He steeled himself against their alienation, then wound his way through the multitude to the kitchen.

Reaching the island counter, he scanned the large plastic trays for food, but only a few carrots, celery, and parsley sprigs dotted the platters. Everything else was eaten. Even the cake. His stomach craved more than rabbit provisions, so he scooted around a few more guests to check the refrigerator. He stooped to see what looked good, and immediately felt a tap on his shoulder.

He craned his neck to see Kate, dressed in a knockout red-velvet formal. Her long, auburn hair was swept off to one side with a pearlized hairpin of some kind. She held out a plastic-wrapped plate filled with BBQ chicken, pasta salad, jo-jos, and a slice of cake.

"You're *late*," she remarked above the noisy crowd, her eyebrows curved, scoldingly. "But I saved you some," she added in a reserved, but kind way.

Ignoring the food, Daniel absorbed her appearance. His gaze traveled eagerly from the side-slit that revealed her slender ankle and calf, up the shapely form of the dress, past the fitted sleeves, and over the modest neckline that graced her velvet-covered curves. A silver chain held a teardrop pearl below the hollow of her throat

He remained silently stunned with the refrigerator door wide open. All Daniel could think was, *Wow!*

She closed the fridge door for him. He offered his warmest, most grateful smile. "Thanks for thinking of me. But wouldn't you rather feed me to the lions?"

She displayed a *don't-tempt-me* look. "It's Christmas Eve," she commented. "It's only right to show good will."

"You're too kind," he added dryly. He sat at the barstool beside the kitchen island counter to eat. She stood beside him, sipping her cup of steamy spiced cider. Cinnamon, apple, and orange aromas wafted around her, teasing his senses. He watched her pearl earrings swing delicately next to the creamy skin on her neck.

Daniel was suffocating from her beauty. He reached to loosen his tie. "May I have some . . . cider, please?" he asked, taken by her loveliness.

"Sure." She turned to the stove, ladled out a cupful, and placed it in front of him.

"Thanks." He looked into her eyes, tried to convey how appreciative he was for her benevolence in the midst of personal conflict.

But she glanced away. "Big turnout, huh?" Kate said.

"No kidding. I should have called a cab to bring me down my driveway. How many showed?"

"Seventy-one at last count. Nearly everyone's here, except for some on the evening shift. They are needed at the hospital."

Daniel nodded. "Yeah, things are going to be very different with Henry gone," he said and turned to see Kate turning pale. "That wasn't a decree for slavery. I just meant that Henry is a wonderful man, and no one can adequately replace him. *Especially* not me," he added convincingly. Her face resumed a normal color.

"Well, I don't think anyone expects a carbon copy of him. But, if you want to make some allies, I know a way," she offered a tiny coaxing smile.

"I may be swimming upstream for a while, but people are always resistant to change. Things will get better." He took a bite of pasta.

She didn't look pleased with his reply. "Henry wanted to wait for your arrival before he gave his farewell speech. I should find him and tell him you're here. Excuse me."

Daniel ate while Kate wove her way through the mass of aides, nurses, doctors, technicians, staff, and volunteers. He stayed in the back, out of the hubbub of well-wishers and lamenters. Someone gave a loud whistle, the crowd hushed, and the music was turned low. Kate stood a few steps up on the staircase to be visible as she spoke.

"Welcome everyone, and Merry Christmas! Thank you for coming and making this part of your Christmas Eve celebration. I know many of you have families to get home to, so we want to proceed." She reached for a globe-sized, beautifully wrapped box, which was being passed from person to person. Then she motioned for Henry to join her. He stood beside Kate, folding his hands humbly.

"Henry," Kate began, getting a tiny choked up, "from all of us at TLC, we wish you a wonderful, blessed retirement. Your contributions to our hospital and our lives are without number. Only heaven knows all the good that you have done. We will greatly miss you, but we are very happy for you and Louise, and we wanted to give you a reminder of what a 'Tree of Life' you have been to each of us."

"Thank you," Henry barely spoke. She handed him the sizeable package, and he sat down a few steps higher so all could see him open the gift. He slipped off the bow, then the paper. Then he lifted the lid. Tears welled in his eyes. A nurse from the watchful crowd called tenderly, "We love you, Henry." He fought to restrain his emotion, wiping his eyes.

Carefully, he lifted out a large, golden, hand-crafted Banyan tree on which hung a multitude of tiny, tinkling colored ornaments, each bearing a locket-sized photograph of someone who had worked with him at the hospital.

"Go ahead—read it," a doctor announced. But Henry couldn't speak, even more hindered by the sentimental engraving.

Kate leaned over and read the inscription on the tree's trunk: "It says, 'To Henry—Father, Friend, Favored leader. You helped us reach out for our dreams, and our lives bear the fruit of your love. Go with God and our best. Love always, TLC staff and volunteers.'"

She gave Henry a long hug and everyone cheered. Now weeping, he pulled a handkerchief from his pocket and blew his nose. He gently placed the tree on the stair beside him, and stood next to Kate, hugging her again. He looked over his audience and strained a smile.

"*Thank* you. Thank you all. You have no idea how much you mean to me. And your gift—it is wonderful beyond words! I couldn't be more proud. You've been such a fine group to work with." His voice weakened. He took a deep breath. "All my life I've enjoyed overseeing hospital centers. But these last several years at TLC have been far and above the reward of the others combined." He shook his head and smiled warmly. "If I weren't so old, I'd stay."

Everyone chuckled. Many dabbed their eyes.

"I would like to add that I appreciate what you've done in my life every bit as much. And I wish you all the gift of God's peace—this Christmas and always. Thank you."

The audience applauded and cheered again.

Daniel's head dropped. *Peace?* So far, this Christmas was wrapped up in turmoil.

Henry's speech also really got to Daniel. The man was a legacy—one that could never be replaced.

But there was something else that bothered him: Henry loved being an administrator. And, as a result, he was as heroic in his position as Daniel had been as a neurosurgeon. How could Daniel ever succeed at this new endeavor, having run from the one passion and desire in his life?

He didn't know.

Chapter Twenty

*D*aniel held Kate's coat open for her while she slipped it on. She was the last to depart, having stayed with two other helpers to clean up. Just as she'd promised, they did not leave a messy house.

It neared 9:15, and Daniel felt drained of strength. More so emotionally than physically. The announcement to sell the carousel had unleashed a tidal wave of uncertainty inside of him. After spending the entire day dodging looks from employees, he had stayed near the corners of the party, avoiding social interaction as much as possible.

He did, however, find an opportunity to give Henry his own gift—a journal. The idea stemmed from something Daniel had heard him say several times, "I ought to record that in a journal," when he referred to special occasions or memories of the hospital. Henry really appreciated the booklet and had given Daniel a grateful hug.

Now, as Daniel walked Kate to the carport he suddenly remembered his car. He begged her for a ride to his vehicle. She took him down the lengthy drive and stopped beside his car. When he started to get out, he hesitated. "Kate, you did a super job tonight, organizing all of this. I could have never pulled off something like that."

"Thank you. I've gained a lot of experience directing the hospital's events. Actually, this party was a cinch—TLC's undertakings have been far more complicated!"

"Well, you've certainly proved your gala-hosting expertise. Thanks again. It was a nice party for everyone."

She smiled in the dome's light. "I really appreciate hearing that from you, Daniel. Thank you, again, for providing your cabin. We would have been stuck in some restaurant back room, otherwise. This was much nicer, in the woods. More like being home for Christmas."

"Yeah." He fell into a cloud of despondency. "I . . . guess I won't see you until Monday, so I hope you have a nice holiday."

"Thanks." She smiled graciously. Then her expression became more thoughtful. "Daniel, what are you planning to do tomorrow?"

He rubbed his chin and stared out at the mixture of moonlight and headlights on the road. "I don't have any plans. My relatives are all back in San Diego, so I'll just hang out, relax, maybe watch a few games on TV."

Her face turned up a playful smile. "Do you think you could help me with something, in the morning?"

He grew suspicious. "Another beast needing sanded?"

She laughed softly. "No—toys. Every year on Christmas morning, Henry and I would distribute wrapped toys to each of the kids retained at the hospital. He's not available, with their flight to the Virgin Islands. I'd really like it if you joined me. You could meet some of the kids in your charge. Maybe even improve your reputation with the staff." She raised her eyebrows and gave a challenging grin.

"Very funny. I won't be winning any 'Man of the Year' award, I can tell you." He shook his head and looked down.

"Fortunately, the kids don't know about your plans for the carousel yet," she remarked. "Why don't you give this a try? Please?"

He looked at her soft face in the moonlight. Her eyes sparkled from the lunar reflection. With the way she gazed at him and gently pleaded, he couldn't refuse.

"So, how early does Santa have to wake up?"

Kate drove home, singing to "Silent Night" playing on the radio. She felt satisfied. Though she had still been agitated with Daniel about the carousel, the gift delivery idea had swept over her with a fresh wave of hope. It was worth a try. Any exposure with the children might sway his heart toward doing what delighted them, even if he couldn't be persuaded by the staff to change his mind.

She arrived at her house before 10:00 p.m. and soon changed out of her evening dress. She smiled. She had recognized Daniel's absorbed stare when he first saw her at the party. For a moment, she'd even savored his admiration. After all, he was a remarkably handsome man. It had played on her mind many times, wondering what he'd be like in a romantic way.

But she didn't feel like a suitable match for him. Mostly because she saw no evidence of his faith. And she was not interested in a relationship where God was not honored by both parties. Such mismatched combinations only invited disaster. Plus, he'd probably dated a hundred women—without boundaries. She had only attempted two serious relationships, neither of which worked out well.

Though she always hoped for a loving marriage and children some day, she was content to remain as she was. If God wanted her married, He would bring that man into her life. And, thanks to Jocelyn's vigilant prayers for Kate's perfect man, she could relinquish worrying over that area.

Too emotionally charged to sleep, she pulled on her sweats and headed for the garage. The lion needed a few highlighting touches to its recent topcoat before it was finished.

As midnight approached, she painstakingly added the final strokes of light and shadow to the curls and swirls of the mane, rendering the wooden creature a real-life appearance. Though she gave it a valiant effort, her hands became shaky during the meticulous labor. How had Daniel done such a precise job sanding the animal? The lion was one of her most difficult pieces to restore. Most men didn't possess the knack for such minuscule details. When she had painted the primer earlier, she noticed there wasn't a single flaw on the wood surface. No careless scratches. No digs. No mistakes!

The quality of Daniel's work probably wouldn't have caught the average person's attention. However, Kate had been restoring these wooden creatures for several years now, and she recognized excellent handiwork. Patience and deftness *that* superior didn't come from talent alone; it was learned, trained into someone through intense discipline.

Her curiosity lingered, but she couldn't imagine what had honed Daniel's ability to function so skillfully.

When the lion was finished, she sprayed it thoroughly with a sheen coat of polyurethane to protect against wear. It glistened, enhancing its life-likeness. She set down the spray can and admired the masterful "king of the jungle." How like Daniel it was. Rough roar and claws on the outside—harmless, playful cat on the inside.

Kate smiled ruefully at her mental comparison. "Too bad we can't see more of the gentle cat at the hospital," she muttered her wishful thinking, then flipped off the garage light on her way to bed.

Chapter Twenty-One

$\mathcal{F}$rom the hospital lobby, Kate watched Daniel enter the Admin. wing promptly at 8:00 on Christmas morning. Casually dressed in jeans and a Nordic cream/tan/blue sweater, he looked like a handsome model that stepped from the pages of a men's clothing catalog. Daniel's staggering appeal coaxed her stare. Her throat went dry. She tried to swallow.

Kate was used to seeing him solely in a dark suit and tie, but she really admired his informal attire—and the wonderful transformation it seemed to create in his attitude. He seemed unusually happy, less apprehensive than the night before. Yet, Kate was sure it was more than a change in clothes that caused the easygoing way about him.

He approached her cheerfully. His slightly dampened hair and fresh clean scent evidenced his recent shower. It tantalized her nose. But the mischievous grin on his face hooked her curiosity. "What? *What* is that look?" she questioned him and almost started to chuckle.

"Oh, nothing you should be thinking about right now."

She smiled, still suspicious. "Hmm. OK, I'll have to trust you because we are out of time. The kitchen crew will be starting breakfast rounds in less than an hour. We only have a few minutes with each child, so be happy and say something nice."

"Yes, mother."

She glowered. "I'm making sure you have the rules down."

"Shouldn't I be wearing red or something?"

His humor always touched a soft spot in her. She suppressed a giggle. "No. In fact, . . . you look great."

"Thank you. So do you," he suavely answered. She noticed his eyes taking easy roam over her white and gold angora, Angel sweater, and the white stretch leggings beneath.

The presents had been collected and previously wrapped by the volunteers and were all tagged with the children's names. Over the last few weeks, the volunteer staff had been observant to learn what special toy each one wanted, and had compiled "The List." Kate greatly appreciated their help. It was one more task she didn't have time for, along with her other administrative responsibilities. Plus, the volunteers were often among the kids, so it was easiest to have them gather the information.

Inside the Admin. office, Kate and Daniel loaded the gifts high on the bright red wagon according to floor, room number, and name. Then they started down the hall to the ground-floor patients.

Kate entered the first room. She handed sleepy looking Marissa Jane a little red box with a big white bow. "Merry Christmas, sweetheart!"

Marissa's blue eyes opened wide. Joy covered her tiny four-year-old face, perfectly framed by soft strawberry-blond ringlets. "For me?"

"Yes. Go ahead and open it."

She sat up to unwrap the gift. "It's a Cinderella heart pendant! I wanted this one for Christmas. Oh, thank you!"

Kate gave a large golden box to Daniel and silently pointed to Marissa's roommate behind the privacy curtain.

An older girl, about eleven with chestnut-brown hair, woke up and wondered what the noise was about. Kate pulled the curtain back so Marissa could watch as Daniel gave the gift.

"Hello, Reyanne," Daniel greeted her. "This is for you. Merry Christmas."

She looked dubious at first, then reached for the rectangular flat box with an IV-fastened arm. Reyanne opened her present, and her disbelief melted into joy. "Wow! It's an art set! How did you know?"

The sheer elation in her ginger eyes must have done a number on Daniel. He smiled bashfully. "Well, we have some important connections."

Reyanne didn't seem to really care how her wish was discovered. She sat up to hug Daniel around the waist. "Thanks! I thought this was going to be the worst Christmas ever. Now I can draw!"

Kate and Daniel moved on to the next room. This time Daniel led the way, handing a five-year-old boy, Mason, a shoebox sized gift. "Merry Christmas, Mason."

Surprised, the boy ripped the paper off in record time. It floated down to the floor beside his bed. "Cool! A spaceman!"

Kate went to the handsome African-American teenager next to the windows and handed him a round gift. Duane looked disheartened by the circular gift. "I know what that is. A basketball. I already have one, but thanks for tryin'."

Kate smiled patiently. "Why don't you open it, Duane, see if you're right?"

Duane listlessly tore the shiny green paper off. He was right, it was a basketball—but signed by Shaz Rippen, the Sonic's new top center. "No way!" he yelled, his voice rising an octave. Signed by Shaz! What a day! What an *awesome* day!" His beaming grin flashed approval, and he kissed the ball, then kissed Kate on the cheek. "Wait till the guys hear about this. They're gonna green!"

Kate turned to Daniel, who looked confused. "I think that means 'be jealous.'" Daniel nodded and grinned.

They made their onward journey with the wagon, room after room, then floor after floor. First-floor patients were easy. The kids were mostly independent and needed only light care and medical supervision. Second floor was more difficult to serve, with youngsters impaired by pain medication or hospital apparatus. Kate and Daniel assisted several in opening their presents.

ICU, on third floor, was the toughest challenge. Some of the children opened their eyes for only a short time and smiled briefly at seeing the toy or gift, knowing they couldn't play, yet still inspired that someone outside of their family also thought of them.

Others were unable to respond. Their gifts were simply placed on the bedside tables. Kate knew this would be the last Christmas for some of these kids. Silently, she prayed for God's blessing as they visited each one.

A short while later, Daniel and Kate approached the last room. A single occupant lay inside. Daniel picked up the last gift to read the name: Andrew.

His stomach twisted into a hard knot. He'd been so caught up in the special deliveries, he didn't realize they had yet to see the Champ.

A sixth sense alerted him this visit would be the most distressing of all. Not for the boy—but for him.

Daniel waited until Kate entered the softly lit room. She pulled up a rolling stool to sit beside Andrew. He lay sleeping, and Daniel watched Kate lightly caress her fingers over the boy's hand. "Merry Christmas, Champ," she said just above a whisper. Andrew didn't respond. She glanced up at Daniel. He saw her eyes were growing moist—obviously the young lad held her heart, as well.

She touched Andrew's shoulder and spoke a little louder. This time Andrew's eyelids fluttered and opened slowly. He turned to see her and attempted a weakened smile. He nodded, unable to do much more.

Daniel felt the pressure building inside him. It made him tense, anxious. Just standing there was virtually impossible. In his mind he was pacing, a caged animal, yearning to be free. He longed to help this boy. Everything inside of him yearned, ached to rescue Andrew from the dreaded tumor embedded in his head. Daniel believed he could beat it. But he was effectively paralyzed, unable to do a thing about it!

He numbly watched as Kate spoke yes-or-no questions to the boy. Andrew sluggishly moved his head to answer.

Daniel had seen this stage of brain tumor illness many times before. It wouldn't be long before little Champ would lose the fight.

Unless someone took action.

Daniel's palms started to sweat. There was a time when he would have risen to the challenge and fought valiantly on the boy's behalf. Now he was imprisoned by fear.

Kate glanced back and looked unsettled at seeing him. No doubt, she immediately sensed something going haywire inside of him. Whatever it was that gave away his dread, he couldn't hide it from her. She was too perceptive. Hopefully she wouldn't ask about it later.

Kate motioned with a nod of her head for Daniel to grab the other chair. He did and sat close beside them.

She turned to Andrew again, who still hadn't opened his gift. "Hey, Champ. You want to see what it is? I'll help unwrap it."

He nodded once for yes.

Kate pulled back the silver-bells paper on the box and lifted out a shiny, glass ornament fashioned into a three-dimensional star. The young boy smiled big despite the pain.

"Andrew, do you know what this stands for?"

He turned his head once to each side for no.

"It represents your miracle, Champ. We're still praying. And we won't give up on you. . . ." Her voice started to crack.

The boy opened his mouth, straining to speak, "Th-ank . . . you."

"You just hang on, OK? Your miracle is coming."

He tried to smile again, but his cheek muscles quivered from a twinge of pain. He looked suddenly drained from the brief visit. Kate turned to Daniel. He thought he was going to burst from the pressure.

"We'd better go," she said. "He's getting weak now."

Daniel didn't know what to do, but he couldn't leave. "You go ahead. I'd like to stay with him for a minute," he softly answered. She complied with his request, but first hung the star ornament where Andrew could easily see it, beneath the television braced high upon the wall. Then Kate slipped from the room.

Daniel moved over to the stool where Kate had been sitting beside Andrew. He paused for a long time, then reached out to tenderly clasp the boy's hand through the side rails. Tears stung behind Daniel's eyes at the contact. He tried to swallow them back, but they welled up anyway and nearly filled his vision. He bent to wipe them away, struggling under the tremendous weight of compassion that blanketed him.

He sniffed, took a deep breath, then closed his eyes. "Jesus, you're the only one who can do this. I can't go back to surgery. I want to, but for some reason, I can't. I'm *pleading* with you—help this little guy. Please, don't let him go. Prove your love and your mercy by helping, by healing Andrew. . . . *I'm begging you,*" he choked out the last few words.

He couldn't say Amen, but he knew he'd expressed all there was to say, and he'd meant it with all his heart. He held the boy's small hand up to his closely shaven cheek and stroked it gently. "Merry Christmas, Andrew," he whispered.

Andrew barely squeezed Daniel's hand, but otherwise the boy didn't respond. Something inside of Daniel did, however—in a major way.

Strangely, for the first time in many agonizing months, Daniel felt peace sweep over his soul.

Chapter Twenty-Two

K ate waited in the cushy lobby chair, hoping to see Daniel before they went their separate ways. She assumed he would exit the same way he came in. So she tarried by the entrance.

She wondered what had kept him with Andrew, and she worried. When Daniel got that intense *on-the-edge* look, something serious was battling inside. Had eavesdropping not been a breach of his privacy, she'd have stayed by the door to learn what he needed to do. But her conscience would have never allowed that, and she'd come to the lobby, deeply concerned.

The elevator *dinged*, and Daniel stepped into the lobby, seeing her immediately. His countenance was sensitive, heartened—altogether opposite from the pallored expression of dread she'd witnessed moments ago in Andrew's room! She examined his face, observed the swollen, pinkish tint around his eyes.

He's been crying. Her heart nearly rended in two. She knew he had a tender side, but he was usually much tougher to crack. Yet, Kate had witnessed before that something about Andrew reached the core of Daniel.

He smiled cordially. "Hi. I'm glad you are still here," he said, earnestly.

"Daniel, are you all right?" she had to ask. "You seem pretty affected by Andrew. There's nothing wrong with that—it's just . . . I'm concerned about how you're doing, that's all."

He glanced down past her feet. "I can't say Andrew's condition doesn't get to me, but I'm fine, really. Thanks for caring."

She nodded, still attentive.

"Do you have a minute?" he asked.

"Well, yes—just a few. I'm headed for my grandmother's nursing home."

"This will just take a few minutes. Wait here."

She thought she saw a hint of the mischievous smile from this morning, the one he'd walked in with, that caught her curiosity. He walked briskly to his car out front and promptly returned, holding a cylindrical-shaped gift, wrapped in metallic purple with a large gold bow on top.

"This is for you. Merry Christmas, Kate." He handed her the beautiful package.

Surprised, she accepted it and blushed. It was heavy, and she wondered at the contents. "You really didn't need to do this."

"Yes, I did. Go ahead. Open it."

Kate gingerly unwrapped the lustrous paper and untaped the round lid from the container. She opened the top and carefully pulled out a tissue-wrapped item. Lifting the paper away, she discovered a musical creation: Its entire top piece, a carousel, was sculpted exquisitely from marble. Four distinct, diminutive horses, all in different shades of marble, encircled the centerpiece. She wound the t-bar underneath. Clear, soprano tones *plinka-plinked* from the smooth, revolving platform as each horse raised and lowered in succession to the melody.

Kate's emotions were turned loose in an instant. Her heart raced. Her face felt warm and taut. She fought hard to keep from weeping in front of him. "It's so beautiful, Daniel. I—"

"I wanted to somehow show you that I'm really not against the carousel—or you. I know you're having a hard time believing that, but I hope you will realize I'm only aiming to improve our hospital."

At his words, she was immersed in a new wave of anguish. It took her a moment, but she poised herself and finally answered. "*Our* hospital?" she asked, unbelieving. If only they could become a team, she thought. But she knew it would never work.

"Yes, ours." He looked serious, pained. "Kate, I really want you to stay. I'm asking you to reconsider your resignation. To me, you are the one that makes this hospital a wonder. Not the carousel."

She had been rewrapping the gift in its tissue and slipped it carefully back into the container. She gazed at his golden eyes, saw the vulnerability there. She could swear they conveyed more than endorsement. Something else. Maybe interest . . . devotion. Her heart pounded, tears stung her eyes. This time she lost the struggle. The first two fell, and a stream quickly followed. "I can't, Daniel. I'm sorry!"

She turned and hastened out the doorway, unable to face him while her heart and dreams crashed to the floor.

An hour later, Kate still lay dressed and propped up on her bed with her Bible in her lap. Its freshly tear-stained pages and a nearby mound of damp tissues evidenced her aching soul.

Since Daniel Brakken had walked into her life, she'd faced more inner vexation and shed more tears than she knew she possessed of either!

Wearied, she finally folded the Bible shut. Its words normally brought her serenity. Now they only blurred before her eyes. She couldn't find the peace to cling to, even on Christmas Day. And it troubled her. She'd always found it before. God had been her strength when she was weak. She had always sensed His presence, without fail. But, for some reason, she felt very alone, abandoned, left to carry a burden without comfort or assistance.

How could Daniel come so close and not see? She wished for the answer. How could he sometimes say all the right things, then turn around and make all the wrong choices?

"This whole ordeal is insane," she muttered, and collected her pile of tissues to dispose of them.

Mostly, Kate wondered if she was wrong about Daniel. Maybe God had sent him because she wasn't strong enough to lead the hospital in the direction it needed to go. Maybe he was more objective, less vulnerable in a way that she could never be. Maybe . . .

Her mind filled with uncertainty and sorrow. She hadn't felt this anguished in a long time. Not since her father had left home. She'd blamed herself for so many years. Why else would a father walk out on his family in a drunken rage, accusing his young and only daughter—to her face—of ruining his life? Then, take his own life before hope or reconciliation had a chance.

Sure, everyone had tried to explain it wasn't Kate's fault. That it was her father's problem. He was to blame. He'd been dysfunctional and simply couldn't admit his inadequacies. Still, she grappled continuously with the unrelenting guilt and fear that sought to strangle her. *If only I had been a better child. . . . I must not be lovable. . . . Why didn't he want me?*

She'd condemned her young self time and time again. Until, as a adolescent, she'd nearly lost the will to go on with life because of it. Every day had been filled with pain beyond belief.

Because, without love—especially a father's love—a child's life was a miserable place.

Just when she'd given up hope, her Heavenly Father came to her. Hope and love came knocking, promising to stay forever. She met the Prince of Peace—Jesus Christ—and He rescued her from the jaws of despair.

His glorious presence and healing love touched her wounds *so* deeply and completely that all the pain was eclipsed by His divine embrace, the moment she asked Him to come in. *In* to her wounded and broken life, *in* to her ashes and grief, to give them His renewed life.

In one moment He exchanged her agonizing loss for His abundant life. She was amazed at the transformation—amazed that He actually wanted her. Yet He was *real*, and He loved her with an everlasting kind of love. Tangible yet spiritual. And totally unquenchable!

Now, reeling from the recent blows to her faith, she wondered how she'd fallen from such peace and harmony. Where was God? Where was His guidance? Where was His assurance? Why was the Lord letting her feel so confused and alone?

Kate rose from atop her now mussed covers. She was listless, still hurting, but compelled to move on. She slipped her shoes back on and flipped off the light. She was already a half-hour delayed in picking up her grandmother for their Christmas Day together, so she called the nursing home and left word she was on her way.

While retrieving her coat, purse, and keys, she determined this time she would not burden her beloved Grandma Rose with personal struggles. It was Christmas, and her grandmother deserved laughter and cheer.

Besides, Kate felt she had to work this out herself. No one could fight her battles for her. Like *Job* of old, she sensed her faith was on trial. But, it wasn't the Lord who wanted to sift her like wheat; His enemies were intent on ruining her. She needed to stand strong, to believe, to hold on through this whirlwind. . . .

Until God was ready to reveal His glory in the midst of it.

Daniel dialed Kate's home from the office for the fifth time. It was well over an hour since Kate had fled from him. He had tried her number, saved from the night he went to her house, after giving her plenty of time to return from visiting her grandmother. But there was no answer—again! He placed the receiver down, growing impatient and disconcerted.

Plus, he felt horrible, totally responsible for the capsized state she'd left in. Anxious, his mind kept imagining her in a wreck on the side of the road, overcome by her emotional distress. How could he have been so thoughtless? He blamed himself. To presume she'd actually appreciate his gift when it only unveiled the painful territory all over again. Then, to beg her to stay with him, making the gift seem like a bribe. What was he thinking? He felt so dense.

Daniel paced the office. He couldn't wait here a moment longer and contend with the speculation anymore. Finding her home safe—albeit admitting that he'd worried sick about her—would be preferable to this.

He left immediately, trotted to his car, revved the engine, and headed for the freeway.

Daniel made good time to her house with the absence of much traffic. He pulled into her drive, parked, and turned off the motor. He glanced around. No open curtains. No lights, but it was the middle of the day. He got out, prepared to ask her pardon for his witless actions, but still needing to see the glow of her face before he could leave.

Daniel knocked at the front door. No answer, as expected.

Uneasiness mounted, but he was able to keep it in check. He'd come the same way that she would have driven home, and he didn't see any cars crashed along the road. But, neither did he see her car parked out front. He would just have to sit tight until she showed.

In the break of noonday clouds, sunshine poured as strong as Christmas in Washington could offer. It wasn't the temperate, coastal weather he was used to, but it wasn't the freezing spell from two weeks ago either. Comfortable in his sheepskin-lined leather coat, he sat on the porch and waited.

Nearly a half-hour passed before Kate's car tires crunched along the gravel driveway. And sitting on the passenger side, Daniel noticed, was her grandmother.

At first, he had swelled with relief that Kate was all right. Now he stewed, not expecting to make his apology in front of others. Suddenly he felt tongue-tied. Though he'd had hours to think of how to apologize, all words escaped him.

Kate stepped out of the car, visually questioning his presence. She wasn't smiling. Which clued Daniel that, undoubtedly, she was still hurting.

Daniel mustered all the social grace he could. This time he wanted to do it right. He stepped down from the porch.

She disregarded him and went around to the back of the car, where she opened the trunk to retrieve a wheelchair.

"Let me get that for you." He came beside her and lifted it out with ease, then opened it as well.

"Thanks," she said politely but guardedly. She pushed it forward to the passenger car door and opened the door for Rose.

Daniel glanced at the unstable gravel, the short distance from Kate's car to the house, and the three-step porch. "How about I just carry her in?"

Kate looked agreeable. "It's fine with me. Grandma, this is Daniel. He works with me at the hospital. Daniel, this is my Grandmother Rose."

Rose smiled at him. "Nice t-to mee-t y-you," she reached out a shaky hand. He cupped her warm palm between his. Her eyes were filled with great kindness, and Daniel sensed much wisdom beyond her disorder. "Thank you, but the pleasure is all mine."

"Grandma, Daniel suggested he carry you in. Is that OK with you?"

Rose looked back to Daniel, smiled approvingly, then nodded.

"Here we go," he said, bending to hoist her gently into his arms. Her small, frail body didn't weigh much, and he was at the door in seconds, waiting for Kate, who fumbled with her keys.

Once inside, he placed Rose upon the couch next to the fire that was dying down. While Kate brought in the wheelchair, Daniel stoked the fire and added the last log from the bin. As the flames took, he stood to one side and gazed at a framed, old black-and-white photo hung upon the fireplace wall. It displayed a young man, probably after the turn of the century, sitting on a carousel horse in motion—his contented face revealing his enjoyment as he waved.

"Th-at feels ni-ce," Rose commented on the fire.

Kate closed the door. "Yes. Thank you, Daniel."

Her eyes still silently questioned his unexpected company. He realized it was discomfiting for her, but he hadn't anticipated her grandmother's company or else he wouldn't have come without being invited. Since it wasn't the best situation for them to talk privately, Daniel asked Kate to show him the woodpile so he could bring in more logs.

She took him outside and around to the side of the house.

"All right, we're alone," she said, somewhat reserved.

His gaze dropped to the ground, and he ran a hand through his hair. "I, uh, tried to call, but no one answered." He paused. She waited. "You left in such a state that I . . ." he glanced up at the trees surrounding her house, then to her face, "I wanted to make sure you made it home OK. And . . . I wanted to apologize."

Her expression softened. "I'm touched you were that concerned about me. But, you claim you are doing what's best for the children. Why the apology?"

"Because I feel awful about upsetting you. When I bought the musical carousel, I just didn't consider that you would react so . . . emotionally. I was only thinking about how pretty it was and how much you might enjoy it. Honestly."

She stayed silent, considering his explanation, while the evergreen branches swayed in the breeze above them.

"I'm sorry, Kate. I didn't think it would hurt you."

The winter sun shone through a break in the billowy clouds and spilled around them, lighting her face. For a moment Daniel thought she might cry again. But, she granted him a modest, gracious smile. "I forgive you. I am glad you cared to explain, though."

Relief coursed through Daniel. Impulsively, he reached around her shoulders and hugged her. "I was really worried something had happened to you." Holding her felt good. Daniel realized suddenly that he was embracing her with more in his heart than goodwill. Quickly, he released her.

She looked up at him, baffled by his intimate contact. Her eyes sparkled beneath the sunlight. Her lips glistened. He encountered a desire he hadn't faced with a woman in years: a yearning to kiss her. It hooked him, lured him closer. He'd always found her attractive, especially last night at Henry's party. Now, he was drawn by her simple beauty and charming nature. He wanted to lean down, just once, to feel the softness of her lips against his own.

She seemed aware of what he was thinking and backed up a half step. "Will you stay and have dinner with us?"

He longed to stay for more than that. Certain he was about to reach for her and carry through with the kiss, Daniel swallowed hard and fought the impulse. This wasn't the time to let a sensual craving overrun wisdom. He bent to grab an armload of wood instead.

The endeavor gave him a moment to think. He was baffled by her unexpected, congenial offer. However, the *last* thing he'd intended on doing was to barge in on her Christmas dinner with a family member! Anxiety tensed his stomach. He surmised the polite thing would be to decline. Yet, the desire to accept and spend the afternoon with her overruled his qualms.

Finally, he raised upright holding several logs. He smiled awkwardly at her. "Yes, I'd really like that."

Chapter Twenty-Three

$\mathcal{K}$ ate sighed. She, Daniel, and Rose had just finished eating a nutritious dinner of turkey, cranberry sauce, lots of fresh vegetables, and nine-grain rolls. She had even fixed a tasty gravy and mashed potatoes—with butter—knowing Daniel craved something that wasn't low-fat. She was pleased with her holiday meal and started to clear the dishes.

Daniel sat back in his chair. He was gazing at her. "That was terrific. I haven't eaten so well in a long time."

"Thanks," she said, blushing a little.

Rose gave Kate her compliments as well, then asked for help in laying down for a rest.

Having gotten her grandmother nicely tucked in, Kate reached to turn off Rose's bedside lamp.

Rose touched her arm. "Ka-tie."

"Yes, Grandma?"

"He is a n-nice m-man."

Kate nodded. "Yes. But sometimes—"

"The h-heart is deep. Don't ju-dge too quick-ly." Rose looked up at the ceiling, searching for words. "Real l-love is al-ways a chal-lenge."

Love? Kate didn't want to argue with her well-meaning grandmother, but she wasn't sure she could accept that advice. Besides, there were many things about Daniel that Rose was not aware of. She kissed the elderly lady's forehead. "Thanks for caring. See you later."

She rejoined Daniel in the living room.

He stood to leave. "Thanks again for dinner."

She felt a tug in her heart. She enjoyed his company when he was so easygoing and relaxed, and she hoped he would stay a while. "You really don't have to go. I was just about to make some mint tea. Would you like a cup?"

He winced. "Any coffee?"

She shook her head. "Only tea."

He mused a second, then nodded. "OK—that is, if it's no trouble. I know you have a garage full of fun waiting for you." He grinned briefly.

Kate remembered his finished piece. "Oh! I have to show you. Come see." She walked toward the garage. Daniel followed. She led him through the door and flipped on the lights, saying, "Voila!" She gestured a hand toward the Monarch lion.

Daniel looked astounded. "Incredible! He's so real." He walked over to admire it more closely and smoothed his hand over the glossy, muscular shoulders of the beast. Then he ran his fingers down the rippled mane. He glanced back at her. "He's outstanding. I can't believe he is the same figure."

"Isn't it amazing? The color enhances their distinct character, but the eyes really give it life. That's why I always do them last."

"Do they ever. If he'd been sitting on your porch I would have run."

She smiled, glad for his approval. "Actually, Daniel, you did the hardest part. Your skilled handiwork is unmatched. That kind of precision doesn't just happen. What has made you so disciplined at using small instruments?"

He paused and looked cautious. "Well, I guess I was always good at things like that." Then he held up both hands in a stop position. "Now, don't get any ideas. I owed you that one. Next time, I'll be charging an hourly rate." He grinned.

She smiled. "I was only curious. But if I'm ever stuck in a jam, I know who to call."

"Kate?" he asked gently, looking pensive. "What are you going to do with him now?"

She grimaced. Why did this thorny subject continue to fester? "I'm not sure. In fact, I haven't really crossed that road with any of this." She waved her hand at the surrounding mass of creatures and paraphernalia.

"Grandpa Joe's carousel at the hospital was the only full setup I've had to work with, even though it was just a portable 2-row." She avoided looking at him, not wanting to make matters emotional again. "Since that is no longer an option, I guess I'll have to find good homes for them as they are finished. There are some carousels in the area."

"What would the lion sell for at auction?"

She felt defensive. "Don't get any ideas about my garage! These are not part of the hospital carousel."

"Relax—I'm just curious."

"Well, it's a Dentzel, and a 'king' figure."

"Why's that? Because of the crown?"

She started to smile and suppressed a laugh. Daniel didn't realize he was wearing his ignorance on his sleeve.

"No," she answered. "Actually, it's because of his *superiority*. 'King' horses and figures are always outside row pieces. They used to serve as a marker point for the ticket-takers, but that practice was considerably diminished by all the pay-one-price parks we have now. You see, the outside row is usually made of 'standers,' meaning they don't go up and down like the 'jumpers' do. But 'standers' are more intricately carved and flamboyant—especially the right side: That's called the 'romance' side. They are made more striking and alluring for a reason: They are the most visible and attract all the riders."

She smiled and patted the lion's back. "The 'king' figures, however, were designed to be the premiere eye-catchers. This lion's worth about thirty thousand, more or less, depending on who's buying."

He shook his head. "That will never cease to amaze me."

"What?"

"How lucrative they are. After all, they're not masterpiece paintings or antique cars. They're just wooden animals."

"True. They're unusual for antiques. You wouldn't let a child put his cotton-candy sticky hands on an expensive painting. But, contrary to your statement, they *are* masterpieces. And because of that, they are also collectors items. *Unfortunately*."

"Why so unfortunate?"

"Because the people who buy them solely to collect are killing off what remains of the carousel industry. They want them strictly for profit and selfish gain." She paused, hoping he would see his own name in that infamous category. "Some merely use them as a conversation piece in their ritzy home. But, their collections remove the figures from the market for the working carousel owners, making it more difficult each year to preserve the wonder for everyone."

He looked uncertain. "Which wonder is that?"

"Of riding a carousel," she answered, a little too pointedly. "Imagine an amusement park without a carousel. It's unthinkable. The trouble is most people take its presence for granted, like it will always be there." Kate strolled through the rows of figures and past the rounding board paintings. "Sadly, the original wood carousels are fading away. Their production ceased after World War II, and the last one was built around 1930. Of the five thousand plus carousels built between 1880 and 1930, less than two hundred are accounted for today—and about fifty of those are no longer in operation." She folded her arms and leaned against a workbench. "But, thanks to support groups and organizations like the American Carousel Society and the National Carousel Association, they are being located, restored, protected, and preserved to a large degree so future generations can enjoy them."

"There's still one on the Santa Cruz Beach Boardwalk in California. I haven't ridden it in a *long* time," Daniel added.

"Most people haven't been on one since they were a kid, but that wasn't the intent when they were created." She walked over to the nearby ostrich and placed her hand on the scooped seat. "When you were little, did you ever wonder why the seats were so big? And the stirrups so far away from your feet?"

Daniel nodded in agreement.

"It's because they were made for adults. The sculptors weren't aspiring to make children happy—but adults. Although kids love riding carousels every bit as much. If you look at old photos, you'll see mostly grown-ups on the machines. In fact, I have an old picture of my grandfather riding one when he was a young man. It's hanging above the fireplace in the house."

"Yeah, I saw that. I didn't realize he was a family member, though."

"That was Grandpa Joe when he was eighteen. Anyway, it wasn't until after they became popular that children were allowed to ride. The craftsmen intended to create a euphoric art to experience with more than the eye. A place of wonder less chaotic and complicated—full of dreams and yesterdays—where things are enchanting, pleasurable. It was their design to transport you *away* from the tensions and labors of life."

"Sounds pretty captivating."

"It is. And all for two pennies a ride—well, back then anyway." She paused, looked at him. "Maybe it's time you rode one again, Daniel?" she asked with gentle challenge, not wanting to start a tug-o-war, but hoping to make him think. He glimpsed at her but didn't respond.

Daniel peered through the open side of a nearby horse, dismantled at the torso box for repairs. "Are they all hollow?"

"Yes—well except for some of the first ones. They're far too heavy if they aren't. That made moving them around pretty difficult. Plus, a carousel loaded with solid wood animals would require massive machinery to support and operate them. The hollow pieces gained favor fast."

"What's this?" Daniel pointed to a long stand with an angled metal shaft hanging down and open at the end.

She smiled. "That's an arm to a ring machine. They used to be on many of the carousels. In fact, the one down in Santa Cruz still operates as a ring machine. Maybe you were too young to notice it when you rode the carousel. See—this arm lets down a brass ring, which flies out for someone to grab. The idea is to catch the ring as you're riding past. If you can seize it, you win a free ride. The concept was quite famous for many years—and mourned greatly when they were made inoperable or removed."

"How come?"

"The high cost of liability insurance, mostly. It was rare than anyone got hurt, unless they were goofing off. Really, it's too bad. The rings were far safer than some of the high-tech, modern rides allowed today."

He looked solemn. "Has the hospital ever suffered liability from incidents on the carousel?"

"Not even once. But, we do have waivers signed by the parents before the kids can ride. No one has refused. The parents and doctors are all in support of it, especially for what it does to benefit the children."

"Well, I've seen the hospital's reports. But tell me from your perspective: What influenced you to pursue this from a medical standpoint?"

"First, we found improved health all around. The lively ride makes the children laugh. It's true that laughter is like a medicine. And also the spinning sensation, in particular, causes a sense of exhilaration—euphoria—that releases the endorphins. Somehow, it also helps the body's system. A notable doctor wrote about his studies on the effects of spinning. He found that it generates a natural boost that people inherently enjoy. Just look at any kid who discovers how much fun it is to spin around in a circle. Adults get the same euphoria from ballet and square dancing."

"And riding carousels," he added.

"Exactly. The spinning, or circling, sensation is more than enjoyable, it's physiologically beneficial."

He nodded, still interested.

"Then we discovered that one child who'd had no success with chemotherapy started improving rapidly within a few days after he began the rides. When he was released a month later, his health declined. He was eventually readmitted and immediately improved again, until his health was stabilized. We could only conclude that the carousel was the significant change in his life. Nothing else matched."

"Sounds like he got addicted."

"He did, in a way. Kind of like taking vitamins. Your body has a letdown when you stop. But the process works similarly to other kinds of treatment, in that you benefit more by doing it repeatedly. The continuous onslaught against the cancer by a boosted immune system seems to be what fights it. Eventually, his cancer went into remission and he got to go home again. He hasn't had a recurrence in the years since." She watched Daniel growing more contemplative.

Kate continued, "Well, needless to say, his initial reaction made us curious, so we started checking the other kid's charts. Almost ninety-percent showed a significant improvement in strength and feeling of well-being. Several had either stabilization or a decrease in cancer cell growth, which appeared to correlate directly with the period after they started riding the carousel. When we realized the growing number of successes, we started keeping detailed records, all of which I showed to you. The hospital board considered the recoveries remarkable. So we started calling the carousel the Miracle Machine. It has become the *envy* of many hospitals nationwide." She sighed. "I wonder what they'll say when they learn we're selling it." She slowly looked at Daniel, sorrow choking away her Christmas joy.

He gazed back, thoughtful but unmoved. She feared a reversal was futile, but still she hoped he would see his error and change his mind.

Daniel checked his watch. Another hour had quickly passed since their meal. "Guess I'd better be going. Thanks for the tour." He wandered back to the house entrance and stepped inside.

Kate followed. She felt like a balloon exhausted of air. "Maybe we can have that tea some other time."

"Sure," he answered, but didn't look at her.

His walls were clearly back up. She walked him to the front room, and he retrieved his coat. He stood by the door and gazed down at her solemnly. "I really appreciate being your guest today and meeting your sweet grandmother. Thank you."

"You're welcome," she said. "I'm glad you did not have to spend Christmas alone." He regarded her silently. She saw that look in his eyes again, the one she'd seen by the woodpile, the one that made her insides tumble, her pulse beat faster. She felt arrested by desire that beckoned her heart: Anticipation of a kiss that she was certain wasn't wise, but seemed like a splendid choice at the moment.

Daniel reached for the door, however. Kate's expectation fell through the floor. Again sober-minded, she remembered she hadn't yet thanked him for his gift. "Daniel!"

"Hmm?" He stopped at the porch's edge, turned and fixed his dark, honey-golden eyes on her.

She stayed at the doorjamb and leaned upon the knob. "I forgot to thank you for the musical carousel. It's remarkable! I adore it—really."

His rigid expression softened. A small, tender smile broke through and he nodded. "I'm glad."

Chapter Twenty-Four

*A*t home, Daniel paced the floor. He wanted to pick up the phone and make a call. His instincts were imploring him to get hold of Jerry Nabor and cancel the auction. Impressions wrestled with reason, tugging and straining against prudence and sensibility.

Every time Kate explained the carousel's benevolent existence at the hospital, he wanted to believe her. Moreover, something in him *did* believe her.

But there was another side.

One that knew failure and feared it. One that had forsaken vision, innovation, and the courage to brave undiscovered territory. Daniel wanted to cross over the line to Kate's side, but he froze. Trepidation settled over his desires. Memory flooded in of his past error.

To add to that, Nabor had made it very clear to Daniel that in his business, advertising costs and placement fees were charged in *advance*, regardless of whether the figures made it to auction. A distasteful sum of five thousand dollars had already been paid as Daniel's deposit to hold the spot, which didn't include the extra fifteen hundred dollars for printing the catalog exhibiting Nabor's pictures of the hospital's inventory.

That expense—along with his misgivings—kept Daniel from calling the whole thing off. He would appear reckless if he cancelled at this point, having wasted the hospital's money on an impetuous decision.

No, he thought. He *had* to go through with this. After all, he had been certain before—even if he wasn't now. Currently, Kate's appeal and loveliness were clouding his reason. Daniel felt he just needed to trust his initial decision, and he would be fine.

He hoped.

Late on Christmas night, Andrew lay on his bed heavily sedated and starting to dream.

He envisioned himself on his bed in a dark place. No light. Only fear, thick as a black cloud, surrounded the place. Then, behind him, he sensed a presence—an awful, harmful presence. It scared him. He prayed for God to rescue him. Then, in his dream, someone walked through the door, someone at the hospital: Mr. Brakken. He glowed like an angel, but he didn't look like one. With his appearance, the darkness quickly diminished, retreated from the light, but it remained on the edges of the room. Mr. Brakken smiled down on Andrew, took his hand. He had something to say. Like an angel bringing a message, he spoke: *Don't worry. I'll help you. You'll be OK.*

Andrew awoke. A warmth blanketed his room. He was alone, and yet he didn't feel like it. Someone *Good* was there with him—he knew it. Maybe it was an angel? he wondered sleepily.

With vision still blurry, he tried to look around the dimly lit room to see who was there. He lifted his head slowly to one side, then the other. No one. He rested back on the pillow and stared through the side rails. Something shiny caught his eye. He paused his obscure gaze on the glimmering object. Seconds passed. His vision finally adjusted, and he recognized the gleaming piece. Pirouetting on a string in the moonlight, Andrew's Christmas star hung where Kate had placed it. It's twinkling seemed to convey a silent promise.

Andrew smiled from the hope it imparted.

Then he fell back asleep.

Sunday afternoon, Kate waited for Jocelyn at the Wild Burger restaurant after church, and after returning her grandmother to the rest home. It was Kate's idea to meet her friend. She'd wanted to run some ideas past her about setting up a fundraising campaign to buy back the carousel.

Jocelyn approached her table. No longer on duty, her long black hair flowed freely from its usual confined state. She sat down, swung her purse off her shoulder and stared at Kate with incredulous crystal-blue eyes.

"Kate, you're *not* going to believe this!" Jocelyn exclaimed.

Kate wondered at her eagerness. "What?"

"It's amazing!" Jocelyn blurted.

"What's amazing?" Kate pressed.

"Andrew. I checked on him this morning, right after he woke up—it's incredible!"

"Joce, what? Fill me in, here. Is he getting better?"

"No—he says he's seen an angel."

Kate blinked. "Really?"

Jocelyn nodded. "Well, in a dream he saw one. But when Andy woke up he said its presence was still in the room. And that's not all. . . ." Her eyes opened wide.

"I'm waiting." Kate was growing frustrated.

"He insisted the angel looked like Mr. Brakken."

"Daniel?" Kate grimaced, staggering at the thought. "You're right, I don't believe it. Daniel Brakken is *not* an angel."

"Andrew didn't say he was the angel, just that he looked like an angel."

Kate frowned. "Joce, you're losing me." The waitress appeared just then. They each ordered a teriyaki chicken burger and iced tea. Then the waitress left.

Jocelyn nodded. "I know, I know—it took me a couple explanations, too. But I think I finally figured it out."

"Really?" Kate leaned forward, ready for the explanation.

"Andrew said he brought a message."

"Daniel or the angel?"

"Both."

Kate rolled her eyes. She was more confused. "*What?*"

Jocelyn rolled her eyes. "Just listen. Andrew said it was really weird. At first, the room in his dream was dark, scary. Then Mr. Brakken walked through the door, but he was radiant, enveloped in a light that somehow pushed back the darkness. He didn't have wings, but Andrew felt the presence was really an angel because of the light. Then, the angel touched his hand and said, 'Don't worry. I'll help you. You'll be OK.'"

"What then?"

"Andrew woke up, but he felt the same *Good* presence in his room. He believed the angel was still there, even though he couldn't see him."

Kate was bewildered. She peered at Jocelyn. "Do you think it really was an angel?"

She nodded, her blue eyes revealing her excitement and conviction. "Yes, I do. But the fact that the angel appeared as Mr. Brakken *has* to mean something. Because he said, 'I'll help you.' I'm betting the 'I' part really does represent Mr. Brakken. I think this all means that God knows Mr. Brakken will—somehow—help Andrew get better. He sent an angel to deliver the message, looking like Mr. Brakken in Andrew's dream, so that Andrew would trust Mr. Brakken." Jocelyn looked as satisfied as a cat that had seized its first mouse.

Kate blinked. "And what if this is just a dream?"

Jocelyn's expression changed and grew solemn. "Kate, I've worked night shift for most of the sixteen years since I was licensed. A lot of the sick kids pass on at night, when I'm on duty. I check their pulse, I turn to inspect their I.V., then I turn back to adjust their blankets. They're gone—to heaven in a split second."

Kate listened with interest. She'd never heard this personal account from her close friend.

"I've actually witnessed a few go. It's *beautiful*." Jocelyn got slightly choked up, misty-eyed. "One little girl last year, Lindsey—you remember her?"

Kate nodded.

"She was laying in bed—asleep, I thought. All of a sudden she sat up, pointed toward the corner of the ceiling, and smiled the biggest smile I've ever seen. Then she said, 'Look! The angels! Aren't they pretty? And they sing so sweetly!'"

"Then, in the faintly lit room I watched Lindsey's face start to glow with the reflection of light. But there was no beam shining down—just the reflection showing on her. It grew brighter, then quickly dispelled. Her little body slumped back on the bed. She'd left with them."

"That's amazing!" Kate said, touched and enthralled. "Did you share it with her parents?"

Jocelyn nodded, "Um-hmm. They were grateful, too." She looked straight at Kate. "So, yes. Even though this may have something to do with Mr. Brakken, I think what actually appeared to Andrew was a real angel. I sense it, too, by the way he is behaving."

"But you said he wasn't any better."

"He's not—physically. But his spirit is soaring. I'm sure he encountered the real thing, even though it was through a dream. They aren't uncommon experiences; hundreds of people have written about these happening to them or someone they know."

Kate glanced down at the table. The waitress brought their iced teas and said their burgers would take another few minutes. Jocelyn excused herself to the ladies' room.

Kate reflected while looking out the window. She recalled Daniel staying at Andrew's side on Christmas morning. Then she remembered his words in the lobby, how he'd admitted that Andrew "got to him." She wondered how it all fit together and what piece she was missing—the one that would help the puzzle make sense. She gave up. *Nothing* made sense with Daniel. He seemed out of place—more so than a fish plucked from the water.

The waitress set two plates on the table and left again. Kate's stomach rumbled from the smell of the grilled chicken, but she waited for Jocelyn to return. When she did, Kate offered a quiet, brief blessing for their food.

They both reached for their burgers. "Well, you sure beat out my piece of news," Kate said.

Jocelyn picked up her burger and peered back, raising her eyebrows. "Oh, yeah—what was this meeting about anyway?" She bit into her hot sandwich.

Kate smiled confidently. "I'm going to buy back the carousel for TLC."

Chapter Twenty-Five

J ocelyn almost choked on her bite of chicken burger. Kate waited until her friend swallowed, took several drinks of her tea, and squeaked out her response, "*You what?*"

Kate explained her entire secret plan for the carousel: The fundraiser, the fliers, the list of donors, the reality.

Jocelyn looked doubtful. "Just how do you expect this to stay a secret from Mr. Angel?"

"Very funny. You know as well as I do that Daniel is human."

"Yeah. And a very good-looking one, too."

Kate moderately glared at her compatriot for the distracting personal comment, then continued, "True, keeping this quiet could be tough. Especially if any phone calls and mail leak through the shortcuts."

"Shortcuts?" Jocelyn's eyes widened with curiosity.

"I'll have all the benefit mail forwarded to a PO Box in care of 'Carousel,' and route all calls to my place. I have automated voicemail at home. I can change the message for the next few weeks and make it a benefactor acceptance line."

"What about the press? If they do this story, your secret is history."

Kate frowned. That was true. She needed coverage, but it might only hurt the project. There was no sure way to keep Daniel from watching the news or reading a paper. It would be hard enough concealing the arrangements from him at the hospital.

"I'll just have to do without much media. Besides, I won't need it if God is supporting this."

"Kate . . ." Jocelyn looked troubled, "what if you come up short? Do you give the money back?"

"No. I thought it'd be wise to make a disclaimer. If the funds raised are less than we need, the money will go toward the hospital's future endeavors."

"And the Board? Are they in the dark, too?"

"They won't be. I'm confident I'll gain their support. I plan to ask Henry to talk to them. My efforts will be totally independent of the hospital. All my time spent on the fundraiser will be conducted before or after work. But I need to recruit some volunteers, and get some personal stories from the kids and their parents—including original drawings from the kids, to help appeal for support."

Jocelyn nodded. "It's daring, but I like it." She smiled. "However, if Daniel finds out, this could mean your job."

Kate sighed. "At this point it wouldn't matter." She paused. "I gave him my notice."

Jocelyn looked stunned, then sad. She placed her burger down and said, "Oh, my." Silence followed for a moment. "How much time do you have?"

"Thirty days from last Wednesday. Look, Joce, I know you probably think I'm a quitter, but I had to back out. Something keeps telling me this is all backward. I don't know why, but I can't shake it. Consequently, Daniel and I don't work well together, and I don't think we'll make a team, *ever*."

Jocelyn frowned. "Too bad. You were our hope for next time."

"Thanks. But maybe God has had other plans all along."

"I don't think so." Kate's longtime ally was suddenly not in agreement. "*You* are the best thing going in that administration. We all loved Henry, but you excelled him a year ago."

"Perhaps. But Henry is gone, and Daniel is here. I'm not so sure this is meant to be my place anymore. And if saving the carousel for the children is the only thing I can do to help them, then I have to give it everything I've got."

"Noble choice."

Kate shook her head. "I feel like I really don't have a choice in this. My heart said jump—and I did."

Monday evening, Kate finished talking with Henry on the phone. She was elated. The Board had given full support to her endeavor—as long as everyone's efforts were done on personal time. She was fortunate with their decision. Had they not been so partial to the carousel, they would have decided against her plan, she was sure. Now, she not only had their blessing, but their financial backing as well. Several had promised to send her their personal donations!

Kate went to her spare bedroom, which doubled as a home office, and sat at her computer. She had a lot to prepare in precious little time. Already this morning, Daniel had given her a teardown date—the Monday after New Year's—when a hired crew would disassemble the carousel. The mention of it sealed her fate, along with the Miracle Machine's. Anguished, she had looked pleadingly at him, silently begging him to call it off.

His eyes were also filled with torment. He wanted her to stay. He seemed to be struggling close to the surface of her pain, close to a recision.

But not close enough.

Recalling the teardown date fueled her fire to get started. She copied the file of donor names and addresses onto her hard drive. The hospital Board had graciously consented for her to use them in connection with her fliers.

She worked steadily, creating the flier and mailing labels until 3:15 a.m. Exhausted, but feeling like she'd accomplished what she needed to, Kate turned out the light and headed for bed.

"Help me, Lord," she prayed aloud for the project's success and protection while turning down her covers. "Help this all work out. Please!" It bothered her that she needed to keep the undertaking from Daniel, but she knew there wasn't a chance he would be agreeable, since the fundraiser basically made him out to be the bad guy.

But Kate had run out of options. She *needed* to make this work. It was the only way to protect the children's carousel.

Kate stopped at the local copier business at lunch on Tuesday and had ten thousand copies made of her flier. Only seven hundred labels were on the list, but she needed extras to pass out and post in local civic centers, libraries, malls, grocery stores, and other establishments that would permit them. Since Daniel lived in Issaquah, it was safe to hope he would never see them.

That evening she called everyone on staff—with the exception of the night crew on duty. People were very generous, not only promising to take and hand out a few hundred fliers door-to-door, but also volunteering some of their own ideas for fundraisers, since the flier merely asked for donations.

Kate appreciated their recommendations. She knew she needed other avenues to raise money, ways that wouldn't interfere with the hospital's regular solicitations. Fortunately, a few of the suggestions could be easily effected without Daniel finding out.

After compiling her list of helpers, she prepared two new fliers: one announcing twenty-five dollar benefit rides on the carousel before the teardown date. The other allowing the public to have their pictures taken with the animals from the petting zoo for a *premium* donation—ranging from one hundred to one thousand dollars—depending on how exotic their choice of animal. Both events could take place on New Year's Day—a holiday when Daniel wouldn't be around!

By early Wednesday morning, Kate had the new fliers completed and copied. Finally, everything was ready for the multitude of helpers who were asked to discreetly pick up their stacks on their way in to work. Fully stocked with paperwork, envelopes, and postage, the small, private conference room down the hall from the Admin. offices temporarily looked like a postal office. Once everyone had shown for their pickup, though, it was normal again.

If things went as planned, the staff would spend their lunch hours folding, stuffing, and stamping some mailers to go out that afternoon. The remaining fliers would be passed out in portions that evening in a vast area surrounding the hospital. Hopefully, her phone would start ringing by tomorrow afternoon.

Kate plopped into her chair after completing her own stack during her lunch hour. She was fatigued, but pleased with what she had accomplished in the speedy project. The passion that filled her heart felt wonderful. It was the same kind of zeal she'd experienced directing many of the activities at TLC. In recent years, though, her responsibilities had become more administrative, and a fundraising supervisor had been selected to carry on the work.

The intensity of this cause was deeply satisfying! Yet, it also conveyed a sense of *challenge*. There was no way of knowing the outcome in advance. Still, when the familiar fervor was there, Kate believed she was on track.

Chapter Twenty-Six

*D*aniel's eyes were tired of reading. His vision had gone bleary an hour ago. He laid the nurses' report on his desk. It was just one of nearly twenty that had stacked since the week before Christmas. From nursing to patient advocate, therapy to ER, volunteer to lab tech—and many more—every department had a monthly status report.

Though science and research had always intrigued him, reading was never one of Daniel's strong suits—especially when it came to deciphering substantial data and numbers. He was a visual person. Masterful with his hands. Competent with procedures, not in analyzing repetitive statistics and amounts. So, each day, he'd kept pushing the reports aside, until later.

Later had come. He needed to sign off on several reports that, according to Kate, were already two days overdue in being returned to department heads. Five more were due today, and a string of them needed returning by Friday. He could understand now why they were due in stages.

He rested his head in his hands. Lisa buzzed the intercom. "Mr. Brakken? Line three is for you—Pamela Hinz."

Daniel scrunched his eyebrows. He'd never heard of the woman. "OK." He grabbed the receiver and punched the line's button. "Daniel Brakken. May I help you?"

"Mr. Brakken, this is Pamela Hinz, from North Beach Realty. How are you today?"

He winced. *Sales call.* "I'm swamped. How are you?"

"Curious. That's why I tracked you down. Our offices are located in L.A., and one of my clients has an interest in making an offer on your beachfront house. Have you considered selling, now that you are obviously relocated?"

Daniel was stunned by the surprise information. Though he knew selling was inevitable, he had wanted to give things time before making the move permanent. That way, he would still have a place to go to if everything collapsed in Seattle.

"I'm not sure that is possible at this present time. But, just for the record, what is their offer?"

"One million, two. Half in cash."

Daniel reeled from her answer. "You're serious?"

"Serious enough to find you out of state. It wasn't easy, I'll tell you."

"How long do I have to decide?"

"They opted to give you one week to consider it, which is very generous, considering the surrounding homes are comparable, and those on last season's market went for less."

Daniel wasn't sure he wanted to loose a hooked fish from the line. True, he hadn't been in a rush to sell, but this bid was better than he'd hoped for. He'd paid eight hundred thousand for the refurbished place five years ago. "Tell them I'm interested, and that I'll have an answer for you by Friday morning."

"They will be glad to hear that. Here's my number. . . ."

Daniel wrote down the information and thanked her, then said goodbye. He hung up the phone just as someone knocked.

"Come in."

Kate poked her head through the opening. "Daniel, the JCAHO surveyors are here."

He blinked, gave her a puzzled look. "I'm sorry—who?"

She looked a little perturbed. "The Joint Commission on Accreditation of Healthcare Organizations—for the hospital's quality assurance review. Remember?"

He couldn't recall the meeting, nor did he yet understand what JCAHO *really* meant. And what he was supposed to do with them. "Why don't you handle it, Kate? I'm buried here."

She seemed suspicious, then pursed her lips. "Sorry, this one's out of my league. I would officially need your title to pull it off. It's in the Admin. department manual, if you want to look it up. Section 12."

He wasn't happy with that answer. He realized it meant he'd have to handle something important—of which he probably knew little about, even with his years of hospital work. "Section 12? Terrific. Would you please tell them to give me ten minutes?"

"I'll tell them, but don't be long. These guys keep a tight schedule." She closed the door.

Daniel grabbed the Admin. manual off the shelf, which Henry had mentioned would be of help to him from time to time. He opened it to "Section 12: JCAHO Surveys" and proceeded to read the half page of material. He immediately became discouraged to learn it was an independent agency doing a triennial walkthrough—

one that required the administrator's participation to answer questions along the way. Daniel closed the manual and rubbed his chin. There was no getting out of this one. He needed to skate his best or sit in the grandstand. But, did he really have to skate solo? Surely Kate could accompany them, since he was not fully accustomed to this hospital.

He pulled on his suit jacket and reached into the inside pocket for some mint spray. After spritzing some into his mouth, he replaced it in the pocket. Daniel emerged and shook hands with the two reps, introducing himself.

"Thank you for coming. You may not be aware that I'm fairly new to this hospital, so I'm going to ask my Assistant to join us."

They nodded, seemingly unconcerned by the change.

Daniel glanced around for Kate, but she wasn't at her desk. Nor was she in the office.

"Lisa? Where's Kate?"

"She left a few minutes ago. Said she had a personal appointment and needed to take off for a couple of hours."

Daniel made a sarcastic face. "Great," he whispered loud enough for only her ears. "Say, Lisa?"

"Yes, Mr. Brakken?"

He whispered to her, "Henry never reviewed this procedure with me. Can you point me in the general direction."

She shrugged. "I'm not sure what to tell you. Mr. Freeman has always given them the tour before."

Daniel closed his eyes, feeling the walls caving in on him. He sighed, then turned and faced the reps waiting anxiously near the door. "It seems my Assistant stepped out for an appointment. Perhaps you would like to reschedule, so she could join us."

"That won't be necessary, Mr. Brakken."

Daniel blinked and swallowed hard. "Oh, . . . well then, shall we begin?"

At 12:30 that afternoon, Daniel finally returned to his office, vanquished, whipped by his lack of knowledge during the review. He couldn't recall answering even one question competently. Sure, he knew lots of hospital procedures from L.A. General. Trouble was, procedures varied greatly across hospitals. He had hoped to adequately pull off the walkthrough. But the isolated conference only unveiled his shortcomings, where administrative matters were concerned.

The surveyors had grown so visibly wearied over Daniel's apologies for being new and without answers that they finally gave up questioning him and just took notes of what they observed.

Now Daniel sat and shook his head, glad that it was the lunch hour and everyone was out for a while. He sifted through his growing in-box, amazed at how it had nearly doubled during his absence. Spying the medical journal article that Kate had given him last week, featuring laser surgery, he decided to work on something he could easily tackle. Hopefully, it would boost his self-esteem in the process.

He read the piece with intense interest, fully trained in the technical procedures described as groundbreaking. Most doctors would be stumped by their title alone. Yet, at the conclusion of the article, Daniel was shocked to read of the "new" strategy the medicine field was now supporting—the *same* laser surgery method that he had argued in favor of implementing over a year ago! The same one he had attempted with Sammy.

Not only was the procedure being successfully performed now, but was being recommended for certain brain stem ops!

"Unreal!" Daniel couldn't accept it easily. He reread a paragraph, flabbergasted at how the Chief of Physicians being interviewed commented that a "daring colleague from Los Angeles had first tried the new technique, but failed to correctly execute the procedure," and that "they owed their gratitude to him for pioneering the way." Albeit they withheld his name for confidentiality, Daniel knew they were speaking about him. Especially from their declaration that his attempt had *failed*.

"That's for sure!" He slapped the magazine shut, then tossed it onto his desk, incited over how the "notable success in neurosurgery" at Daniel's expense had never prompted L.A. General to call him back—with laud.

Daniel rubbed his chin. "So, I was right after all," he pondered, as he dared to reflect once more upon the grievous day when his former career came to a screeching halt.

The memory reeled forth all too quickly, ever present below the surface of thought and emotion. He recalled the morning: the high confidence, the anxious boy, the excruciating hours in the OR, the complications, the critical point, the decision to go ahead, . . . the tragedy.

Daniel winced. He heard again, in his mind, the frenzied tumult when things turned for the worst. The long, piercing tone of the monitor announcing the heart had stopped beating. Doctors shouted for defibrillator assistance. Nurses raced around, responding swiftly to orders. Emergency technicians barged in.

Daniel's own voice hollered, "Pack him—hurry up! We're losing him!"

"Clear," the tech declared. They sent a shock but no response.

"Do it again!" Daniel yelled.

While the technician used the paddles, Daniel's desperate pleas followed, "Come on Sammy. Come back, you hear? It's not your time, yet. It's *not* your time! Come back, kiddo. I promised I wouldn't let you go. Come back, . . . please! Sammy!"

Then the silence—the awful, heart-wrenching silence—that followed an impeded rescue, when the monitor was shut off and everyone lingered by the lost patient. No one dared speak a word; they all felt the same anguish when defeat choked the air. Efforts thwarted, they stood motionless, conquered by a puny, malevolent mass of gray tissue that took lives without mercy.

Even so, Daniel felt the slayer. He'd been the one to push them to this point. He could have retreated, called it done, and progressed with chemo follow-up. He could have played it safe.

But he had refused.

And it was *his* call to make. The others would not interfere. He was the top surgeon, the one with the answers. They trusted him to make the right decision.

He failed them all.

Chapter Twenty-Seven

*K*ate watched Daniel storm into the staff meeting room the following morning and swiftly call the audience of doctors, nurses, and staff to attention.

They were gathered for the promised assembly, in which they could *discuss* the sale of the carousel. Though most everyone had already heard of the teardown date—and knew it was unlikely that Daniel would reconsider keeping the carousel—they came anyway, prepared to confront their fearless leader. To make him answer their questions and defend his reasoning.

Kate was relieved that Daniel kept his word to have the meeting, and she prayed fervently for a turn of events. Though her intellect told her that wasn't apt to occur, she entreated heaven's help anyway—desiring that, somehow, this final chance would succeed. Then she could forgo resigning from her job. She could cancel carrying out her secret backup plan. *Then*, she knew, everything would be fine.

You're dreaming, she advised herself as she sat next to Jocelyn. They watched Daniel stand before them, rigid and as powerful as an oil-drilling rig. Black suit. Gold tie. Hair impeccable. Steel-faced. Surely he'd known to expect warfare, and in Kate's eyes, he'd come iron-clad, ready to take on any opponent.

One by one, she witnessed the staff members fire their questions and accusations. One by one, Daniel shot them down.

After an hour of disputing, the air grew even more charged through zealous supporters. At that point, Daniel appeared somewhat vulnerable. His rebuttals turned verbose, less harsh, and he paused more between sentences to collect reasoning.

That's good, Kate regarded his shift in answering. *Maybe his shell is not too hard to crack.* But, just when she thought the hospital personnel showed promise of winning him over, Daniel called an instant cessation to the meeting.

"The rest of your comments will have to be submitted in writing by the end of the day," he flatly stated and looked at his watch.

"Hey—that's unfair!" "You can't do that!" Protests burst forth from various attendees.

"I'm sorry, but we are out of time," Daniel answered, obviously flustered yet not giving in. Then he left more swiftly and resolutely than he had charged in.

"So much for hearing *our* side," Jocelyn murmured her reluctant acceptance of the whole scenario.

"Guess so." Kate frowned, closed her eyes, and shook her head. Her last hope for a turnaround withered away.

Later, that day, Kate covered the phones in the office while Lisa attended an afternoon training session on some new software being installed by their Information Systems manager. Fortunately for Kate, the phones were quiet and Daniel was away for another of his renowned meetings. She was more than a little despondent after witnessing the morning assembly.

Such a shame, she dwelled on the pathetic event. Daniel was truly a likeable person—when he wasn't in charge of the hospital! Every decision he made "in the best interest of TLC" worked contrary to his favor. Since arriving, he was accruing enemies by the day. Though Kate knew the staff didn't hate Daniel, she could see they were growing deeply disappointed with his presumed leadership capabilities. Morale was at an all-time low, and several staff members were pulling the plug on their full support of him. Though *hers* was the only resignation so far, she knew it wouldn't be long before others flooded in.

When she wasn't frustrated with Daniel herself, Kate felt sorry for him. From the beginning, she'd sensed something didn't sit right. Something seemed out of place and festered beneath the surface of his life. Yet, she just couldn't put her finger on it.

"Help us, God," in the quiet office, she pled once more with the Lord to do something—anything—to improve the situation.

The phone rang.

"TLC Hospital. May I help you?"

"Yeah. Dr. Brakken, please."

"You mean, Mr. Brakken?" Kate was surprised by the medical title. "I'm sorry. He's in a meeting right now. May I leave him a message?"

"Please. It's Dr. John Robinson—his buddy from L.A. General Hospital. Tell him I've got good news for him."

"Well," Kate smiled, "I'm sure he can use some today." Her curiosity was peaked, but she didn't feel it was right to inquire into Daniel's personal affairs. "I'll leave him the message, Dr. Robinson. May I take your number?"

The man laughed softly into the phone. "Don't worry, I'm sure he still has it memorized, after practicing here fifteen years."

"Wha—?" Kate nearly choked on the word. She cleared her throat and blinked in confusion.

"Tell him my 'ops' are done for the day, so he can reach me here until about 5:00. Thanks."

"Excuse me, Dr. Robinson? May I ask what practice you are in?"

"Pediatric Neurosurgery," he replied.

"And how did you come to know Daniel in that field?"

"Are you kidding? He taught me everything I know. Since he's been gone, though, I've had to blaze my own trail. It's been good, but I sure miss him."

Kate was getting more confused. "I guess I don't follow you."

"Daniel was the best. When he left L.A. General, I had to learn to take the lead here with the team."

"What team is that, Dr. Robinson?"

"The *neurosurgical* team, of course."

The light of the doctor's meaning finally broke through Kate's clouded thinking. She rubbed her forehead. "Umm, Dr. Robinson, you aren't saying that Daniel is a—"

"A neurosurgeon? Yes—the finest we ever had. Probably the best in the country. Hopefully, we can get him back. That's why I called, to share some good news with him. Funny, I thought everyone in a pediatric hospital had heard of Daniel Brakken. You must be a new employee."

Kate smirked. She drummed her fingers on the desktop. "No, just a little out of the picture, that's all. Thanks for the education. It helped to fill in the missing pieces."

"You're welcome. Have a good day." He hung up.

She replaced the phone and stared into space, still baffled by the news. *Daniel, a doctor? A neurosurgeon? The best in the field?* With each thought she grew more amazed, yet everything started to make sense like never before: Daniel's knowledge about surgery, his lack of knowledge about administration, his precision in sanding the lion, his attendance in med school, his push for the emergency-room upgrade, his reluctance to trust nonconventional methods like the carousel. And—most of all—his hypersensitivity toward Andrew's condition.

Kate could only wonder how it must have torn at Daniel to witness Andrew losing the battle and not be in a position to help the boy. No doubt, it was why Daniel looked like a caged animal whenever he saw or talked about Andrew Tucker.

Suddenly Kate questioned why Daniel would remain so silent about his former occupation. Why was it necessary to keep it a secret? And Henry, too! It dawned on her that Henry must have known of Daniel's career. In fact, he'd been the one to tell her that Daniel was "accomplished" instead of explaining his medical credentials. And if Henry knew, the Board knew! They were all in it together.

Kate nearly fell over from shock, though she was relieved at finally getting some answers. Now that the secret had sprung loose, there was no way to stop it from getting some attention.

Daniel returned from meeting with a hospital equipment distributor. His mind was swimming with figures, but the upswing of the meeting was that the hospital could manage the ER upgrade without going into any debt, as long as the carousel auctioned as expected.

He came to retrieve his messages from Kate, who was on the phone. She looked earnest when she saw him. Eager or anxious—he wasn't sure which. He wished for the former, but didn't rest his hopes upon it.

These days it was all he could do to keep his mind from wishing every time he saw her. He'd come too close to kissing her on Christmas Day, and now he struggled with the alluring desire continuously. He wondered if there was even a chance that she was interested in him. But even if that were true, she wouldn't want the real man—the wounded one that he was inside.

He closed his door most of the way and reviewed his handful of messages. Not a lot, but more than he wanted to deal with. The morning had been stressful enough, with having to defend his judgment for the carousel in front of the entire staff. What supporters he may have had were gone now, he was sure.

What he really wanted to do was write his own resignation, but that didn't seem a smart thing to do. The last time he'd quit, it had nearly ruined him.

He read the last message, from Dr. Robinson. "He has good news for you," Kate had written.

Daniel's stomach did a backflip. If anyone could sprout a leak in his watertight plan for secrecy, it was his buddy John. John was an easy talker. Daniel wondered how much conversation had transpired while his friend was on the line with Kate.

A soft knock sounded from the door. Kate poked her head through the opening. "You have a few minutes?"

He tried discerning in a split second whether this had anything to do with his past. And if so, whether he should deny, avoid, or refuse to explain. Or, whether he should just tell her everything and let the chips fall where they may.

After the failures of the last week, Daniel was bent on the latter choice. He was tired of running, tired of pretending to be someone he wasn't. Tired of trying to impress a woman who was stealing his heart but would never love or trust him.

Besides, there was no reason to influence her now. She was planning to leave him here to flounder alone. And she certainly hadn't changed her mind, even after he'd humbly begged her to stay.

"Yeah. Come in," he muttered, and folded his hands.

"First, I wanted to applaud you for keeping your word about having the carousel meeting. I know that wasn't easy for you."

Her words seemed to pierce right through to his heart. How did she always know to say things that reached the core of him? "Thanks. I'm sure the anguish was mutual, however." He tried to show empathy over what she must be feeling.

She glanced away. "I've had better days."

"Thought so."

Silence spanned the room. She looked at him but couldn't continue her conversation.

"You didn't come to discuss the carousel, did you?"

"No." Her green eyes looked moist.

"What is it?" he pressed slowly, but resolutely.

"Daniel, are you happy here?"

Happy? Her question stunned him. No one had been interested in what he was enduring. Answering her was all too easy.

"Honestly? No."

She nodded, waiting. It encouraged him to explain.

He gave a near-mocking laugh at the situation. Against his better judgment of personally confiding in a subordinate, he followed his heart to entrust her. "In fact," he continued, "*miserable* would be a far more accurate description."

She nodded again, tenderly. "Why are you here if it's not what you love?"

He rubbed his chin and looked away from her compassionate eyes. He realized that John Robinson had said more than enough. He blew out a sigh. "I don't know, for sure."

"Do you want to stay?" she continued.

He truly didn't know the answer to that question. If work were the only issue, he would have flatly said no. But Kate had become the other reason he wanted to hang on here. Even if it seemed futile to gain her personal interest.

"I don't have another option."

"That wasn't what I asked," she continued.

"Well, it doesn't matter if I don't have a place to go."

"What your heart *longs* to do matters, Dr. Brakken," she pleaded, giving him a sympathetic look. "It's the driving force of life inside of you. And if practicing neurosurgery is what you long to do, then you need to follow after it."

He grew uncomfortable. She obviously didn't know all the facts about his leaving the practice. "You don't understand, Kate. It's not that easy. In fact, I only wish it were."

"For someone who's 'the best' on the West coast, it should be easy as frozen pie. You should have your pick of jobs."

"Not when 'the best' screws up," his voice rose and he stood to pace the office space beside her. "No matter how good you are, when you blow it they don't want you back. People want a flawless hero."

She stood in front of him, halted his pacing by grasping his forearms. The warmth of her contact surprised him, then calmed him. Kate looked him straight in the eyes.

"What happened, Daniel? Tell me—why are you running? If you won't explain, I'll just find out from Henry. But I'd rather hear it from you. Please, Daniel? I want to help, but you have to tell me what is chasing you."

He searched her eyes with near desperation. If he explained, his insufficiency would ever be before her. Yet, he felt he would die if he didn't unload the burden that had held him prisoner for so long. "I told you. They don't want a failure."

She loosed her grasp and folded her arms. "What do you mean? You failed a surgery?"

"Yeah, I messed up. Big time! I gambled with a kid's life and lost."

"But, every surgeon has to face the losses at times."

"Not when they are avoidable!" He paced again. "I walked right into this one, boy—me and my hotshot reputation for the edge!" he spat the words. "Oh, yeah, I knew I was the best, and that is why I failed. I let my ego make the choice instead of my brain."

Kate was starting to cry. It wrenched his heart to see her reaction. She thought the worst of him, for sure.

"Failing is not unforgivable," she insisted, tears cascading down her velvety cheeks. "You can still go back to neurosurgery."

"*Really?*" He mocked her innocence. Daniel stopped pacing and faced her squarely. He felt the rage of condemnation and the pain of guilt crushing in on him, squeezing the life out of him. "I can never forgive myself for what I did," he said the words resolutely. Then he paused, his throat choked up. "And *that* is why I can *never* go back!"

He abandoned the conversation and abruptly left the office, unable to face her disappointment a moment longer.

Daniel wasn't surprised when the migraine hit with a vengeance. Fortunately, his intense exchange with Kate had compelled him to leave for the day, and he was nearly home by the time it came on strong.

He muttered under his breath the entire drive. Never had he felt so caged, so close to insanity, not since he'd left his practice in L.A. He wanted to believe Kate's simple hope was possible: that a broken life could be mended. But she didn't realize how impossible her proposal had been.

If Daniel had been capable of returning to surgery, he'd have done it long ago. The fact was, he was imprisoned, locked in a dungeon from which he couldn't escape.

And no one held the key.

Kate knocked at Henry Freeman's front door just after 5:30 p.m. She knew he and Louise were due to return from the Virgin Islands that afternoon. Though they were probably tired from their trip, she couldn't wait to talk to Henry about Daniel.

The door opened and Louise peeked through, her aging face lit with cheer. "Kate! What a pleasant surprise!" Louise hugged her without a moment's hesitation. "Come in, dear."

"Thank you. Is Henry resting?"

"No, he's putting the suitcases in storage downstairs. I'll tell him you're here. Sit down. Do you want some tea?"

"Yes, please," she nodded her pleasant appreciation.

"All right. I'll put the water on and be back in a minute."

"Thank you," Kate sat on the comfortable sofa while the butterflies launched flight in her stomach. She hadn't anticipated being this nervous over pinning Henry into confession.

Henry emerged from the stairs that led to the basement, looking a little tanned and healthier than ever. "Kate!" He reached out and gave her a fatherly hug. "It's good to see you."

"Same to you," Kate responded, relishing the familiar warmth of their friendship. "How was the trip to the islands?"

"Wonderful! We should've gone every Christmas."

"That's great. You look fantastic."

He chuckled. "Can't say I'm not enjoying my time away from the paperwork, but I deeply miss you all, and the kids."

She smiled, acknowledging his sentiment. "We miss you."

He sat on the edge of the couch. "So, tell me what's happening." His gaze turned curious. "How's Daniel managing?"

Kate's smile faded, and she sat beside him. "Not too well. That's why I came."

He seemed concerned. "Remember, Kate, it will take time to adjust to a new person in charge."

"She shook her head. That's not what I need to talk about."

The teakettle whistled, and Louise got up to fix their cups.

"What is it, Katie?" Henry's tone softened. His blue-gray eyes were gentle yet searching.

She took a deep breath. "I found out about Daniel, about his practice in neurosurgery."

Henry nodded, looking somber, then folded his hands beneath his chin. "I knew you'd learn the facts eventually. It was just a matter of time."

"What I don't understand is why you had to hide it from me."

"We didn't have a choice. In order for TLC to hire Daniel, that was what needed to happen. He didn't want anyone to know, and we didn't want it to become a nasty news issue. So we promised him his former career would be kept under wraps, as much as possible."

"What do you mean we? You make it sound like it was your idea."

Henry gave her an apologetic look. "It was my idea, Kate. I recommended that the Board hire Daniel. I felt he was the right choice—for the time being—and they followed my recommendation."

Louise returned with a tray, balancing three steaming cups. She placed each one down onto individual coasters.

Kate was beyond stunned. "But . . . but you said—you trained me all those years, you said I was your choice." Her emotions started to tumble inside. She'd expected confronting him about keeping a secret—but not about this! She fought back the tears. "How could you lie to me?"

Henry looked hurt and reached out to clasp her hand. Louise shook her head sympathetically. Henry lowered his gaze, then looked at Kate. "I know it's difficult for you to hear this, but I didn't lie. I was your highest supporter, and I still am. But, for some reason, God impressed upon me to call Daniel and interview him. And, ultimately, hire him over you. I don't know why to this day. I can't even say that I support Daniel personally. I only know that the Lord pressed me to do it, and I had to be obedient. Do you believe me, Katie?"

She couldn't believe what she was hearing. "If that's true, why didn't God tell me? I've felt Daniel was wrong from the start, and he is clearly not capable of handling this position. He's falling apart at the seams. And the hospital is crumbling as well. Staff morale is at an all-time low."

"Then you've got to set a good example, Kate. Stick it out. Stay behind him, because God has a purpose for him being there."

She stood and threw her hands up in a show of relinquishment. "I *can't* support him!"

"But you must," he pleaded. "Without you—"

"Henry, I can't. . . ." She sighed heavily and turned to face the window, crossing her arms and steadying her voice for her confession. "I already turned in my resignation."

"What?" Henry stood. He turned her to face him. "No! You must stay, or he'll fail for sure."

"He's crashing to the ground, even with me there. I'm telling you, there is *no* way Dr. Brakken is going to make this position work—with or without God's stamp of approval! God may have called him up here, but I think it was merely to prove to Daniel where his heart really was. And it's not in managing the hospital."

Henry now appeared twice as aged as when she'd come.

"Please, Henry, you must hear what I'm saying. Daniel cannot do this. He's miserable; he told me so. He wants desperately to return to surgery, but he can't forgive himself for failing an operation—one evidently bad enough that the hospital asked him to leave. Even so, I know he is not destined to do this job. I feel it with everything in me," she implored him to accept her words.

"OK, OK. I promise I will talk to him. But that's all I can promise. He may not listen to me."

Kate shook her head. "I'm not asking you to talk to him, Henry. I'm begging you to pray for him, to go back to where he belongs . . . before he destroys his life and everyone else's at the hospital."

Henry, Louise, and Kate spent nearly twenty minutes praying fervently for TLC, and interceding for Daniel to find God's plan for his life. Afterward, Kate left the Freeman home a lot more at peace than when she'd arrived.

She made a surprise visit to see Grandma Rose on her way back. Her grandmother was in good spirits, but she looked more pale than usual, and was resting early in bed. So, Kate didn't stay long.

Once home, she spent hours retrieving the hundreds of messages from her voicemail, then opened a whole box full of responses from people sending money and pledges for the carousel. To date, she had raised over fifty thousand. It wasn't bad, but she was a little behind her goal for this point. Hopefully, the fundraisers scheduled for New Year's Day would close the gap.

She prayed they would.

Chapter Twenty-Eight

riday, New Year's Eve, Kate rose very early in the morning. She turned on some worship music, as she often did, softly—enough to break the silence in the house and give her something to hum to. She spent a particularly long time reading her Bible—the Psalms—to gain encouragement and wisdom.

She always liked to start her day reading scripture, but today she needed a larger portion before she faced Daniel. After his departure from the office yesterday, she had no clue what to expect. It wouldn't even surprise her if he failed to show at all.

Unlocking the Admin. wing an hour and a half before her usual time to open, she found the office dark and quiet. She turned on the lights and started to tackle her in-box items leftover from yesterday. She hoped Daniel would show this morning to give the physicians' Roundtable—unlike last time. How foolish she felt now, understanding why he nearly laughed at her when she'd handed him the article to read on laser surgery techniques.

It wasn't long before Daniel came through the door, tense as a rubber band stretched to its limit. She looked at him, compassion unfolding over their previous encounter. "Good morning," she said tenderly.

Daniel only nodded, and walked past her to his office.

She called him on the intercom. "Daniel, will you be able to give the Roundtable this morning? I've got to catch up on several things today, before the holiday tomorrow."

"Yeah," he grunted a reply. She didn't press for further conversation.

As soon as Daniel left for the meeting, Kate dialed the nurses' station on third floor. Jocelyn picked up the line. "ICU. This is Nurse Greenbeck."

"Joce. It's me. I need a favor."

"Now—or after I get off? We're just starting to chart, and then I have to do final rounds."

"Call me when you're done. I'll meet you in the cafeteria. And bring Andrew's chart with you."

"Why? What's up?"

"I'll tell you later, OK?"

"Hmm, . . . all right. It will be after 8:00," Jocelyn answered.

"Thanks. See ya."

Kate resumed her duties and awaited Jocelyn's call. They would have a little while to talk before Kate was due to give the kid's their carousel ride—the last one of the year, the last one she could expect to give . . . for certain.

Jocelyn met Kate in the cafeteria and, as promised, she had with her Andrew's chart.

"This better be important. It's not a good idea to remove those from the unit."

"I know. I'll take full responsibility if anyone asks. Besides, I only need it for a short while."

"You have one hour until rounds start again. They'll notice it missing for sure if it's not returned before."

"I promise I'll be done before then."

"Kate, what is this all about? I trust you and all, but something tells me this is chancy. What is going on?"

"I need your confidence, and your prayers, Jocelyn."

"No problem with that." She removed her nursing hat and let down her shiny black blanket of hair.

"Daniel's in trouble. Well, not trouble with the law or anything like that. But he really needs our prayers. He's not supposed to be here, in Admin."

Jocelyn leaned forward. "Kate, you're not making any sense. Just give it to me straight."

"Right—put your seat belt on!" Kate drew in a large breath. "Daniel is a pediatric neurosurgeon. He left neurosurgery because of what he says was a botched operation, one he feels responsible for, which evidently caused his former practicing hospital to lose confidence in him—and they asked him to step down. I've felt since Daniel arrived that he wasn't meant to have this position, but Henry knew for certain that God told him to hire Daniel for His divine purpose to be fulfilled in Daniel's life.

"The only thing we can surmise from those contradicting leadings is that God had a reason for Daniel coming here *temporarily*—I think it was to save Andrew's life. You said yourself, Joce, that you felt Daniel would have something to do with helping Andrew, and that's why you concluded Andrew saw an angel that looked like Daniel. Well, Daniel may be the *only* person capable of helping Andrew, since he's been the top neurosurgeon in his field and maybe in the country. But, that's only going to be possible if we can convince Daniel to return to neurosurgery. And that is how Daniel is in trouble."

Kate stopped for air.

Jocelyn blinked from the barrage of information. "Mr. Brakken is a *surgeon?*" her voice elevated along with her dismay.

"I know—I was shocked too." Kate looked at her matter-of-factly. "But he has already admitted it to me."

"How did you find this out?"

"One of his former colleagues called yesterday to talk to him. Lisa was in computer training while I was covering the phones. The doctor unveiled a lot of Daniel's history before he realized I had no knowledge of what he was talking about."

"Hmm," Jocelyn nodded slowly.

"Incredible, isn't it?"

"It all makes sense. But why won't he return to surgery?"

"He feels he's an irreparable failure. Says he can't face it again. I think he has a confidence problem."

Jocelyn shook her head. "Maybe he really can't go back."

"What are you getting at?"

"Trauma. If what he experienced with his last operation really did a number on him—crippled him, somehow—he may be, in a sense, traumatized. Unable to conquer the wall that's holding him back." Jocelyn explained. "Does he suffer from symptoms of sleeplessness, nightmares, flashbacks—stuff like that?"

"I don't really know. He looks tired almost every morning, fatigued—you know, like he's not sleeping very well. And Henry mentioned Daniel had a problem with recurring migraines, but those aren't uncommon for people."

"Could be part of it. They increase with stress."

"So what do you think will hoist him over the wall?"

"Healing of the scar. And a good dose of motivation—something with a 'slingshot' effect to catapult him from the trap he's in."

"I think I've got the 'slingshot' factor covered," Kate said, tapping on Andrew's chart with her polished nail. "But we'll have to trust God for the healing, so start praying!"

"Absolutely. Keep me posted," Jocelyn answered, and they both went their separate ways.

Daniel returned from the physician's Roundtable exasperated beyond imagination. He'd been certain he could deliver the information and lead the discussion without faltering. But, standing in front of those doctors and explaining the benefits of laser surgery only fanned the flame that Kate had sparked the previous day.

Just touching on the basics of his former profession proved impossible. Daniel's constant inner questioning, whether he should—or could—go back to neurosurgery, triggered a fresh conflict inside of him.

He was now beyond stressed. Aspiration and anxiety pulled him in two different directions to the point where he was having difficulty breathing. He admitted to himself that he wanted to return to neurosurgery, but for whatever reason, he couldn't determine to make that happen. He wasn't content at all in his new role at TLC—nor adept at it. Kate would do far better than he! Yet, he could not make himself quit.

He had nowhere to turn for solace. No place to hide from his inadequacy.

And, now that his past had been revealed, there was nothing to keep it from spreading across the entire hospital—or beyond.

He had failed. There was nothing further he could do to hide the truth. He'd wanted to open up to Kate for a long time. The call from John Robinson only pushed him through the door. Now, Daniel would have to wait and see what Kate would do with the knowledge she'd gained about his former career.

A knock rapped at his opened door. Daniel glanced up to see Kate. In her slim, raspberry-colored dress suit, she looked more attractive than a delicacy, and perceptive as a female hawk. Lately, engaging in conversation with her had been a losing battle for him. He wondered what victory she had her mind set on winning this time.

"Hi," he managed a weak greeting.

"Daniel, I need a few minutes to ask you some questions."

"Sure," he replied, reluctant to tackle another controversy.

She closed the door behind her. "Did the meeting go OK?"

His stomach turned at the revisited memory, but he didn't want to confess his inner struggles to her. "Fine."

"Good." She smiled and sat in front of his desk, clutching a chart to her waist. "Well, . . . after our talk yesterday, I wanted to ask your opinion—as a physician."

"I can't give that to you. I'm not practicing."

"Granted, but I don't want your *advice*, so much as I want to find out what you think."

"What's the difference?" he countered.

"One is completely off the record. You won't be held accountable for your testimony in any way."

He glanced at the chart she held. "Is this about Andrew?"

"Yes," she answered soberly.

He paused a long time, but she didn't cower from his silence. "OK." He reached for the chart. She passed it over.

He reviewed the pages in a few minutes, flipping back and forth, then over them again, comparing notes from each operation with the same level of skill and refinement he'd had before leaving his profession last year. It amazed Daniel how smoothly the once-familiar process re-engaged. He read the various hospital jargon, medical acronyms, and doctors' scrawl with surprising ease.

The facts of the young boy's case gripped him—and didn't let go. Plain and simple: Andrew's brain stem tumor placement was—though bleak to many doctors—a well-rehearsed operation to Daniel. He'd performed similar ops at least forty times.

On the other hand, most neurosurgeons were green to the groundbreaking procedure Daniel had originated, which was likely necessary to save Andrew's life. Many had yet to ever hear of it. Fortunately, according to the med journal's article Kate had given Daniel, and John Robinson's good news, *that* was soon destined to change across the nation.

But not soon enough.

It won't help Andrew, was the ruthless fact that clawed at Daniel's heart. He knew the coming wave of newly-trained neurosurgeons would never make it to TLC before Andrew's time was up. The best Daniel could do was refer Andrew to a trusted colleague, like John, one Daniel believed might be able help the boy. But this specialized procedure was even a little beyond John's expertise, though he'd assisted Daniel on numerous occasions. Without Daniel, Andrew could be taking a large risk.

"Well?" Kate asked, obviously anticipating an affirmative answer. "What do you think?"

"With the right surgical help, Andrew has a very good chance to live another five to ten healthy years. By then, he can try radiation." He handed the chart back to her.

"Do you know who can help him?" Her eyes were softly pleading him to agree to take the case. His heart wanted to comply, for both Kate and the boy. But it just wasn't possible.

"I know I once could have." He looked at her, hurt, ashamed, then shook his head with frustration and despair. "Now, all I can give you is a recommendation."

"But, Daniel—"

"Kate, it's the *best* I can do." He was firm, and though she looked disappointed, she nodded her surrender. "Thank you. I'm sure your best is better than what he's facing right now."

"I'll give you a very short list of names." He began scribbling names on a piece of paper and placed it on his desk in front of her. "There are many capable neurosurgeons in this country, and several in this area, but these three are the only ones that studied and practiced under me while I was developing the procedure. If they won't agree to take Andrew's case," he looked down, placed the pen upon the desktop, and covered it with his hand, "then there's nothing further I can offer you."

"OK," Kate quietly responded. She turned and rested her hand on the doorknob. "Daniel? Have you considered that doing this op for Andrew may be the *only* way to win the war you're in?" She regarded him compassionately.

Chapter Twenty-Eight

"Yes. I have."

"That would make quite a special New Year's, wouldn't it?"

He only nodded, acknowledging the tenderness behind her sincere nudge.

"If I can help that happen, please, let me know," she asked.

"Thank you."

"You're welcome." Kate gave him another sympathetic glance, one that nearly tore him open—heart and soul.

Then she left with Andrew's chart.

Daniel rubbed at his temples. A hollow feeling ached from deep inside.

Chapter Twenty-Nine

*L*ong after everyone had left to ring in the new year, Daniel remained in his office. He had tried to work, but his thoughts were elsewhere . . . on Andrew's case. The more he endeavored to push the data from his mind, the stronger it returned to trouble him.

Help him, a compelling voice persisted.

"Terrific!" He slapped the pen down and rubbed his forehead again to reduce the mounting tension. New Year's Eve was shaping up to be just as distressing as Christmas Eve.

Well after 11:00 p.m., Daniel decided he'd better hit the roads before the mass of holiday partiers did. He closed up the office and headed out, thankful that the drive home would be virtually clear of traffic, being so late.

He reached Issaquah and passed through town, then turned onto the road that led to his area of the woods a few miles away. The jet-black road glistened in the path of his headlights. Daniel drove carefully along the icy street in the moonless night. He knew the way, but extra caution was warranted with all the curves along the backwoods road.

He passed houses every once in a while, most of them dark, shut down for the night. Only a few bore evidence of their occupants waiting up for the new year.

Finally, he came to the four-way stop, the last sign of life that preceded his gravel driveway two miles ahead. The deserted intersection was landmarked solely by Lighthouse Community Church, squarely positioned upon the Northeast corner. Its tall doorway and stained-glass windows were well lit. The church was humble in size, but gracefully built—belltower and all.

Daniel glimpsed the lit message board as he drove torpidly by: "Healing our Past—the Door to God's Future." The New Year's Watchman Service, as labeled on the sign, was in full swing. Daniel could hear lighthearted music and singing even through the windows of his car.

His gaze lingered upon the words announcing the message. He pondered them, mesmerized by the hope of healing they offered. Daniel's thoughts wandered . . . then his car drifted. He tried to remedy his course, but the road was icy. He steered headlong into the ditch!

The car dropped to a jarring halt. The engine died. Headlights were dimmed to two faint greenish-gold beams smashed against the grassy bank. Daniel was hunched uncomfortably over the steering wheel at a sharp angle—his seat belt still intact around his hips. His forehead pressed against the cold windshield.

Stunned and gasping for the air that the constraining wheel cut short, he realized he wasn't hurt but also that he needed to get out before he fainted from lack of oxygen. He grabbed the dash to gain leverage in hoisting himself backward from the wheel. Bracing himself against the downward grade, he pushed open the driver's door and slid out one leg. Then he guardedly stepped from the vehicle. Freed from the contraption, his lungs inhaled with need. He hiked up out of the ditch, still panting.

While catching his breath, he gaped at the tilted, stuck car. To anyone else it would be a ludicrous scene. With all the intoxicated drivers on the road tonight, Daniel knew the tow-truck driver was going to get a good heckle out of this stunt—performed stone-cold sober by a man reading a church signboard!

But to Daniel, it felt like he was a pawn in the hand of a manipulative God. Suspicious of the "bigger picture" surrounding his plight, he grew furious with God for putting him in another predicament. He glared at the night sky and yelled, "If You wanted me to go to church, You could have asked!"

Offended, Daniel went back to the car, reached inside, flipped off the lights and grabbed his keys. He then closed the door and started for the church.

Fortuitously, the small building was still open for the service in progress. Daniel blew a sigh of relief for that, and it eased his outrage. At least he could call for a tow truck.

He climbed the steps to the church and opened one tall wood door. As he entered, the warmth of the inside blanketed him in a way greater than physically. Oddly, it comforted him, took the edge off, as though *Someone* good had welcomed him, embraced him with a pleasant yet strong *beckoning*. Daniel sensed a serenity that graced the unpretentious "house of God."

The music quieted, and switched from the lively tune to a slow, adulating solo. A splendid soprano clearly and reverently filled the air from the platform up front. Her angelic voice was accented perfectly by soft, celestial tones from an electronic keyboard. The moving song reached something deep inside of Daniel. It somehow awakened his spirit, watered a parched and dry area in the depth of his soul that he had abandoned long ago.

Discomfited by his perception of what was occurring, he focused instead on the task of finding a phone. No one was in the lobby to ask for help. He peeked

inside the open sanctuary doors for an usher, seeing only the fractional attendance of the midnight group seated up front. The back half of the sanctuary
wasn't even lit. Gladly for him, they were out of earshot and his arrival hadn't
disturbed them. On the other hand, no one came to see what he needed, either.
He scanned the lobby to see if a phone hung on the wall. Nothing.

It was reasonable to assume there would be one in the church office, but he
dreaded hanging around until the service ended just to gain access to a phone.

Nonetheless, he wasn't about to disrupt the small group of worshipers and
cause all attention to be directed upon him! Daniel set off to explore the hall-
ways himself. He peeked in each room, but no telephone. He had no choice but
to wait until they were done.

Quietly, he came into the sanctuary and sat in the back pew. He was at least
forty feet from the nearest person. Only the concluding soloist seemed to notice
his arrival.

The group stood together with the pastor to recite a scripture passage. Daniel
sat and listened curiously to see if he would recognize the text from former days
of Bible reading.

The leader began with a Psalm, number 147. The first verse didn't especially
perk Daniel's ears with all the praise to God. He was mad at God and found it
difficult to appreciate the words.

They read on:

The Lord builds up Jerusalem; He gathers together the outcasts of Israel.
He heals the brokenhearted and binds up their wounds.

At the mention of those words, something responded inside of Daniel and
fastened upon them. If anyone was wounded, he was. He knew all about deep
wounds. Yet, he had always thought it was *his* responsibility to deal with them.
He'd never heard that God wanted to bandage them and bring him healing. He
continued listening more earnestly.

The next passage was announced, Isaiah 53, verses 4 and 5:

Surely, He has borne our griefs and carried our sorrows: yet we esteemed
Him stricken, smitten by God, and afflicted. But He was wounded for
our transgressions, He was bruised for our iniquities; the chastisement
for our peace was upon Him, and by His stripes we are healed.

This time, the inspired words sank in easily. They gently reached the torn
and jagged parts of his soul with their assurance of hope. He thirsted for them,
longed for the promise they carried: Jesus suffered the penalty for us, so that we
could be healed of the results of a sin-scarred life.

Like never before, Daniel saw his utter brokenness before God—an awesome, blessed God, whom he had bitterly walked away from. The God he couldn't

forgive for allowing failure to plunder his life. The God who loved Daniel in spite of his abandonment.

Daniel realized God hadn't forsaken him—it was he who had run away from God.

Hot tears started to burn behind his eyes. He held them back. He was a long way from running publicly to an altar, yet something powerful had laid hold of his heart. He put up a wall against the emotion and tried to keep listening without letting the aching truth undermine his fortitude.

The small gathering concluded their reading and sat down, while the kind-faced, silver-haired man with round glasses remained standing at the pulpit. "As you know, this service is meant to be a celebration of the new year more than anything else, so I didn't prepare a full sermon for tonight."

Daniel blew a sigh of relief and glanced at his watch. It was already a quarter to midnight.

The devout man continued, "There is, however, something the Lord has impressed upon me to say. This beautiful, redemptive word of encouragement is for someone who *desperately* needs to hear it." The man removed his glasses and dabbed at his eyes with his handkerchief, then replaced the spectacles.

"At the turn of the calendar page, we will enter a new year, a fresh beginning. A clean slate for a new, promising future. But†.†.†. for some, it will merely be the continuation of a torturous prison, a life-stealing grind from day into painful day. Sadly for some, it will be a lonely, mournful journey in a wilderness that you have been traveling for too long."

The pastor's voice was low, sensitive, persuasive. He held every eye captive. No one moved, nor made a sound.

"If that is how you feel, this message is for you. It is meant to reach you, to stop you from running any further with the pain. If that is you, . . ." he gently smiled and looked out with compassion, "then I have good news from the Lord Jesus Christ: He came to heal the brokenhearted and set the captive free."

Daniel felt his insides tumbling. The preacher's words couldn't have hit the bull's-eye more perfectly. He sat in the pew and rehearsed again the strange chain of events that brought him to this place tonight. He thought back to something Henry had said about a divine plan working in his life, that he was still in God's hand.

Daniel shifted his position, sniffled, and blinked at the compelling tears that now rimmed his eyes.

The pastor stepped away from the platform and came down to the audience's level. He walked along in front of one side of the people and looked honestly at them. "Whatever you've been through, He hasn't abandoned you. He still loves you. Whatever suffering you've endured, He knows about it and He deeply cares. Whatever fears have ransacked your faith, He can dispel them in an instant with His divine peace. Only if, . . . yes, *only if* you will let Him touch your wound and heal it with His marvelous grace." He walked over to face the other half of the meager congregation.

"Jesus never said this world would be free of trials. He said, 'Be of good cheer, for I have overcome the world.' Jesus never claimed our walk with Him would be protected from grief and anguish. He said, 'I will never leave you nor forsake you.'"

The man returned to the center isle and smiled knowingly at his flock. "How often we cry, complain, and fuss over the pain of life, begging God to mercifully remove us from the situation. But He doesn't—because of 'the Fall,' because sin and rebellion has ushered pain through the door of our lives. So you naturally ask, 'What then do we do with our hurt, with our pain, with our despair?' Simple . . ." The preacher looked up to the high ceiling and raised both hands just above his head. "You *surrender* it to the Lord. Ask Him to touch it, to heal it." He lowered his arms. "*Then* the pain will lessen, transform into something beautiful, as He sees fit." The man paused to dab his eyes again.

Daniel wasn't sure how much more of the message he could take before the dam broke. He was on the verge of weeping, and his heart ached painfully so—to the point he thought it would burst inside of him.

The pastor went back to his platform and looked over the listeners. "You see, God is a perfect gentleman. He will never barge His way into your life. He longs to bless you, but you must *ask* for Him to enter. You must ask for His presence, His power, and His love. You may not realize it, but God loves you so much that He risked everything by giving you a free will, so you could choose whether or not you wanted Him in your life. He will never alter that principle, nor transgress it—even though He has the astonishing power to lift you to His throne in an instant!" He snapped his finger. "He could compel you to stand before Him to witness His awesome splendor." His voice raised with the expressive declaration. "But that's not His way."

Then he looked meekly at them again. "No, . . . God will never force you to want Him. But, even more incredible than that, He will never give up calling you. You see, He desires to have a close relationship with you. And He longs for you to be healed of the pain. He longs to comfort, to guide, to strengthen and rebuild the broken places."

The pastor switched his Bible opening to a different section and lifted it up to read.

"Before we dismiss, I want to leave you with one more scripture, from Jeremiah, chapter 18." The audience followed suit in locating the passage.

The word which came to Jeremiah from the Lord, saying: "Arise and go down to the potter's house, and there I will cause you to hear My words." Then I went down to the potter's house, and there he was making something at the wheel. And the vessel that he made of clay was marred in the hand of the potter; so he made it again into another vessel, as it seemed good to the potter to make. Then the word of the Lord came to me, saying: "O house of Israel, can I not do with you as this potter?" says the Lord. "Look, as the clay is in the potter's hand, so are you in my hand."

The pastor closed his Bible and looked forthrightly at the group. "*You* are still in God's hand. Maybe you have become marred by life in the process, but God has not given up on you. He will remold your life. He desires to bless you and use your life. Let His hand shape you as He sees fit. Trust Him, for He can make something beautiful from something broken."

Then he bowed his head for a brief prayer, "Lord, let no one leave here tonight still carrying the pain of the past, for You came to heal the brokenhearted. Set them free to find Your good purpose, and Your will for their future. Amen." He then invited anyone who wanted personal prayer to come forward.

Daniel couldn't move. His broken heart was laid open, vulnerable, exposed, deeply in need of mending.

He closed his eyes and no longer fought the tears. They streaked down his face, washing away a year of anguish and bitterness with each cleansing stream. He turned his palms open in a sign of surrender and dropped his head in his hands. Then he wept. "Forgive me, Lord. Forgive me for blaming You, for not trusting You when You loved me all along. Help me, please, to forgive myself for failing."

Low sobs coursed from his aching soul. Daniel placed his agony and despair into the hands of a caring, healing God. Finally, the burden of untold grief began to lift and disappear.

He heard people file past quietly, but none disturbed him. When Daniel's weeping relented, he finally dared lift his head. The room was empty. Most of the lights were off, except for one on the front wall, illuminating the cross, and another dim one that lit the exit from the sanctuary.

Daniel wiped his face and took a deep breath. As he did, he sensed a distinct tranquility from outside of him enfolding him. The notable presence and overwhelming peace was wonderful. It soothed *all* areas of his soul. He relaxed in the pew and let it wash over him in healing waves.

The last time he'd felt remotely peaceful was after praying at Andrew's side on Christmas morning. Before then, it had been years.

"Excuse me—young man?" A kind, elderly woman's voice broke into his placid state.

"Yes?" He looked into her remarkable eyes—they were the purest blue, clearer than the waters on a tropical beach, and emanating love. It felt refreshing just to look into them.

"I'm sorry to disturb you, son." She sat beside him and placed her warm, aged hand on his hand. The contact surprised him with another peculiar emission of love. He could actually sense it radiating from her hand. "Do you own a fancy black car?" she asked pointedly.

"Yes—it's in the ditch, I know. I came in to use the church phone to call a tow truck."

She raised her eyebrows and almost smiled. "I don't know what you're referring to—it's sitting right out front. You will need to move it, though. That is a fire zone; we can't let anyone park there." She patted his hand and got up to leave.

Daniel blinked, politely withholding his correction of her information. He followed her through the lobby and out the locked church doors, certain the old lady was talking about someone else's car . . . until he stepped out of the building.

There—parked in front, just as she had said—was his Lexis, evidenced by some grass and leaves stuck to the front bumper. He stood in amazement and gaped at his car.

The elderly lady teetered down the steps, pulled on her gloves, and turned to wave at him. "Goodbye, Daniel. Happy New Year!" she called while she ambled along the sidewalk.

He was still dumbfounded but had the presence of mind to wave back, assuming her home must be within walking distance. He stared at the car again.

Suddenly the realization hit of her calling him by name. "Hey, how did you know my—" He looked in the direction she'd headed, but she had rounded the high bushes on the corner.

The bells in the tower above him immediately rang their grand toll, declaring the new year. Startled, he covered his ears from the loud peal, then descended the stairs to catch up to the elderly woman. But when he turned the corner she was gone. He looked every which way of the intersection of roads but, other than the church, there wasn't anything around. No houses, no cars.

And no old lady.

He recalled they were the last and only two to leave the locked building. She couldn't have been whisked away in a car in a split second; he'd have seen or heard the car. In fact, *his* car was the only one around—miraculously rescued from the ditch, at that! He marveled at the reality of it.

Daniel was at a loss to fully understand what had happened. He realized there was no other explanation than divine intervention. He shook his head at the incredulous event and breathed out a sigh with elation and relief. Then he gave a soft laugh.

"Thank you, Lord!" He felt true praise rise from his spirit. "I see, now, that you are *still* in the business of angels and miracles!"

Chapter Thirty

K ate finally reached the phone on the sixth ring, after smacking her hand on the nightstand corner while trying to turn on her bedside lamp. She rubbed the sore spot as she answered.

"Hmm—'ello?" she groggily mumbled into the receiver and propped herself up onto her shoulder with her pillow.

"Hi, it's Daniel. Happy New Year."

Her jaw fell open as her eyes finally focused on the bright red numbers of the digital clock glaring 1:00 a.m. "Daniel, do you realize—"

"I know, it's late—in fact, it's very late. I just hope it's not too late," he rambled on, his voice reflecting a dual tone of joy and urgency.

Kate moaned softly. Though she didn't drink alcohol, she wondered if Daniel had gone out for the evening depressed and gotten himself drunk at a New Year's Eve party. "Are you all right? Do you need a cab or something?"

"I've never been better! I need to see you."

"Huh? Fine. I'll call you back later, when I get up."

"No, I *have* to talk to you. Right away."

"Now? You're joking."

"I'm very serious," he stated tenderly.

"Daniel, I can't—I mean, I'm sleeping here. It's the middle of the night!"

"I won't take no for an answer. And I promise, you won't be disappointed. At least, I'm confident you won't," he added.

Kate really moaned this time. "Where are you?"

"About two blocks from your house. I'm calling from the gas station on the corner of 216th and Cedarwood."

She sat up in bed. "You're already *here?*"

"I'll wait if you need some time to . . . well, get dressed and all."

"I am dressed!" She huffed, wondering where his mind was trailing. "But I'm not presentable, so give me fifteen minutes. Not a minute sooner, or I won't open the door."

"Fair enough. See ya." He hung up with a click.

Kate placed the receiver back on the stand and sighed. She really wanted to sneak in a few more minutes of sleep, but she knew she would never wake up before he arrived. So, she dragged herself out of bed, freshened up in the bathroom, then brushed her hair and teeth. She changed from her silky nightgown into sweats and then padded into the kitchen to put the teakettle on. *What is this all about, Lord?* she wondered, totally baffled by Daniel's call.

Something had changed. His choice of words, his tone of urgency, his excitement—it all painted a bizarre picture. One very peculiar for a conservative, non-spontaneous man like Daniel Brakken!

About the time he was expected, Kate went to turn on the front porch light. Then she padded in her pink slippers into the kitchen to prepare two cups of tea. She owed him a raincheck on the tea, anyway, from Christmas. And they may as well visit a while, since she was up and dressed.

Not too long, she coached herself. She needed to be back at the hospital by 8:00 to set up and host the all-day benefit with carousel rides and zoo animal pictures. As it was, she'd been in bed for less than two hours, after sorting and recording eleven thousand dollars in donations and pledges.

Kate jolted to a stance at the thought of the money. The box overflowing with the mass of paperwork and donations was sitting on the couch, right by the door. Daniel would see them for sure once he walked inside. She needed to hide them.

She shuffled back to the living room just as Daniel was approaching her door. They saw one another clearly through the large picture window behind the couch. He gave a polite wave and moved to the front of the door.

Out of time, Kate grabbed the afghan off the back of the couch and, attempting to not be seen by him through the window, she draped it over the box. Then she opened the door for him.

"Hi, Daniel."

"Good morning," he responded gratefully.

His soft, honey-colored gaze roamed over her like he'd waited a lifetime to see her. Kate went weak in the knees. On more than one occasion before, she'd been attracted by the handsome qualities in Daniel. But, tonight there was something more appealing in him—a deeper luring. Something more revealing. Sincere. No longer brusque.

Intimate. Her heartbeat raced with the impression. She offered to hang up his coat.

He removed it and stepped close to hand it to her. "Thanks for doing this," he said above a whisper.

She smiled tiredly and attempted to collect her thoughts, which kept wandering down to his lips. "You didn't exactly give me a choice, remember?"

"I'm sorry. I know this is rude—waking you. But I want you to know that I appreciate your indulging me."

Kate nodded, feeling very drawn toward the man who *looked* like Daniel, but was not behaving like him. "It's OK. Come on in the kitchen; I made that tea we canceled at Christmas."

She brought two steaming cups to the table and sat down. He settled in the chair beside her—near her. She regarded the soft blue/green/gold plaid pattern on his thick flannel shirt. She had always liked seeing flannel on a man, the way it softly covered his broad shoulders was . . .

Kate realized her mind was drifting again, and she reigned in her musings. Briefly closing her eyes for extra focus, she sipped her tea. The cinnamon, chicory root, ginger, and other spices awakened her nostrils.

He sipped his along with her in a moment of shared silence. Then, she waited for him to explain.

Daniel glanced at her twice, obviously ambivalent about beginning the talk. After a few minutes, Kate grew sleepy with his silence. She covered her yawn. "Do you want to think about it while I go take a nap?" she attempted to break the ice.

He grinned, innocently embarrassed for stalling. "No. There's just so much. I don't know where to start."

She rested her chin into a propped-up palm. "How about with whatever happened after I left your office today."

"Right." His face lost the innocent look and became very serious. "I stayed fairly late, until about 11:00."

"That is *really* late. How come?" She winced sympathetically. "You aren't that backlogged are you?"

"No—not really." He dropped his head and talked. "I guess I tried to work, but I couldn't. Andrew's chart wreaked havoc on my concentration. I thought over and over about what you said—about his condition and winning the battle I'm in. As the hours ticked by I felt caged, furious with the whole thing. I guess I knew deep inside that I wanted to help Andrew, but—for some reason—I couldn't go back to surgery. I couldn't take that chance. And I didn't know what was stopping me!"

He paused and shook his head sideways. "I had always taken the most challenging route, before. . . ." He seemed hindered by reflection, like the memory was too painful. "Now, I was being pulled in two directions: Heart one way, and my head—rather, my fears—the other. It was excruciating."

He met Kate's gaze. She saw the expression of hurt in his eyes.

"What do you mean, it *was* excruciating?" she asked. "Has something changed? I mean, you seem different. You certainly act different. And you talk—well, like someone else." She tried to be frank without insulting him.

"I know." He nodded, leaned forward, and looked candid. "The most incredible thing happened to me tonight—it was a miracle!"

Her heart beat excitedly at his statement. She tilted her head forward and opened her eyes wider, curious over what he experienced. "A what?"

"Kate, I will never doubt God's love again."

Obviously, Kate was not expecting to hear those words, for she stared dubiously back at Daniel. He thought she would never believe him. He couldn't blame her for doubting his sincerity. After all, it was difficult even for him to admit such a dramatic change in heart within such a short time.

"Did you say *God?*" she finally spoke.

"Yes—God. The everlasting, omnipotent King and Lord of the universe. *Him.* I will never doubt His love again." He sipped his tea again.

She blinked, then sighed, then chuckled softly. "Wow—this is too . . . You don't . . . I mean, I didn't know that you believed in God. . . . *Do you?*"

He nodded. "Believing He exists is one thing. Trusting Him with your life is totally another."

She smiled, seemed pleased with his insight. "You're right. A lot of people 'believe' in God, but it's not the same. Only those who've trusted in Him have been touched by Him. You have really experienced something tonight!" She grinned.

He nodded eagerly.

"So, *that's* the change in you. How did it happen?"

"God chased me into a ditch."

Kate started laughing but immediately stopped herself and sobered her expression. "I'm sorry. He did what?"

"I was driving home and the roads were a little icy. I was careful, but when I passed a church I got preoccupied with the sermon caption on the reader board. That's when I coasted headlong into the ditch, where the road turns."

She smiled at him. He knew she found it a little amusing.

"I realize it sounds funny, but I was irate with God. I felt tired of being His little pawn that He toyed with from above, knowing every once in a while He would trip me up, just to see how I would deal with it."

Kate shook her head, looking pitiful. She replied, "No, God is *not* like that. He loves you."

He nodded in agreement. "I realize that now. But as warped as my concept was, it's what I was believing beneath all my pain and my confusion. I was hurt and thought God didn't care—that He was playing us all like pieces in a game, merely watching how we would react when things didn't go our way. *Now,* I understand how wrong my thinking was. I'm embarrassed to say I believed He abandoned me when I messed up—when my successful practice washed down the drain. In truth, I was the one that left Him. In my misery, I blamed Him and walked away from His love and His comfort, away from any relationship with Him."

Kate looked suddenly curious. "So how did you get here?"

"Well, that's the strange part. I left my car in the ditch and went into the church to call for a tow truck. They were having one of those midnight services for New Year's. Unless I was willing to make a scene, I was forced to wait until they were done. So I sat in the back pew and listened. But while I was there this wonderful presence draped all around me. I first felt it when I walked in the doors. Then it increased, until it reached inside of me."

"The pastor began speaking on healing your past as the key to your future. Every word he said seemed like it was sent straight from heaven to me. By the time he was done with his brief message I was a wreck, sobbing my eyes out. But it felt good—it was right. I knew I needed to surrender again, to trust God again with my life. I've been running from Him a long time, blaming Him for my pain. I was offended by what happened in my practice. I wanted Him to chase me down and apologize for treating me like a puppet. Tonight, I realized it's better we turn toward Him when we're hurting, instead of daring Him to bowl us over to get our attention."

She gave him a crooked smile. "So that's why you ended up in the ditch."

"Exactly."

"What then?" She drew in a long swallow of her tea.

He watched her mouth draw the liquid in. For a moment it snagged his full attention. Finally, he recalled his thought.

"Then, this old lady approached me and asked me if it was my car outside—except she wasn't really a lady."

Kate's expression turned sour. "You mean she was a man?"

"No, . . . she was an angel," he answered firmly. "She was different from a normal, human woman. Her eyes were the purest crystal blue I've ever seen, and—I know this sounds weird—but I could feel the love of God in them. It was noticeable! Her hands, too! She patted my hand when she stood to leave, and I felt this awesome love flowing through her hand. Believe me, I realize it is very strange! But, I know it happened."

"I don't doubt it for a minute, Daniel. I've never seen an angel—at least, that I realized was one, anyway. But I firmly believe they are all around us. Just like the Bible describes. They continually help us to serve God and to do His will. And they protect us from spiritual enemies."

He agreed with her. "So, I told the old lady yes, my car was in the ditch, and that I came in to use the church phone to call for a tow. But she claimed my car was parked in a fire zone out front, and that I needed to move it! Then, she smiled at me—you know, like people do when they are pulling your leg or planning to surprise you. I figured she was mistaken, so I followed her outside. There was my car parked right in front, just as she'd said!"

"Maybe someone pulled it out for you while you were praying after the service?"

"I wondered the same thing, but there wasn't time. I only stayed for about fifteen minutes. Besides, I thought, how would they know for sure that the car's owner was in the church? Why would they park it in the fire zone, instead of on the side of the road. And, if they had pulled it out, they would have stripped my gear, because it wasn't in neutral. Yet it drove just fine."

"It does sound pretty unusual," Kate added.

"Yeah! But what convinced me it was a miracle was the angel. She watched me recognize my car. Then she said, 'Goodbye, Daniel,' and walked around the corner of the bushes in front of the church sidewalk. I hadn't told anyone there my name. So, I hustled after her. Too late—she was gone in a split second!"

Kate looked surprised. "Really?"

"Yes! I'm sure she removed my car from the ditch after everyone had left—seconds after I prayed and placed my life back in God's hands."

Kate nodded, cupping her hand over his, softly. "Thanks for sharing this with me, Daniel." The heat from her touch and the way she looked at him lit Daniel with fireworks. Her simple compliment touched every nerve in him, and roused the desire to kiss her, just as it had a week ago. This time he wondered if it would be worth the risk. He felt something in his heart for her now that he'd never felt for any other woman. It made him bashful to think it was love, but he couldn't imagine it being anything else.

He gazed at his tea and stroked his finger around the rim of his cup with his free hand, not daring to remove the other one from her warmth. "You were the first person that came to mind. I knew you would understand, and be happy to hear about it."

"I am." Kate smiled, then gradually pulled her hand back.

Kiss her, his heart entreated, this time with a dire pull to follow through. But the ridiculous thing was, Daniel wasn't used to following his heart. In fact, he wasn't used to any of the passions that were bombarding him right now.

A moment of silence lapsed. He raised his cup and drained the last swallow. "Well, I'd better get going and let you sleep. Thank you, Kate."

Kiss her! The desire entreated him again, this time with a dire urgency to it.

He leaned forward, raising up to scoot back his chair. Kate's face was so close at that moment, Daniel felt something inside him kick into gear. He seized the opportunity. He tilted her chin and kissed her quick, but soft—just to the side of her lips.

She touched her mouth. She just stared at him, speechless. He didn't know how to interpret her response, so he figured he'd made a wrong choice. Heat filled his face. He turned to leave the kitchen, embarrassed.

Kate followed him and met him in front of the coat closet. She hesitated by the door. "Daniel, . . . what are you planning to do . . . now that things have taken on a turn?"

He looked at her matter-of-factly. "I'm not certain what you mean exactly, but I am planning to do one more surgery. Hopefully, Andrew and his parents will let me."

"And then? What will happen at the hospital?"

"Doing one operation won't change everything else. I haven't contemplated any long-range plans to return to practice. Just this one, for Andrew."

She appeared disheartened, as though it wasn't the answer she had hoped for.

"Kate, my offer from Christmas still stands, though. . . . I really want you to reconsider your resignation. The hospital needs you, the kids need you. . . ." He stepped closer to her and brushed a tendril of her auburn hair away from her face, stroking the velvety pad of her cheek with the gesture. "And I need you," he added tenderly, hoping to persuade her. He gazed intensely at her, unsure of how to convey what he was feeling any other way.

Now the look in her eyes bordered on heartache. The last time he had raised this subject she'd fled from the room in tears. This time—though she was clearly hurting from his proposal—she stood firm.

"And what about the carousel, Daniel? Are you going to reconsider?"

On that point, he knew he was pegged. Not only had Daniel already paid Jerry Nabor the nonrefundable deposit to reserve the auction date, but he'd also hired a teardown crew, scheduled to arrive the day after New Year's to haul the carousel away, piece by piece.

Even more obligating, per Daniel's request Nabor had done considerable last minute advertising, announcing the auction in multiple city newspapers across the Northwest and on the Internet. He claimed four to five hundred people would show, at a minimum, with such a full set of pieces for sale.

Backing out of it seemed impossible. He couldn't, though he deeply wanted to remove the pain he could see in Kate's eyes.

The pain he had caused.

He offered the only response he could, the most lamentable expression he could manifest. Silently, he hoped she would see his deep-seated remorse, because he didn't know how to answer her.

Kate closed her eyes and turned to retrieve his coat. "That's what I thought," came her emotion-choked reply.

Daniel's insides were really tearing him apart now.

She handed him the leather garment and stood before him, visibly in anguish. "Goodbye, Daniel."

Chapter Thirty-One

*T*he next morning, Kate drove to the hospital in a mental fog. She hadn't fallen asleep until well after 3:00 a.m. Then, she'd slept fitfully through a strange recurring dream:

The hospital was on fire and the carousel burned down. The fire spread fiercely until it threatened the lives of the children. Kate was trying to save the children, but she couldn't do such a feat by herself. And yet, no one else was there. She screamed for help while the conquesting fire continued to spread, but no one came to her aid. Then, finally, an approaching fire truck blared its emergency horn with an elongated blast. It sounded and sounded incessantly and wouldn't quit. . . .

Kate then woke up to see it wasn't a fire engine horn at all, but the blaring of her alarm clock. She reached over and shut it off, releasing a heavy sigh of relief at the returned silence.

She knew she'd gone to bed worried and upset over the state of the carousel, so it made sense that she dreamed it was in danger. But, what really disturbed her was dreaming that the children were also in jeopardy!

Her spirit was troubled. She prayed about whether the dream was a signal from God, warning her that the safety or tragedy of the children somehow rested in her hands. If Kate's presence at the hospital played that critical of a role, it would stand to reason the children were at stake, since no one else came to their rescue in her dream.

Daniel had pleaded with her to stay at the hospital—told her frankly that the children needed her, that they all needed her. And she had turned down his request—twice—focusing only on her problems and inconveniences, without realizing what impact her leaving would have on everyone else.

Now she became very worried. She prayed as she drove to TLC, "Lord, if this is a dream from You, please give me wisdom. Show me what I must do—no matter what it costs. I don't want the children to suffer."

She felt better, immediately, just by placing her concerns in God's sovereign hand, and asking Him to guide her.

She soon arrived at the hospital. Kate was thrilled to see the large crowd already convening outside the door next to the carousel's dome. It wasn't quite 8:00 a.m., and they weren't due to start the benefit rides until 9:00, but there were already close to seventy people lined up with kids. Kate couldn't see the need to make them wait so long. As soon as the volunteers showed and a donation table was set up, the Miracle Machine could go to work.

Carrying her box of contributions, she walked past the crowded lineup, relating to sections of people that it wouldn't be long before they got started. She hurried inside and turned toward the Admin. wing, where she'd asked all the benefit helpers to meet. Well before she rounded the corner to Administration, she heard lots of excited voices.

People filled the entire hallway. Kate was stunned by the considerable show of support! Not only were volunteers and staff members *en masse*, but they brought others to assist, as well. She pulled a chair out of the office and stood upon it for visibility. Whistling loudly, she brought the troops to silence.

"I don't know how to thank you for coming today." She smiled gratefully. "In fact, there are so many here, we may not have anything for some of you to do—except spend your money." They all laughed. "So I'll start by asking you to divide into two groups: If you want to help with the carousel, please move to the right wall. If you want to help with the zoo, please go to the left. If you don't have a preference, we will need about twice as many helpers with the carousel."

The mass noisily divided into two uneven groups, then Kate quieted them again. "Great! Now, I need to know if Harriet and Zinnia are here." She scanned faces for the women.

"Over here!" Harriet called out and waved a dark arm from behind the carousel's grouping.

"O, yez!" Zinnia also waved from the center of the zoo crowd.

"Terrific!" Kate said. "I have cash boxes and receipt books to give both of you." The two women wove their way forward to reach for their supplies. Kate called out again, "Now, everyone in the carousel crew, you'll need to follow Harriet. Those with the zoo team, Zinnia will be organizing the petting zoo pictures." They were all ready and eager to start.

"Let the benefit begin!" She dismissed them with a rousing cheer. They matched it with a brief roar of applause and hoorays. Slowly, the masses migrated from the crowded Admin. wing to their stations of choice.

Kate made rounds each hour, checking in with both Harriet and Zinnia, emptying their cash boxes, and keeping on top of the multiple questions raised by people.

It was also good that they started early, she thought. At 9:00 a.m., the line had increased to three rows deep in a switchback filling the dome's outside courtyard. By noon, it was up to ten rows. The zoo lines were similarly increasing but shorter. Not once did Kate see the lines diminish at either station. People must have come from all over the surrounding region!

Thank you, Lord! She praised Him for moving hearts to come. She was extra grateful for the added blessing of temperate weather. The sky remained light gray, but it wasn't raining. If it had, the turnout would have been reduced by half, she was positive.

"How's it going, captain?" Jocelyn walked in on Kate and caught her off guard as she was locking up another batch of money in the Admin. office.

"Hey!" Kate said with a grin, then glanced at her watch. "It's only 2:30. Aren't you supposed to be in bed, still?"

"Who can sleep when the carousel is in peril?" she countered in her usual humorous but caring way.

"You're right about that." Kate recalled her own sleepless night. The dream unsettled her whenever it surfaced in her mind.

Jocelyn looked discerningly at Kate. "Yeah, I can tell by the bags under your eyes that I still got more rest than you."

"My mind was working overtime."

"No kidding. So—what's our count look like?"

"We just broke the hundred thousand mark."

"That's great!" Jocelyn raved.

"It's fair. We're still behind the goal," Kate commented.

"Where should we be by now?"

Kate winced. "About double."

Jocelyn gave her a sympathetic smile. "Hmm. That's a ways yet."

"I figure we'll pull another thirty-six thousand before the end of the day, then see what comes in through mail and call-ins the remainder of the week. If we get fifty thousand more by Friday evening, we'll be close enough that I can buy back the base and a good number of figures—that is, if the auction prices don't climb too high." Kate sighed, and let her head drop.

Jocelyn lifted Kate's chin with a finger, "Hey—don't worry. Something is going to work out. OK? God has never let this hospital suffer, because we have always put Him first. We trust Him to supply our needs."

Kate smiled. "Thanks, Joce."

Jocelyn winked. "Anytime."

By the end of the day, two hours after the original closing time due to the long lines of people, Kate and Jocelyn counted—and recounted—the donations.

"That's one hundred seventy-five thousand, plus—confirmed," Jocelyn said.

"Good," Kate answered. "We covered some extra ground with the extended hours. Now we'll wait out the week."

Kate thanked her friend and hugged her goodbye. Then she locked the money in the safe again, shut off the lights, and locked up the office. She went home expended from the tiring day, but she felt that a burden had lifted from her heart. Now that most of the money had been raised, she could finally relax a little until the auction next Saturday.

She prayed for God's favor on the hospital's funds.

Then she prayed fervently for Him to show her if she should stay at TLC.

Early on Monday morning, Daniel called the Medical Licensing Department of the Washington State Board and Certification Office to inquire about the process of transferring his surgical license. *Amazingly*, it turned out to be a very simple procedure because his former license to practice had not yet expired. With just a faxed, signed application and a fee charged to his credit card, he was back to neurosurgery—in a snap!

Whoa! Daniel thought, reclining in his office chair, ruminating on the ease of the transaction. It was practically too easy. In fact, he'd been so stunned by the newer, quicker procedures that he'd asked the rep lady on the phone, twice, if she was giving him the correct information. She assured him that was all he had to do, since his license was still current.

Finally, he was content to believer her, and he thanked the Lord for the pleasant surprise.

Since he'd made peace with God, though, everything seemed to be riding with the sail of his desires, instead of against them. Or, maybe it was his desires being in line with God's will now that caused things to flow more smoothly.

He was certain the latter was the reason. Either way, it was much more favorable than the way things had performed over the last year in seclusion.

Another incident that happened fast enough to make him dizzy was the sale of his California beach house. The interested buyers had become anxious when Daniel stalled on their offer, and they raised it by ten thousand—switching their offer to full cash payment! He was astounded! Somebody wanted that beach house a lot worse than he did. Daniel had enjoyed the beautiful home and location, but he knew he would never see this liberal sized offer again.

Beyond the money, though, something inside encouraged him to pounce on the bid. He was sure that the keen impression he was feeling was God's way of leading him, of showing him the path for his life, just as He promised his followers in the Bible.

So Daniel had taken the offer. In a couple of days, his bank would be very happy having him as a customer.

Now, I need your help with something else, Lord, he prayed, knowing he would talk to Andrew's parents soon. He had to get their permission to perform the brain stem operation before mentioning anything to Andrew. If they wouldn't agree, there was no sense getting the boy's hopes up.

But, prior to seeing them, he needed to regain Kate's support. *Especially* after his pathetic and calloused act this morning!

While he'd been on the phone with the real-estate agent and the buyers, his teardown crew had arrived. Insensitive to how she would be hurt, Daniel had instructed Kate to show them where the carousel was housed. She was visibly displeased with him for being unavailable due to the conference call. Then, she'd accused him of cornering her into "carrying out his dirty work."

From Daniel's perspective, he was merely wrapping up important final arrangements—long distance. He wasn't about to hang up on them just to direct a work crew down the hall a ways.

Nevertheless, he now felt heartless and guilty over it, and he knew he'd have to make it up to her somehow. Though the notion seemed impossible while she was irate with him! At best, rapport between them had been minimal and tense since his visit New Year's morning. Now he wouldn't be surprised if she refused to speak to him.

It'd serve you right, he cajoled himself. *You can't win her heart while you're busy stomping on it.* His own admonishment added shame to Kate's earlier rebuke. He feared bringing out the worst in her by approaching her now for a favor. Regardless, he had to talk with her right away, to find out if she would visit Andrew's parents with him, this afternoon.

He approached her desk. "Kate, may I see you in my office for a few minutes—please?"

He received a glower, but at least it was tempered. "Fine," she muttered her compliance.

She entered after him and stood rigidly beside the desk. He closed the door behind her and backed up against it. He wasn't going to let her leave without reaching a partial reconciliation.

Daniel looked apologetically at her. "I'm *very* sorry about the teardown crew this morning. You're right—it was something I should have dealt with. But honestly, I could not postpone that conference call this morning. It was just bad timing, and I apologize for putting you through a difficult situation."

She regarded him rigidly, without a hint of forgiveness. "Daniel, you have no idea how horrible that was for me. My grandfather—actually, my only real 'father' in the world—rebuilt that carousel with me at his side, since I was a child." Her eyes conveyed emotional anguish. "It was hard enough to accept that you were tearing this away from me—and from all of us who love it so much. But, it was entirely too painful to take part in!" Her voice rose with condemnation.

Now she wouldn't look at him. He felt even more despicable after her reply. A snake had more pride at that moment.

He tried to sound as repentant and sorrowful as he felt. "Kate, I realize more than ever that this machine has meant a great deal to you. What I don't know is how I can reconcile this issue. I want to—believe me! It just doesn't seem possible." He paused, then added, "Isn't there *someplace* where we can meet in the middle?"

"Not that I've found," she stated flatly but less harsh than before.

"Then . . . I beg your forgiveness. I never wanted to hurt you. Please—will you forgive me?"

Her tears flowed at his appeal. Daniel retrieved a tissue box from the shelf above his desk and drew out sheets for her. She went through several before speaking again.

"That . . . is going to . . . take some time," she answered in a shaky voice.

"I understand," he conceded, then fell silent. He waited patiently for her streaming emotions to subside.

When she was more collected, he finally mentioned, "There's something else I need to discuss with you, Kate. I am going to Andrew's home this afternoon to talk to his parents about the operation procedure . . . and I want you to come with me."

She appeared uncertain and curious. "What's the advantage of having me there?"

"Plenty. You've known his parents longer, and you know Andrew better. Why, you even know the hospital inside and out. They will feel a trust, a *bond* with you, that they don't yet have with me."

"I guess so." She sniffled.

"However," he continued, "for this meeting to be successful, I will need you to act favorably on my behalf—regardless of what a despicable, insensitive jerk I've been recently."

She gaped at him, then chuckled on hearing his self-chastisement. "I hate to admit that I agree with your analysis."

He nodded, still serious. "Can I count on you, for Andrew's sake?"

She paused, looked in his eyes a few moments longer. "Yes. What time do we leave?"

"2:00."

"I'll be ready." She dropped her arms and waited at the door for him to move aside.

"And Kate . . ."

"Hmm?"

"For all the pain that I've caused you, I'm going to make it up to you. *Somehow*. I don't know how, but I promise I will find a way. God help me."

Her expression softened, her eyes misted over again. She didn't smile, but nodded to acknowledge him.

"No! Not another operation!" Mrs. Tucker asserted, obviously unnerved at the mention of the procedure. Her lip began to quiver. She wrung her thin hands together. "I can't take any more."

Daniel had faced this sensitive situation before. Parents who'd been through the mill—way beyond the average—almost always hit a ceiling. They often felt they could not go on. *Unless* something gave them hope.

"I know you're afraid for Andrew, Mrs. Tucker. I know you want what's best for him. All I can say is, I think . . ." he paused, still trying to regain the confidence he once exuberated in the profession. "I can almost guarantee that I will succeed in removing eighty to ninety percent of the tumor with this newer procedure. It's already been accomplished in my practice various times. Chemotherapy would, of course, still follow the operation. Though, I advise against doing radiation treatment on younger children. It can seriously harm their growth pattern. Also, my fee will be completely waived, if that is a concern for you."

Mrs. Tucker started weeping.

Mr. Tucker held her hand, then he spoke up. "It's not the money, and it's not that we don't think you are sincere, Dr. Brakken. We just feel that we've put Andrew through too much already. And for all the effort and pain, it only buys a little time for him. No kid should have to live like that." His eyes welled up also.

"I couldn't agree with you more, Mr. Tucker. That is why I pursued this method of removal. It's called Laser Extraction Duo-Therapy. It involves two lasers and is more aggressive on the tumor mass. Yet, it is far safer than cutting. The former procedures that Andrew underwent have not been used in my practice for almost half a decade. I've been utilizing other laser techniques for five years now. But LEDT removal is even more effective. And, provided we have no complications, I think Andrew will gain several years of fairly normal life, possibly even reach adulthood without many problems, if any. Some of my kids made it into their twenties before needing further treatment. By that time, they tolerate radiation better, which can more effectively combat tumor growth than chemotherapy alone.

Mr. Tucker looked at Mrs. Tucker, a faint willingness to try evident on his face. It was apparent to Daniel that Andrew's mom was having a much harder time agreeing to another surgery.

Daniel softly added, "I know you must feel like you've done this before, but I'm telling you the honest truth: His previous surgeries haven't covered the same territory as this one. According to Andrew's file, his other operations debulked only between sitxty to seventy percent of the tumor. Of course, I won't know for sure until I'm inside, but I'm confident this approach will reach ninety percent—maybe more. It's well worth trying, for Andrew's sake. I wouldn't suggest it, otherwise."

Mrs. Tucker continued to shake her head no.

Daniel felt the tension rising in the air. He'd hit a stalemate. He glanced at Kate, tried to convey through desperate eyes his frustration over the meeting's impeded progress.

Kate nodded modestly, in agreement. "Mrs. Tucker, I have known Andrew as long as he's been at our hospital. From what I know about him, he's always been a fighter. That's why we call him Champ. He always tells the other kids to never, *ever* give up. And he prays all the time for a miracle to make him well." She paused, hoping the family had some faith in God. "Maybe *this* is the answer to Andrew's prayers."

Mrs. Tucker looked at Kate. A spark of hope glinted in her eyes. She then gaped at Daniel. "Dr. Brakken, are you certain this will work?" she nearly demanded a guarantee.

That was the *one* question he hadn't missed during his sabbatical from surgery. He sighed deeply. "Nothing is for certain, Mrs. Tucker. But Andrew's chance of surviving five to ten years after this procedure is pretty good—maybe longer. I believe I can safely get him to that point. And, I would be grateful for the honor of trying." He regarded her earnestly. "But . . . beyond that, I can't promise miracles. Those are only for God to grant."

Mrs. Tucker looked suddenly resigned, peaceful. "OK. How soon can you do it?" she asked.

"Yes," Mr. Tucker added, "when can you help him?"

Daniel swallowed, surprised by the turnaround. He stared at Kate with relief, then smiled gratefully at Andrew's parents.

"Right now, he's my only patient," Daniel replied. "You pick the day."

"Hi, Champ," Kate roused Andrew from his drugged, drowsy state. Daniel stood across the boy's bed from her. "Andrew, Mr.—that is—Dr. Brakken wants to talk with you for a minute. Is that all right?"

Andrew gazed back with sleepy eyes. "Yeah."

Daniel leaned over the railing where Andrew could see him easily. "I'll bet you didn't know I am a doctor, huh?" he asked.

Andrew rolled his head from side to side, indicating no.

"Well, it just so happens that I am a Pediatric Neurosurgeon. Do you know what kind of doctor that is?"

Andrew seemed concerned. Then he nodded for yes.

"Andrew, I have seen your medical charts, and I believe I can extend your life for several years by doing a newer kind of operation on this tumor."

The boy shook his head. "Other . . . doctors . . . tried."

"Yes, I understand. But, you see, I know how to operate on the tumor in a way that some doctors haven't learned yet. I've done it with other kids, just like you, and many of them are doing well today. Would you be willing to let me try?"

Andrew looked to Kate. His widening eyes revealed increasing fear.

She reached for his small hand, trying to think of what to say. "Andrew, do you remember when you told Nurse Jocelyn about a dream you had—the one with Dr. Brakken and the angel?"

Daniel stared curiously at Kate, obviously surprised by her information. She knew it was news to him.

Andrew nodded his confirmation of the dream.

"Well, Nurse Jocelyn and I both believe God gave you that dream to help you trust Dr. Brakken to make you better. Do you remember Dr. Brakken saying in the dream that he would help you?"

"Yes," Andrew answered, then looked back to Daniel. "Are you . . . an angel?" he asked innocently.

Daniel smiled tenderly at the boy, then glanced at Kate. "No, I'm very human." He looked back down at Andrew. "But, I do realize that God sent me to this hospital for very special reasons, and I believe one of those reasons was to help you. Your mom and dad have given their permission to operate. But, I won't do anything unless you say it is alright with you."

The young patient seemed to contemplate it seriously for a few seconds. Kate hoped he would have the courage to endure one more surgery.

Andrew spoke slowly to Daniel, "In my dream . . . you said . . . I will be OK . . . once you help me."

Daniel sighed. "I'm very glad to hear that."

Kate smiled.

"Alright," Andrew replied, "you can . . . help me." He then closed his eyes, showing exhaustion from the conversation.

Kate nodded to Daniel. "We'd better let him rest."

They walked out to the hall, and Kate closed the door.

Daniel nearly fell into the hallway chair beside the room's entrance. He sighed with relief at the outcome. "Thanks, Kate. I was losing that one, too. Without your support, this would have never worked out."

She gave a modest grin. "If it weren't for the dream, I would probably have my own concerns. He's been through so much."

He cocked his head to look up at her. "Yeah—what about this dream? How long ago did he have it?"

"Christmas night."

"And you weren't going to tell me?" he asked, sounding slighted by the concealed incident.

"What difference would it make by telling you? The dream was for Andrew's benefit. If it was truly from God, I knew it would come true. If not, why mention it and raise false hopes?"

He seemed to accept her reasoning, though he still looked a little hurt by her secrecy. "It just would have been nice to know about, beforehand," he emphasized.

Looking him straight in the eye, she calmly said, "Daniel, you weren't ready to hear it before now. You had to find God's direction in your heart, first."

He nodded, spreading a humble smile. "You're right."

Chapter Thirty-Two

K ate sat in Daniel's office, agreeing that he needed to take the next two days to strictly review his medical notes and journals from former surgeries. He also wanted to spend time interviewing and getting acquainted with the team that would assist with Andrew's operation.

She was glad he was focusing all his concentration upon Andrew. It was a safe move, since Daniel hadn't been in an operating room for a year.

But, it also took pressure off of her at the hospital. She was effectively back in charge, and efficiently managing the hospital the way she did best during Henry's final year of service. In one day, she plowed through a week of backlogged items that had piled in Daniel's in-box throughout the holidays. She knew he'd be happy to hear that!

His absence from the office also gave her added privacy to update records on the benefit funding during her personal time, without having to wait until she got home to check a slew of voicemail messages.

The money continued to pile in. She had nearly met the goal of two hundred thousand by noon on Thursday! Grateful for God's provision for the hospital once again, she spent a moment in private prayer before heading back to the office.

"Lord, thank You for all You've done—for Your guidance and Your help. Thank You for touching people's hearts to give money for the carousel. I ask that You give me favor at the auction on Saturday. You know I've done this for the kids. Even though it hurt me to see the carousel taken down, You know my motivation has been for the good of the children. I ask You to crown my efforts with success. Amen."

As she walked to deliver finished departmental reports, she passed kids occasionally—some in wheelchairs, some on crutches, others playing with various items in the carpeted halls. A few just staring out the windows at the rain. She waved or chatted a moment with them as she went, giving each one a tender hug. She needed their love as much as they needed hers. They all held a special place in her heart.

As she turned the corner toward the Admin. wing, something inside of her snapped. Kate couldn't explain what gave way, but it felt like the plug had been pulled on her confidence. It stunned her—halted her in her steps. Remorse washed over her concerning the auction outcome, and she strangely knew that she would *not* be successful.

The imparted knowledge hit her instantly, like an invisible person had whispered it in her ear. The more she tried to shake the perception, the more she recalled the troubling dream she'd had on New Year's morning. If the carousel would really be taken from her grasp, then it was feasible the other part of the dream—about the children being in jeopardy—held a very likely caution: She must stay at TLC.

That insight deeply concerned her!

She had prayed earlier for God's guidance about the dream. Kate now considered whether the deep impression on her spirit was His way of confirming it.

She didn't hesitate to respond. "Lord, I don't understand all of what I'm feeling, or even what I'm supposed to do. But if You show me, I'll obey Your leading. Please show me clearly, so I don't miss Your direction. Please don't let anything happen to the children!"

Thursday evening Kate's telephone rang. She had just finished dinner and was catching a bit of the local news. She turned the volume down and answered the phone. "Hello?"

"Kate. Hi, it's Daniel."

"Well, hello, Dr. Brakken. How are your preparations going?"

"Great. But please—I would really prefer it if you stayed with calling me Daniel. Besides, you're not my patient, and . . . I rather like the way you say my first name."

She smiled. They'd had no contact for over two days, and it felt good to hear his voice—the new one that wasn't tied up with emotional chains of his past. Moreover, it touched her that he liked something personable from her. "OK, Daniel. Are you nervous about tomorrow?"

"I'd be lying if I said no."

"I think everything is going to be fine," she encouraged him. "Plus, you have two extra things going for you this time."

"What are they?"

"One, you have an entire hospital staff praying for you."

"That is terrific! What's the other?"

"You have the knowledge of Andrew's dream."

He paused. "You're really sure it was from God?"

"I believe it was. God is always trying to communicate with people. It's we who aren't cooperating with God, like we should."

"Well, regardless of the dream, I feel better knowing that people are praying. Especially you, Kate."

She paused, collecting her thoughts. "Daniel, I've been praying for you—and about you—since before you arrived at TLC."

"Hmm. Doesn't sound like they were all thankful prayers."

"No, but I'm very grateful for what's happened in your life, and about Andrew, even though I had no idea what the Lord was doing by bringing you to our hospital."

"You're an inspiration to me, Kate. I want you to know that."

"Thanks. That's kind of you to say."

"No—I really mean it. During the times I was struggling the most with my last failure, I would observe you. I wondered how you could stay so together, so on top of everything, despite the trials I was putting you through. After watching your example, I would feel the strength to continue battling my own challenge. You are a blessing to me, Kate. I'm sure that helping Andrew was not the only reason I was sent to Seattle."

She was getting choked up from his sincere compliment. "What—what time do you start tomorrow?"

"We scrub at 7:30 a.m. By the time he's prepped and set up, we should be working on the tumor between 11:00 and 1:00. That's when I'll really need your prayers. I can't be too aggressive near the brain stem, but I have to be aggressive enough to get as much as possible. Besides, . . . that's where I failed last time."

Kate was filled with compassion for him. "What happened, Daniel? You never really explained."

"I pushed the limit. I sensed I shouldn't have gone any farther, but things looked good, medically, so I did. My confidence was soaring, and I wanted to destroy more of the tumor than ever. You see, passion can be a two-edged sword in this profession: It gives you the courage to battle the enemy, but you must master it. Otherwise . . ." He paused. "I lost control over my zeal and went too far. Sammy's blood pressure plummeted. We lost him within minutes." He paused again. "In effect, my zeal took Sammy's life. If I'd held back when I felt I should have, he would be alive."

"*Possibly*," she amended his statement.

"Yeah, well, the hospital board considered my move unwise, and L.A. General paid one million in a settlement to Sammy's parents. Though the act was never deemed reckless, nor did it revoke my license, I was politely asked to leave the hospital because of the liability increase it probably would have caused, had I remained in practice there."

Kate wanted to cry, both for Sammy and Daniel. "I'm very sorry," she managed to say despite the tightness in her throat.

"Me too. It took me a long time to forgive myself—and God, for allowing Sammy to die."

"But you can't expect that will happen with Andrew. If anything, you'll be more careful now."

"That's why I need your prayers—for discernment. I don't want to be too conservative and end up leaving tumor mass that is safe to debulk."

"You have them. I'll ask specifically for God to give you wisdom and show you the *exact* moment to stop."

"Thanks," he said, sounding relieved.

"How long will it take?"

"The entire procedure takes about seven-and-a-half hours. Closer to four hours for just my part."

"That's a long procedure," she marveled at the endurance it must take.

"Especially toward the end, when my muscles start getting tired and sore."

"Daniel, I know you'll do a fine job tomorrow."

"You have a lot of confidence in me, considering you've never seen my work."

She observed the Monarch lion that now commanded the front entrance of her living room. It made her softly laugh. "Oh, yes I have! He's right beside my door, better than a watchdog."

"Who? Oh, him—that's right. To think I tried to keep my profession a secret from you. You actually mentioned once that I was as precisioned as a surgeon." He chuckled. "I guess there's no way to hide who you really are inside, is there?"

"No. It just becomes a lesson in futility."

"How true. Well, I'll call you as soon as I'm done—that is, if you want."

"I look forward to it. I know you will have a good report. So don't worry. You're walking in God's path again," she expressed her faith in divine help as well her assurance over Daniel's ability.

"Thanks, Kate. I look forward to sharing it with you."

Andrew lay on his bed, a little on the edge of sleep in the late evening hours. He watched the star ornament pirouette slowly from the ventilated heat in the room. He was thinking about the operation tomorrow.

He wasn't scared, just a little disappointed. Unable to speak out loud very well, he prayed silently:

I know You know what's best, God. It's just, I was hoping You would do my miracle differently. But if this is the only way, it's OK with me.

Dr. Brakken thinks this operation will be different from the others. I hope so. I really want to go home. I miss my family. Please help Dr. Brakken do a good job. Even though he's not an angel, he says You sent him to help me. That makes me feel better. None of the other doctors said that before. Thanks for sending him.

And, please . . . bless all the other sick children. Amen.

Chapter Thirty-Three

*D*aniel drove to the hospital on Friday morning, an hour earlier than expected. He had wanted to avoid further anxiety by arriving before the traffic madness began on the I-90 bridge.

There was a strange but welcome deep-seated peace in his spirit. But he also sensed a noticeable challenge taking place in his soul, like a contention of wills. For a year he had run from this very thing.

Now he was running toward it.

Over the last several days, his mind rehearsed operating scenes with almost every patient he'd had. The reflection flowed like a stream from his memory banks. He saw how he'd made a difference in many lives, how he'd extended the joy of living, even for those he'd brought only a little time. It was a gift he'd been given to share. A gift of time. A gift that precious few others had to offer these children. With over thirty-five hundred neurosurgeons in the United States, less than fifty were specialized in pediatrics, and far fewer were performing the newer, advantageous techniques.

Daniel parked near the hospital entrance at exactly 6:40 a.m. With nearly fifty minutes before scrub, he went into his office to pray. He sensed there was going to be a difficulty of some nature today. He also sensed that God wanted him to succeed—which meant God's enemies wanted Daniel to fail! They were bound to put up a spiritual fight in his direction.

Humbly, he knelt beside his office chair. "Lord . . . thank You for granting me a fresh start. I know that You are watching over me. Please grant me Your wisdom as I perform this operation. Guide my hands in the right direction. Please guard Andrew from any harm, and bring him through this healthy and strong enough to return home to his family for several years. I'm depending upon You to help me, Lord. In Jesus' name I ask this. Amen."

He then spent a while sitting and reading from a pocket New Testament that he now kept in his desk drawer.

Forty minutes later, Daniel emerged feeling like a warrior heading off to battle. He walked the halls to the operating ward. TLC wasn't big, but they afforded a pair of essential, fully equipped ORs, which—thankfully—had been upgraded the year before the ICU.

He greeted the attending surgeon, the assisting resident, and the three-nurse team. With morning salutations all around, they dressed and then scrubbed. Andrew was brought down, already sedated for pre-op. They wheeled him next to the operating table and, by lifting the sheet beneath him, transferred him from the gurney to the op table.

The scrub nurses unwrapped sterile, stainless steel microsurgical instruments and placed them in perfect rows for easy selection. Then, they placed a pulsoximeter over Andrew's big toe to monitor the level of oxygen in his blood.

Daniel came over to the boy, sterile hands held palms upward, light blue mask and cap on. He wanted to connect with Andrew before they put him under.

"Hi, buddy," he peered down at the boy.

Andrew nodded, his eyes blinked lazily. "Hi."

"Feeling a little drowsy?"

"Yeah."

"That's good. Don't worry. You'll sleep through everything."

"Dr. Brakken, promise me you will—" Andrew couldn't finish the sentence without taking a deep breath.

Daniel's heart raced. *No—Lord, I can't promise life.*

". . . leave some of my hair," he concluded. "Please?"

Daniel smiled and sighed with relief. "I promise I'll leave a lot of hair. I only shave about three inches, OK?"

Andrew smiled, noticeably pleased with Daniel's answer.

Daniel nodded toward the anesthesiologist, and he came over to administer the halothane. Andrew's eyes closed in seconds.

"Let's hook him up," Daniel said, and the attending physician and resident attached electrocardiogram leads to Andrew's chest to monitor his heart activity. Following that, they connected a breathing tube and a respirator. A catheter was carefully inserted, and the boy's eyelids were gently taped shut with salve, a precaution to keep any particles from getting in.

"Time to turn him. Watch the lines," Daniel said.

Once connected to various monitors and support systems, Andrew was carefully turned. His head was propped up onto a headrest and held in place. Pads were placed under his chest and shoulders to allow unrestricted breathing. Finally, a rectangle of brown hair was shaved, and the skin was immediately swabbed with Betadine to ward off infection.

One nurse kept steady watch of the digital monitors, maintaining a sharp eye for any changes in body signals that would mean an immediate need for more or less anesthesia.

By this point, it was two hours into the operation, and Daniel had yet to make an incision. "Wipe," he asked for assistance from the nurse in removing the sweat from his brow.

He reviewed Andrew's recent MRI and CT scans one more time, making sure of the exact location of the tumor.

"Tape on?" he asked, giving the cue to record the operation on video for later instruction to other neurosurgeons and students.

"Rolling," the resident answered with a thumbs-up sign.

Daniel held his right palm open, knowing it was time.

"Scalpel," he directed. The nurse passed the tool to him. He clutched it—but suddenly hesitated.

The room started closing in on him. The beeping monitors grew louder in his ear. He squeezed his eyes shut, fought the whirling fears that mounted.

He prayed silently for help: *Lord Jesus, You are the Master Physician. Help me do this. Guide my every move and tell me when to quit.*

After sending his urgent plea, he opened his eyes again. Strong peace settled like a blanket over his nerves. Andrew was in Daniel's hand, but Daniel knew they were both in God's hand.

"You ready, Dr. Brakken?" the attending physician asked.

"I am. Time?"

"10:52," the head nurse replied.

"OK, team. Let's begin."

Kate grew extremely anxious as 11:00 a.m. approached.

She closed the door of Daniel's office and began pacing inside, praying as she had promised him. She told Lisa to hold all calls because she would be "in a meeting" for the next few hours. And it was true—a meeting with God.

She prayed for everything she could think of: from clear thinking to the right temperature in the room. Having never studied neurosurgical operations, she didn't know what specific needs were the greatest, but her nursing education gave her ideas of what to ask for.

An hour passed. Lisa checked in with Kate. "I'm going for lunch, Miss Montgomery. You want me to grab something for you?"

"No, thanks." She clutched at her waist and gave a sour look. "I don't think I can stomach anything until this is over."

"I understand. In fact, everyone is praying as they work right now." Lisa closed the door behind her.

Kate continued making her appeals.

Daniel stared at the gray tumor mass through the three-dimensional operating microscope positioned over Andrew on the OP table. A retractor instrument adequately held the opening in place, while the attending physician suctioned bits of bone and blood away, enhancing Daniel's view of the enemy. He had easily debulked most of the major portions of the mass, holding back from the more exacting remnants.

He and the attending physician evaluated Andrew's blood loss; they determined it was minimal and safe.

The flickering and soft beeping of monitors in the background kept Daniel alert, ever aware that he wasn't watching one of the myriad of medical films he'd seen in his practice. The noises reminded him that someone's life was really on the line.

"Wipe," he called, and the nurse dabbed again at his forehead. He was really sweating now. But that was nothing compared to the pain that was beginning to trigger down his back from the inflexible positioning. He pulled back, straightened, moved his head and shoulders around for the temporary relief it would give. Then went back into position.

He had made it through the easy part with flying colors, "Just a walk in the park" his friend and colleague John Robinson used to say after a favorite line in a movie. Now came tougher terrain. In the brain stem there was no margin for error. If he touched even a tiny portion of brain tissue with the laser, he would disable one of Andrew's normal operations—anything from standing upright, to swallowing, to breathing his next breath.

Daniel stared at the thin gray tumor tentacles that twisted around and wove through pink living tissue. The sight was such a harrowing paradox: Life versus death, intertwined in a battle for reign!

How tragic that death is winning, Daniel contemplated the struggle. His heart pounded with anger. He hated the way it taunted him, dared him to make a brave—and yet unnecessary—move. He couldn't allow that to happen. *Never again,* he calmly coached himself. He needed to remain in control. Every move calculated, every millimeter guided by the peace in his spirit—not by a zeal to conquer.

He worked his way down one tentacle, vaporizing tumor mass into smoke. The whiffs rose in a weird dance of departure. A blessing for Andrew's sake was that the tumor had been mostly firm—avascular—without blood vessels and easier to fight further growth with chemotherapy after the operation.

After decimating one thin finger of deadly tissue, Daniel went on to another, then another, until he had vaporized between eighty-five to ninety percent. A respectable stopping point, he thought. And safe—he'd touched no brain tissue.

Yet, the plan called for ninety to ninety-five percent. And it *was* possible. He wasn't there yet.

Daniel hesitated. He thought hard about his next move. This was where he'd been with Sammy when he had dived into defeat. Only with Sammy, Daniel had felt invincible, like nothing could stop him. His attitude and motivation were altogether different.

This time he was humble, pleading with God for help. Pleading for permission to annihilate just a few more percentages.

"Dr. Brakken, do you want to close?" the attending physician noticed his hesitancy.

Daniel blew out an aggravated sigh. *No!* His inner resistance roared. He was at the big crossroads—the one he knew had tripped him up last time. With Sammy he'd felt the need to quit. But, this time he felt the need to continue.

Even with the persuasive contrast, he questioned his leading to go on.

"Dr. Brakken?" the attending physician asked again, growing concerned with his stalled response.

"Stats," Daniel called for figures on the heartbeat and blood pressure. Andrew was holding up fine.

Help me, Lord. Do I stay, or do I close?

Kate felt queasiness mounting in her stomach. She would have written it off as jitters, if it hadn't come with such dark foreboding. It felt like unseen blackness entering the room. She prayed more intensely for Daniel, claiming his success, and for Andrew's life to be protected, in Jesus' name. She felt the need to verbally repeat the affirmation, over and over.

So she did, until a strong peace finally blanketed her. Then the dark foreboding dissipated, and a definite calm encompassed her.

Daniel felt a distinct urge to continue. *Jesus, I'm trusting that it is You leading me forward.*

"Dr. Brakken, what is your decision? Are you ready to close?"

"Not yet," he finally answered the doctor. Then, after a moment's hesitation, he slowly began vaporizing the tinier trails of gray mass with surprising precision and dexterity. He proceeded another ten minutes. Then twenty. Then thirty.

He passed the ninety-five percent mark. Instantly, he felt something arrest his hand. It went numb, impeding him from further movement with the laser.

Time to get out.

Daniel's spirit felt satisfied. "We're done. Close him up!" he announced, and handed the laser to the head nurse.

The team collectively sighed with relief after his prolonged extraction of the remaining safe percentages.

Over the next two hours, they closed up the layered opening carefully, efficiently, with no complications. Piece by piece, they put Andrew back together like a fragile puzzle. They bandaged him after leaving a shunt in place to drain any fluid, then rolled him onto his back. His head was propped in a way to leave space behind the bandaged incision, and keep pressure off of it. With exception to the I.V. and a few other vital monitors, they unstrapped much of the apparatus and tape surrounding him, freeing him from unnecessary bondage.

Daniel took a fresh sponge and wiped the damp, dark bangs from Andrew's brow. He leaned closer to the unconscious boy's ear and whispered for his spirit to hear, "You're going to be fine, Champ. Just rest. I'll see you in a little while."

Daniel went to clean up. He pulled off his cap and mask and tossed them into the disposal bin, then started to wash.

"Well done, Dr. Brakken," the attending physician complimented him while they finished cleaning. "You executed the last five percent beautifully—more smoothly than the first ninety, I thought!" They began toweling off, in sync.

"That's interesting." Daniel smiled uncertainly at the doctor's laud and rubbed his chin with the back of his hand. "I'm sure I *wasn't* performing the last five percent."

"Pardon?" the surgeon gaped at Daniel, perplexed.

"I mean, it just felt like something was guiding my hand. I can't explain it, but it was real. Then it stopped guiding; I couldn't go any farther. My hand felt numb."

The other physician cocked his head and raised his eyebrows. "Well, it sounds like you had some divine help. But if I were you, I wouldn't put that on the boy's record." He winked and patted Daniel on the shoulder. "It's been a pleasure, Doctor." He reached to shake hands.

"Thanks. Same to you, for your fine support," Daniel answered.

"Hello!" Kate answered Daniel's office phone so quickly that it hadn't even finished the first ring.

"Hi. We're done," Daniel responded in an easygoing manner.

"Yeah? How'd it go?" she ventured.

"Pretty good, up until the end. Then it was—"

She felt the blood drain from her face. "No—what? Is Andrew all right? Is he—?"

"Andrew's fine. It was just peculiar."

He explained the odd sensation of guidance to her.

She beamed, overjoyed at his account. "I don't know what is so strange about having prayer answered. You should feel honored. It was like having a 'hands-on lesson' from the Creator."

"Believe me, I'm very humbled by the whole thing. I know what a dilemma I faced. But then I *knew* I needed to continue."

"How is Andrew?"

"He's resting well right now. All vitals are good. When he rouses, we'll do the piggy game."

"The what?" she asked, stumped by his phrase.

"You know, 'This little piggy . . .' I use it to entice kids to wiggle their toes. That way I can perform a checkup without worrying them."

"Very clever, Dr. Brakken."

"Yeah, but not original. Lots of neurosurgeons know that one." He paused. "Well, I just got done washing up. It's time to talk to his parents."

"Congratulations, Daniel."

"Let's make certain he moves before you start applauding."

"I don't doubt for a moment that he will be fine," Kate added assuredly.

Daniel walked through the double doors of the operating ward. Mr. and Mrs. Tucker stood immediately. He could see Mrs. Tucker had cried a bucket full of tears, evidenced by her red and swollen nose and the wastebasket filled with tissues beside her seat. Only her acute anticipation held them back, even now.

"He's fine and resting," Daniel began with a smile. "It's a little early to tell, but everything in the operation went well—actually, better than we'd hoped for!"

"Oh, thank God!" The dam broke on Mrs. Tucker's eyes, she sobbed in her husband's arms as they hugged each other.

"When can we see him?" Mr. Tucker asked, fighting his own flood of tears.

"In about an hour. Once he wakes and shakes off the remaining anesthesia, we'll do some sensory tests to check for movement."

Mr. Tucker nodded. "Thank you. God bless you, Dr. Brakken."

Daniel nodded his appreciation at the blessing. "I'll check back in an hour."

Andrew woke to a radiant room. He wondered if it was heaven. It was so bright. He turned his head and saw thick, stalky figures moving around. Slowly he focused, and they looked more like people. Like nurses. No—he realized he was still on earth.

The next thing he realized was that his head wasn't hurting anymore. But his throat made up for it—parched and sore.

"Wa-ter," he squawked hoarsely at the nurse nearest him.

"Well, look who's awake!" the pretty blond lady turned and cheerfully addressed him. "How are you feeling, son?"

"Thir-s-s-ty," he managed another raspy utterance.

"I can't give you anything yet, but hold on a little while I let Dr. Brakken know you're awake. I'll bet you can try a popsicle soon, OK?"

That sounded terrific to him.

It seemed an eternity before she came back. He thought sure she'd forgotten about him.

"OK, kiddo," she chirped. "Cherry, lime, or grape?"

"Cher-ry."

She unwrapped his choice and placed it tip-down in a Dixie cup on the bedside tray. Then she gingerly turned and propped him a little onto his side with pillows behind his back, to keep him from choking on the juice. He reached for the popsicle.

"Take it easy with that. If you start to feel nauseated, just put it here on the tray."

"All right," he answered, regaining some of his voice with the added moisture in his throat."

Andrew heard approaching voices. Then Dr. Brakken came around the drawn curtain. "Hey! You look great. It's good to see you up, pal!" he inspired the boy. "How's the head feel?"

"A little funny, but I think it's just the bandages. It doesn't hurt anymore."

"That's really good news! You are on some medication, so you shouldn't feel any pain from your operation, but if it begins to ache or feel like pressure, I want to know right away. OK?"

Andrew nodded. Daniel tugged the blanket off of his feet, exposing them. "Now, I want to play a little game with you. Remember 'This little piggy?' I want you to wiggle your big toe on this foot."

Andrew followed as requested.

"Great! Now try this one."

He succeeded with the second try.

"Terrific. Now pull your feet up and back. . . . Good. Now point your toes. . . . Superb!"

His doctor continued until Andrew had wriggled nearly every part of his body. He'd finished his popsicle, as well.

"Andrew," Daniel sat on the rolling stool beside his recovery bed, a broad smile on his face, "you passed all my initial tests. It seems to me, at this point, that you are going to be fine for quite a long while."

Andrew tried to "hooray" with joy, but with his sore throat, the cheer sounded like the raspy honking of geese.

Dr. Brakken patted him on the shoulder. "Whoa, there! I think you better stick to smiling for a while, until your throat gets back to normal."

Chapter Thirty-Four

*I*n the surgeon's suite at the hospital, Daniel showered to freshen up, and then changed from his surgical blues into some comfortable, casual office attire. While combing his hair, he caught the sparkle in his eyes. He felt good. *Really* good!

He had been nervous about the operation earlier, but once in the saddle, his nerves settled and he started feeling . . . at home. He relished the deep satisfaction of being in his element. He had felt out of place for so long. It was wonderful to have a sense of belonging again.

Daniel sat down at the desk. Peacefully alone, he opened Andrew's file, reviewed the films and stats one more time, then he journaled all of the detailed information from the surgery.

After a while, someone knocked. Kate poked her head in the room with a smile. "Hi," she said. "The nurses said I could find you here. Hope I'm not disturbing you."

"No. I just had to do some post-op recording and wanted a quiet place to concentrate. Please, have a seat. You want some tea? There's a pot of hot water over there by the copier."

She closed the door and took a few steps in but stayed standing. "No, thanks. I need to get back soon. I just wanted to say . . . congratulations."

"You did, on the phone."

"Yeah—well, I wanted to say it in person." She then looked serious. "Daniel, I really appreciate what you did for Andrew. Your sacrifice—stepping out in faith to conquer the past—was heroic in the truest sense. And . . . it has softened my heart about you in many ways. All along, I think I've been seeing only your protective shell. Now, since New Year's, I believe I'm seeing the real you. I wanted to say that it was an honor working for you today."

He nodded, pleased with the personal nature of her statement. Then something in his heart grabbed him. "How about saying it over dinner?"

"What?"

He chuckled. "Just kidding. I don't need any more of your applause, Kate." He rose and walked over to where she stood and looked deep into her green eyes, "But, I would love to have your company for dinner tonight. Would you join me in celebrating?"

She looked suddenly shy. "That depends."

"On?" He moved closer as he looked her over with longing.

She blinked and stepped back a little. "On whether you consider it a date."

He tilted his head, understanding the game of words set before him. He slipped his hands into his pockets and slowly stepped nearer to her. "What if I said yes?" he asked bravely.

She moved back another step. "Well, then I'd want to know what elegant place you're planning to take me to, and what time I can expect to be home," she answered with playful challenge.

"I promise to have you home by midnight. And I thought the Space Needle would be nice. I hear the view is great. It's supposed to be a clear night—lots of stars. How does that sound?" He took another stride toward her, reaching to touch a lock of her soft hair.

She now seemed a little shy by his intimate contact and continued backing up, but came against the closed door. "Midnight is too late for a first date."

He grinned. "All right, 11:00. I promise, no parking gimmicks—and I will open all the doors for you."

She smiled tensely. Her breathing had accelerated with the closeness between them. She was obviously considering it.

"I like fresh flowers, too. Roses."

He closed the gap between them, giving her a gentle, earnest smile. "I'll buy out the nearest florist."

His avowal made her softly laugh. "All right, Dr. Brakken. You have a date. But, I insist on keeping things professional around the office—agreed?"

"Agreed. Now, I have a little request."

"Oh?"

"Promise me you'll wear that red dress, the one you wore at the Christmas party."

"The one that made you so tongue-tied?" she teased.

He raised his eyebrows. "That's the one."

"All right," she answered.

"And, one more thing . . ." he stared at her lips earnestly.

She looked a little unsure of his next request. "What?"

"This." He leaned quickly and kissed her, long, fervently. She responded favorably and raised her hands to cup his head. Daniel didn't want to stop but wasn't going to ruin things either. He'd won her trust thus far; he still needed to play it safe. He pulled back and tenderly kissed her cheek, an accent to his preceding affection.

Kate was speechless.

"You'd better go. I hear the boss you work for is a real *tyrant*." He winked.

She smiled at his amusing remark and cleared her throat. "Yeah, I thought that at first, too. But once I got to know him . . . he really took me by surprise."

"See you about 6:00 p.m.?" he asked as he opened the door for her.

Kate slid past, listlessly. "7:00 would be better—and not a minute before."

Kate sprayed a faint mist of sweet perfume on each side of her neck as she finished getting ready for dinner with Daniel. She checked herself in the mirror. Fresh makeup flawlessly applied and her hair swept up the way she had worn it on Christmas Eve. She was ready.

Except, she was still in shock. She wandered into the living room. It staggered her mind to think that she was dating the very man who had so incensed her only days ago. What had taken hold of her heart?

She had to admit that, although on some issues she and Daniel were diametrically opposed, there remained a mutual pull between them, a magnetism that brought them closer than the time before. No matter what the differences, they didn't have enough influence to keep Kate and Daniel from being drawn together.

She questioned what enticement caused this. It was certainly deeper than his handsome physical attributes.

Love? she wondered. Kate had never really been in love. The only thing she discerned about her feelings for Daniel was a deep, flourishing desire to be a part of his life. Was that love?

Daniel obviously felt something for her, or he wouldn't have kissed her so passionately.

Yet, she considered whether he was just on an emotional high after a triumphant day. She speculated about how he *really* felt about her, before Andrew's surgery, before New Year's, before Christmas. Being inspired by her, as he'd said, was not the same as having true love for her. Kate needed to be careful not to release her heart until she was sure of what Daniel's genuine feelings were.

Exactly at 7:00, she heard him knocking.

"Hi." She opened the door with a smile. Then she gasped. "Oh, my goodness!" She laughed.

Daniel leaned against the doorjamb. His arm was barely halfway around an overwhelmingly large bouquet of multicolored roses—at least twelve dozen! "You look heavenly," he drawled in a low tone.

The longing in his eyes tugged at her. She was warmed by his compliment, and the enormous bouquet. "Thanks. Come on in." He passed the flowers to her. She couldn't help but giggle at them. "You weren't kidding about buying out the shop, were you? I don't think I have enough vases to hold them all."

He waited in the living room and admired the Monarch lion near the door. "The lion looks really good here. Quite a guardian."

"Yeah," she answered from the dining room. "It's a nice feeling having him there. There's finally someone to watch over me." She glanced at Daniel as she finished arranging flowers.

He seemed thoughtful after her remark, but didn't comment.

"OK, I'm ready." She approached him by the door and pulled her black formal coat from the closet hanger.

"May I?" he reached out to assist her. When he had helped to put on the coat, he faced her, tugged the white, imitation-fur collar to her chin, and snugly covered her neck. He gazed deeply into her eyes.

Kate didn't know how to interpret the yearning she saw in his eyes, but she realized it was intense. Her heart started beating rapidly. All she could think of was how remarkable his kiss had been earlier. No other man's affection had touched her so deeply!

She wondered, with mounting anticipation, what the night held for them together.

Daniel's insides were melting. He stared at Kate—transfixed. He couldn't move, couldn't speak. His complicated and often challenging world was suddenly reduced to one isolated, imperative thought: *I need this woman.*

She looked up at him—soft and vulnerable. Lips parted, eyes trusting. Her escalated breathing slowly caressed his face in minty waves. He thanked heaven above for bringing her into his life. Then he desperately hoped she wouldn't walk out of it.

He decided to keep the pace slow and safe. He swallowed hard. "Shall we go?"

She nodded and led the way out.

After the engaging moment in the house, words escaped Daniel. Their drive downtown was fairly quiet, with only a few pleasantries about the office.

He parked in the lot nearest the Space Needle and came around to open her door. She gracefully rose to stand beside him. Their eyes met again. The exchange of intensity once more held him captive.

Gradually, he put his arm around her as they made their way to the Needle. The elevator filled with the maximum people, and the pack forced her to stand right against him. Her back brushed against his chest. The flowery aroma in her hair had an intoxicating effect on him. He wanted to nuzzle the nape of her neck, but he reigned in his wandering thoughts.

Soon, the elevator ride slowed to a halt, and everyone exited. After Daniel and Kate waited a few minutes, the hostess led them onto the rotating platform and to their table beside the window. A single red rose and a soft, glowing candle graced the center of the white cloth. Daniel pulled Kate's chair out for her first. He then sat across from her.

Once he was seated, the waiter appeared. "Good evening, and welcome to the Space Needle. My name is Rick, and I will be your server tonight. Would you like to start with something to drink?"

"Raspberry iced tea, please—if you have it," Kate began.

"We do," the waiter nodded and smiled, jotting down her request. "And for you, sir?"

"Just some coffee with cream. Thank you."

"Here are your dinner menus. May I recommend the evening special? Broiled, lemon-herb halibut filet with almond shavings, wild rice, and mixed fresh vegetables in a mushroom sauce."

"Mmm—that sounds wonderful!" Kate replied.

"It sure does." Daniel agreed, looked to her, and she nodded eagerly. "Very well, we'll each have the special. And some calamari for an appetizer. Thanks."

The waiter scooped up their menus with a smile and carefully stepped onto the stationary floor. Seattle's sun had long set, and stars were brightly visible through the restaurant windows. A curved quarter moon hung prominently against the black, cloudless sky.

To Daniel, Kate looked luscious. Her eyes twinkled and lips sparkled in the soft candlelight. He sipped some of his lemon water in lieu of the kiss he was yearning for. The beverage didn't do much to quench his thirst for the real thing, but it helped.

"Did you see Andrew's parents again this afternoon?" Kate asked.

"Yes, just before I left, in fact," he answered.

"How are they?"

"Relieved, and holding up nicely—considering the post-op period for neurosurgery is at times a little tricky. Stats and vitals can look fine on the routine checks—then suddenly change, and you discover an organ or muscle isn't working the way it used to. So far, though, all of Andrew's neuromuscular exams scored well." He sighed, recalling the hugs he had received from Andy's parents that afternoon. "I think his mother and father are really glad they agreed to go forward."

"Me too," she added, and granted him an honoring smile.

He nodded at her compliment. "Me three," he jested, then reached across the table to take her hand. "Kate, I don't know how to thank you. If you hadn't persuaded me to do his surgery, I never would have had the courage to try."

She raised her free hand in a gesture that declined accepting praise. "No—I only gave you a boost over the wall. God did the real miracle by healing the pain that had kept you in prison. Now, you are free!"

"He sure did something powerful. I feel like a new man. All that time, I was so wounded by those memories, scarred by the guilt and misery of my failure—even blaming God for allowing it to happen. And yet, all along, the Lord wanted to help me get released from the hurt. I just didn't see it. I was blind to His larger picture."

"We all are, sometimes." She appeared withdrawn, focused on something internal. "We get too caught up in our own small world and fail to see how God is using us in other's lives, even when we don't want to be used."

He sensed she was referring to herself. "Are you saying you weren't eager to be the springboard that helped me bounce back?"

She gave a resigned expression. "To be totally honest, at first I was more concerned for Andrew's well-being than your best interest."

"Well, I have only myself to blame for that," he answered. "It's true—you reap what you sow."

She didn't comment. Instead, she tugged her hand back and looked sorrowful.

Daniel sighed. He could only speculate how much distress he'd caused her over the last several weeks.

The waiter brought their beverages and a basket of hot rolls. Daniel poured far less than his usual amount of cream in his coffee. Then he reached for a roll, and after splitting off half he began to mildly butter it. He'd become a lot more health conscious since getting to know Kate.

"It's not all your doing, Daniel. I may not look the ambitious type, but I've always stepped out boldly to achieve what I desired. Unfortunately . . . sometimes I neglect to watch out for those around me."

"I'm not sure I follow you."

She squirmed a little in her seat. "I mean that I haven't been a model Christian to you, Daniel."

He was stunned by her disclosure but couldn't agree totally with it. "Personally, I think you are more the real thing than many others I have seen. Besides, none of us are perfect—only Christ."

"I know, but I haven't treated you . . . honorably." She looked down remorsefully, then continued. "Granted, I haven't agreed with everything you've enacted at the hospital, but recently I had a dream that showed me how I've been following my own selfishness. All this time, I was thinking my motives were only for the children, when in fact . . . it was my *own* heart I was trying to shield from pain."

He looked straight at her. "Are you referring to giving your notice?"

She nodded and looked sad, "That, among a few other things."

He felt a twinge of anxiety, but didn't want this to stifle the romance of the evening. "Kate, is this something that you *have* to confess tonight?"

"No," she shook her head. "Even if I don't, you will find out soon enough."

"Then wait. Please?" He wasn't sure what she was alluding to, but right now he wasn't concerned. "Look," he gazed at her sincerely, "whatever you felt, said, or did, you probably wouldn't have done so if I hadn't been such a beastly boss. You have my *complete* forgiveness—no matter what it was." He reached for her hand. "Let's not let it spoil tonight. Promise?"

She looked a little uncertain about putting the matter aside, then gave a soft smile. "If that's what you really want."

"Absolutely. I'd like this night to be a fresh start for us. And right now, all I want to think about is how beautiful you are—sparkling like one of those stars outside."

After dinner, Kate wanted to drive down to the piers on Puget Sound. Though the night air was cold, she loved walking out on the docks and watching the lights sparkle upon the dark water. They stood side by side against the log railing that surrounded the pier, and talked. The salty smells of the Sound filled the air. Waves lapped the pier pilings and sloshed every so often.

Daniel told her about his parents, Norma Mills and Theodore Brakken, how they met and fell in love. It was a classical "doctor meets nurse" story, and Kate could see how Daniel's future—being that he was an only child—was easily shaped into a successful medical one.

Kate in turn shared about her mother, Sophia, before her death, and then about her grandparents—what it was like being raised by a loving, older couple.

They talked for as long as she could endure the cold winds. When her toes became numb, she finally asked to return to the car. Daniel took her arm and escorted her back.

Later, when they arrived at Kate's home, Daniel held her hand as she walked along the unsteady gravel to her front porch. She retrieved her keys from her small handbag, unlocked the door and stepped inside, then turned to say goodnight.

Once in the doorway, he didn't hesitate to wrap her in his arms and kiss her. Long, gentle, and warm—his kiss easily awakened every sense in her lips, and then set her heart and soul ablaze with a yearning for more. For love. For intimacy. For that *missing* piece in life: The "right man" Jocelyn talked about.

She finally ended the kiss and pressed her face against his. She was grateful he hadn't wanted to hear her confession—it kept the night special.

But the truth was riding in on the wings of morning. Daniel would learn that she had secretly rallied the whole hospital, and the city, to support the carousel—all to his dishonor.

Guilt twinged inside. She looked up at him, appreciative of his actions, but ashamed of her own. "Daniel, thank you so much for tonight. If things do change between us tomorrow, I just want you to know that I'll always cherish this special evening."

He brushed the hair from her face. "What difference could tomorrow possibly make?"

"Tomorrow is the auction. I'm not sure it will be possible for us to remain . . . close."

He looked downcast. "That's too bad. Maybe we should make a full night of it before it ends," he teased, and wrapped his arms tightly around her waist.

"Daniel!" She started to feel heat in her face.

"I'm only kidding!" He chuckled, then grew earnest. His embrace eased to a gentle hug. "I would never take advantage of you, Kate. I'm not that kind of man. Doesn't mean it hasn't crossed my mind, though." He kissed her softly again.

She felt even more ashamed at his declaration. If only she'd been half as noble toward him in the last few weeks! "Daniel—seriously—if things are different tomorrow, . . . please understand that I thought tonight was wonderful. And I'm so sorry I didn't see the real you sooner."

He nodded, seemingly touched by her honesty. "Kate, this was the best night I've ever had. It's strange to hear myself say this, but I've fallen for you. There isn't anything I wouldn't do for you." He kissed her lightly on the nose, then on the cheek. "And, as long as it's within my power, I'll *never* let anything take you away."

Kate closed her eyes and rested her head on his shoulders. Tears seeped between her eyelids. Too many insurmountables lay upon her heart, and it started to crumble beneath their weight.

What would Daniel think of her after the auction, when he would discover her secret plan to buy back the carousel?

What if he couldn't forgive her, after all? And, even if he was able to pardon her unkind treatment, what was she going to do about leaving the hospital? Should she stay, regardless of whatever happens between her and Daniel?

Yet, she also wondered if he was *really* in love with her and would do anything for her, why hadn't he stopped the carousel from being auctioned, knowing how much it hurt her?

She was caught in a vexatious web of confusion. Her feelings tumbled down a mountainside of uncertainty, getting more fragmented and bruised along the way.

Daniel released his embrace and noticed her tears. She saw the concern in his eyes. "Did I say something to hurt you?" he asked.

She shook her head, wiped at the wet streaks on her face, then crossed her arms. "No, it's just . . . things are kind of difficult right now. I'm not sure I'm ready for us to be—well—like this. I want to, and I wish I could. I just . . ."

He waited, listening.

She sighed. "Sorry, I need to give this some more time."

He looked disheartened, but not in despair. He reached for and squeezed her hand. "As long as it takes, I'll wait for you."

With that he turned to leave. More tears rimmed her eyes. Through blurred vision, Kate watched him get in his car and drive away. She should have been touched by his affirmation, but the ache of knowing what separation the auction might bring was all too real. She wasn't going to deceive herself into thinking everything would be fine.

After all, she thought, life rarely turned out like happily-ever-after romances.

Daniel stepped into his cabin and closed the door. He flipped the lights and slumped onto the sofa. There, he viewed the diverse pieces of mail numbly—not really seeing them.

He had prayed the whole way home, hoping there was still a way to redeem himself in Kate's eyes, and win her over. He'd certainly done a number on her heart by stripping away the one thing that was so special to her. He wanted to make it up to her, badly. But how?

He tossed the unopened mail onto the coffee table in front of him and dropped his head back against the couch. "Lord," he pleaded, "how can I turn this around? Show me if there's a way to mend things. Please, God. I can't bear to lose her."

After a moment he sat up and just stared at the strewn pile of mail—mostly junk, but not all. A thin, express-mail package had been placed between some larger magazines and papers.

He plucked it up. It was from the real estate agent of his buyers—copies of the signature pages from his house sale . . . and a *very* large check.

Daniel stared at the amount. He would never need so much to buy a house in this area. Even *half* would purchase a magnificent place! He got an idea. His eyebrows raised up at the inspiration.

Then he looked up to heaven and hollered, "Thank you!"

Chapter Thirty-Five

Kate arrived at the auction almost an hour before the start time. She wasn't alone. Hundreds of others swarmed the local public facility rented for the occasion. As she passed through the various exhibits, seeing her grandfather's pieces on display, her heart was in agony. It hurt almost as terribly as when she'd been forced to show the carousel to the teardown crew.

This time she had hope.

There was more than two hundred fifty thousand dollars in travelers' checks in her purse. She'd felt sick to her stomach yesterday afternoon while ordering them, just after being kissed by Daniel at the hospital.

Her insides were torn in two. Daniel wasn't the only one in love. It became clear to her last night that her feelings for him were way beyond friendship. That was precisely why it made her ill to go ahead with something she knew could hurt him.

But, it was too late to back out. She had to carry through with the rescue operation. The kids were counting on her. And, after the generous support from people, she couldn't change her mind—though she now wanted to give it all up for Daniel's sake.

With him on her mind, she glanced around to see if he would actually come to the event. There was no real need for him to show, since everything was being handled by the hired auction master and crew. But she wondered if she would see him, just the same.

Time grew close to the auction start, and people were settling in the sloped auditorium chairs. Kate went around the main crowd to the other side and got a seat fairly close to the front, and furthest from the entrance. She had her bidding card ready. People were chatting excitedly around her. Being alone and anxious, she silently prayed:

Lord Jesus, please help me. Make this work out for the best. Whatever happens today, I ask You to divinely guide everything by Your loving hand. Amen.

The auction master took the stage, and two men carried out the first piece: a carriage. He gave a brief description of the item, then shouted, "We'll start at five thousand—who'll give me five?" The numbers rose steadfastly, and the serious contenders narrowed to three people. Kate was one of them, and she was aghast at how high the price had climbed for only a carriage piece! How would she purchase some of the more treasured pieces if she paid top dollar for the lesser items? Reluctantly, she dropped out of the bid, choosing to wait for some of the better selections.

Roughly a half-hour passed. The two carriage pieces were quickly sold, as well as the core paintings, base, and trims. She didn't feel too badly sacrificing those, because her grandfather had owned others that were in her garage, though they were not yet restored.

Finally, they started on the animal pieces—a giraffe. "We'll start the bid at nine thousand," the auctioneer called. Kate couldn't believe the price he was initiating. Yet, others around her didn't seem daunted by the high cost, and bidding numbers shot up, one hundred dollars after another. Kate tried her best to stay in the competition, though the expense was far beyond what she'd anticipated. She hung in the round and finally won the bid at ten thousand, eight hundred.

Kate mentally did the math. Pieces were selling about double from what she'd planned. She would have to sacrifice bidding on a few more of the lesser pieces in order to have enough to buy the best.

Through the selling of the next ten pieces, she purchased every other one. It was a far cry from her anticipated victory, but it made her feel good to have rescued a third of the listing so far.

The auctioneer took a short break, then dove into the second hour. The next item was a Dentzel horse—one of the best pieces. They were down to choice selections now. Kate slipped up her number and soon found herself pitted against one other serious bidder, way in the back of the room. She couldn't even see the person, but whoever it was wanted that Dentzel as badly as she did. Amid the excitement she went higher than she would have allowed, but that didn't stop her rival. He boosted the price in jumps of three hundred, whereas she was only bidding in minimum increments. The cost grew too expensive to reasonably consider, and she regretfully backed out. She'd have to forfeit that one, as well.

The sale had definitely taken on a new challenge with the second hour. After weeding out a few other bidders, Kate and her fearsome contender ended up pitted against one another with every shot. Each time her rival was willing to pay twice, even three times what the creations were worth. That person obviously had money to spend, and their affluence eliminated all other competition.

The next three figures were also sold to the other bidder with lots of money. Kate grew very concerned. There were only three left! The choicest creations. She had to ignore her sensibilities and "shoot the moon" for these last selections. Otherwise, she would let down the hospital kids. Besides, that was what the money was raised for.

She tried to outbid her persistent challenger, but the buyer kept boosting the price, now in increments of five hundred, then by one thousand dollar jumps! It became obvious to Kate that whatever she bid—no matter how high—this contender had enough to surpass her. And he *certainly* seemed bent on doing just that!

"Thirty thousand!" he cried aloud from the back, a full three thousand dollar jump from her prior bid. The crowd gasped at the exorbitant price. Kate was speechless. She had only a little over thirty-one thousand left. She knew he would outbid her, but she tried anyway.

"Thirty-one," the auctioneer called when she lifted her number, then he looked back to the man. "Do I have thirty-two?"

"Thirty-five thousand!" he called out another jump in price.

Kate closed her eyes and sighed. *It's over!* She'd lost out on another one! The two remaining were the top ticket items; unless her contender was out of resources, there was no way she'd beat him on those. The auctioneer waited for her to show a decision. She shook her head, somberly.

"Thirty-five going once, . . . twice, . . . sold!"

He whacked the gavel, and the stage crew shuffled the purchased horse offstage and another one on.

During the remaining bids, Kate didn't participate. A couple other brave souls tried to outdo the rich man in the back row, but they fought the same useless battle that she had.

Soon, the formalities were finished and people noisily stood to leave. Kate stayed in her seat and dropped her head. Amid the bustle around her, she reflected, *I'm sorry kids. I tried my best, but it just didn't work.*

She wondered how she would explain to the hospital staff and the children that her efforts had floundered. They would be disappointed; they'd had so much faith in her pulling it off. Now, she was leaving with only seven of the eighteen pieces, and none of the accessories or machinery. She'd never before felt like such a failure!

Once the large room was nearly empty, Kate finally rose to pay for her pieces. She made her way to the Claimants' table out in the lobby and placed down her bidding card, then retrieved her travelers' checks. After she signed over the majority of the checks, the attendant asked if she wanted shipping services, cautioning her that the only slots left now were two days away. She answered yes and signed over another check.

She then collected her receipts and turned to leave.

At the exit doors, she saw Daniel. He leaned against the doorjamb, an astute look in his eyes. He held a piece of paper and repeatedly ran pinched fingers over the fold. Though attractive in blue jeans and a burgundy flannel shirt, his rigid expression spoke clearly that he *knew all*—and it gave Kate's stomach the willies.

She figured he must have arrived after the auction had started, because she hadn't seen him anywhere before. *Time to test the waters,* Lord, she thought, wishing for a positive resolution.

Since she wasn't about to resort to immature games and walk past him without speaking, she greeted him, humbly. "Hi."

He glanced her over, perceptively. He seemed both pleased and irritated at seeing her. "Doing a little post-holiday shopping?" he asked dryly.

There was an edge to his voice—one that revealed displeasure. Unfortunately, there was nothing she could do to erase that. He would either keep his pledge to forgive her "no matter what," as he'd claimed last night, or they would go their separate ways.

"Daniel, I tried to confess this to you last night, but you *pleaded* with me not to explain." She wasn't trying to be prudish. The simple truth was, she had attempted to come clean already, and he'd begged her to wait.

He nodded. "Yeah. You're right about that."

"For what it's worth, I'm *very* sorry. What I did without your knowledge was unkind. As I started to explain last night, I was not looking out for your best interest, at the time, because I was too busy trying to conquer my own pain."

"The entire community knew about this behind my back." He looked at her soberly, hurt.

Kate nodded in shame. "How did you find out?"

"When I got here, one of the attendants heard I was from the hospital, and he asked if I was the one raising all the money to save the carousel for the hospital kids." Daniel now unfolded the piece of paper he held. "When I answered that I didn't know what he was talking about, he gave me this." He showed her the benefit flyer that asked for donations to be mailed or pledged to Kate. She took it and refolded it. "Then, he told me that he and his boy rode the carousel, twice, at the New Year's Day benefit. Oh, yeah—he also mentioned what a complete *fool* he thought the new administrator was to want to give up such a wonderful part of the hospital."

Kate felt horrible over how it must have hurt Daniel to hear that. "I'm sorry, Daniel—"

"You know what?" he interrupted her, "He was right. I did something very foolish. Something I came to regret. Yet, I never expected to find that you had enacted such an *underhanded* strategy." He looked pained. "Kate, . . . I was always truthful with you. I never held back the facts, even when I knew they would be upsetting to you. I gave them to you honestly."

Tears formed in her eyes. "Daniel, I'm so sorry. If only I could take it back—believe me—I would have given it all up this morning! Except that hundreds of people supported this. True, my heart has changed about you, but I couldn't let everyone down by quitting—just like you couldn't find a way to reverse sending the carousel here, . . . though I believe you wanted to." She paused, blinked back her emotion, and hoped he would identify with the constraint she'd felt to go forward with the fundraisers.

Regardless, he didn't appear the least bit sympathetic to her motive. She raised a hand to rub her forehead. "Maybe you'll never trust what I'm saying, but it is true."

He waited in silence, then nodded. There was a heavy, strained feeling between them. "Well, I've got to go. Goodbye, Kate," he finally said, and strode out the door.

She swallowed hard at the knot in her throat. No use—it was lodged too well. "Bye, Daniel," she barely whispered, then walked slowly to her car. Her heart grieved over the hard reality of Daniel's unforgiveness.

Kate's phone rang late that afternoon. It stirred her from her sleep upon the couch. She'd come home in utter heartache and spent hours just sitting by the fire, wiping away the stinging tears. She'd gazed sorrowfully at the burning flames as they seemingly condemned her for mistreating Daniel. Then, finally, she'd fallen asleep in her anguish.

"Hello?" she said, realizing by the darkened sky it was almost dinner time.

"Hi—it's Joce. Congratulations! I see the carousel is back. Nice work, lady! Wish I could have seen you in action."

Kate blinked her eyes and tried to get a clear understanding of what Jocelyn was talking about. "Jocelyn—you're not making sense. I *didn't* do very well, and the horses aren't being shipped here for two days."

She paused. "Are you kidding?"

"Not in the least."

"Hmm, . . . then who can explain why the carousel is being resurrected over here?"

Kate was stunned. She sat upright. "I certainly cannot! But I will be there, right away. Meet me by the glass dome in twenty minutes."

"You got it. See ya." They each hung up.

Kate tossed off the afghan and slipped her leather ankle-boots back on. She put on her winter coat, then remembered to quickly stoke the fire before heading out. She shivered after stepping outside. The cloudless sky and north winds had brought in record low temperatures. But, inside she was warm with excitement.

Arriving at the hospital, Kate parked in the lot closest to the glass dome. She exited from her car. With the dark evening surrounding the dome, its interior light was akin to a beacon, illuminating a good portion of the parking lot. Kate walked in astonishment. She saw—indeed—that the machinery was set back up, and two crewmen were still assembling panels and lights. Two others were unpacking carousel pieces from padding and shipping crates.

Her heart leapt with amazement and joy. "I don't believe it," she whispered as she neared the glass structure. Obviously, the rich man at the auction had been a hospital benefactor. She praised God for a miraculous turnaround. She stopped briefly outside the dome to gaze at the operation. Then a feeling of hilarity came upon her. She laughed out loud, spun in circles, and raised her mittened hands above her head, thanking God for what she was witnessing! It didn't matter to her whether the men inside thought she was nuts. She was too ecstatic to care about appearances.

After a minute of rejoicing, she finally went inside.

Jocelyn evidently hadn't gotten away yet. Kate asked one of the men, "Excuse me, can you tell me who the benefactor was that sent you here?"

A crewman in his late forties looked at her matter-of-factly. "Yeah, Mr. Brakken."

She chucked at his miscommunication. "No, I think you have it mixed up—Mr. Brakken is the one who requested the teardown. Who hired you today?"

"Mr. Brakken," he answered decidedly and used a pocket handkerchief to wipe above his reddish gray moustache, and then his shiny forehead.

"Are you absolutely sure?" she pressed.

"*Absolutely.*" He looked at her like she was peculiar. "Excuse me, lady. We've really got a lot of work to do here."

"Thanks," she offered her gratitude, then went to glance down each of the four halls to see if Jocelyn was coming. Still no sign of her anywhere. Kate waited another minute, then decided to go into Administration and see if Daniel was around.

Typical for a Saturday, the Admin. door was locked. She tugged her keys from her purse side pocket and opened it. The office inside was dark. She flipped on a switch and the front reception area lit up. "Daniel?" she called, and walked over to his closed office door. Light showed through the crack at the base. She tried the doorknob, but it was locked. She wondered if she had forgotten about the light last night when she'd left, eager over her dinner date.

She softly knocked. "Daniel, are you there? It's Kate."

No sound. Nothing. She had keys to his office as well but didn't want to create a bad scene.

"Daniel—if you're in there, I'd really like to talk to you. Please? May I come in?"

A few seconds passed. Sounds rustled from inside. The lock popped. He opened the door, then went back to sit in his chair. Two open-ended boxes were on the floor with his things packed. He twirled a pencil by its ends, between thumbs and fingers.

"Wow—" she almost choked on the word, at seeing the stark evidence of his intended departure. "You're leaving?"

He looked solemnly at her. "No need to stay with you here, Kate. You can run this hospital better than I." He gave a small mocking laugh. "Let's face it, everyone would prefer it if you were the administrative head. I've done enough damage, don't you think?"

"Daniel, once again—I apologize for the benefit, but if you're doing this because of it, that is not the right reason."

"True—but, shocking as the benefit was, I'm not leaving because of it. It's because I don't belong here. And you obviously do." He placed the pencil down and, with elbows resting on the chair arms, he propped his chin upon two fingers pointed upward in a teepee. "And, because I got an offer doing what I love to do. You once asked me if I liked working here. Truth is, neurosurgery is the only thing I've ever loved . . . that is, before I met *you*."

Pain gripped her heart. The tears that flooded all afternoon threatened to spill afresh. She remembered the call of good news from his former associate John Robinson. "Do you mean, in Los Angeles?"

He nodded. "Seems L.A. General has renewed esteem over my performance— now that the procedure I developed is hot news around the medical industry. They've asked me to return."

She couldn't answer. It felt like her heart was beating in her throat.

"I already called Henry, so you won't need to tell him. He's glad. Said he felt my time here was just a necessary bend in the road of my life. I assume that I already have your blessing. After all, you have earned this position. I'm sure you are happy that I'm leaving." He glanced at her.

She was hurting beyond belief! She didn't want him to leave at all, but there was nothing she could say to change his mind. Yet, if it was what he really wanted, she didn't want him to go without her support. "I would never have said it that way. But, you have my blessing and my prayers for whatever it is you desire. I know you will be far more content doing what you love. I just wish . . ."

He didn't interrupt her delayed speech.

She swallowed and took in a bolstering breath. "I wish things would have turned out . . . differently."

"How so?" He gazed at her, questioning her with his eyes.

"Well, that you could have set up your practice here. We definitely need someone of your expertise."

He seemed disappointed with her response. "That would have been too difficult."

"Kate?" Jocelyn called from the front desk.

Kate suddenly recalled her agreement to meet Jocelyn. She glanced back at Jocelyn and raised a finger to indicate she'd be a minute longer.

"Oh—sorry," Jocelyn remarked, realizing the conversation taking place. "I'll wait for you by the carousel."

"Thanks." Kate nodded to her friend, then returned her attention to Daniel. "When you were at the auction today, were you the one in the back, bidding on the carousel?"

"I told you I would make it up to you, remember? I told you that I would find a way to mend all the damage I caused."

She paused, felt overwhelmed by his genuine love and benevolence. "Why didn't you tell me?" she asked in a whisper.

"I didn't realize what I needed to do until I got home last night. When I saw the check in the mail from the real estate agent, I knew it would be a great surprise to you, and the kids," he said looking down, folding his hands. "I wasn't expecting to see you down in front, bidding against me."

He was clearly still hurt by what she had done in putting on the benefit. She nodded and raised a hand to nervously rub at her temple. "I sincerely hope . . . some day . . . you will find it in your heart to forgive me, Daniel."

He didn't respond.

"Regardless," she stared straight at him, earnestly, "thank you for buying back the carousel. The kids will always appreciate your gift. It's such a joy to them."

"And, to you?" he risked her personal sentiment.

She smiled bravely through the pain and rimming tears. "To me, your gift is *priceless*."

He acknowledged her answer with a pained expression. He nodded, then bent to add another book to his box of items.

Kate tore her aching heart away from Daniel's presence and walked back to the carousel to meet Jocelyn.

Chapter Thirty-Six

$\mathcal{K}$ ate opened the Admin. office on Monday morning. She placed her purse on her desk, and walked over to Daniel's former office. She knocked, yet there was no answer. After a minute, she unlocked his door. It was useless to hope he'd be there, she knew, but she had to see to be sure.

The scant office was sufficient proof of his departure. Only paperwork and some manuals remained. But further confirmation was the set of keys laying on the desktop with an envelope addressed to her. Kate's insides were already suffering from the mournful weekend. She didn't know if she could bear any more heartache.

She slipped her finger beneath the envelope flap and lifted it open. Slowly, she unfolded the contents—a short handwritten note, and two checks payable to the hospital: one from the auction bookkeeper, and another from Daniel's account. Together they totaled seven hundred thousand dollars!

She read:

Dear Kate,

I will never regret my experience with TLC. Moving to Seattle brought me back to the Lord and healed me of a devastating wound. It also led me to you, which I'm grateful for, even though things between us didn't work out. Enclosed are the proceeds from the auction, plus an extra donation from me, for making everyone's life here miserable. There should be enough to remodel and fully equip the ER. My prayers will always be with you. Thank you for helping me find my miracle.

Warmly,
Daniel.

She reread it several times before finally allowing the guard on her heart to release. She sat in the desk chair and cried over the note. "How can this be happening?" she begged God for an answer. "He said he would forgive me no matter what—but he didn't, even though I tried to explain," she sobbed out her hurt and bewilderment.

Eventually, Kate stopped crying. She realized, in thinking things over, how God had answered all her prayers. The children's carousel was rescued. . . . Daniel became a blessing to TLC. . . . Andrew's life was prolonged . . . and, she was granted the administrative position she desired.

Though each answer was wonderful to behold, right now they seemed small in light of the need in her heart.

When Daniel arrived a month ago, falling in love with him was the furthest thing from Kate's aspirations. Yet, it had happened. Now, it was slipping away, and she didn't know how to rescue it. She had only one hope: to plead with God to bring Daniel back.

"Lord, please, do whatever it takes to help Daniel forgive me. I need him. Please bring him around."

Kate dried her eyes and unlocked the safe behind the desk to place the check inside.

Jocelyn poked her head in the door. "Hi," she said. She glanced around Daniel's office and frowned sympathetically. "No show, huh?" Jocelyn looked closer at Kate's swollen eyes and must have known instinctively to hug her.

Kate wept on her friend's shoulder, releasing the sob she'd fought hard to spare Jocelyn on Saturday when she'd explained Daniel was leaving. "I've lost him, Joce. Just when I realized how much I needed him!"

Jocelyn held Kate and didn't say a word. Kate finally pulled back. She reached for several tissues, wiped her face, and blew her nose. "Thanks. I needed a compassionate shoulder."

Jocelyn smiled tenderly. "Hey, that's what nurses do best!"

"Especially the good ones," Kate replied and patted her friend's hand. They fell into shared silence.

"Say, Kate . . . I don't want to rush you, but I was sent to fetch you for an 'emergency' Board meeting. Seems *you* are the honored guest."

Kate nodded. "It's funny. This position was the one thing I wanted more than anything in the world. Now, it's just a shadow behind what my heart is aching for."

"That's called true love."

"You mean lost love," Kate sadly remarked.

Jocelyn looked indeterminate. "I'm not so sure he's out of the picture, completely. Let's give it some time. When he cools down over the benefit ordeal, I think he'll realize the same thing you do, that he can't live without you."

Jocelyn put her arm around Kate, ready to escort her through the office. "Come on, Kate." She pleaded softly with her. "You *deserve* this. Don't let go of it. Besides . . . we want our fearless leader!"

Kate laughed. "I'm not half as dauntless as Daniel."

"Maybe not. But to all of us here, you are the best!"

Daniel adjusted his seat in the airplane to a more comfortable position. The takeoff was smooth but not without trepidation. It wasn't flying that bothered Daniel—he loved being in the air. Something *uneasy* was camped in the pit of his stomach since he'd accepted L.A. General's plea to meet with them about a renewed affiliation. Everywhere Daniel looked "red flags" seemed to be flashing warning signals.

He pondered the inner reservation—mostly because he'd had the same foreboding when he decided to sell the carousel. *What a disaster that decision brought!* he reflected.

In addition to his hesitancy over leaving, his mind had been captured by memories of Kate all weekend. Even now, a hundred images paraded through his thoughts, they lured him into deep reflection as he listened to the constant drone of the airplane engines.

He almost smiled as he remembered when they'd met—her crashing into him with the towering binders. Then the resulting astonishment at learning she was not his secretary.

He recalled her sanding lesson, as she showed him how to expertly transform a wooden beast into a beautiful creation. He reminisced over how warm her hand was touching his.

He envisioned her at the Christmas party, looking more beautiful than an elegantly wrapped present.

He easily reflected on kissing her in the surgeon's suite. It flooded his memory and sparked a flame of desire. How he had longed for the touch of her lips that day! He still did—every day since. *Even now.* And the thought of losing her kiss forever sent a wrenching pain into his midsection.

He also recalled the agony in her eyes after the auction. It made him ache all the more. He hadn't wanted to leave, but Daniel had felt he'd had no other choice. Kate said that she wished he would stay in Seattle to practice at the hospital. But no mention of wanting him in her life. Though he'd told her he was in love with her, and given her several opportunities to respond whether she loved him, she had not answered with anything close to a confirmation.

Still, something in his heart told him he'd be a fool to believe otherwise. He sensed she did love him.

Daniel closed his eyes and reclined his head, hoping to catch a little sleep on the two-and-a-half-hour flight. He knew the chances of that were slim. Endless visions held his mind hostage, of a beautiful woman with lush auburn hair and bright green eyes.

Daniel roused from a near sleep to the flight attendant's voice on the intercom. She announced their imminent landing in L.A.

He blinked and glanced out the window, somberly. He had expected to be at least a little glad over returning. Evidently, it was going to take time.

The passengers deplaned. John Robinson met Daniel inside the terminal gate with a huge grin and a firm handshake. His tall, portly stature was familiar—except for the shiny, large wedding ring on his left hand. Daniel recalled the wedding was held the same weekend that he had moved to Seattle.

"Welcome home, Dr. Brakken."

Home? He didn't want to make his friend feel bad, but Daniel felt more like he'd just run from home than returned. "Hey, John. Thanks for meeting me here. Hope the traffic wasn't too bad."

"The usual," John casually retorted. They made their way to baggage claim and soon after picked up Daniel's sole bag from the luggage conveyor. "Is this it?" John asked with surprise, lifting up the small suitcase. "I brought my four-wheeler because I thought you were moving back?"

His friend's incredulous question made Daniel recall why he'd packed so light. Something inside him just wouldn't let him go for broke. Besides, nothing was firm with L.A. General—yet.

"I already paid rent through the month," he quipped to stall John's curiosity. "Besides, I have to go back for my car."

They made it to John's truck and stowed Daniel's suitcase on the small passenger bench behind the front seats. They both hopped in and were soon winding through the airport parking; minutes later they herded through the crowded toll lines.

John turned to Daniel and said, "A lot has changed since you left."

Daniel pondered over the truth of that from his own perspective. A lot had changed in his life, too. In fact, he wasn't the same person anymore! All in a months' time.

"I hate to dampen your excitement, John, but L.A. General and I haven't signed a contract, yet."

"They made you an offer, didn't they?"

"An offer to return, but nothing is final yet." He felt better saying something noncommittal. The nervous knots in his stomach eased up.

John looked suspicious. "Are you saying you've got cold feet about this?"

Daniel rubbed his chin and just stared out the window at the California sunshine. Somehow, its brightness seemed to bother his eyes in a way it hadn't before. He wasn't sure how to answer that question.

"You can be straight with me, bud," John continued. "If this job isn't 'the mountain,' you know you won't be happy."

"*Neurosurgery* is the mountain, John. I can be happy anywhere, as long as I'm doing that."

"Oh, yeah?" John didn't sound convinced. "Then what is eating you to pieces?" he asked, concern rising in his voice.

Daniel knew the answer to that, but he wasn't sure he wanted to expose his personal feelings to a co-worker, even though John had become a close friend in recent years before Daniel left for Seattle. "It's complicated," he said. "Something about it feels awkward, that's all."

"Um-hmm." John gave Daniel a skeptical look. "You want to know what I think?"

"What?"

"I think, if I were you, I'd take a really hard look at whatever made you say that. Because whatever it is, it's not going to go away at the meeting, or tomorrow, or next month. Something has captured your focus, Daniel. It's hooked your heart and seized your zeal along with it!"

Daniel looked at John, flabbergasted. He laughed nervously at the pointed comment. "That's unbelievable! So I feel a little unsure about returning to an employer that essentially fired me, rocked my career with scandal in the process, and then begged me to come back just to benefit their own pocketbook. Is it beyond reason that I should be a *little* leery over making a comeback, here?" He felt red in the face and wondered if John was seeing right through him.

"No. But that's not what is eating you. Is it?"

Daniel gave a low groan. He was pinned.

"It's OK, you don't have to tell me. I'll find out down the road. But it's your life, Daniel. If you don't follow your vision, no one else will do it for you. Then, day by day it will slip through your fingers. One day, you'll look back with only regret because it will be gone."

"What are you now, my psychiatrist?" Daniel was growing a little edgy with the spotlight on his personal issues.

John paused, pursing his lips seriously. "Hear me out a little on this, Daniel. We've been friends a couple years, and I've never seen you this bewildered. Not even after you left L.A. General. Promise me you'll give this—whatever it is that has your attention—some serious thought, all right? If I can see it written all over you, so will they . . . and, so will your patients."

Daniel sighed. "OK, I promise," Daniel answered, and his buddy finally seemed mollified.

"Good. Now, let's hit the next steak house. I'm starved."

After lunch, John dropped Daniel off at a nearby posh hotel where his reservations were—all expenses paid by L.A. General. He checked in, made his way to the suite, and flopped onto the bed, expended. He couldn't forget John's emphatic declaration: *If you don't follow your vision, . . . one day, you'll look back with only regret.*

Though he was tired, Daniel knew he wouldn't be able to sleep, so he picked up the phone and dialed information. At least he could handle *one* thing that was heavy on his mind.

"Yes, please give me the address for Ricardo and Margarete Paredes in East L.A." He scribbled the number down, thanked the operator, and hung up.

Then he thought about checking his recorder at the rental cabin in Issaquah. He wondered—actually hoped—there would be a message from Kate. Though it was totally unreasonable to expect one. What did he suppose, anyway? That she would come running after him? She couldn't even say that she loved him. Why would she contact him?

He decided to postpone calling the cabin until that evening. Presently, he needed all the fortitude he could muster to accomplish the visit ahead that he *had* to make.

Mrs. Paredes opened the large door of her stucco, tile-roofed house. Her dark brown eyes were curiously set on Daniel. Her light-brown Spanish face looked jaded, afflicted by pain, and her hair had grayed considerably since Daniel had last seen her in the waiting room, only a year ago.

She didn't recognize him at first, then it dawned on her who was calling at her home. Her countenance quickly changed to a defensive glare.

"What do you want?" she asked, a bitter edge lining her question.

"Mrs. Paredes, I'm Dr. Brakken, your son's Neurosurgeon."

"I know who you are."

He swallowed hard. "I came to talk to you and your husband. May I?"

"Why?" she grilled him. "Haven't you caused enough pain?"

"Please—I know you've been through a lot. This is very difficult for me. I came a long way to meet with you. Please, let me talk with you, for just a minute."

She still seemed reserved, but his sensitive pleading worked to break the ice. "Alright, you may come in—but only for a minute."

"Thank you."

"Wait here. I will call for my husband." She went to the back room, and returned a moment later with Mr. Paredes, a handsome but weary-looking Spanish-American. Daniel offered a handshake, but the other man did not accept it.

Mr. Paredes looked him over with confusion and some disdain. "What is it you have come for, Dr. Brakken?"

Daniel took a deep breath. "I came . . . to apologize. After Sammy's surgery, I told you about the complications we experienced," he began. Mrs. Paredes started to whimper, and she quickly sat in the middle of the L-shaped couch beside where the men stood. They followed suit, and sat across from each other near the two ends.

Mr. Paredes held his wife's hand. "What about the surgery?" he questioned.

Daniel folded his hands. His head hung low, remorsefully. "Well, as you may recall, I utilized a new procedure that day which, evidently, was . . . not the best choice for Sammy. I had been extensively researching a new aspect to our standard laser procedure, one that would verifiably help improve success rates of brain stem surgeries. In fact, its accomplishment is sweeping the nation today." They didn't share his mounting enthusiasm. He toned it down.

"Well," he continued explaining, "At the time, I felt strongly that it could have extended your son's chance at life—and it probably *would* have . . . except, Sammy apparently wasn't in the best condition to battle the risk. I felt uncertain whether it was wise to try on him, but I also knew the potential it had to offer. I *truly* believed it could help your son, provided Sammy remained stable."

Daniel looked at them both. They hadn't thrown him out yet. He continued explaining. "In looking back, I now see how I took a risk that I could have, and possibly should have, avoided. There are always risks involved in surgery, especially neurosurgery. Yet, I have come to realize that I shouldn't have gone forward in his particular situation. I know these words must seem terribly empty to you, but I am so sorry. And, I'm asking . . . actually, I'm begging for you . . . to forgive me . . . please."

Mrs. Paredes was crying harder now. Mr. Paredes's expression softened, but he was still guarded and obviously hurting from the revisited emotional issue.

"Please, believe me," Daniel continued, "I intended to do only what was best for your boy. Unfortunately, I let my instincts get clouded by the hope of a chance to beat the odds. The possibility of something better for him lured me to go forward. Only, it was too far for him. I wanted to succeed, for his sake, with something that would have effected a better outcome, but it wasn't a conservative move. Because of that, the chance I took inadvertently took Sammy's life."

Mrs. Paredes's weeping subsided a little.

Mr. Paredes commented, "The hospital informed us that you acted unprofessionally. They claimed you resigned as a result of your negligent approach."

Daniel wasn't happy to hear of the hospital's inaccurate and negative slant on the facts. He shook his head and felt patches of heat rising into his face from the injustice. "I'm afraid that what you were told by them was only a partial truth, to keep the hospital from looking bad. It was mainly handled that way for insurance reasons."

Mr. Paredes seemed keenly aware of Daniel's disclosure. "And what is the rest? Tell us the whole truth."

"Please, . . . this wasn't why I came here today."

"Regardless—I insist on knowing," Mr. Paredes directed.

Daniel sighed. There was no way around clearing the air, even though Mr. Paredes would not be happy to learn that he'd been partially mislead by the hospital. "Actually, they asked me to resign during the handling of the matter, and I complied. Of course, if I hadn't, they would have fired me due to a rise in the media exposure of the situation—and to keep a lawsuit from occurring. Those drive up their malpractice insurance."

"And what you say about your part—is that true?"

Daniel sighed heavily. "Yes. With Sammy, I sensed inwardly that I should have held back. Though, from a medical standpoint, there was *no reason* to follow a more conservative approach. I felt confident the newer technique would help him considerably more than the conventional one, so I went forward with it. Even though I sensed something caution me against it."

"What do you mean when you say 'you sensed' and 'something cautioned' you?" Mr. Paredes asked.

"Well, it wasn't medically necessary to quit at that point. There were no vital signs that indicated we should retreat. Any other knowledgeable surgeon would likely have continued, the same as I, if he had known the procedure. It was something inside me—a sixth sense or spiritual nudge of some kind—that sort of urged me to back out. Unfortunately, I didn't heed the signal. I looked at the situation medically and intellectually, instead of listening to instinct. Now I know I should have gone with my gut feeling." He paused. "In my profession, I've lost some children, but only due to unforseen complications—never because I failed to follow my intuition.

Mr. Paredes looked intrigued. He squinted his eyes and sat up straighter. "You say that you conduct your surgeries with *instinct*, as well as medical knowledge?" he inquired earnestly.

"Yes—usually. I've always been kind of a natural at surgery. I guess you could say I have an inherent gift to understand the process—when to trust certain aspects of it, and when not to. Some men are great at football or fixing cars. Others master accounting or law. I'm good at using surgical tools and understanding the human brain."

Mr. Paredes closed his eyes and whispered something in Spanish. He appeared both surprised and at peace with the information Daniel had shared. Daniel considered whether his hopeful reaction arose more from miraculous intervention than human response.

Finally, Mr. Paredes stood next to Daniel. He reached to place a hand on Daniel's shoulder in an honoring fashion. "Dr. Brakken, . . . the world needs more doctors like you," he commented with respect while tears brimmed his eyes.

Daniel couldn't believe what he was hearing. "I appreciate your esteem, but I only came to beg your forgiveness."

"Yes, I forgive you," Mr. Paredes announced, resolutely. "Even if you could have done differently. I believe in what you say—following instincts. And I have more respect for you now than any physician I have known. We all have gifts from God, and you have recognized yours. But no one is perfect in them. I forgive you of any fault."

Daniel was speechless. He nodded his thankfulness.

Mrs. Paredes had finally stopped crying. She looked at Daniel with blood-shot eyes, tissues clutched in both hands. "Now I know you tried your best. Everyone makes mistakes, Dr. Brakken. I, too, forgive you for what happened with our Sammy." She looked toward the sunny window. "He is with God now. We miss him, but he is in a better place. No more pain."

Daniel was getting choked up and misty-eyed. He stood to leave and tried to breathe deeply to relieve his building emotion. "Thank you," he managed and reached once more to shake Mr. Paredes' hand. This time the man not only accepted Daniel's hand, but leaned forward to embrace Daniel and pat his back.

"Go with God, Dr. Brakken," Mr. Paredes said warmly.

Daniel's eyes clouded over with tears. "I will. Thank you." He looked to Mrs. Paredes with overflowing gratitude. She nodded and dabbed at her eyes. He reached to give a tender squeeze to her hand.

"Thank you, so much."

Chapter Thirty-Seven

K ate decided to wrap up for the day—her first day as the hospital's new Executive Administrator.

She reflected on the urgent board meeting earlier that morning, when the council straightaway inaugurated her as Daniel's official replacement—in front of the entire TLC staff. They were also asked to attend, much to her surprise! The applause left her tongue-tied and tearful. She'd already been walking on sensitive ground with Daniel's departure, but the reception she received so warmed her heart that she could barely say a word of thanks in response.

Then she recalled a meeting not so long ago when her pride had wanted the accolades, but *she* wasn't ready—yet. Now the Lord had worked everything out using His timetable to orchestrate her calling in life. She was so much more grateful for the position now that a change had been effected in her heart.

Amid the stream of congratulations by staff members, her thoughts had wandered periodically to Daniel. Even now, she wondered where he was, what he was doing, and what his heart was feeling. She wondered if he missed TLC, the children, or her.

He had certainly made an impact on her life in more ways than one. Not only had she learned to love him, his character taught her things that she would never have learned from Henry's personality. Daniel's caution—though caused by his inner wounds—warned her to be more discerning with her innovations. His apprehensions about the carousel and petting zoo were extreme, but they brought to light the need to put some extra precautionary measures in place. For that, she was thankful.

His life also demonstrated to her how easily wounds can keep a person down, and the tremendous need to run *toward* God when trying times hit like a tornado. It was tragic how suddenly Daniel's career had fallen, leaving him with dishonor, fear, hurt, and condemnation over Sammy's death.

She realized more than ever how many people must really be suffering on the inside. Too often, it seemed, Christians were burdened into thinking that they must live like only joy and blessings abound in their lives. As though only wonderful things and victory took place—unless, of course, there was something wrong with the person's faith! Kate realized now how narrow that thinking was.

She knew how Jesus had told his disciples that "in the world they would have tribulation" and pain, but they could *still* have cheer in Him overcoming the world and it's sorrows. He was telling them He could heal and conquer the pain in their lives. He didn't say that all pain would be removed from life—that would only come when they went to Heaven. He wanted His followers to realize that joy was still available through His power and healing for the miseries and grief of life.

That was a big part of why he had come: to heal the brokenhearted and set the captive free!

Rarely had she heard of churches teaching the need to receive emotional healing for failures and other past hurts. Forgiveness, yes, but not healing for scars and wounds. Now, Kate had witnessed firsthand the tremendous blessing of someone receiving such healing from the Lord. What a change it had made in Daniel, she remembered! His whole countenance was different—lit up! Even though he had been a believer in Christ already. The genuine healing broke his chains of fear, failure, and pain from off his shoulders. Once again, he was able to rise in integrity, to walk in freedom, joy, and wholeness of heart.

Kate locked up her office and strolled toward the parking lot. Just a month ago she had prayed, *desperately*, for God to work a miracle. To her amazement, He had come through—not only with one, but several!

She hummed a familiar melody of praise to Him as she approached her car.

Daniel walked into the catered dinner meeting promptly at 6:00 p.m. on Monday evening. The large conference room was filled with the heads of L.A. General. After shaking hands and extending the obligatory greetings, they asked him to sit down and review their proposed contract.

Daniel didn't need to even see it. His heart had been dealing with him all afternoon. Since the visit to the Paredes' home, he realized he needed to forgive Kate, just as they had forgiven him. And, after the nearly prophetic warning by his friend in the car that morning, Daniel *knew* what he needed to do—and it didn't involve moving back to California.

Daniel pushed the contract aside a little and sat forward. He folded his hands on the table. "Ladies and gentlemen," he nodded to each person in attendance, "I think I can spare us a lot of wasted time this evening. I'm sure that what you have agreed to offer me, in terms of a career move, is very generous." He looked around the room of twelve people, their broad smiles were starting to go limp. "But I'm going to have to decline."

The gathering of distinguished directors erupted into protests.

"But you haven't even looked at the contract, Daniel," Lou Westfield, the chief administrator of the hospital, charged and stared at Daniel, incredulously.

"I know," Daniel answered. "But something inside me tells me this is the wrong choice—not bad—just wrong for me. I'm sorry to come down here at your expense and disappoint you. The truth is, I didn't know until I arrived today what I needed to do. And my understanding was that this was to be a precursory meeting."

"That's true. Nothing is final until you sign. But we understood from our telephone conferences with you that that was your full intention," Lou added, still perplexed.

"Honestly, it *was*. But I can't say that it is any longer." They broke into another string of objections. "Please," Daniel held up his hands to quiet them, "I understand this wasn't what you expected, but it really is what I must do."

"Are you sure that is your final decision, Dr. Brakken? Don't expect that we'll be calling you with a higher offer," Lou declared an end to future opportunities at the hospital.

Daniel was repulsed that they assumed his reasoning was to stall for more money. It fueled his fire to turn them down completely. "Oh, *yes*, it is my final decision," he answered. "I'm sorry. Good evening, everyone." He pushed his chair out from the large conference table and walked toward the door.

"Hey, Brakken!" Max Donnelly, his former Chief of Surgery, called to him and met him at the door. Daniel had always enjoyed working for Max and was a little hurt to learn from Mr. Paredes how the hospital had placed such a harmful slant on Daniel's performance, just to keep their insurance premiums from rising. He hoped Max hadn't been involved in their politicking.

Daniel paused and waited for his comment, whether good or bad.

"It's been a real honor having you on my team," Max said and held out his hand for a farewell shake.

Daniel accepted. "Thank you, Max. I'll miss working under you."

"I am real sorry to see you leaving—again," Max continued, then glanced behind himself cautiously. "It was hard enough losing you the first time, with all that rubbish about your technique! I want you to know that I supported you without a flinch, as I will support you in this. You deserve to reach whatever you desire, Dr. Brakken. Good luck." He gave Daniel a final, supportive pat on the shoulder.

"I really appreciate that," Daniel answered.

A few others had now wandered over to shake Daniel's hand. In one sense, it was sad to be leaving—like the final chapter of a book—the "resolution" that had been missing when he'd left the first time. But, a tremendous peace settled in Daniel's spirit. He knew he was doing the right thing. He *knew* where he belonged. And—hopefully—Kate knew it by now, too.

With the farewells over, he hustled down to the drive-through and caught a cab back to his hotel. Since he hadn't even unpacked, there was nothing to do but check out.

Daniel grabbed his bag and overcoat and left the hotel suite. With a spring in his step, he bypassed taking the elevators and sprinted down the seven flights to the lobby.

He placed his magnetic keycard on the counter. "I'll be checking out, please. Daniel Brakken."

"Yes, sir." The hotel desk clerk pulled Daniel's name up on the computer, then looked confused. "Mr. Brakken, it says that you just arrived this afternoon."

"That's right."

The attendant looked concerned. "May I ask if everything was all right with your accommodations?"

"Wonderful—I just can't stay any longer." He almost smiled, excited to get back to Seattle.

"Very well. I see your account is already taken care of, so if you will sign here to show that you have checked out, that is all we need."

Daniel signed the paperwork and practically fled through the lobby to the front entrance of the hotel. He hopped in the first cab available.

"To the airport, please."

Kate changed into something comfortable and started a fire before checking her mail at home. She sifted through the junk and advertisements to glean the important pieces. Surprisingly, she was still receiving donations for the carousel from people around the city who'd either just heard of the benefit or forgotten to send their gift in earlier.

Fortunately, the number of messages on her voicemail had reduced to almost nothing. She realized she still needed to remove the benefit message, and re-record a new one for herself. For now, she just turned off the messaging mode and let it merely ring until she had the energy to go through the motions.

She sat by the fire with the stack of letters in her lap. She loved reading the enclosed notes and cards more than the joy of raising the money. It was incredible to hear how the carousel had touched the lives of so many people who knew a child that had been a patient of TLC. Sometimes, they just wanted to bless the hospital.

After opening over thirty letters with donations, she piled them together and slid them into a large envelope on her coffee table that had previously jacketed other mail.

She folded the flap inside and placed the envelope on the coffee table beside the lion. Kate smiled and gazed at the majestic piece. He was by far the best piece she had—and certainly wasn't doing her as much good being a house guardian as he would by being added to the carousel at the hospital. She and

Daniel together had lost five of the early pieces to other buyers, so the gaps would need to be filled.

"I've found you the *perfect* home," she said, and tapped the lion figure on the nose. "You're going to love it."

Kate sighed, thinking once more of Daniel. It was next to impossible not to think about him. She closed her eyes. *Lord, please, just one more miracle. . . .*

Daniel approached the airline-booking attendant and asked about his options for evening flights. She explained the few nightly selections, and he purchased a one-way ticket. He was drumming his fingers and tapping his toes, growing more excited every minute. With a little over an hour wait, he would soon be flying north again. Back to his newfound home state.

Back to Kate.

He prayed fervently that she would open up her heart before he asked her to marry him.

The attendant stapled his tickets and handed them to him. "Boarding at Gate 7," she said.

"Terrific. I like the number 7; it's God's number of completion." He smiled at her. "Have a pleasant night."

She smiled back. "Thank you, Mr. Brakken."

"Umm, that's *Dr.* Brakken," he added kindly and winked at her in good spirits.

She checked the computer screen and smiled. "Oh, yes. Have a pleasant flight, *doctor*," she responded.

"Thanks. I will."

Daniel tucked his tickets in his inside coat pocket and soon checked his bag with the airline. Then he hustled back to the cab lines to catch another quick ride. He hopped in the nearest one.

"Where to, sir?" the cabby asked.

"I need a fast, round-trip to the nearest, nicest jewelers and back in less than forty minutes. If you'll wait for me while I shop, I'll pay double for the time, plus a tip."

"Your wish is my command!" the eager cabby responded, looked behind them, and punched the gas pedal to move into the exit lane.

The telephone rang as Kate finished up her dinner. It startled her at first. Then adrenaline coursed through her. She wished with every chamber of her heart that it was Daniel, even though she knew that was senseless to hope for.

"Hello?" she answered.

"My name in Winifred Poll. Is this Kate Montgomery?" the woman asked.

"Yes."

"I am one of the nurses at your grandmother's rest home."

Kate's heart plummeted from hopeful anxiety to fear, in a second flat. "Yes—is something wrong?" She ran her hand through her hair and held her breath.

"Your grandmother is not well, dear. She's had a heart attack. We had to send her to Highlands Hospital by ambulance. She requested for you to know immediately, to be with her."

Kate was seeing spots from not breathing. She closed her eyes and fought the dizziness swirling around her head. Her world seemed like it was caving in. *No, God! Please, not Grandma Rose. She's all I have left. Please!*

"Miss Montgomery? Are you all right?"

"Yes. I'll leave right away," she finally answered, and hung up the phone without thinking to say goodbye. Kate grabbed her coat and purse and rushed out the door.

Chapter Thirty-Eight

Daniel reached the nearest telephone after deplaning at Sea-Tac airport. He wanted to call Kate and ask her to meet him—to "talk" over dinner. He grinned as he listened to the first rings. He had his suave plan all figured out.

Her phone rang several times. Not even a recording picked up. Daniel wondered if he had misdialed. He hung up and tried again, this time looking intently at each digit on the paper instructions he'd kept in his wallet since the day he went to sand the carousel piece at her house.

He waited through ten more rings. No answer.

Daniel sighed, and finally hung up the receiver. He'd have to wait and pay her a surprise visit.

For the last time that day, Daniel hailed a taxi—this time to take him home.

🐉   🐉   🐉   🐉

Kate found her grandmother's room. Rose had been taken from the Emergency ward and was now in Intensive Care.

"Hi, Grandma," Kate said, and sat beside her grandmother at the hospital. Rose was hooked up to monitors and oxygen. She was coherent, but frail. She reached out a shaky hand toward Kate as soon as she saw her enter the room. Kate took Rose by the palm and kissed the back of her soft hand. Tears streamed. Kate's heart was breaking once more.

"Ka-tie. Don't c-cry. . . . I can't l-live for-ever, *here*," Rose said weakly.

Kate saw the heart monitor beeping unnaturally. She understood the dangerous signal it revealed from her brief sojourn in nursing school. She wiped her tears and smiled through the pain. "Everything is fine, Grandma. You'll make it through this. You'll see." She couldn't bear to lose hope.

Rose closed her eyes and gently shook her head. "No, dear."

Anguish gripped Kate's insides. She wasn't going to let her only loved one go that easily. "Really, Grandma. You're going to be OK. I'm praying for you."

Rose smiled sympathetically. "Let m-me go home. You'll be f-fine. Grand-pa Joe has been wait-ting for m-me, . . . and y-your Mom-ma."

Kate sniffed back the tears. "But I don't want you to go. You're *all* I have. Everyone else is gone. I love you, and I need you here!"

Rose looked at her with tremendous love. "No, you h-have Je-sus, dear."

Kate let out a whimper. "I know, but He's not here, like you are."

"Yes, He is, hon-ey—He's stan-ding right t-there. D-do you see Him?" She raised a finger to point at the corner of the room.

Kate looked up, incredulously. Her tears subsided for a moment. She thought her grandmother was speaking metaphorically, that Jesus was with her *in spirit*. Now, she wondered if Rose actually saw the Lord's form near her bedside. "I don't see Him, Grandma. Do you?"

"Y-yes, dear. He says to t-tell you, 'It's alright.' And that 'y-you will not be lone-ly.'"

Kate clouded up with emotion. "OK." Her throat was so constricted she couldn't hardly talk. "Grandma? When you see Momma and Grandpa Joe, tell them that I love them." Her tears streamed.

"Yes, hon. L-love you, Kat-ie."

"I love you, too."

Rose's eyes stayed open, and a peaceful smile crossed her face. She looked suddenly serene, out of pain. The heart monitor went to a monotone. A nurse came immediately into the room and looked expectantly at Kate.

Kate nodded and tried to smile, but her lips quivered. "We said our goodbyes."

"Bless her heart." The sympathetic nurse looked both sad and relieved. She turned off the monitor, knowing Rose had requested no life-support beyond this point. Then she touched Kate's shoulder. "You can stay as long as you like. I'll notify the nursing home."

"Thank you," Kate said, and sniffled again.

The nurse left, and Kate turned to her grandmother's still form. She gracefully closed the elderly woman's eyelids and squeezed her hand one last time.

Daniel's ride home in the cab was growing more agitated with each mile. He sensed something amiss, but couldn't put his finger on it. He had asked the driver to stop first at the hospital, but Kate wasn't there either. The Admin. offices were locked.

He stared out at the rain as it dripped down the window. Thankfully, his driver was not the chatty type. Daniel was on pins now and didn't feel like conversing with anyone—but Kate.

Once home, he paid the cabbie and headed in to call Kate's house again. No answer. It was after 10:30. He figured she had either turned off the ringer on her phone or gone to visit someone.

In either case, it wasn't going to work out as he had planned. Now, he'd just have to wait until morning.

Kate drove up to her house late that night, after visiting Henry and Louise to share the news of Rose's death. It was closing on midnight as she undressed for bed and crawled beneath the covers. She lay in the dark, half praying, half thinking.

Considering the anguish she had felt upon arriving at the hospital, Kate thought she would be even sadder now. But she *wasn't*. She had been wrapped with a warm, tremendous peace the moment Rose left her side. It was as though the tranquility that she saw on her grandmother's face spilled over and blanketed her, as well.

She contemplated the things Rose shared before departing. Then she remembered talking to Jocelyn about witnessing children enter the heavenly realm at the moment of their passing, even seeing beautiful angels, and hearing music, and singing.

Kate felt blessed for having been there to experience her grandma's *homegoing*. She knew where Rose was, and that Jesus had come to escort her to Heaven.

She realized God had given her a wonderful gift in seeing what had happened. It helped comfort the sorrow of her grandmother's farewell. And Kate cherished it.

The next morning, Daniel showered and shaved as fast and thoroughly as he could. He wanted to look his best—even though he couldn't do much about his tired-looking eyes.

After lying awake a long time excited and thinking, he'd realized the *perfect* plan. Going to sleep afterward was next to impossible. He was running on adrenaline.

And hope!

If Kate turned him down, she would have to do it in front of the entire hospital.

Jocelyn put the last few charts away and looked up to see whose heavy foot-steps were coming down the hallway. She couldn't believe her eyes! Instead of a parent, Daniel Brakken walked determinedly toward her at the nurses' station.

He stopped right in front of her face, then whispered, "I need to talk to you, *right now.*"

Stunned and eager to find out why, she followed him to a nearby supply room, then turned, expectancy filling her heart.

"I need your help, Jocelyn."

"Yeah? For?" *God, please let this have something to do with Kate!* she prayed inwardly.

"I came back because I now know I'm supposed to stay and practice, here. I also know that I'm in love with Kate."

"I'm extremely glad to hear that!" she smiled.

"Thanks. There's more—that's where your part comes in."

"Just say it."

"How quickly can you rally everyone down by the carousel?"

She grinned.

Chapter Thirty-Nine

*A*fter making arrangements with the funeral home for Rose's service, Kate hauled the wrapped lion off the front porch and carried him to the back of Jocelyn's borrowed van. She lifted him in and slid him to the front. It was tight but workable.

She locked her house door and turned with a sigh. The bright, sunny morning graced her face with its mild warmth. She had just called Lisa to let her know she would not be coming in to work until Friday, after Thursday's funeral. Kate was sad over Rose being gone, but the peace that filled her was real—and comforting.

She was also glad about the "special event" of the day: The carousel was finally back in place, and the children would be able to ride it again! She just had to be there to give them the first ride of the morning. Granted, it was missing a few animals, but it was safe to ride and mostly intact.

Thanks to Daniel. The impact of his gift touched her deeply. She missed him *terribly*. It seemed every moment her thoughts raced to him, wondering what he was doing, whether he was happy, if he . . .

She would always arrest her thoughts before letting them trail into fantasy. Obviously, Daniel had to pursue a direction in life that didn't involve her. She understood the reasoning in her head, but her heart did not want to accept it. She had fallen completely for Daniel, . . . and she had blown it.

Now, he was gone. She knew it was going to take a long time to get over him.

Andrew was just finishing his pancake breakfast when someone knocked on his room door.

"Come in," he responded, his young voice echoed in the room. To Andrew's surprise, Dr. Brakken stepped in, immediately shading his eyes from the light of the morning sun pouring through the Eastern window.

"Hi, Dr. Brakken!" Andrew cheerfully greeted the man God had used to answer his prayers, and extend his life.

Dr. Brakken smiled big at seeing him. "Hey, Champ! You look really well. How are you feeling?"

"I feel great!" he chirped, and turned his head from side to side. One small patch now bandaged the incision on the back side. "Look! I can move, and it doesn't hurt."

"That's wonderful." Dr. Brakken opened Andrew's chart and sat on the edge of his bed to review it.

"I thought you were gone! My mom said you had to move away. Are you going to be my doctor while you live in California?"

Dr. Brakken laughed, though Andrew wasn't sure what he had said that was so funny.

"Uh—no. I'll be your doctor *right here*. It turns out that I'm not moving, after all." He smiled.

Andrew was glad about that. "Great! I like having you for my doctor. I didn't want you to leave."

"Thanks! But I hope you're not the only one here who's happy to see me back."

Andrew was puzzled by Dr. Brakken's reply, but it didn't concern him for long. "Will I be able to go home, soon?"

Dr. Brakken read over the pages in the chart, this time looking more seriously. "Well, . . . maybe . . . by Friday." He flapped the chart closed and grinned at Andrew. "It appears everything has checked out nicely on your post-op CT. I feel safe about releasing you by the end of the week."

Andrew drew in a big breath. "Alright!" he squawked, unable to believe he was really going home, once again!

"In fact, you're doing better than many adults! But let's give it another few days. Shall we? Just to make sure nothing changes."

"OK!"

"Good. Now, there's something *very* special that's about to happen downstairs with Miss Montgomery, and I would like you to see—that is, if you are done with your pancakes." Dr. Brakken retrieved Andrew's wheelchair and pulled it close to the bed.

"I'm done." Andrew pushed the breakfast tray cart aside and swung his feet around to the floor.

Once arriving at the hospital, Kate drove straight to the back entrance to unload the lion and set him up. She'd remembered to grab her tools before leaving, and had earlier called for Harriet to meet her and help hold the piece steady, while Kate secured it to the carousel. Everything should go smoothly, she mused, and the carousel would be ready by 9:00 a.m. for the children.

She hauled the covered animal into the hospital and into the carousel's dome. Then she started stripping off the taped, padded paper.

Harriet came up behind her as she pulled off the wrapping. "Mm-mm! Doesn't he look handsome!" She exclaimed, with hands posted on rounded hips. Her plum-colored lips and shiny teeth gave a beautiful smile.

Kate also smiled. "He sure does. I'm glad he was already done. Only four slots to fill.

Together, they lifted the lion onto the carousel and Kate started working with the hardware to hold him in place on the floor. She completed those attachments, then checked for sturdiness. The piece was secure at the base, so she carefully stood upon the lion's back in her tennis shoes and worked away at the top of the structure.

She held the last screw in place, and without looking down she reached toward Harriet. "OK, screwdriver."

Harriet handed her the tool, and Kate wound the screw into place. "There. It's done!" She inspected the hold once more for safety as she handed the screwdriver back down.

A man's voice responded, "Catcher of the ring wins a free ride." He took the tool from her hand and placed something square and solid in her palm, closing it around the object.

Daniel! Kate immediately recognized his voice. Her heart raced, she looked down. There he stood, more handsome than she'd ever seen him before! A twinkle lit his eyes, and he gave her a warm, favorable grin. She blinked back the tears, and offered a silent prayer of thanks. "Daniel?!" she barely squeaked out his name from surprise.

"Hello, Kate."

She then glanced down at the velvety red box in her hand. Recognition exploded. With her other arm still wrapped around the pole, she raised her free hand to cover her gaping mouth. She looked back to him, amazed.

He was gazing earnestly at her. "It's not brass, so I hope it will do," he added with mock-seriousness.

"What?" she finally asked, not understanding what brass thing he was talking about.

He cupped her elbow to steady her while she hunkered down and sat upon the back of the lion. "Remember what you told me? 'Catcher of the brass ring gets a free ride.'"

She gazed at box astounded, unable to open it just yet. "Why—why are you . . . I thought you moved to Los Angeles?"

"I had to come back. I've been acting foolishly. I forgive you, Kate . . . I need you."

Kate blinked, absorbing the words. Then she realized several people were quietly gathering behind the gate around the dome to watch. They all had grins on their faces. Andrew sat in his wheelchair in the very front, a huge smile on his face. Even Henry was there, standing next to Jocelyn and Zinnia.

"What did you do?" she asked Daniel, curious and bashful over being the center of attention.

"Please forgive me, Kate. I should never have left the way I did. I knew I wanted to stay. And I want to live the rest of my life with you. I love you, and I believe you are God's chosen mate for me." He reached to open the tiny box lid for her. A gorgeous diamond ring sparkled and glistened. "Will you marry me? Minister in medicine, along with me? Each of us will do what we do *best*."

The crowd behind Daniel had now increased to a large congregation of nurses, doctors, volunteers, and children lined up in front. They all kept quiet and just beamed.

Kate gazed longingly at Daniel. Her lip quivered a little. She swallowed and said, "But, I can't marry a man when I haven't yet confessed that I love him."

He looked her deep in the eyes, undaunted by her delay.

"Do you love me, Kate?"

She smiled, but felt all choked up. "With all my heart."

He smiled handsomely. "Will you marry me? Have my children? Be my wife until death?"

"Yes, yes, yes!" She reached to hug his shoulders, and he pulled her close. Tears rolled, wetting her cheeks and mouth, and she started to laugh with joy.

Then Daniel pulled back a little. He bent over and kissed her lips—a long, fervent kiss of unquenchable love.

The crowd of onlookers burst into applause, shouts, and whistles!

"Hold on, you two!" Harriet called from behind the podium that operated the carousel's controls. She flipped on the switch, and it started to slowly spin.

Daniel clutched Kate tightly. She smiled again. "I thought I had lost you forever," she confessed over the cheerful music.

Daniel shook his head no. "I'll love you forever, Kate. For all eternity!"

Dear Readers,

If this story has touched you in a significant way, I would be especially blessed by hearing from you. I realize this book is not a perfect work, but it is a labor of love from my heart. So, if these pages have helped you to find "restoration" in some area of your life, please write me to share what the Lord has done. Then, we can rejoice in His work together!

Sincerely,

Monica Coglas

To order additional copies of

MIRACLES
OF THE
HEART

have your credit card ready and call

(800) 917-BOOK

or send $12.99 plus $3.95 shipping and handling to

Books, Etc.
PO Box 4888
Seattle, WA 98104